HEXES GO WELL WITH TEQUILA

- MOCKTAIL VERSION -

LeAnna Ehrsam

CONTENTS

DEDICATION

To all the women who have looked up and wondered when they became
invisible.
You are magic.
And to the women who have ever stood in the paper goods aisle wondering
why
in the world The Brawny Paper Towel man is so attractive.

CHAPTER ONE

THE UNEXPECTED INVITATION

Ursula Cambridge answered an ad in a newspaper she had never heard of, but found inside the rusted belly of her twenty-year-old mailbox on a particularly rough day. It was one of those days that hung on the precarious hinges of a heavy decision that would alter the rest of her life.

She got up that morning to a quiet but full atmosphere, something only a person who understands war-like silence can name. Her coffee was bitter, and her toast was underdone. Her greatest friend was a great, big Irish wolfhound named Casper, and even he stretched his lanky limbs as though a weight had been hung on his long body for far too long.

Their daily walk around the worn-down neighborhood was slow, but filled with anxiety that jumbled Ursula up on the inside and transferred to her hound who would throw her large-eyed looks as his lanky body padded next to her along the cracked sidewalk.

Their neighbors were friendly enough in a neighborhood of fifty houses built in the early 2000s, but there was a halting air in even the "hello's" and "good morning's" as though everyone was just a little afraid of being too much to a not-quite-stranger. There was a tension in a certain age group, where the pull of wanting to dig in deeper than the perfunctory "How are you doing?" pressed against the absolute terror of having to answer that question on a deeper level for themselves.

Ursula always thought she had a superpower of understanding the simplest thing about humans: they all wanted to be seen but were afraid of what would be found and therefore the socially acceptable amount of greeting and farewell would have to do and was settled upon.

She wanted more.

She craved intimacy in a way that dusted off questions like, "What did your mother teach you about who you were allowed to become as a child?" and "If you could perfect your relationship with your partner to create absolute peace, what would you change with how you interact with each other?"

But those questions terrified most and she had found that the risk of finding out the small percentage of people who didn't get squeamish and wiggle in their seats was exhausting.

The ones that leaned forward and dropped their carefully created guard with relief in their eyes, and desperate truths on their tongues ...those were her kind of people.

They were hard to find, rare and precious, and she had lost the one whom she could sink with, allowing her bones of holding herself too tightly inside of herself to dissolve so that she could floppily just be.

The one person who not only required no social battery to be around but recharged her exhausted self for just having to manage to be a human woman.

It was her fault that she lost that. She didn't often buy a ticket down memory lane, the price was too high, but every now and then she would think of penny-colored hair and an infectious laugh. Today the weight of that would press her down, for she already felt heavy. She could envision a piece of straw floating down from the sky to land on her shoulder as she stood on the grayish and muted brown block of sidewalk looking at the front of her house with Casper by her side.

She thought of the air inside that house: not loud in volume, but loud in its silence, created from years of asking for more and for change from someone she deeply loved and receiving half-hearted promises with no honest action. Cycles of this went on and on until the reality of settling for feeling lonely next to someone who should make her feel just about anything but, became her world. And she had allowed it.

But today something bold bloomed inside of her.

She didn't want to go back inside, she realized. It was like a skeleton key had turned inside an old, victorian lock and, *click*.

She was done.

She looked at her beige door that needed repainting and the faded green shutters that needed refreshing, and she thought of the man inside who had once been someone she didn't have to hold herself so tightly around.

How long had it been? How long had it been since she felt that walking through her own front door was truly home and that sagging against the cushions of her sofa was a relief rather than an unwelcome pose of a woman pushing towards forty ought not make?

She ran her hand over the bristled head of Casper as he sat steadily next to her, his head coming up to the middle of a rusted rib cage that was tired of holding captive the beat of her worn-out heart.

"I think I'm done," she whispered that day.

Click.

The lock was undone at that moment.

Looking back she would wonder if magic had found its way to an aging Midwest neighborhood as she decided not to carry on with that trajectory of her life and relationship. A sharp breeze which was alien to the Midwest heat in September pressed through the young trees trying to become something older and wiser than their twenty years, and she would remember shivering and frowning at the unexpected intrusion. Though, not unwelcome, as she was made for cooler weather, she was sure. Every year summer lengthened its stay and wrapped its sticky fingers around their suburban world, she would long for a world of a more crisp nature: tart apples, crackling fires, cool air, and winds just like that one that interrupted now.

Casper, having the blood of an old Irish man, closed his eyes, and tilted his normally drooping head up to catch that refreshing breeze as they swayed together, making some kind of pact between woman and beast, a pact that had no formed words and yet held the open possibilities that came with change.

But where and how?

What a terrifying and wild thing to decide to stop what you've been doing for nearly a decade and simply not do it anymore. And why? Because it hadn't settled kindly against her aging bones and she was dreadfully desperate for peace and purpose so glorious and lovely, that she could barely remember how and when she lost herself in the mediocre and damaging world she had allowed to develop around and inside of her.

"What now?" she asked her wise, grey companion.

She supposed she still had to walk into that house, face him, and then do whatever one had to do between the decision of starting over and the act of starting over.

It was a bit overwhelming for her, a person who in particular liked the start and the end of things but the middle tended to get tangled and frustrate her need for resolution. She was a woman who needed to learn to enjoy the middle of something.

Like a six-layered cake.

Or a perfectly baked and spiced apple pie.

But first, she got her mail. When she pulled on the stubborn door of the chipped black mailbox that needed a new wooden stand, the pop and groan that had become familiar at some point in the last decade brought a new burst of cloud and glitter that made Ursula jump and Casper hop up at attention. She waved her hand through the falling embers of curious starlight as she watched in wonder and absolute confusion, her very ordinary human brain trying to make sense of what seemed like a cruise line magic trick.

When the white cloud and glitter motes had dissipated, she looked around at anyone who might be watching a practical joke unfold, then bent down to tilt her head at the curious object that sat happily inside. Casper, too, looked like he was on the edge of his paws as she carefully reached inside and pulled out what looked like a pumpkin made of newspaper.

"Well, this is odd, isn't it?" she mused. She briefly wondered if she should be more wary, but then she had unlocked something rather grand in her life just moments before, and with that came a robust bravery she felt was like meeting up with an old version of herself that she had left behind at some point.

The newspaper pumpkin sat in the palms of her hands, light and yet full of some mystery she could feel brimming beneath the black-oiled words.

She looked at Casper as though asking him what he thought and his grey-bearded mouth turned up in a look of encouragement, so she nodded her head and while holding it carefully in the palm of one hand, plucked the paper stem with the other, untwisting what had been twisted until the paper rustled, shook and then opened itself into a perfectly smooth newspaper that looked as though it was fresh from the press.

No wrinkles and no hint that it had been wrangled at any point into a Halloween decoration.

"I'm going to wake up any minute," she said as her eyes scanned the newspaper, feeling a dreamlike sense of wonder.

The title read, *The Crescent Courier.* The script was rather fanciful and there were stars and the phases of the moon scattered artistically across the top. Underneath the title read, *The more magical news of Salem, Massachusetts.*

"Well, that certainly adds up," she said with wondrous awe. She had been to Salem, Massachusetts once when she was eighteen years old with the penny-haired friend she could be exquisitely herself with and had lost through years of pulling herself in and in and in. What she remembered of the famous little town was how touristy it was, with funky shops named after witchy things like *The Black Cat Tattoo* and *The Cauldron Coffee Shop.*

They had stayed in a small old house for a night just outside of the witchy town, and watched Practical Magic with margaritas and tacos, slightly musty blankets, and flickering candles that smelled like overly perfumed linens while the October night threw ice-cold rain at the windows creating the perfect autumn night. A twinge of pain pierced her at the memory of the easy conversation that came with a soul friend and a heart not yet told to become less.

She smiled gently as her eyes scanned the paper, her mind tugging on that memory like little threads from a plush throw until she caught something at the bottom of the page. She pulled it closer, scrunching her face in absolute astonishment as she read the ad.

"Looking for a new tenant, preferably a woman in her late thirties, pushing towards her forties and feeling it when she sneezes too hard and pulls out her back. Also preferred that she has VERY recently decided on a rather large change in her life, ready to move to a magical place with her baggage, both physical and emotional, packed up tightly with the intention of unpacking it and letting it air out in this rustic gothic-style mid-century six-bedroom house situated on a few acres of rolling land. She must have an absurdly large pet that is young but looks old and wise and gives comfort wherever they walk or lope."

She looked down at a suspicious-looking Casper whose head was tilted to the side, her black eyebrow arched high in awe.

"You do lope. And you do look like an old man even though you're two years old," she said slowly, a note of caution entering her voice. Casper whined, his large white and grey paw lifting to stroke her arm holding the paper encouraging her to keep reading.

"Tenant would live in the house, bringing warmth and life back to the old bones for an insanely low price, utilities included, with one odd request required. Please call this number IMMEDIATELY as life-changing moments do not linger. They tend to spark and then float off into the world as if they never happened so that most people end up not chasing change or revolution, but slide back into their worn-out humdrum life, never to find true fulfillment or magic ever again."

She paused, both eyebrows rising to the middle of her forehead as she looked back at Casper who she swore was nearly laughing.

"I think this newspaper just insulted me?" She turned the paper over seeing an article about the mayoral election and more ads of the magical and funky variety, then turned it back to scan the ad. "I...do you think I should call? Am I crazy? I am absolutely crazy, but I want to call the number, old boy. What do you think?"

But before Casper could bark or groan his response her phone buzzed inside the pocket of her nearly too-tight shorts she was begrudgingly wearing because she had recently found a dislike for her pushing-forty thighs. When she fished it out she let out a gasp recognizing the number from the ad dancing across her phone in the most friendly greeting.

The words of caution about change and magic floating away made her answer without much thought, which when she looks back on she may berate herself for such a flippantly dangerous action, but in that moment it felt like fate.

No greeting had left her mouth when she heard the most gentle and inviting automated message float into her ear as though the words were spun from cotton candy and wishes.

"I hope this message finds you precariously on the edge of a new life, making you feel like a completely different creature ready for adventure. If it does, you are invited to the magical and historic town of Salem Massachusetts where black cats are plenty and the peculiar is found to be rather normal after a spell of time. You have been specifically chosen to apply to be the tenant, along with your rather hairy friend, of The Lost Souls House, an old but beautiful house on the edge of Salem. If you're not too bothered by the oddity of this message, which is clearly and remarkably impossible, please select 7. If not, just hang up and enter your house where you won't be seen or valued for another decade. Have a lovely and magical day!"

Ursula looked at Casper, her mouth open in wonder as she pressed the 7 key on her phone and waited with so much awe and anticipation that she feared she might need to schedule a CT scan soon.

"You chose a new and magical journey! Welcome! An envelope with instructions and a contract will show up at exactly the right time before you start your trip to our cozy town. You will be both welcomed and treated with curiosity when you join our town and we do hope you find yourself on a road of discovery, magic, and peace!"

And then a little magical ring of tinkling bells sounded before the call went dead.

"What do you think? Call the doctor or lean into the obviously crazy and see where it takes us?" she said, her chest brimming with something she couldn't define. But it didn't feel sharp or burn, or weigh her down. That was new and she felt invigorated by it.

So, that was the day, and those were the bizarre circumstances that led a nearly forty-year-old Ursula Cambridge and her beloved wolfhound Casper to pack up minimally, leave a, (what some would call cowardly and others would call more than she owed), note for her partner of ten years bidding him farewell. If she hadn't left the note, he might not even know she was gone for at least five days.

They answered an unexpected invitation to an unexpected adventure and the thrill was so strong, coursing through her entire body, that she felt certain that even if this was the most dangerous mistake she had ever made, the hours of absolute thrumming excitement made it worth it.

CHAPTER TWO

A BLACK CAT WELCOME

U rsula followed the phone's instructions in a lackadaisical manner because for some inexplicable reason, she never quite believed the GPS at all times. Which was why she often found herself turning around or hearing the word, "rerouting" ring through her car's speakers.

She would look every now and then at the large black envelope that was tied with twine and sparkled in the sunlight just the slightest. When it had arrived on the hood of her car just as she had loaded the last box, (exactly as the message had said), she had picked it up and read the white flowing script that instructed her to open it once she was sitting at the kitchen island with a cup of black coffee, (exactly how she took it), after her first night in the house.

By the time she started seeing signs for the historical town of Salem, she and Casper were tired from their unnecessarily-long journey.

She navigated her black SUV through town. September was softer here, and when she rolled down her window she pulled in a breath and smiled as she held it inside of her lungs, reveling in the crisp edges of the air and the overall feeling of autumn that had already decided to grace the town, unlike where she had fled only two days ago which had left a sticky residue on her skin. She couldn't wait to get to the house and sent up hopes to whoever seemed to be running this show that there would be hot water and a comfy bed waiting for her.

She remembered that the town pressed itself against a harbor that let itself out to the ocean and as the wind ribboned its way through the car windows, she and Casper sucked it in like a delicious treat. Casper was perked up, the size of an adult human as he sat erect in the front seat with the seatbelt over him. His grey head was tilted up, the way it did when a cool and fresh breeze came his way. He was a cold-weather creature, which was one of the reasons Ursula was so certain that they were such close companions.

Whenever the Midwest decided to allow autumn to enter its bounds, which was far into the year, and just for a short blip until winter came swooping in to take over the show, she and Casper did it up. They went to a pumpkin patch together and someone at the farm always helped push his great big body up into the back of a hay ride. They sat on the tiny back patio that was a cracked slab of concrete, only six-by-six feet, something that she had wanted to expand for years but didn't due to no agreement from her partner; with blankets and burning candles, fall treats, and a good book which she would read aloud as Casper nodded his head at the appropriately interesting or shocking bits.

They had skirted around the main part of downtown Salem, where she knew driving would be a nightmare no matter the time of day. After about ten minutes her phone suddenly made a lovely sound of tinkling bells and a new voice took over the directions. This voice sounded like a sage older woman who had learned to take great care with words, as many older women do. The soft, lilting voice directed her to take a sharp turn but the directions were centered around landmarks and things like, "There will be a large boulder that looks rather like a sleepy cat. Turn left there." And sure enough, there was a boulder that looked exactly like a sleepy cat, though Ursula could not have guessed what that would have looked like until she saw it.

"Interesting," she mused.

Once they found a large tree filled with wooden birdhouses painted in an array of autumn colors, they followed the woman's voice down a narrow, wooded lane that stretched through a wood that filled their car with quiet darkness and the smell of damp trees.

"Oh, let us brighten this up, shall we?" the voice said, and before they could wonder at her words, dancing orbs of small lights turned on along the lane. The lights looked as though they were bobbing up and down in zig-zagging lines, creating a soft glow that would make for a lovely magical nighttime walk for her and Casper.

"I still feel as though I should be waking up soon," Ursula whispered, moving them slowly down the packed dirt trail, watching the lights twinkle and invite them further in.

Finally, the woods gently pushed them out to a small clearing where she stopped the car and she and Casper leaned forward, taking in what was in front of them. Before them stood a great black house with the most perfectly wrapped, wide porch, and dormer windows on either side of an intricately gabled roof. The windows looked lead-paned and ancient but large lending that sharp and dramatic gothic style that had been promised in the ad.

"Wow," she said. Casper answered in a short huff then whined tipping his head forward and looking at her with his large, sad eyes. "Alright alright. Let's get on."

She inched the car forward until she found a cleared area with gravel for her to park. Unfolding her cramped body from the car was a relief and once she opened Casper's door, he did the same, letting his lanky form find its natural pose slowly with a long arched stretch.

The front porch was a very welcome thing, almost like the architect of this great house started here in her or his mind and then worked in. She made a mental note to look up porch furniture once she was settled as there currently was none.

She imagined a set of black wicker with outrageously comfy cushions and outdoor rugs in blood red and orange that would add color.

The chipped black wooden stairs were creaky and she and Casper both stopped short when seven black cats of various fluffiness or sleekness came into view. They sat or lounged in different positions of off-handed indifference. A few slept, a few cleaned their paws with their reddish pink tongues. Two sat with flipping tails, curious green and gold eyes, sitting sentry on either side of the large wooden door.

Casper was not like other dogs, who chased anything with paws and or tails. He sat beside Ursula with a calm sort of gravity, leaning into her legs and offering her his steadiness.

"Uh, hello," Ursula said cautiously, to which all seven sets of feline eyes lazily flicked up in response. "I should probably knock on the door, yeah?"

She wasn't sure who she was asking, perhaps herself or no one, or perhaps the cats who might understand what she was saying because until two days ago she hadn't believed in magic. But with each minute and mile that got them here to this exact spot she becoming more open to the possibility.

She raised her hand to the dark, impressive door with a lovely stained glass window depicting the phases of the white moon against black and blue glass.

The door swung open before she could knock with a rush of wind and the overall feeling of something momentous about to happen. Her breath caught and held as a woman of absolute beauty stood before her with long white-grey hair gently curling around her shoulders. She was tiny, coming up to Ursula's eyes, which were already closer to the ground than most. Her body was swathed in a flowing and diaphanous kimono of caramel and copper with matching copper flowing pants and bare feet. Her toenails were painted a light taupe color adding a classy and put-together touch to her already classy and put-together flowy aura.

"Oh, you're here! Not a moment before Sulphur thought you'd show and not a moment after. And you do have the greenest eyes, so perfectly captured with your black hair."

Her voice sounded like the one that had guided them the rest of the way here and Ursula immediately felt a rush of ease.

"Come in, come in you two! I'm Crystal, the in-between caretaker of the House of Lost Souls."

She and Casper crossed over the threshold into the foyer of the home. "Nice to meet you. And who is, did you say Sulphur?"

Crystal laughed, the sound robust and filled with years of practice. "She's the main cat here. Don't worry, the cats don't often come inside. They prefer the woods where they can hunt and climb their favorite trees. And I will get to the history of the house in a bit. For now, I will show you around down here and put on the kettle for some tea for us as it's getting chilly. You could probably use a refreshment and some food, then I will leave you to explore."

Ursula nodded as she took in the house. They walked over polished herringbone floors, the ceilings high and beaming with beautifully warm wood and the oddly blank walls. There was nothing inside the house other than the structure itself. As old as the house was, the inside looked like it had been built and then left to sit. There was a large sitting room on one side of the foyer and an empty library with built-in bookshelves of wood that matched the beams. How sad to see an empty library. She could feel the craving for words and ideas coming from the room as they passed it, noting the empty fireplace. Casper padded alongside her and she lightly ran her hand over his back as they moved down a dark hallway, also with bare walls, and then dropped into one of the largest kitchens she had ever seen. The island was its own triumph, at least twelve feet long with a thick wooden top. The countertops were made of the same wood and the cabinets, which were many and of varying sizes, were unpainted and plain. There was a large, black hood over the massive stove and triple oven she wanted to run to and lean over with an absolute squeal of joy. But she refrained. One wall of the kitchen was made completely of those arching lead-paned windows, that gothic style with the top arches holding moons and Moravian stars. It was now dark, because of the setting sun and the cover of the trees, but she could just barely make out that thick forest and wondered what the view would be when she woke up the next day.

There was no table and no chairs. The cost of furnishing this house was going to add up quickly and with all of the plainness inside, no color or personality other than the beauty of the architecture, she wondered again if she could paint. This was the perfect canvas for her dream home filled with thick, dark, and plush colors. She had always leaned toward the more dramatic end of decor, which she hadn't surrounded herself with in years. No, he liked light grey and white or beige everything. It was "breathable" was what he had said.

"Now," Crystal interrupted her thoughts as she pulled down the only two mugs in the otherwise empty cabinets. They were clear glass with black, delicate spider webbing in a lovely design that almost looked like lace. She then proceeded to pull out a copper canister that she hadn't noticed before and pulled out two satchels of tea. "You have your packet, yes?"

Ursula immediately had the urge to run out to the car and grab the black envelope like a good student.

"Yes, it's in my car. And I didn't open it," she added hastily.

Crystal smiled gently. "I know, dear." She slid the beautiful cup of tea over to where Ursula and Casper leaned against the other side of the island. "Unpack your belongings, get settled and I am certain you will have a spectacular night of sleep."

"The instructions said not to open the envelope until tomorrow morning."

She nodded. "With your black cup of coffee, yes."

Ursula thought for a moment but then decided to say what she was thinking, a habit she had formed at quite a young age and then tamed in the last ten years. Well, strangled really. To death.

"It's a little...well, creepy, that strangers know how I take my coffee."

Crystal's light blue eyes crinkled in mirth as she sipped her tea. "Is it? Black coffee is quite common."

"Sure," Ursula said, a note of being unsure. "So I see there is no furniture and nothing of any..." she looked around the wide space of the empty kitchen for the right words.

"Nothing of a personal nature you mean?" Crystal guessed.

"Yes! This is an incredible house, don't get me wrong, but it's very ..." Again, she looked for words that wouldn't land quite so ungratefully.

"It's empty. Has no heart. Yes, yes I know. Do not fret, Ursula with the green eyes. I am sure you will wake up after a deep sleep and find a way to make it your own." She took one last sip of tea, set it down in the sink, and washed it. "I will leave you two to get on and then check in on you tomorrow night after you've had time to read the contract and spent some time in these bones," she said wistfully looking around the kitchen.

She gently clapped weathered and thin hands together with a bright smile. "I'm off now!" As she was moving through the doorway back the way they had come, she threw over her shoulder, "And if you get hungry, just open the fridge. There is something left for you and this dear soul," she winked at Casper who looked besotted with her and then waved regally as she floated down and away, the only sound her light footsteps and then the opening and shutting of the front door.

A great breath filled Ursula's lungs as she pressed her fists to her hips. "Well, let's have a look, shall we?"

They quickly poked around downstairs, finding a large walk-in pantry and 5 guest rooms. Still, each room was empty. The obvious, and empty, master bedroom held a bathroom the size of her previous master bedroom, with an empty space under a wall of high-arched windows that started halfway up the wall for privacy.

"A tub should go there, don't you think?"

Casper trotted alongside her as she checked out the large closet. "This is insane. This can be your room," she said jokingly to which Casper huffed and walked back into the bedroom. "Kidding," she called after him.

Casper's excited bark pulled her from the closet and bathroom and into the bedroom where she found, to her absolute astonishment, a massive, four-poster bed, high off the ground. The frame was made up of gorgeous dark wood with spiral-like posts and a bed frame with a herringbone headboard. The bed was outfitted in a mossy green velvet spread with too many pillows of cream and different shades of brown and copper.

It was exactly what she would have picked out for herself.

"You move this in here?" she asked with a smile and then laughed when she saw a matching dog bed just the size for Casper next to her matching nightstand. He immediately curled his large body up like a snail and let out a tired sigh as he closed his eyes.

"Not a bad idea. I'm going to grab some things and then take a shower."

She emptied her cup of cold tea, filled it with water, and started moving things into the house, feeling with every load, one lift from her shoulders.

A few hours later, a lot of boxes unpacked and her now-no-longer-empty bedroom and bathroom, she turned on the large but plain shower to as hot as she could stand. Bracing her hands against the wall of the shower, the hot water poured over her perfectly as she ruminated on where she was.

Which was currently in a shower inside of an amazing house she normally couldn't afford, in a town she had loved when she was eighteen and surrounded by the most peculiar circumstances that could only be considered magic.

Or she had a brain tumor.

And frankly, she was fine either way.

In one scenario she might be delusional and face the Grim Reaper, but she was still living an incredible delusion that she was quite fine with.

And in another, she was finally embarking on a journey that she could only begin to imagine the possibilities of. She could think of many, in great detail, as she burrowed into the most luxurious bedding that smelled softly of vanilla until she drifted into that deep sleep promised by Crystal.

CHAPTER THREE

A FRONT PORCH SOIRÉE

S unlight tickled Ursula's eyelids, the rays bright and playing with the lack of boundary between the windows and its fingers. When she opened them and paused, taking in the arched windows, with no curtains, and the motes of dust dancing around, her mind quickly pieced together that she wasn't waking up in her Midwest home. She stared at the antique windows and chewed on the thought that she was now alone, but felt less alone than she used to every morning when she woke up next to someone.

She rolled to her back and then let out a soft gasp when a large, hairy head pressed against the side of her face.

"Casper. Off the bed, buddy."

Casper groaned and replied by pressing his wet nose against her cheek. He wasn't a licker, and Ursula had always appreciated that about him.

When he let out a high-pitched whine that she knew would turn into a wolfhound bay soon if she didn't get up, she grumbled and got herself out of the most comfortable bed she had ever slept on. She hadn't slept that hard in years.

Perimenopause had brought many nights of tossing and turning, and even some nights where she had shot up in bed, out of a deep sleep because of suddenly feeling like her entire body was on fire, covered in sweat and needing to change.

With the bed made, and a long, black robe tied around her waist, Ursula and Casper made their way down the wooden staircase.

When she walked into the kitchen, she smiled at the beautiful wash of sunlight that bathed the large room from the wall of antique windows. The forest was thick and verdant, creating a lush atmosphere that she reveled in. The back door was one of those Dutch half doors which took her a few minutes to figure out, but once she was able to get it open, Casper bounded outside into the trees giving her a moment of panic as she realized there was no fence. Or at least, she was fairly certain that there was no fence. But her grey beast ran a few loping laps around the back garden and along the treeline, did his business, and then made his way back to the brick patio which spanned the entirety of the back of the house. The garden was lush, more lush than it ought to be in this early autumn bite. She couldn't begin to identify anything other than the white hydrangeas that gave the yard a plush feel.

There was so much she could do out here with some furniture and lights. As she ushered him back into the house she was thinking of how she would add a firepit when she stopped short to find a glass and copper french press sitting on the island with a mug shaped like a cute, white ghost next to it.

She frowned and looked at an equally curious Casper who suddenly ran toward one of the corners to find a great, big copper bowl of his favorite food and another filled with water.

Ursula rubbed her eyes and then walked toward the French press which held the elixir she needed.

"Wait," she said as she noticed the eight new stools that she was sure had not been there moments ago, and certainly not last night. They were a beautiful warm wood with plush velvet pintuck cushions in a mossy green similar to her bedding, perhaps a shade darker like the darkest part of the forest outside. She pulled one out and then threw up her thick, black hair into a messy ponytail as she reached for the coffee and poured herself a cup. It was steaming hot and smelled perfect; a hint of smokiness wrapped around smooth earth and a hint of chocolate. The large, black envelope sat waiting next to the coffee and she picked it up feeling it in her hands. Heavy, ominous, and darkly fabulous.

This felt momentous. Once she opened this, she would possibly find out why she was here, and what was happening in this new, spell-like world she had found herself in.

"I'm just going to drink half of this first," she said to no one. Casper certainly was only interested in his magical dog food. The coffee was divine. Dark, complex, smooth with hints of chocolate and rich berries. She didn't like light and bright for her coffee. She liked dark and twisty. Which was another transgression her partner had liked to point out.

Once half of the cup was gone she set the little ceramic ghost down and picked up the envelope, sliding her finger under the seal and letting the weight of her hand pull the seal from the back. The moment that it was completely open, a tinkling of bells sounded making her smile.

With the thick, cream paper, which smelled like rosemary and juniper, laid out on the warm wood of the island, she picked up her mug of coffee and sipped as she read it slowly.

Dearest Ursula Nova Cambridge,

This is a contract for your tenancy at The Lost Souls House.

You were specially chosen to enter and live in this house, on this property for the foreseeable future. The Lost Souls House and property are indeed special as not just anyone can live here.

The terms are as follows:

Tenant must keep the house and property in good shape and may add whatever they deem necessary to create the perfect atmosphere that would make them feel safe and at home.

Tenant must only invite those onto the property who do not turn their nose up at the impossible.

Tenant must water the garden when rain has kept its distance.

Tenant must be cautious of unexpected visitors.

Tenant must spend time outside in the wildness around the property regularly. Your presence is needed on these earthy grounds.

Lastly, and arguably most importantly, the tenant must commit to walking the graveyard after the sun has set at least four nights a week to keep the lost souls here company.

They're friendly, mostly, and simply need a grounded soul to remind them that they're not alone.

Should you accept the terms, please place a piece of your black hair in your empty coffee cup and then say these words:

I, Ursula Nova Cambridge, accept the terms of my tenancy and promise to uphold the odd and exciting rules of living here.

By the end of the contract, Casper had his chin resting on the top of the island looking at the paper as if he too were interested in the terms.

Ursula pet his head gently and looked in her, yes empty, mug and then looked into Casper's big hound eyes.

"So, we have to play host to dead souls? That may or may not be friendly. This could either be the most delightful setup for a grisly death, or this could very well be one of the most magical adventures I could never have imagined," she mused. She wondered if she should have added a shot of bourbon to her coffee this morning. Then she looked at the French press suspiciously and wondered if someone had added a shot of something to make all of this seem acceptably unusual.

Casper nudged her and let out a grunt.

"You want me to sign us up? Because I'm telling you now: you're walking the graveyard with me. No way in hell I am going to a grave-yard alone to talk with ghosts. And if you whine like a baby, I'm buying the dog food that smells like feet that you hate."

Casper let out a sound that told her he most certainly did not want the food that tasted like feet.

"Alright then," she said slowly, sliding the ghost toward her. She reached up and pulled a hair from the root, feeling the pinprick sting against her scalp, then dropped it into the mug to float and settle starkly against the white ceramic.

She pulled in a big breath, bigger than any breath she had probably ever pulled into her lungs for she felt like this was the beginning of something bold and extravagant.

"I, Ursula Nova Cambridge, accept the terms of my tenancy and promise to uphold the odd and exciting rules of living here."

Immediately upon the uttered last word, a pop and a bright flash of light exploded from the ghostly mug, the sound and theatrics making both her and her hound jump. With a hand over her wildly beating heart, she and Casper leaned forward slowly to look into the cup.

Nothing special; just the lone piece of her hair and the absolute silence and stillness of the moment feeling full-to-bursting.

But then they jumped, (she screamed and he whimpered), when the sound of three loud knocks popped the moment, their nerves buzzing and causing a bit of a high. When they realized the sound was someone knocking on the front door she looked at Casper and let out one of those laughs filled with nervous energy trying to calm down, and he bounded toward the hallway, always eager for a new friend.

She followed his excited body through the house, thinking again briefly and with slight misery how much furniture she would have to buy until she came to the wooden front door and got up onto her very tippy toes to look through the moon-stained glass. She could make out the blurry heads of a few people and she looked down at a wiggling Casper.

"The contract said to be cautious of unexpected people." She placed her hand on the old brass knob with its delicately carved sun and clouds and made an expression that was a cross between a smile and a question as she pulled it open.

On the wide porch stood three different women. Ursula quickly scanned them. One looked incredibly young, possibly in her early twenties, and the other two could be around her age. Too late she realized she was dressed in her long black robe and wool socks with her hair in that long, messy ponytail. As it often goes, the appearance of other women could make you harshly criticize yourself.

"Hi! I'm Jen. We're the welcome wagon here and Crystal told us that you moved in last night so we brought you some snacks." The woman talking was of average height with beautifully coiled braids twisted and then plopped beautifully on her head adding a good six inches to her height. She had dark skin and a look in her brown eyes that said she didn't show much fear. Her cheekbones were sharp and her eyes keen like she was built to arrow through life and its obstacles.

"Oh, I'm Ursula," she responded as she bumped her hip against a straining Casper. One of the other women was looking at him with slight trepidation so Ursula hip-checked the great beast so that she could close the door behind her. She ran a hand down her satin robe and tightened the sash self-consciously. "Sorry, Casper is over-friendly and he's...well, quite large so I like to warn people before I release him on them."

The three women laughed and the one that had been looking at him with worry smiled softly.

"I'm Tilly." She ran a hand through straight, shiny black hair that was colored light ash at the ends. She held up a colorful dish in her hand and her golden cheeks pulled up in a bigger smile. Her glasses were a classy red cat eye and she was dressed like she was about to go to work at a law firm.

"And this is Kelsea," Jen introduced pushing the younger woman forward who had perfectly curled blonde hair and a soft presence. "She just recently joined our little welcome group. I own a business in town, Tilly works behind the scenes at our local radio show and Kelsea just finished her degree and is doing freelance writing."

Ursula smiled, nodding her head and looking around the women. There was that slight awkwardness lingering and weaving between them and Ursula realized in that moment that she had completely forgotten how to make friends. She had no idea. How was she nearly forty years old and standing on the stoop of a new house in a new town and completely drawing a blank on how to be even the tiniest bit friendly? What do women do when they get together? Her mind briefly flashed a scene of women pouring and drinking red wine while laughing.

"Wine," she finally blurted. Oh dear god. It was mid-morning, and she just yelled an alcoholic beverage at strangers like a lush.

But then the eyes of trepidation on Tilly twinkled and she bent down only to pop up holding in her hand an actual bottle of wine.

"I see you speak our language," Jen said with a bold smile.

Ursula let out a laugh that felt like breathing. The bubble of fear popped as the four women giggled and the younger one said, "We could just sit here on the porch and get to know you a little?"

"I don't have any sitting furniture yet other than the chairs at the kitchen island," Ursula started saying and then regretted it as she thought of the caution rule in the contract. She didn't know these women. Should she be letting them into her possibly magicked new house?

But before she could say anything further she realized the three women were looking at her oddly and then Tilly shifted pointing to a lovely conversation set on the porch. It was gorgeous. Black wicker with thick, dark blush cushions covered in a pattern.

"Oh! Right, those. I completely forgot that was delivered," Ursula quickly improvised with a nervous laugh. "Moving brain," she knocked on the side of her head in a silly gesture as they all moved toward the seating. She paused. "Uh, I'm going to change really quickly. You get settled," she said as she opened the door and closed it before anyone could respond. She let out a breath and then hastily got dressed in jeans, a black, loose shirt, and flats. When she made it back to the porch they were sitting easily and comfortably, talking the way old friends did without pause or insecurity.

There were two plush chairs, a loveseat, and a chaise with a warm wooden table in the middle.

"I love this seating set! The pattern is so beautiful," Jen commented sitting in one of the chairs. Ursula took the open chair they left her.

The pattern was lovely with different birds, snakes, and plants made for a dark and moody pattern that was interesting and eye-catching.

"Thank you. I tend toward the darker side of decorating," Ursula said, which was true. She would have picked this out had she found it shopping.

Tilly sat the wine and the dish on the table.

"Oh! I, uh, don't have..." Ursula started.

But Jen cut her off with a quick and easy gesture. "Don't expect you to have much in the way of entertaining, which is why we brought everything."

Kelsea had gotten up and carried over a large, woven bag left by the top of the stairs. Out of it, she pulled wine glasses (real glass), a corkscrew, black napkins, small clear plates (also real glass), forks, a serving utensil, a vase of flowers (how big was this bag), and an entire chocolate bundt cake.

"Wow," Ursula whispered. The table looked ready for a home magazine to take pictures of a dark academic-styled picnic complete with a bouquet so dark red it was nearly black inside a moss-green vase.

"Kelsea makes the best chocolate cake in the world," Tilly praised, reaching forward and cutting slices.

"This is all really kind of you," Ursula said as she was handed a plate of the blackest cake she had ever seen.

"We are kind and fun," Jen said nodding her head as she took a bite of the cake. She was poised and slightly on the intense side. Her cream sweater and dark chinos complete with cream leather loafers said she liked being in charge and also comfortable. "But, we are also nosy as hell and really wanted to meet the woman moving into The Lost Souls House."

"Jen!" Tilly admonished shaking her head, a smile trying to come out of the corner of her mouth.

"What? I'm not lying."

"Definitely not lying. I have wanted to see inside this house for as long as I can remember," Kelsea added.

"Be honest with our new friend here that you cannot wait to see the inside of this house," Jen said pointing a fork at Tilly who rolled her eyes behind her red frames and then smiled.

"Fine, fine. I admit it," she relented throwing up a hand and then reaching out to pour a small amount of amber-colored wine into the four glasses. She raised hers up, prompting everyone to follow suit. "To new, nosy friendships."

CHAPTER FOUR

HONEY WINE

"Here, here!" Jen bellowed. Her voice was like dark wood, warm and enchanting.

They clinked glasses as they laughed and more of that anxiety between strangers flew off of the porch and out into the world where it would not bother these four. In its place sat an easiness that filled the space, softening the edges of the unknown and giving each woman a rush of excitement to learn about a new person, or people in Ursula's case, and embark on new friendship.

"I like your use of plants," Kelsea commented looking around.

And to Ursula's great inner surprise, which she tried to keep off her face, there were new plants around the porch. There were fall mums of burnt orange and burgundy traipsing up the steps and a few wooden plant holders with the same colored mums mixed with ferns and a spindly-looking plant bursting from the top. Hanging plants of various shades of dark green to light hung from corners and a few were placed along the ledge of the side of the porch where the railing was wide and flat.

She also noticed a new rug with a dark floral pattern that perfectly tied together the wicker seating and warm wood.

"Thanks, I like plants," she said, smiling because she did like plants. In fact, she had left many plants behind at her Midwest home. She had found solace in growing and sometimes fixing the living things in her house, checking on new growth or a sickly fiddle leaf fig she was trying to bring back.

"Love, this wine is incredible. New batch?" Jen asked holding the clear glass up to the sunlight, inspecting the rather unusual color. It was a deep amber color, more the color of Ursula's favorite scotch that she sipped now and then.

"It's the latest batch and you should notice some notes of butterscotch. I did more experimenting with the profile," Tilly said with an excited nod.

"You made this?" Ursula asked, astounded as she held up the glass to inspect the sweet liquid. It was strong and just sweet enough, perhaps more sweet than she would have chosen, but it was rounded out with a buttery note that made it smooth and warm. The overall effect was lovely.

"I make small batches of honey wine that I sell at our local market and some restaurants," Tilly replied with a smile.

"Well, it's so good. I would drink this regularly, and I don't typically enjoy sweeter wines," Ursula said.

"I am usually a vodka soda girl myself," Jen agreed, "but then Tilly let me try her wine and converted me."

"And me!" Kelsea added. "This has to be the wine of the gods because I hate wine. And this is the only wine I will drink."

"Maybe it's magic," Tilly said with wide eyes and a secret smile.

Ursula looked around the other women's faces with a slight uptick in her pulse but when they started laughing she let out a breath and joined their laughter.

Right. No magic here. Just really good wine.

They talked and laughed, the ease of which delighted Ursula who felt like she didn't have to try and relax. She could sit and join and offer little tidbits here and there. It was oddly satisfying to find herself immersed suddenly into a foursome of women who wanted to be near her. She wasn't a pariah before, but she hadn't attracted much in the way of friendship and she hadn't realized just quite how lonely that had become.

She learned that Tilly worked behind the scenes of a local radio show, and she made amazing wine. Kelsea was a freelance writer for an online newspaper in town and did other writing for small magazines. Jen, she learned, was a nutritional coach and owned a business helping people in all stages of life live their fullest.

"This cake and wine in the morning couldn't be a good health move," Ursula said with a laugh.

Jen tilted her head and considered her. "Are you happy right now?"

"I...in life?" The large question caught her, but also stirred something inside of her.

"No, at this moment," Jen said. She pointed to the nearly empty glass of wine and plate that no longer held a full piece of cake. "Are you happy and feel good?"

"Yes, I am," Ursula replied with a note of surprise. Because she truly was.

"As long as you don't eat cake three times a day along with wine then the occasional sit down with friends that helps you feel relaxed and unwind...then this is a good health move. We must devour life by lifting our glasses in celebration and laughing with friends and cake whenever the occasion calls for it."

"Here, here!" someone shouted and then commenced another round of raised glasses and drinking in feminine tandem.

Ursula smiled widely at that. So wide was her smile that she felt a little stretched and silly, even, but in the best sort of stretched and silly way.

"And what do you do?"

All three pairs of eyes swung to Ursula in a dramatic pang of attention and she swallowed a sip of her wine as she tried to ease the nerves that had left a while ago but came flying back. She wasn't used to this much attention on her.

"I am a C-suite strategist."

Blank stares met her response and she realized she would need to explain. "Right, so I connect companies with people who are high-level and looking for new opportunities and jobs that will best utilize their skills. When a company needs a new growth director, for example, I find a few and connect them with the hiring team to see if they would be a good fit. I also help people with their resumes and improve how they position themselves when looking to move up in their current role."

"You're a networker," Jen said nodding her head. "That's quite interesting."

"It pays the bills and I have fun connecting people." What she didn't say was that it was a job, and mostly unfulfilling at that.

"You must have been the busiest bee wherever you lived before," Tilly commented. "Connecting people in your neighborhood, having wine nights with people and dinner parties."

The reality of what she left leafed through her mind. Working from home alone, keeping the house that rarely became untidy tidy, simple dinners for two dwindling from nightly to a couple of nights a week over the last year. She broke up her days with walks with Casper and ended most nights alone on the beige couch she had compromised on, with a finger or two of scotch or tea and a book or her thoughts that meandered down the lonely hallways of her mind. She should probably hide that from these lively women, right? But as she smiled over the words that would paint a different picture, the open faces of these women stopped her.

"No actually. I didn't have many friends, to be honest. I," Ursula stopped, looking for words, and shook her head. "Honestly, this is long overdue for me; connecting with other women and sharing time. I haven't done this in a very long time. This," she said gesturing around the small group, "is not the usual for me." She tilted her head thoughtfully. "I don't think I have met with people without a cause or agenda in a very long time." What an odd realization. And now they knew that she was a loner. Great.

But then Jen's face stretched showing off her straight white teeth and Tilly nodded her head eagerly.

"I completely get it. It's like the older we get the more we forget how to make friends," Tilly said, her voice full of passion. "I swear I developed social anxiety later in life. Afraid to intrude on anyone's lives with my offer of friendship."

Ursula's eyebrows rose with the woman's words that resonated deeply with her.

"Yeah, and college makes having friends seem like it's always going to be easy," Kelsea added. "But you're all thrown into the same stage of life with like-minded people all with similar goals and you all live in your own little world together. I graduated and moved back here and it was probably some of the most lonely times for me."

The young woman's poignant analysis of relationship after college struck Ursula. She'd never thought of the time after college that way, but it was spot on. Going from various groups of friends and sisterhood to bursting into the great big world had been shocking.

Maybe that was why she had made so many concessions in her life that tumbled and grew into the stifling life she finally left behind.

"And I'm a black lesbian," Jen said. "My chances of rejection of offered friendship triple." Her words were bold and unwavering, not meant to make them uncomfortable, but not holding back truth. But then what slapped softened when she smiled again and leaned forward. "Until Crystal basically kidnapped me and these other ladies and we formed a friendship. Which we all craved."

Excitement that felt a lot like nourishment rushed through Ursula. Sulphur and another black cat meandered onto the porch, weaving their bodies among legs feigning indifference until they found sunny spots.

"I used to host a dinner club back in college and I loved it," she said, remembering long-ago friendships that were unfiltered and easy. Remembering a time of lovingly putting together meals with a friend that was no more.

"What happened?" Kelsea asked. Her young curiosity was so pure and sweet that Ursula wanted to tell her to keep it close to her and hold it tight.

"Oh," Ursula waved a flippant hand through the air. "The usual. Like you said, we left that world where it was so easily accessible."

"Well, we should start a dinner club." Kelsea threw out the idea like she was hopeful but tentative. She was refreshing in her sweetness. She wore a simple long-sleeved striped t-shirt dress with white tennis shoes which seemed to fit her easy-going softness that was simple and energizing.

"I could absolutely go for that," Jen replied.

Tilly joined in with her excitement. "I could bring wine. Kelsea, you're our dessert queen. Jen," she tilted her head considering the intense woman.

Jen rolled her eyes and sighed. "I'm actually quite good with appetizers."

Ursula watched both women give her a skeptical look.

"I am. I just hide that fact so that people don't ask it of me." She shrugged a slim shoulder. "And then only offer it when I want to with people I want to."

Her secretive smile pulled bursts of laughter from Kelsea and Ursula, and Tilly threw a balled-up black napkin at her calling her a "little sneak" that had been holding out on her for years.

"Hey, we all have secrets. Any woman worth her salt does, anyhow," Jen said with a knowing look in her brown eyes.

Another round of cheers for that and Ursula thought on her words. She certainly had secrets, and more so in the last few days than ever before. She wondered if any of them would ever be unburdened from her bones, or if she would carry them with her to her own grave.

But sitting here now with three other women and good conversation, (and the homemade wine was possibly going to her head), she was suddenly offering up The Lost Souls House as the hosting kitchen for dinner club. No one was more surprised than herself, but enthusiastic agreement was met all around.

By the end of their conversation plans had been made, the women packed everything up, and Ursula walked into the house to find a sad wolfhound lying on the ground directly in front of the door with large, puppy eyes.

She gave him a comforting smile and got on her knees to pet his wiry head. "Sorry buddy. They had cake, for which we both know you have a weakness, and your food-snatching skills are frustratingly impressive."

Casper let out a huff, the heat of his breath fogging the dark wood of the floor.

"Next time, okay? Which apparently will be in a few days because I invited them over for a dinner club. And," she threw in with a pat on his head, "I'll take you for an extra long walk today."

That perked the hound up and when he lifted his head his eyes took on a less melancholy gleam. Ursula stood up and looked around, hands on her hips as she took in the hollow house.

"Right. I will need furniture," she said nodding and trying not to allow the overwhelm to drown her. "Into town, I go," she said.

Two hours later, wearing an oversized checkered cardigan with comfortable jeans and boots, Ursula exited the third furniture store with less hope of finding what she wanted to fill the house with and an increasingly growing appetite which made for a frustrated mood.

She stopped on the sidewalk to check a message on her phone when her body was suddenly and violently jolted to the side pushing her up against a shop window. Her face met the cool, slick surface of the glass in what she knew would make for an amusing picture of her distorted face for any people on the other side of the glass. Which there were.

When she opened her eyes, the faces of two employees in what looked like a barber shop were staring wide at her. The two men sitting in their seats at different stages of haircuts were also paused at the sudden intrusion of her being pushed against the glass. One of the men now had a stark line of missing hair that was slowly falling from poised hair clippers in the barber's still hand. She blinked a few times and then registered that a large hand was lightly resting on the top of her back and a low voice was saying words she wasn't registering.

When she pulled herself from the embarrassing position she had found herself in, her cheeks flaming and heart racing, she looked up to see a man scowling down at her.

Truly scowling.

He was wearing a thick, good-quality flannel in red and black check and she didn't dare move her eyes, or any part of her body, as his angry face held her captive.

"Are you okay?" he asked again.

His voice was low and it didn't hold the note of concern that the words were trying to convey.

"Uh," she brushed her bangs out of her eyes and shook her head a little. "Yeah, sorry."

"You were just standing in the middle of a sidewalk."

Again, with the scowling and the angry tone, she quickly turned from embarrassed to annoyed.

"I was distracted," she replied, adjusting her feet to give her better purchase on the aforementioned sidewalk.

"Which is why I ran into you," he said slowly. He even dipped his head a little as if he were trying to get on her level in a condescending move. Which would be difficult because he was at least a foot taller than her.

She squared her shoulders, a flare of anger inciting her. "You should watch more closely where you're going. I do not think I am the only guilty party here. It takes a lot of," her eyes scanned his tall, lean body and she waved a hand up and down trying to not embarrass herself further, "momentum to shove an entire human across a sidewalk and into a shop window." Dammit, this was embarrassing. Her words were wobbling even as her indignation had been ignited.

His dark eyes narrowed slightly and he lifted his chin. "Maybe get off your damned phone and you'll be more aware of your surroundings. Those things are more of a hazard than helpful," he grumbled. "They make people mindless."

Ursula was suddenly so filled with rage, an emotion she was sure she hadn't felt in a very long time, that it made her skin warm. Her blood was heating up, bubbling, and making her jumpy and full of energy. A tall, extremely handsome man just bowled over her, pushing her into a storefront window and he had the audacity to treat her like an idiot?

"Well," she said dramatically placing a hand over her chest, "I am so sorry that my mindless little self got in the way of Mr. Brawny Man's walkway. Please, don't let me keep you from tripping the elderly or yelling at children."

She gave him what she hoped was her best glare, though admittedly she hadn't tried to glare at someone in a very long time, and then stepped off the sidewalk to walk around the still-scowling man and go on her way.

"Jerkface," she whispered as the anger was still simmering. She was thankful for the chilling breeze and the overcast sky as she made her way down the sidewalk with no destination in mind because her skin felt hot and she needed the cool-down. And frankly, she was a little mindless at the moment from the literal collision she'd just had.

She was still thinking about the run-in with Jerkface when she saw a sign that read, "Sandwich Witch", and sighed in relief at the same moment that her stomach gave a great gurgle.

Food first, then she would decide where to find the perfect furniture for her new house.

CHAPTER FIVE

HOW TO JOURNAL

A day of shopping and the only thing that Ursula had liked enough to buy and bring into the house was an antique desk. It was scratched and dented in a perfect footprint of age and use, the dark wood matching the beams and flooring as if it had come from the same trees. There were three drawers with small, brass metal hoops for pulls. Lifting one to pull a drawer open in the antique shop, the sound of dropping the pull, the metal clanging against the face of the drawer, took her back to her mom's writing room.

Her mom had been a poet. Always sad and a little melancholy, her mom had been a strong woman who tended to veer toward being a damsel with her energy rather than slaying dragons. Ursula wouldn't have been able to see it when she was a child, but she learned from watching her mom be a victim too often that she would have to become a knight herself in place of the emotionally stable mother she had needed.

So she did.

She learned how not to need people, and how to figure things out. She learned that being an independent woman felt good, strong, and attractive. And that attracted an independent man. They mirrored each other in how ambitious and autonomous they were.

It would take years for her to step back, look in, and realize that wasn't what she wanted, that what they had created wasn't healthy.

She ran her hand over the worn wood, thought of her mom, and bought it. After setting up the delivery, she stopped at the small French patisserie and bought an almond croissant. The shop was so small that there was no seating inside, only a few white metal tables and chairs on the sidewalk. The pastry chef was a man named Michelle, who lived half his fifty years in a small French town called Cassis and the other twenty-five here in Salem.

"I was made to make pastry for witches. What more glorious and fearsome creature is there?" He'd made her laugh, and it was easy promising him that she would frequent his little shop and tell him all about the small Midwestern town she had come from.

And now she was back in her empty house, with the sun bidding farewell, and the silence making itself thicker the darker it got.

She'd opened the refrigerator to find a small copper pot full of cooked bowtie pasta with a note directing her to grab a tomato from the garden with basil. The garlic was in the fridge drawer with a ball of fresh mozzarella and soon the kitchen was filled with the smell of Italian food. Casper got a few bites from her and once the dishes were put away she decided it was time.

Time to find the graveyard of lost souls and walk around, keeping them company.

"Ready for this? Because if a ghost pops out, I'm running. You running?"

Caspar tilted his head.

"Alright, let's do this." She kept him off the leash because the property was large enough that they wouldn't run into people. He was a giant furball of gentleness, but when people saw him there was often a spark of fear at his sheer size. But here, in the woods and the haunted land of The Lost Souls House, he could run free.

Well, lope. If you have ever seen an Irish wolfhound try to run, the visual is quite entrancing as they move more like a galloping gazelle and only briefly, as they do not carry much energy inside of their large bodies.

The sun was nearly set by now and Ursula was glad for the extra layer of the plaid jacket she had slipped on. The pen-drawn map on the back of the contract had shown the back of the property leading into a thick forest with a path that would take them directly to the graveyard. She wondered how easy it would be to find or identify.

"I could use those bobbing lights that ushered us in the other day," she mused.

The trees were so still, that when she and Casper stepped from the backyard over the threshold of the forest into its belly, sound became different. It was stockier in here. There was an intimacy like the trees enveloped whoever walked into their bounds and promised a kind of canopied protection. Ursula had the feeling that she could whisper her secrets here and they would be kept in the wood of the trunks and the wet veins of the leaves.

The leaves had started their turning already, a beckoning for autumn to hurry and blanket their world in its spun gold and auburn. She stopped and looked up and wanted to smile. What an odd thought. To recognize that you wanted to smile because you felt something you hadn't in so long. It wasn't exactly happiness with its giddy rush and sometimes overbearing presence. No, this was softer and more settled. Maybe it was simply the absence of active loneliness. Was that a feeling? She had been with another person in a relationship for a decade and here among the silent trees, she felt less alone.

Casper looked back at where she had stopped and sat waiting.

She did smile then and resumed walking, catching up to her loyal hound.

"Let's go find some lost souls, shall we?"

Casper let out a low bark in response.

The path was a perfectly meandering thing, laid out like a dried-out river snaking through the trees, guiding them gently and expertly until finally, they found a row of black headstones. Ursula slowed and pulled in a breath realizing that they had made it to the graveyard and she had no idea what they would be walking into.

If this was a graveyard of lost souls, people who had never felt they belonged to this world and were left unseen and then unrecognized in their deaths; what kind of atmosphere had they created? What was left behind? She imagined something dark and unsettled.

Her hand found Casper's head and she took a fortifying breath before they continued.

Three rows of neatly placed black headstones sat on the forested floor. A small break in the canopy of trees above brought down a sliver of waning sunlit sky like a natural fading glow exactly where ten markers lay.

Ursula took her time walking among them. A few had vines of dark green ivy sliding its coiled body around the bases. The ground was mostly packed dirt with soft moss and thick sprouts of lush ferns.

The sound of birds was the only disruption to the stillness here, but there was something otherworldly. It wasn't scary, or dark, but as she stood still at one of the blank stones she felt a cloying overwhelm of something *other*. It was like feeling incomplete.

Casper meandered among the rows for a bit before he found a perfectly plump spot of moss surrounding a fat tree and curled himself up, making sure to face where Ursula stood should she need him.

How long was she supposed to keep these souls company? The sun was gone leaving them in a blanketed darkness that felt cooler than moments before, so she pulled her jacket around her more tightly and hugged herself with both arms.

"Should I talk to them?" she called out to Casper who lifted his head and blinked then lay it back down, unbothered.

"Okay, um," she pulled her lips in, biting as nervous energy filled her. "I have no idea what I am doing," she laughed. "But I'm here. We're here," she corrected, shooting a frowning Casper a look. "So, yeah. I guess you will be seeing a lot of us in the future."

She felt silly; beyond silly as nothing answered her, no great gust of wind or intense feeling of ghostliness. She wasn't sure what she expected, but this blank emptiness wasn't it.

Maybe all of this was one large prank. Like a hazing for the new tenants of this house. The peculiarities since opening her Midwestern mailbox a few days ago could have been an elaborate joke, though explaining the bedding showing up in her new room certainly wouldn't be easy.

She looked around at the dark world around them and finally called for Casper, who lumbered to her side in moments.

"I think this should be good. Hopefully, we won't be haunted because we didn't spend enough time with them," she said as they worked their way back to the house. The trek felt longer going back with the dense darkness, but finally, the back patio came into view pushing a wave of relief through her.

She sat in bed reading a new horror she pulled from her large stack of unread books when something pulled her attention away from the words. It wasn't a sound, but more of a thumping feeling inside her chest and a pulling at the corners of her mind like someone tugging on bedding to make it smooth.

She set down the book and slid out of her warm bed to follow whatever was pulling her downstairs to one of the side rooms with the fireplace where she found to her astonishment the desk she had bought that day.

"What?" she whispered, looking around as if someone would be standing there ready to explain their smart idea of walking into someone's home without permission and delivering the desk at most normal people's bedtime. But no one was there and after checking she found the front door was locked. She wandered back to the desk and stood with hands on her hips, still feeling that odd pulling. When she lifted one of the metal loops and tugged, the drawer in its old wooden way, screeched along the wooden tracks of the furniture until it revealed a black leather journal. She frowned and picked it up. The front held only a golden "U" engraved on its cover and as she fanned through the pages of thick, cream paper, all blank and all humming. She opened another drawer to find a gold-capped pen.

She decided to make herself a mug of tea and as she was dipping the teabag, added a splash of bourbon, because...why not? Perfectly snuggled back into her bed, a ghost mug of steaming tea and bourbon and the journal open, she uncapped the pen and started writing.

At first, it was stilted thoughts, forced from her scattered mind.

I don't understand what is going on.

I feel like I may be going crazy.

Why have I never tried sleepy tea with bourbon? This is amazing.

And then it started flowing like water circling a drain slowly until it poured down with a certain rushing fluidity.

I am stressed out about finding furniture that will be fitting for such an incredible and historic house. And so much furniture. I need so much.

And then she sat back, sipping her steaming tea, and instead of the stress of filling this house, felt a rush of eagerness at the possibilities. She hadn't filled and decorated her own space since college. She'd spent the last decade of her life inside a colorless and tidy home that spoke to his minimalist tastes. She had far different tastes. So she smiled and wrote them down.

I can imagine this place exactly how I would want it with dark mossy walls and a black-as-peppercorn headboard, dark floral wallpapers, and velvet couches you can sink into. Area rugs that are unique and welcoming; thick velvet drapes that tie everything together with gold; intricate curtain rods that match the equally intricate door knobs. Lively plants and accented chandeliers that draw out ideas of the forest and fanciful notions of being set inside a gothic fantasy novel.

I have always veered toward the more macabre and dark. Why do you think that is? I'm a happy person. Or maybe not. No, I do not believe I have been happy for a long time. I think I always looked at happiness like it was a cheap emotion. I wanted more. I wanted the expensive emotions that bled like passion, rawness, unfiltered wildness, and even darkness if it suited my soul. I think I always felt more at peace with a dark sort of reality rather than chasing a bright light that seemed so fleeting. Does that make me macabre? Perhaps. But sitting here now, in an empty house I could not have done a better job dreaming up, with Casper and this tea, a pen with ink the most perfect shade of burgundy, and a sentinel forest surrounding me, I am breathing better than I have in years. I like darkness and the unknown. I like ghost stories and the peculiar. And I like that I like those things.

I do not know what the future holds so delicately in its hands for me, but I do hope to find that it is a great adventure.

And adventure tied up in twine with a tag of my name.

For now, I will breathe and wait and open my life to whatever lay ahead and I will dream and walk the graveyard of lost souls.

Maybe among them, I will find my own.

Chapter Six

Autumn Coffee for Two

U rsula woke to a wet nose pushing against her neck making her groan and push at Casper's large head.

"Your head is huge," she grumbled in a sleepy voice. "And I don't have any coffee in my system to battle your furry ass."

But her grumbling and sliding under the covers did not win out over a precocious dog who gathered the comforter in his mouth and dragged it down until the cool morning air hit her skin causing her to yelp and sit up with a glare aimed at the annoyingly smiley pooch.

"You, are not getting a sweet treat at all today," she said, pointing a finger at him.

He huffed and then trotted over to the door, sat down, and looked at her pointedly. Which was when she realized that she did not recognize the room that she was in.

She gasped and looked around in a panic until she realized the shape of the room was the same, the door was in the right place and the bathroom was where it should be. The peculiar slanted windows with the stained glass were there, and the soft comforter she was clutching in her death grip was right. But no longer were the walls white and bare. No longer was the only decorative piece the lovely bedding that had magically appeared the first night.

No.

This room was now completely redone with a color palette that she felt immediately at home in. The walls, with their original board and batten pattern, were painted the richest reddish brown, like rubbed exotic spices or warm mahogany, the color so cozy and inviting she felt snuggled in. The wooden flooring now had area rugs of moss and brown. She looked up to find that the single pendant light in the middle of the ceiling was now a cascade of twinkling stars made of bronze. The windows now had flowing, gauzy cream curtains that cradled the sunlight like an offering.

She stood, looking around in awe at the enchantment surrounding her.

Casper walked out of the room and barked from down the hallway so Ursula, in a cloud of amazement, followed after him. She threw the bedroom one last look before she followed him down.

When they emerged from the stairwell she gasped again, her mouth fully open in absolute wonder at seeing what surrounded them: her dream house.

Nearly black walls covered the main living room with slightly darker bead board and cognac-colored velvet couches that looked as though they were designed after clouds.

The hallway leading to the kitchen had bead board painted in a lovely shade of deep terracotta with the upper part of the wall covered in dark floral wallpaper. She had dreamed up this wallpaper in her head. She knew she had because she had wondered what the delicate lily of the valley would look like with other wildflowers and mossy ferns against a black wallpaper. And it was both lovely and dark, and perfect. She ran her hand slowly along the top of the thick bead board trim as she made her way into the kitchen.

The cabinets were no longer raw wood but were a deep garnet color with bronze hardware in the shape of birds and frogs. One large glass cabinet had friendly foxes as the handles. A new black brick backsplash filled out the space along with a copper and garnet-colored runner along the floor. Copper pots and pans hung from a black rack over the large island and more ferns spilled out of standing pots in various corners.

She turned in circles then took another sweep through the house, after she made much-needed coffee, and took her time admiring the many details she had missed during the first walk-through.

The doorbell chimed, (she was positive she hadn't had a doorbell before), and the sound was a delightful tinkling of bells that made her feel like she would be opening her door to fairies. When she opened it, though disappointed she was with no fairies, she was happy to see Crystal on her front porch wearing a long, flowing black cardigan over a black shirt and black flowy pants. The woman was class.

"Darling," she greeted with a large and gentle smile.

"Crystal, hi! Come in," Ursula said holding the door wide and stepping out of the way. She glided inside and then laughed with a merry clap as she looked around.

"Ah! I see the house took your suggestions for decorating and I must say," she said walking through the living room, running her hand over the grand velvet couch, "this is much better than the last tenant. Their taste was much more," she flicked her wrist, "well, bland. This is spectacular. I feel like I'm inside a gothic novel and a ghost is about to float in at any moment."

Ursula laughed softly taking in the new decor again, still unable to believe just how perfect it was. "It is my dream house," she replied. "So, the house..."

"Takes on the most desired house dreams of its tenant once they sign the contract and begin fulfilling their duties, yes," Crystal said easily as if it was the most normal thing in the world for a house to decorate itself.

"Right," Ursula said nodding her head slowly. "I honestly don't know how to take all of this," she admitted.

"Oh, darling. No one who hasn't lived with magic does. Give it time. Do you have coffee? I could use a spot," she said, leaving Ursula behind as she floated to the kitchen. "I love this wallpaper! You are a clever girl," her voice carried down the hall.

Ursula found Crystal filling the kettle with water and she sat at one of the island chairs watching her. She moved in a way that said she knew this kitchen like she knew a person's favorite color or how they sing softly and absent-mindedly while they work on a task.

"You know this house well," she remarked as she leaned her chin on her propped hand while she sipped her coffee.

Crystal flashed her a smile as she pulled down a mug that she had never seen; this one was a burnt orange pumpkin with a curling sage vine as the handle.

"I do," she said simply.

"I found the graveyard."

Crystal's delicate eyebrow raised telling her to go on.

"It was different than I thought."

"How so?"

Ursula frowned, trying to find her own words. "I guess I thought it would be creepier."

Crystal let out a laugh at the same time that the kettle whistled. She made quick work of filling the French press and then sat a few stools down from Ursula. "It's such an easy thing to believe death is harrowing when we avoid the topic. I always found the graveyard rather peaceful, myself. Though, the wrong sort of person will find less peace and more of an unsettled air there."

Ursula tilted her head. "What does that mean, exactly? The wrong sort of person? And the contract was both ambiguous and stern about inviting people over, which I may have already broken," she said, a note of uncertainty in her voice.

"Oh?" Crystal leaned forward, a spark of excitement in her eyes. "Do tell."

"A few women showed up yesterday and they brought wine and cake and well, by the end of their visit I invited them to a dinner club. Here."

The excitement turned to delight as she pressed down on the coffee slowly until the newly brewed coffee was separated from the grounds. As she poured it into her pumpkin mug she asked, "Honey wine? And the best chocolate cake you've ever tasted?"

"Yes," she said surprised.

Crystal laughed. "Those, my dear, are the right sort of people to invite to this house. Jen, Tilly, and Kelsea," the woman said with a smile like she was talking of fond family.

"They're great. I forgot you would know them." She remembered Jen's talk of Crystal kidnapping them into a small friendship group and now as she sat drinking coffee with the interesting woman, she could not deny that being kidnapped by her would be a happy occasion.

"I know everyone, darling. May I come to this dinner club? I was one in the eighties, and it was wonderful. Though, some of it is a blur and I have suspected for years that there were illegal substances to blame for that."

Ursula burst out laughing and they fell into an easy conversation over food and possible themes for their first meeting as they drank coffee from their perfectly autumn mugs. Crystal talked about the last tenants of The Lost Souls House, and while she didn't say anything directly unkind about the couple that last lived here, her tone and carefully constructed tidbits of information left Ursula believing they hadn't exactly left on good terms. Or together. There was a story there.

"And the house has been empty for three years?"

"Yes. And this house needs to be filled. Salem hasn't felt particularly full since they left. The magic has been imbalanced."

"Does everyone..."

"Believe in magic here?" She shrugged elegantly. "Yes, but there are some who turn a blind eye or worse, would eradicate it."

"How long do tenants usually live here?"

"Oh years and years. Usually until death."

Ursula's eyes shot wide at that. She hadn't thought about how long she would be here. Suddenly every moment from the last few days spritzed through her mind like a fine mist and she felt lightheaded. Was this her forever home? Had she truly left behind everything and vanished from a life she'd lived for a decade? She was glad she was sitting because her knees could have given out at the sudden onslaught of thoughts, fears, and questions. The reality of this new life was becoming more solid than fanciful.

"Well, I must be off. I have some rebel rousing to do."

Ursula gave Crystal what she hoped was a simple smile. She pushed the thoughts aside for a later date. A few years from now might be a good time to walk through a collection of trauma she'd let gather dust.

Ursula walked her to the front door. "You? I cannot imagine you stirring anything up," she teased.

"Oh, I can cause quite a stir," she said, mischief in her eyes. "I have been known to drive a mayor or two to near-madness with my stirring."

"I do not doubt that for a second," Ursula said with a laugh and a smile that was wide and true on her face. She realized that while she had known this woman for a few days, she could see her on the front lines of social issues, pulling others in to join her. She had that air about her, an invitation to join her in whatever she was doing. "Is the current mayor someone you would like to stir around?"

She stepped out onto the porch and turned to her with a thoughtful expression. The lines on her face were faint and not as deeply grooved as one would expect from someone her age. "Not our current mayor, no. She is wonderful. Very wonderful. You should meet her. But a candidate that would overthrow her is causing enough of a ruckus with his wild ideas. You know how men get with their thoughts of being leaders," she said with a flouncing wave of her delicate hand.

Ursula could not contain the laugh that barked out of her lungs. "You are something else."

Crystal winked at her. "Any woman worth her salt could be categorized as 'something else'." She flipped her long hair that was folded into a loose braid. "Oh, before I go, I drew this card this morning and believe it's for you." She reached into a wide pocket and pulled out a palm-sized tarot card.

Ursula took it frowning. "What does it mean?" The inky blue card held a flashing gold man who looked old and worn wearing a cape and holding up a lantern that spread out rays of light.

"Who knows? Until you find out," she said with a wink. "Oh no, looks like you've had a small accident, dear."

Ursula followed where her eyes were focused and gasped when she saw the large branch of a tree lying over the toppled side railing on her porch.

"Oh no. I didn't see that this morning. I wonder when it happened," Ursula said as she tried to think of what she would need to do to fix it. Sulphur sat next to the rubble licking her paw absolutely unconcerned.

"No worries, darling. I have someone who can fix it. I'll have him out here by this afternoon."

"Really? That would be helpful. I mean, I could figure it out," Ursula said, realizing that she probably could. She could. And she didn't want to be an inconvenience.

"Oh sugar, of course you could." She reached out, squeezing Ursula's shoulder with surprising strength. "But if you don't need to figure it out on your own, then don't."

Such a simple, complex thought that pressed into Ursula's thoughts.

And with that, she turned and floated across and down the porch until she was disappearing into the thick line of trees with the road that would lead her into town. She was on foot, Ursula realized, and she wondered where she lived and how far she had walked to get here.

"Maybe she flew on a broom," she said to no one and then laughed. Casper cocked his head at her. "What? That woman is the closest thing to a witch. I can see it." She took one last look at the tarot card and placed it on the desk before she got ready for the day.

Ursula had just finished setting up her home office in the room with the empty bookshelves downstairs when the doorbell chimed again. She had forgotten that Crystal promised to send someone over to fix the porch railing until she peeked out one of the front windows, sliding the heavy velvet curtain to the side, and found a red pickup truck next to her SUV.

Her welcoming smile froze as she swung open the front door to find none other than the jerk who had run into her on the street the day before.

When he saw who was opening the door, his dark eyes narrowed and his already straight stance had somehow become even straighter.

"You," she said, hoping her voice conveyed at least a fraction of her annoyance.

"Me," he said simply, his voice giving away nothing of his thoughts, but the clenching of his jaw said plenty. "So," he said slowly, "You're the new tenant."

"Well, I'm not trespassing," she said.

He raised one of his dark eyebrows, which disappeared under the carefully messy waves of his dark hair. His hair was thick and shorter on the sides than on the top. He was wearing a henley under another nice flannel shirt and she suddenly jerked herself out of detailing anything else about this rude man in front of her. Even if she already had noticed that he was incredibly attractive. "Are you done checking me out? I'd like to fix that and get back to my day," he said, pointing toward the railing.

Oh. *Oh*. She begged her face not to catch fire from embarrassment and decided the best course of action was to ignore what he'd insinuated, though she ailed from having fair skin that tended to scream out her emotions.

She waved her hand toward the broken railing. "Have at it," she said.

"Most people say *thank you* when a stranger takes time out of their day to fix something for them."

"Most people who take time out of their day to fix something for a stranger don't have the personality of a pissed-off teenage boy going through his heavy metal phase," she retorted.

That muscle in his jaw ticked and something passed over his eyes other than a rude scowl, something close to mirth, but it was gone before she could enjoy it. He made a low humming sound and walked over to inspect the damage.

She sighed and stepped out of the house, closing the door behind her as she crossed her arms over her chest. "Will it be difficult to fix?"

He was crouched down, inspecting the damage, lifting the heavy branch easily. "It shouldn't take me more than a couple of hours. Only one of the railings broke. Looks like it rotted at the bottom," he said without looking at her.

Not wanting to make an awkward situation more awkward than necessary, she nodded and opened the front door again. The air was getting chillier each day, and her light sweater was not meant for it. "Alright, well, I'll be inside. Thank you," she added because she was a nice human who understood manners.

The only indication that he had heard her was another low hum so she rolled her eyes and went back into the house where she found a snoozing hound taking up most of the floor in the kitchen.

"You know, there is a very disagreeable and large man on the front porch and you haven't tried to scare him once. You are a terrible guard dog," she said. He opened his eyes, huffed, then promptly went back to sleep.

She leaned against the island, running her hands over the worn grooves of the wood, and pursed her lips. She had planned to go into town for grocery shopping, but she couldn't leave the Brawny Man out there. He may be handsome, but she didn't know him and he very well could be a psychopath.

So, she started on dinner. As the flash of cold had shocked her earlier, it had given her a nostalgic need for something soothing and warm. She got to work on a batch of quick yeast dough, and then as that sat rising for an hour she chopped and sautéed butternut squash, onion, apple, and sweet potato. She threw them all into the oven for roasting with garlic and rosemary from the garden, then prepped the dough to bake.

Less than an hour after that, the aroma of simmering butternut squash and spices filled the air and she was pulling the bread from the oven, perfectly golden and shaped like a pumpkin because of the twine she'd tied around it. She had a glass of wine in one hand as she swayed to the jazz music softly playing from her phone, and with the other hand she was cutting the twine from the bread when she looked up and saw a dark figure in the large wall of windows.

She immediately screamed, jerking her hand and sloshing wine all over the countertop and floor, and a few artfully placed splashes on the front of her caramel-colored top. The scissors dropped from her hand with a jarring clatter and she placed the hand over her rapidly beating heart, the other hand holding the, (considerably less) wine out in front of her like a shield.

The door handle turned and her eyes flew to where it wiggled and then smoothly gave, everything moving in slow motion and heightened. When the door pushed in she reached for her phone, the dial pad reading 9-1-

When she looked up in terror at the smirking and annoying...she paused her thoughts as she realized she didn't even know his name.

Her shoulders straightened and all the fear rushed out of her body as she realized it was just the Brawny Man and her annoyance was immediate, filling the space where the fear had just been.

"You know, the scissors would have been a better choice for defending yourself than the wine. But God forbid a woman loses her wine," his low voice mocked.

The annoyance that had been immediate on the heels of fear after seeing him doubled.

"You are becoming more and more delightful with each word that comes out of your mouth," she said shaking her head.

He tilted his head with a half smirk and she wanted to throw the glass and damn him for how good it looked on his stupid face. "I sense sarcasm. And before you say something cheeky about how much of a genius I am, again being sarcastic," he started as he stepped one boot forward making her frown, "know that I don't do cheesy, cheeky banter. I'm pretty much just genuinely an ass who doesn't like people. This isn't charm," he added indicating himself.

Her mouth opened and closed and she couldn't decide whether to laugh or actually throw the glass at him.

"I would not have mistaken anything about you as charm, rest assured," she said, finally setting the glass down. "And you made me spill really good honey wine."

"Tilly's honey wine?"

She looked up and paused from dabbing a tea towel at her shirt. "Yeah," she answered warily.

"Well, that is really good wine. My apologies."

It might have endeared him to her, along with that smirk, had his first remark not been at the expense of women.

Just then, a large grey creature bounded up from the ground and the tall Brawny Man was pushed back against the window (karma really could be playful) as Casper placed his paws on his shoulders, his head nearly reaching the man's.

A curse flung from the man's mouth and Ursula bit her lip to keep from laughing before she called off the dog. Literally.

Once Casper was wrangled by her side, the man pointed to her hound and said in a deep voice, "That is outrageously large. What the hell is that?"

"*You're* outrageously large," Ursula replied, then regretted immediately when his eyebrows shot up. "I mean, you're..." she waved a hand up and down indicating his tall form, "normal." A smirk started on his annoying mouth so she quickly went on. "This is Casper and he is an Irish wolfhound. And he doesn't take kindly to surly strangers."

His eyes cut to the hound who was leaning against her legs and looked like he had a dopey smile on his face as he looked at the stranger he was supposed to not take kindly to.

"Clearly," the man said dryly.

"You've been out there a while. I would have brought you some water, but I don't like you."

Her bluntness hit his stone face, making it move the slightest, and she could have sworn she saw surprise mixed with slight humor, but like before, it was too fleeting to enjoy it.

"You're really good at being grateful," he mumbled shaking his head. Then he threw his thumb over his shoulder and said, "It's done. Wasn't a hard fix and it should be good for a long time. However, the other rails may need checking for rot."

"Okay," she said nodding her head and then giving him a close-lipped smile. "How much do I owe you?"

But he frowned and shook his head once, a hard look in his eyes. "Nothing. It was more for Crystal."

She nodded, that smile tighter, but then she exhaled softly and said, "I am grateful." Because she was.

He simply nodded his head, his own smile a thin line, forced as if his hard face wasn't used to the expression. Something about him, his straight-lined stance, his guarded expression, and hard eyes made her want to ask if he was okay. But she held back the words as this particular man did not strike her as one who would appreciate the concern. He'd find her meddling and cumbersome, more likely.

"Do you want dinner? I made-"

"I don't date," he cut her off and once again she was thrown by this jerk. By his audacity.

A scorching embarrassment shot through her, again, until she shook her head, making that emotion flee as she was filled with indignation. She did not need to use up the minimal embarrassment she hoped she ever experienced in her life on an assumption from a man who obviously thought he was a gift to women.

She was so shocked that a bubble of laughter burst out of her. She had to brace a hand on the island as she leaned over, the laughter wide and deep. When she looked back at the Brawny Man, his head tilted and staring at her with narrowed eyes, a glint of concern and surprise touching his features.

"Dating is the last thing on my mind," she said, the laughter subsiding and leaving behind an honest smile. "And before you say something not charming or cheeky," she threw his words at him making his eyes narrow further, "know that I wouldn't flirt or hit on you even if someone held a gun to my head. I was only offering you food because you fixed my railing and I felt bad about not hydrating you and *I* have manners. It's called 'Midwest nice.'"

His sharp jaw clenched and the stubble seemed darker as the sun said its farewell.

"And, to that, I don't even know your name," she said, lifting her hand to her chest. "I'm-"

"Ursula Cambridge," he cut her off again and she added the habit to her dislike column for him. "I know who you are. Crystal told me," he said. "Plus, this is a very small community and this is a very famous house."

She widened her eyes and waved a hand for him to continue.

"And," he added grudgingly, "I'm Jenson Lancaster."

It was like the introduction was painful for him. This was the kind of man that she did not like: grumpy and wanting the whole world to see it.

"Great. Nice to meet you, Jenson. Thank you very much for helping fix the railing and in return I promise to never hit on you." She crossed her arms over her chest and leaned her hip against the counter, her face neutral and her tone carefully indifferent. He was an ass, sure, but even an attractive ass can make a girl a little wobbly.

He might have almost smiled, and she wasn't sure, but he shook his head and sighed as he lifted a hand silently and opened the door, exiting the way he had come.

Once the door closed firmly behind him Ursula let out a breath and reached for the wine, downing it in one gulp.

"I swear, Casper, even if I had the urge to date, that man would turn me right back off the urge." She looked down at the hound and narrowed her eyes. "No sweet cuddles for him, got it?"

CHAPTER SEVEN

HEXES GO WELL WITH TEQUILA

The day had come for the first dinner party, and Jen had taken it upon herself to start a text group between them with ideas for a theme and they had landed on comfort foods. So, everyone was assigned a course and instructed to bring the ingredients to make it together and learn new recipes.

She was given a comfort food side, so she decided on the sharp white cheddar and smoked gruyere macaroni and cheese dish she had created once a long time ago. She hadn't made it in a handful of years.

She bought the ingredients quickly and without much thought to the memories that accompanied the last time she had bought these things.

When she checked her phone, she saw the time and another message from him which she deleted without reading. As she was putting her phone back inside of her purse she noticed someone watching her.

When the handsome man she guessed was in his forties realized she had caught him looking, he put on a perfectly inviting smile and walked over to where she was putting her cart away.

"I don't mean to bother you, and I apologize if I made you feel uncomfortable," the man said, ducking his head in respect as he spoke. When he smiled this time it was more hesitant as if waiting to be invited out. "I'm Rob Sandis," he held out a hand which she took with a short and firm shake.

"I'm Ursula Cambridge," she said with a half smile.

"Yes, I am afraid to make you even more uncomfortable," he said with a laugh in his words, "but I know. You're the new and exciting tenant of The Lost Souls House," he said.

She was beginning to recognize how much of a small town Salem was.

"I am," she admitted with a happy nod of her head.

"Well, welcome to Salem," he said cheerfully. "I'm one of the town councilmen here and I make it a point to meet anyone new to town. We're a very tight community."

"It's nice to be welcomed and it's very nice to meet you," she said, feeling both welcomed and the slightest bit put off. She was unable to put a finger on it, but she kept herself in a state of awareness as she listened to him talk about some of the upcoming meetings and casually slipped in that he was married with small children. When he asked if she had any family with her, his smile slipped the slightest before it was righted when she told him that no, she was not married and she was on her own.

"We do love including a host of different walks of life and ideals here," he said.

"Oh, how," she fought narrowing her eyes and forced them wide and her smile bright, "open of you."

He nodded his head, trying to decipher if her sentiments were genuine but before he could decide, she gave him a little wave with her sparkliest smile and told him she was off to a dinner. She thanked him again for the warm welcome and made her way to her car with her two bags of groceries and a curious suspicion about the happy councilman.

Before the women came over, she took Casper on a walk through the graveyard, saying hello to the invisible souls that supposedly lived there. She made sure to spend thirty minutes among the blank headstones. Sometimes she talked, sometimes she hummed with nothing to say. It still felt slightly ridiculous doing this routine and wondered when, or if, it would feel normal to traipse around a graveyard at night keeping spirits company.

But still, she felt a warmth here in this part of the forest. There seemed to be a wall that they stepped through when coming out here and once they were firmly on the other side of it and among the souls, the air was thicker, warmer. She still didn't feel fear, or like she should be cautious. She sniggered as she realized she felt safer here at night in a graveyard than she did at night in a city.

Today she was quiet as she wandered among the stones. Her mind was heavier than yesterday, thoughts of what she had left behind pressing in. Or maybe it wasn't what she left behind, but what she had allowed to become over nearly a decade. She hardly thought of him, and there wasn't resentment or anger, longing or regret. There was a shame, and she wasn't ready to fall into that feeling yet, exploring its corners and middle, so she closed her eyes and pulled in a deep breath, expelling it all out as she exhaled. And she thought instead about tonight with new friends, hoping for good conversation and easy camaraderie.

She needn't have worried about the camaraderie being easy as two hours later, she was doubled over laughing, one hand bracing herself on the kitchen island as Tilly regaled them with a story about her last boyfriend who didn't know his pant size so called her after they broke up to ask her.

"Stop it. Stop it," Jen said, laughing and trying to balance the wine in her hand as she also shook with laughter and held herself up against the island. "That boy treated you like his mother," she got out between laughs. She was dressed in a gorgeous cream sweater that looked lovely against her dark skin and jeans that had to be designer with her coiled hair up in the same style twisted on top of her head.

"I bet twenty dollars," Kelsea said, raising her dark blonde eyebrows, her smile wide, "he had to ask Tilly how to do laundry." Kelsea was in a stylish flannel shirt with black skinny jeans and ankle boots, looking exactly like the twenty-two-year-old that she was.

The women turned to Tilly, who wore a simple light grey sheath dress and red ballet flats that perfectly matched her cat-eye glasses. Their breaths were bated as they waited for an answer to Kelsea's bet. When she nodded her head slowly with a Cheshire cat smile, they all burst into another fit of laughter.

"How long were you with him?" Crystal asked, her long white hair down and flowing tonight. "Maybe you can claim him as a dependent on your taxes," she added with a peel of giggles that brought them into another wave of laughter.

Ursula couldn't remember the last time she had laughed so hard, or so much. Since they had walked into the house, hands full of bags of ingredients and voices filling the nooks and crannies of the old house, she had felt remarkably full and warm. They quickly and easily settled in the kitchen.

Tilly poured the wine and Jen was in charge of appetizers, which were passed around with the wine. The buttery squares of pastry had perfectly charred peppered bacon, brie and a sliver of Honeycrisp apple; they had been so good that they all made various moaning sounds as they ate.

Ursula was certain that there were a handful of things that every woman wanted: great food, laughter that wrapped around her ribs, really good sex and to feel fully herself with the people she allowed near her.

She stood there in the aftermath of rib-aching laughter with women who were near strangers, inside the warmth of her dream kitchen, and she realized that she was more herself right now in this moment than she had been allowed to be for years. The thought was more harrowing than it was relieving.

"I had a boyfriend who told me that women leaders were good, and we needed them," Tilly started, "but claimed that studies show that if women get too much power, it can actually harm society."

A chorus of boos and rolled eyes fired off around the kitchen.

"My ex-father-in-law told me I had acceptable hips when he first met me," Crystal said to each woman's astonishment. "Because I would be carrying their family name along."

"The first time he met you?"

"He commented on your body?"

"He expected heirs?"

Questions were rapid-fire and Crystal laughed with their indignation as they bonded over the most amazingly strong and difficult thing in the world: being women.

Perfectly roasted spatchcock chicken with red potatoes, carrots, and broccolini were placed in the middle of the island along with Ursula's macaroni and cheese, honey and sage yeast rolls, and Crystal's allegedly famous margaritas.

She served them with a warning to sip slowly as they filled their plates and settled around the island in the cozy, velvet chairs.

"I cannot believe he said that," Jen said, anger in her voice as she shook her head.

They had been talking about Kelsea's freelance article for the town's paper, the non-magical one, when the mayoral election came up. She was covering a few of the events that would highlight the candidates, and the topic was bringing out a fiery side to Jen. Ursula decided that if a person had four sides, three of Jen's were fiery, and she liked her vivaciousness.

"He is one of those men who think that saying what misogynistic men think out loud, will create an argument for leadership that cannot be ignored," Crystal said in a strong but gentle voice.

Jen snorted into her half-drunk margarita while Kelsea and Tilly shook their heads.

"Yeah, because banning books in the public library and white-washing our history books has always led to a well-led and harmonious society," Jen commented.

"Who is this?" Ursula asked.

"Rob Sandis," Kelsea replied. "He's a local businessman who is running against Cora for Mayor. Cora is Jen's childhood friend."

"And one hell of a woman," Jen said raising her margarita in the air.

Something she said jogged her brain.

"Wait, did you say Rob Sandis?" Ursula asked, remembering the odd interaction she'd had a few hours ago in the grocery store parking lot. "Handsome, in his forties, kind of gives off the air of a high school quarterback-turned salesman?"

"That's him!" Tilly pointed her finger at Ursula in excitement.

"Dayum girl, you know how to peg them. You know him?" Jen said, respect in her eyes.

"I met him today briefly. It's not surprising he's running for office," Ursula said with a shrug thinking about the careful way he held himself and picked his words.

"Well, the man has an agenda and not the inclusive kind, so be wary," Jen said. "He's been gunning to knock Cora over for years and doesn't like that she's a single, strong woman without kids." She drank another sip of her margarita and then pointed to where Kelsea was looking at her small plate of food. "Kelsea worked for him for a minute while she was finishing her degree, right?"

Kelsea nodded her head, an indecipherable look on her face. "He's a family platform guy," she said diplomatically.

"We should hex him," Tilly said with a smile on her cute face.

"Oh, to hex anyone who acted egregiously against us would be a wonderful power," Ursula added.

"We all have stories and people that could stand to be hexed," Crystal agreed, nodding sagely.

"I had an ex-girlfriend who wasn't ready to come out, which was fine," Jen started talking, her words becoming a little louder the lower her drink got. "Anyways, her parents saw us walking at an outdoor mall, we had no idea they were there of course, and I kissed her cheek after we had gotten into a little tiff. About two days later I got a knock on my dorm door," everyone was on the edge of their seats, leaning in as she sat perched elegantly with one long leg crossed over the other, telling her story. "I open it to find a middle-aged woman I didn't know. Turns out it was my girlfriend's mom, coming to tell me that she would report me to the authorities, both legal and at the school, if I continued sexually harassing her daughter."

Gasps, wide mouths, and eyebrows raises of shock all surrounded the island.

"Wait, she covered up having a girlfriend by saying you were sexually harassing her?" Tilly asked. Her red-framed glasses did not hide the look of disdain in her wide eyes.

Jen nodded her head slowly, lifting her margarita into the air. "To being made a secret and a sexual predator in one cowardly lie."

Tutting and head shaking accompanied raised margarita glasses all around. The clink of glasses got more intense, with spiked liquid spilling over hands bringing out more laughter and fewer filters. The stinging smell of limes swirled around roasted chicken and mixed pleasantly with the burning of vanilla candles sprinkled throughout the downstairs.

"Maybe we should," Tilly said, leaning over the island so that her chest was practically squashed against the wood top. When everyone looked at her she added excitedly, "Hex people who have been, what did you say Ursula? Acted.."

"Egregiously against us," she said tilting her head knowing where she was going.

"Yes!" Tilly said triumphantly. "We should go to the graveyard of lost souls and bring our drinks, then hex those who have acted egregiously against us."

Jen slapped her manicured hand against the top of the island. "You're brilliant, Tilly."

Tilly beamed, the way only a happily tipsy woman on homemade margaritas can beam. Bright and slow.

"Female bonding!" Crystal cheered and was joined by everyone, and then suddenly they were using phone lights to shine their tipsy way through the woods to the graveyard where Ursula used her large travel thermos to refill each empty glass with more margarita as they stood in a circle. There were four blank headstones between them and the setting couldn't have been more perfect for a group of women attempting to hex people, with a blanket of fog hugging the ground and the open eeriness of night's shadow as a cloak.

"This feels like a movie set. Is anyone else getting Buffy the Vampire vibes?"

"What's a vibe?" Crystal whispered to Ursula who laughed shaking her head as she swallowed another sip.

"I could go for a sexy, pale vampire," Tilly giggled.

"Please do not tell me vampires exist, because after the last few weeks and these drinks," Ursula raised a sloshing glass, "I absolutely will believe you."

"Believe me," Tilly said with a conspiring tone leaning her shoulder against Ursula's, "if vampires did exist, I would have manifested one by now with all of the paranormal romances I read."

"Crystal, these are the smoothest margaritas I have ever had. I can barely tell there's tequila in here," Jen said as she tilted her head dramatically along with her empty cup, looking to see if there was any more.

"Oh, there's definitely tequila, darling," Crystal warned with a wide smile on her serene face.

"I haven't had tequila since the night I woke up without pants in the woods four years ago," Kelsea admitted.

"Why didn't you have pants?"

"Why were you in the woods?"

"We were playing hide-and-seek at a Christmas-themed camping ground and we had a golf cart and too much tequila. I woke up in the bushes with no pants, but my boots and socks were perfectly in place," she giggled finishing the rest of her drink. Ursula wondered if Kelsea was thinking of getting rid of her pants now based on the amount of tequila she had just consumed.

"So, has anyone ever hexed anyone before? How does this work?" Ursula asked. The tombstones wobbled some. Were they moving? Or was that her? She opened her eyes wider and grabbed the ground with her boots in a firm stance. That was better. The ivy did seem to be sliding and writhing in her intoxicated state like they were trying to wake up whoever was buried beneath the hard ground.

"I have never hexed anyone, but I say we hold hands, close our eyes, and think of who we want to hex and why. Unless Crystal has a better idea," Jen offered.

"Why would I have a better idea?"

They looked at each other cautiously. Ursula had to bite down on her lips, sucking them in so that she wouldn't say anything, thinking of the hermit tarot card she had given her. When she looked it up, the meaning could be searching for truth and enlightenment or isolating oneself and losing her way. Whether it was a past, present, or future card, she did not know. Both meanings fit, unfortunately for the latter meaning.

An indignant and somehow completely sober Crystal planted a dainty fist on her hip waiting for an answer. "Why would I know how to hex someone?"

Still, no one answered her except for the creaking of thick tree branches and the cawing of a bird, until finally, it was Tilly, with her red glasses wildly askew, who broke the silence.

"Because half the town believes you're a witch and the other say you believe you are," she blurted then covered her mouth with a hand that seemed to have more sense than her mouth.

Crystal's wide eyes looked around at the circle, the women holding their tongues and astonishment on tight leashes.

Then she threw her head back and let out the most lovely laugh that filled the circle, the sound pushing and ricocheting off each woman until they all joined in. And then they were holding hands and rocking slowly.

"I'll hex myself to practice," Jen announced. Everyone gave her various confused or scared looks as she raised her very empty glass to the moon and said, "I hex myself to be unable to say the word *cat*," she paused, made a thinking face, and then added, "or *kitty* or *feline*." When she took a sip of air from her empty glass everyone laughed at the harmless curse that wasn't bound to come true, but gave legs to what they were here to do.

"I hex Jason Harrison," Tilly started, her voice clear and sharp, "for telling me I will never amount to much in this country with my skin and my slanted eyes and that I am just a fetish for men."

Ribbons of rage and sorrow slithered between the women at Tilly's words.

"Okay, now hex him," Jen encouraged. Her eyes were shining intensity as she looked at Tilly across from her. She looked fierce, like a vengeful queen protecting her friend.

Ursula's wavering mind, and therefore wavering mental defenses, brought to mind someone who once looked at the world that way for her, protecting her.

"Give him like...uncontrollable loud gas," Kelsea said, and the interruption was enough to pull Ursula from drunkenly dwelling on auburn hair and fierce friendship lost.

"Or make him allergic to his favorite food."

"Ladies," Crystal said in a soft, chiding voice. She smiled slowly, that knowing look on her face, the one that women learn at a certain point in their lives when they realize how cruel the world is specifically for them. "None of that," looks of being chastised and uncertainty darted around the circle. "If you're going to hex him, darling, make it stick. Be bold, or nothing at all."

Tilly looked at her with a stricken look. "Like, murder?"

If the moon hadn't been gracious in her light that night, they wouldn't have been able to see the sharply raised eyebrows but they would have all been able to feel the palpable holding of breath.

"Heavens no!" Crystal said quickly. "Just, make it inconvenient enough to really sting," she said with a small smile.

Tilly's slow smile broke over her face in a baptism of righteousness at being released into the wild.

Make it stick.

Be bold.

"Then I hex Jason Harrison with a permanent lion's tale."

Kelsea and Ursula laughed. Jen cocked her head with curiosity and Crystal nodded in encouragement.

"He once said a strong man is like the king of the jungle. Doesn't back down and doesn't let a woman get in his way," she explained with a shrug of her slim shoulders.

The kind of laughter that rang into the cool night air was so full of understanding and feminine power that the trees swayed with the force.

Then they took turns hexing those who had wronged them in their lives, squeezing hands and offering encouraging, wide smiles with teeth and bite. They stood around the graveyard as a symbol of their empowerment.

What a gorgeously beastly thing: adult women remembering what it was like to stand in a circle like they did as children, when they were carefree, running in circles with laughter that didn't cost them anything, and hearts that hadn't yet learned how to beg time to move faster through pain. Here stood five women not knowing that they were indeed conjuring magic on hallowed ground.

The fog was slithering and a presence was awoken.

They did not know the power a group of women held when they united and connected. When they let out their most free selves to roam the world without pause. They hadn't weighed the potency of such a thing because when they were young, it wasn't so difficult to find soulmates. As they got older they put on layers of insecurities and fears that the world laid out for them, hoping those insecurities and fears would be worn like armor.

The world and the magic inside of it knows this secret: women who shed their insecurities and fears, stepping out of them like unwanted clothes, are dangerous.

And if those women found each other and grasped hands, the naked truth of being human, embracing their power as women...that was more than dangerous. It was possibly catastrophic.

So magic looked up at them from where it lay in the ground, and called to the magic that ran like blood inside the trees. The magic that ran through the veins of the leaves told the magic that hid inside the red-winged black bird's wings, and that magic soared higher into the night sky to let the magic in the moon and the stars know that The Graveyard of Lost Souls had found something peculiar. Something that this hallowed ground hadn't felt since it had been snuffed out.

And the last time had ended with women being buried in the ground without markers or names.

Chapter Eight

Hex of a Hangover

To wake up in your early twenties with a tequila hangover was an inconvenience. To do so in your late thirties was like being given a preview of death. And not for free, either, because Ursula knew that the headache that was deadly now would turn into a sharp knife-stabbing pain later, only to stick around and turn into a pounding tomorrow. Hangovers took their time the older you got. It wasn't enough that she was fighting the perimenopausal things in life, now she could add this to the list which currently included: hot flashes, trouble sleeping, acne out of nowhere, forehead wrinkles that seemed to deepen overnight and now hangovers that felt like your own ghost trying to get inside of you.

"Ohmygod I feel like I swallowed a ghost and it ran around inside of me screaming before I threw it up," she said to no one except for Casper who was lacking empathy at the moment. He needed fed and let outside and her dying was not going to stop him.

So, she somehow fought her way to her kitchen, (there was some crawling involved), and once Casper was outside, she made quick work of brewing coffee at a deadly strength as she popped a few aspirin.

The sun was blessedly absent today, allowing the sky to cover the earth in grey gloom that suited her pounding head just fine. As she stepped out on the back patio, the bite of the cold air against her alcohol-soaked skin was a soothing cloak and she tipped her head back with closed eyes thanking the sky for keeping the sun tucked away for now. Something tickled the back of her mind. Not her head, like the tequila ghost was, but her thoughts. It started as a feeling of small, painless needles and then her thoughts were homed in on the sensation as a picture of a lacey, light pink flower came into her mind.

She opened her eyes slowly, so as not to disturb the ghost of tequila past, and when she turned her head slowly, she saw in her patch of garden the plant that had been conjured in her mind. Curious, she crouched down and ran the tip of her index finger over the pinkish flowers, something like pleasure running over her mind in a small line. She sat back on her heels and set down her cup of coffee, the little ceramic ghost pushing up steam into the air while she leaned in close and fished out her phone. She took a picture of the flower and then found an app to identify it. Before the app could spit out a name at her that same painless prickling inside her mind whispered, *Valerian*.

And somehow she knew things that she did not know before this moment. She knew that if she pulled this plant up from the ground carefully, keeping the roots intact, washed and dried it, and put the roots in the oven at a low temperature with the oven door slightly ajar, they would dry out.

And so she found herself, an hour later, laying out the dried roots of the plant on cheesecloth allowing it to cool before she would use the mortar and pestle she found next to the bread box to grind it up and sprinkle it in tea with fresh mint leaves. Not too much, or she would get sleepy, but enough to take the edge off her pounding head.

She didn't stop to question how she suddenly knew all of this, like a medicine woman from the late 1600s. And she didn't cringe, too much, when she sipped the steeped mint leaves with the ground-up valerian root powder stirred into it. But when her headache had eased and her stomach found more solid ground less than an hour later, she sat back on her cognac-colored velvet couch trying to do work, and marveled at this new peculiarity.

Less than thirty minutes later she felt no headache and no roiling stomach.

She found Crystal's number in her phone and her finger hovered over it as she thought. But could she voice what was happening and would she sound out of her mind if she did?

She set her phone down and decided to go into town to grab some lunch, wanting more fresh air and to walk off these odd thoughts.

She chased Casper around the backyard for ten minutes to get him on his leash, which he suddenly since moving here decided he was staunchly against, and threw on an army green wide-brimmed hat with a black long-sleeved shirt and jeans. She felt good and fresh, and as they walked the twenty minutes into town, she felt light; like the world had smiled at her.

The air was a gentle and cool caressing hand, the smell of smoke-tinged burning leaves and cinnamon wrapped gently around the bustling town center packed with tourists. She wove between the thick crowd, the sea of grey and black witch hats bouncing around, laughter, and the smell of food ambushing the senses. Passersby would stop her to ask what kind of dog Casper was, the attention loved by the hound.

"You are a vain beast," she whispered happily as she walked and he pranced by her side.

She found the small restaurant Tilly had told her had the best mushroom soup. No one else seemed to be going in or out, even though it was lunchtime and there was a considerable amount of people surely looking for a spot to settle down for a meal. When the door opened, a thin man in his late thirties looked up at her without a smile.

"You must be new," he said.

She looked around at the tiny restaurant which boasted three tables, each full, a counter where the man stood staring at her, and a small drink bar on the side. Everyone, especially during tourist season, was new here. Maybe it was how he welcomed people.

"I uh, Tilly sent me. I'm the new tenant at The Lost Souls House," she said. The moment the words were out of her mouth, the thin man behind the counter stopped what he was doing and looked up at her with shock on his face and the three tables went silent, each conversation cut off. She looked around at seven pairs of eyes looking at her intently and tried to ignore them as she looked back at the man behind the corner.

"I heard you have great mushroom soup."

Finally, the shocked look melted and he smiled widely at her, the transformation incredible. She went from feeling unwelcome and dismissed to being the center of warm attention.

"You must be Ursula," the newly friendly man said. He was balding and his skin had an overall stressed-out look, but when he smiled the stress turned into lines of well-worn happiness. "And we do have the best mushroom soup. Tilly is not wrong. Go, sit, I will bring you out a bowl on the house as a welcome." He looked down at the large, cocked head of Casper and added, "And I have a treat for such an incredible beast."

Ursula tucked a smile in the corner of her mouth. "Thank you. That's kind," she said. She sat and Casper took up sentry next to her.

She scrolled through email for a few minutes and then a thin shadow fell over the counter. While she scanned an email from a company looking to see if one of her clients would be a good candidate for a Vice President of Human Resources role, the shadow became heavy. She swiveled on the stool to look up and see a woman, probably around her age, standing there with a hesitant smile. She had long blonde hair, past her shoulders, that looked perfectly curled and highlighted. She either just came from a salon appointment or she was one of those amazing creatures who had more perfect hair days than the average woman.

Ursula herself had black hair that fell to mid-back, was thick and had the kind of wave that sometimes cooperated to look beautiful, but more often looked like she should have either curled it or straightened it, rather than allowed it the freedom it found somewhere between.

"Hi," the woman greeted. Her brown eyes were large and soft, maybe a little haunted.

Or maybe Ursula was letting this witchy town get to her and there was nothing haunted about this woman and she was perfectly fine. "I'm Jessica. You're the new tenant at The Lost Souls House?"

"I am. I'm Ursula," she said, offering her hand.

"Nice to meet you. We haven't had anyone in that house in a while." Jessica's hand was slight and brittle. Ursula had to loosen her grip and not do the corporate executive handshake she'd mastered in her career, for fear of pulverizing this woman's bones. When she pulled it back Ursula watched her place it gracefully on the face of her Hermes cream bag. The designer purse looked massive on her size two body. She was model tall with a slender body and poised demeanor.

"Yeah, that's what I hear. It's a shame because it's such a neat property. The woods alone are so peaceful."

"I've heard that," she said with a small smile. She tucked thick blonde hair behind an ear in a self-conscious gesture. A sparkling diamond that Ursula was sure was real flashed as the woman moved her hand, and suddenly Ursula felt like an instant connection to her. She couldn't exactly explain it, but the way this woman held herself, like she was unsure about how much space to take up, and the kindness in her brown eyes made her want to ask her questions about who she was and what she was thinking.

"Would you like to come over next month for a dinner club I kind of accidentally started with four other women?"

Jessica's face showed a moment of shock at the invitation which turned into a slow smile that looked like a mixture of excitement and also something else...something like uncertainty. "I don't know," she said, casting her eyes down at her phone. When she looked back up at Ursula, that look of uncertainty won the battle with excitement. "Can I get back to you?"

"Sure. Give me your number and I'll text you."

They exchanged numbers and the blonde gave Ursula a shy wave with that half smile.

The thin man behind the counter, who finally introduced himself as Bruce, gave her the mushroom soup in a to-go bag and Casper a rawhide with his card should she need anything. She wondered how much of the hospitality here was because of this peculiar town, and how much was because of the house that she occupied.

As she walked amongst the tourists again she thought about Jessica, trying to put together what it was that had spoken to her about the woman. There had been a craving behind her eyes, a hunger for something, and though Ursula did not know what it was, she recognized it. She had felt hungry for so long. For connection, more and deeper relationships, a sense of belonging.

As she thought about that, she wound around one of the shops to walk along the back alley, trying to find some reprieve from the throng of tourists. Casper, who loved attention, gave her a mournful look as she steered them from the noise to more solitude. Someone had strung lights between the backs of the buildings, the bubbles of lights creating a cozy path. Luckily, no one seemed to have the same idea as her.

One of the shops had the garage-style door opened and she saw what looked like panes of stained glass. She looked down the alley, which was becoming darker as the day moved along, and with the sun still firmly hiding itself, the baubles of light above cast their warm glow. When she saw and heard no one, she decided to peek into the open storeroom. She had always been drawn to stained glass. The art of it was intriguing and beautiful. She leaned down to see a few colorful panes inside a thick frame of repurposed wood, and she smiled wistfully. The artist had created a forest scene with the trees changing their colors like a snapshot taken in mid-change. Half of the trees were still holding onto their thick green coloring while others had started to lose grip of summer's colors, giving way slowly to the paintbrush of autumn. It was astonishing; how someone could take tiny bits of colored glass and so carefully craft pictures as intricate as this.

"Can I help you?"

Ursula whipped around to find a man in his thirties, with sandy blonde hair and a boyishly cute face walking through the shop door into the garage where she was obviously trespassing. Casper perked up, his grey ears quirked and alert at the new possibility of a friend.

"Sorry," she said quickly, then pointed to the forest-stained glass pane. "I saw this and couldn't help myself. It's beautiful."

He smiled wide, his face the kind of face that looked like it was made for smiles. "I'm Miles," he said.

"I'm Ursula."

A look of surprise crossed his face. He was wearing a blue button-up with nice jeans and loafers. "The new tenant over at The Lost Souls place?"

She nodded and smiled, officially no longer surprised that anyone and everyone seemed to know who she was.

"So, is this yours?"

He nodded slowly and looked around at the various frames and large, thin boxes around them. "My shop specializes in repurposed materials made into art pieces," he said.

She looked back at the stained glass window. "Well, that is art that I am interested in. How much?"

He lifted a hand to his smooth jaw and thoughtfully scratched as he looked at the pane, then back at her. "That one is spoken for, I'm afraid. But you can commission one."

His phone started ringing in his hand and he looked down, a flash of annoyance crossing his face before he looked back up at her with his wide smile. "I have to get this but here is my card." He pulled something out of his wallet and stepped forward, holding the small business card out to her.

Albott Ave Art

Miles Greenfield, owner

"Thanks," she said, pocketing it as she stepped back.

His smile widened, showing nice white teeth, and then he waved. "Call. Phone number is on the back. Tell me what you want and I will see what I can do," he said. "Nice to meet you."

There was no mistaking the interest in his face and brown eyes as they held hers.

"Nice to meet you too. I'll let you go," she said as she waved and turned back toward the alley, tugging a stubborn Casper.

As she was walking something small and black wove between her legs, causing her to lose her footing. A yelp squeaked out of her mouth as she threw out her arms trying to find balance as she went down. Her eyes closed tightly bracing herself for impact, but before she hit the hard concrete, arms scooped around her torso keeping her from feeling the bite of the ground.

She opened one eye and then both to see a pair of dark eyes and a scowling face she unfortunately recognized. His arms felt thick and hard and somehow were cradling her gently which made her body respond in a way that she did not approve of, so she shoved away, concentrating on keeping herself standing upright so as not to embarrass herself yet again in front of this man.

He tilted his head, a piece of dark hair falling over his forehead, as he considered her. Today he was wearing a khaki-colored utility shirt with black jeans and black boots. With the low-strung lights illuminating the narrow space she could see a freckle just under his left eye and his stubble was strong along his chin and jaw. And she really needed to stop cataloging everything about him.

"I don't know you well, Miss Cambridge, but based on our three interactions I would say you are unstable and jumpy."

She sighed, wanting to pick up the nearest rock and throw it at his handsome face but refraining.

"Better that than what I have learned from three interactions with you. Which is that you're a grumpy jerkface that thinks he can get away with being a grumpy jerkface because he looks like the Brawny Man."

He paused, his hard face unmoving before he asked, "Who?"

Casper made a whining sound, pulling both of their attention to the large hound with his shoulders back and up and head down in a protective stance.

Ursula jumped with a yelp again when she felt something rubbing at her legs. When she looked down to see a black cat with one gold eye and one black looking up at her she let out a breath. She reached down to pet the cat she recognized as Sulphur and pulled Casper into her with a reassuring hand before he did something like try and chase the feline.

"What are you even doing lurking around a back alley?"

"What are you doing lurking around a back alley?" he retorted.

"I am trying to avoid tourists as," she stopped shaking her head. "You know what? Nevermind. I'm going to get home. Not nice seeing you again," she said over her shoulder as she started walking away from him.

"Who is the Brawny Man?" he called after her retreating back.

She merely raised a hand up without looking back, waving her fingers. The black cat walked next to her and she looked back down. "Sulphur, right?"

The cat's mismatched eyes looked up at her and she swore the cat understood what she said. Which would not be the oddest thing that had happened over the last few weeks. She walked steadily and slowly, a bag with soup in one hand while a black cat walked along one side and a grey hound on her other. When she was almost home, about to walk into the thick cover of forest that led to the house, her phone buzzed a few times. Multiple texts started coming in from her group chat with the dinner club. She paused along the winding drive, bobbing lights above, to read the slew of texts coming in.

"Holy crap," she said as she read through each one trying to process what she was reading. A link was sent by Kelsea and she clicked it as she continued on the path. A video started playing on her screen of a news journalist and it made her stop walking altogether.

"Today's news is stranger than usual, even in a place like Salem. A man named Jason Harrison went to the emergency room, having apparently woken up with a lion tail. You heard me correctly. A man woke up this morning with the tail of a lion, stumping every doctor in the building. In fact, it took three hours for multiple doctors, nurse practitioners, and other medical professionals from out of state to weigh in on this wild medical phenomenon. Mr. Harrison has promised a news story once he is feeling up to it, but for now has asked for privacy for himself and his family. More to come."

Ursula was standing in the middle of her front porch, mouth agape when she read the newest text from Tilly.

Tilly: So. Our hexes worked.

CHAPTER NINE

MAGIC TICKLES FOR ATTENTION

L eaves changed colors and fell, the town became busier with the Halloween season, and B&Bs, hotels, and rentals filled to capacity. An overall air of proprietor frenzy filled each nook and cranny of Salem. Ursula spent her days working for a few hours and tending (with magically obtained knowledge) her wildly burgeoning garden before the sun dipped out of sight. Most nights were spent at home listening to music and making dinner, then bundling up against the crisp, deep fall air to make her way with Casper to the Lost Souls Graveyard.

The first few nights after realizing what they had done were static with trepidation and agitated looks around the sunless graveyard. She kept Casper close as they walked around keeping whatever souls were there company. Each night got a little easier with less fear and more of an understanding that they walked on hallowed ground; as long as they respected that, she felt like she was more than welcome among the nameless headstones.

One night, she found another tarot card on the top of a tombstone, held down with a pure white daisy. This card had the weights of justice on it and looked to be from the same deck that Crystal had given to her. She wondered if Crystal came here on her own. She pocketed it, the card feeling warm against her palm.

Why were the headstones blank? Who were these lost souls and was their anonymity the reason they still hung around? She thought of the card sitting heavily in her pocket. Was there a deep injustice served for these souls?

A scarier thought: were the souls waiting to exact revenge to balance the injustice?

She thought for the first time in a few days about what she left behind. Who she left behind. Going unnoticed in life was not unimaginable to Ursula Cambridge. She had done it with the person she had thought the most important in her life for the last few years. It was a ghostly thing, to live with someone who forgot to look for you and then stopped seeing you altogether.

One particularly cold and windy day with a mug of steaming apple cider next to her, Casper barked, jolting her out of her thoughts as she sat at her antique desk working on a marketing executive's resume as well as a plan for marketing herself to a few startup companies.

"Okay, let's go for a walk," she said as she stood and stretched slowly, the popping of her shoulders a clear tell that she had been hunched over her computer for far too long. It was the cracking of her bones and the ache of muscles that hadn't been there before that reminded her of her age. She could lay on her college dorm floor flipping through the pages of a book for hours and spring up without aches or pains. Now, she sometimes woke up with a pulled neck because she slept oddly.

She walked to the kitchen to fill a bottle of water for their walk when she paused, something out the back windows catching her eye. She frowned as she made her way out the door, a gust of wind just waiting to squeeze inside the moment the door cracked. As she braced a hand over her eyes against the barb of sunlight that found its way through a small break in the forest's armor, her mouth opened in silent awe as she took in what had caught her eye: green. An abundance of green growth.

The plant she had harvested for her hangover headache, valerian, had doubled its size. Vines with small, purple flowers were growing next to it and up along the post of her back porch. Thick patches of what she knew were mint spread across an expanse of land. Was that a cayenne pepper plant? There were at least ten other plants in various states of growth and bloom that she should not immediately recognize but did and, more alarmingly, had not been here yesterday.

She pulled her phone from her back pocket carefully while keeping her eyes on the plants as though they might have another burst of growth and press their verdant bodies against the glass. Once she found Crystal's number, her eyes shot back to the wild garden as she waited with the buzzing ring against her ear.

"Ursula, what a pleasant surprise," Crystal's voice filled her ears with her lilting and comforting tone. She knew immediately that she had been the right person to call.

"Crystal, I..." what? How did she tell her that there were magical plants growing where they hadn't been mere hours ago? She would sound bonkers. But this was a woman who had stood in a graveyard and hexed people. And they worked. Then she thought of the two tarot cards sitting on the island. "There are tons of plants growing in my backyard that were not here yesterday," she said quickly. "And I think I know what all of them are. And I shouldn't," she said, slowly now. "Like, I have never seen these plants but I know their names and what they do." She paused. "Medicinally," she added.

There was silence on the other end and she tried to imagine what the woman was thinking or what her face looked like.

Sure, they drank tequila and hexed some people together, but that didn't mean she didn't sound crazy right now. What if Crystal thought she was out of her mind?

"Do you have any mint? My stomach is a bit upset and I was thinking some nice mint tea would be lovely," Crystal finally said.

Ursula smiled into the phone, a whoosh of relief sluicing through her. "I do," she said. "I can pick some and bring it to you?"

"Let's meet in town," Crystal offered. "There's a rally that I am quite interested in," she said. "See you in a half an hour?"

"Absolutely. See you soon," she replied. She slid the phone into her back pocket again and shook her head at her new plants, then leaned forward with her eyes squinting as she watched the vine stretch and slowly wrap itself around the post in a slithering movement before it sighed and settled. "Wild," she whispered, shaking her head.

A sharp bark made her jump and spin to find a tall Casper standing on his back legs with his front paws braced against the glass looking out at her.

"I'm coming, boy," she said throwing one more look at her magical garden before she grabbed kitchen shears and threw some fresh mint into a brown paper bag. With Casper leashed, mint in her backpack, and water bottle in hand, they made their way to town. Sulphur decided to join them on their trek, her sleek body walking in sync with the woman and the beast.

Crystal was easy to find at the edge of a rather impressive crowd that had gathered in the parking lot of the local grocery store. She was wearing a long, flowing cream dress with bell sleeves and a leather vest over the top of it. Her hair was twisted into an easy chignon at the back of her head. When she saw Ursula her eyes lit up and she waved her over where she pulled her into the kind of hug you got from someone who truly wanted to see you. Ursula wouldn't delve into her thoughts deeply on this right now, but as they released each other from the hug she felt a mixture of absolute awe at feeling welcomed with sadness that the embrace ended.

Had she gone so long without feeling loved and pulled into another body?

She shook the thoughts off as unwanted lint.

"So, what is this?" she asked looking around and seeing an unusual amount of American flags as if they were celebrating Independence Day early. The crowd was large and music was playing, its notes weaving between the words of conversation.

"This," Crystal said with raised eyebrows and a look of gentle wariness, "is a rally of support for Rob Sandis running against Cora for mayor."

Ursula whipped around immediately looking at the crowd of people and at what was a makeshift stage to the side of the parking lot. There she found the impressive banner with Rob's name and his slogan: A brighter future for Salem.

"Hello!"

The crackle of the mic sound system filtered through the crowd drawing words to a snapping halt and bringing everyone's attention to the stage where a woman wearing a fancy blazer skirt set in pale pink stood. She looked to be in her late sixties with perfectly styled white hair.

"Thank you for coming out to show your support to, who I believe, is the right man to bring us a brighter future!"

"That's Cherry Sandis," Crystal whispered into Ursula's ear. "She's the head of the school board."

"Sandis?"

She nodded. "And Rob's mother. Fancies herself a matriarch of Salem with blood that runs deep in its history. Richer than Solomon."

A woman in her fifties gasped when she noticed Casper next to Ursula and gave her a beady, angry look. Ursula frowned and pulled Casper to her other side between herself and Crystal.

The man of the hour jumped onto the stage with the energy of a man who hadn't faced many obstacles in life. It was the way he had his head tipped up just so, not having felt the gravity of what tribulation can do to someone's stance.

"Thank you! Thank you! I want to thank the many people who made this possible today," he said. He braced his hands on the lectern like he was dominating it and something about his posture, his smiling face that beamed, his hands that were holding onto the sides of the lectern as though he were communicating that he was the one in charge made Ursula want to turn and walk away.

"And why are we here?" she whispered to Crystal.

"Because it's important to know both sides."

"This is a big crowd," she said nervously looking around.

"I believe our town is under attack." His strong words brought her attention back to where the handsome politician stood before his crowd. "I believe that we are watching things across our beloved country happen every day that could have been prevented. Crimes against our children." A murmur of approval rippled through the crowd. "We have the opportunity to get ahead of those crimes now," he said punctuating his words with a firm fist on the lectern. "We need to start now, in our schools." More voices of agreement were shouted.

Ursula tilted her head. "He's for protecting children and keeping them safe," she said with a note of confusion. She looked over at Crystal. "And we are against that?"

Crystal answered with a raised finger telling her to wait.

"So," his voice boomed out over the eager and hungry crowd below him. "I petition, with the support of our school board, to bring our Christian, wholesome values back into the schools." Oh no. "We need to give them the right armor!" Cheers. "We need to strengthen our children the way our long-ago fathers did!" More cheers. "We need a leader who understands family values. Understands the foundation of this great country. We need a leader who can strip down all of the noise and bring us back to our simple roots and culture!" Loud applause rippled and broke the air. "Let us pave the way for a brighter Salem!"

The crowd went wild. Ursula watched in awe as this town rich in its history with persecution danced with this fine line. Cherry Sandis stood behind him with head tilted up, an austere and satisfied look.

She felt a tug on her sleeve and looked to see Crystal had turned and was walking away from the crowd. Ursula gladly followed, but she threw one last look over her shoulder at the crowd and the polished man who was now walking down the stage to talk to his supporters.

Once they were sitting at a wooden table outtside of a Black Cat Coffee, strong black coffee for Ursula, a cup of whipped cream for Casper, and tea for Crystal, Ursula leaned forward as though to keep her words protected from the surrounding bustling world.

"A conservative mayflower man running for mayor in Salem seems like the perfect tagline for a cozy mystery," Ursula said with a half smile.

Crystal popped off the black lid of her to-go cup of tea, which was the perfect mix of pink and peach with the black cat logo on the front. She pulled what looked like a small jeweled compact out of her purse, plucked something between her index and thumb then sprinkled it over her open cup before she swirled and then took a satisfactory sip. "Good heavens this tea is good, and yes," she answered her question. "Rob, who I have known since he came into this world screaming and demanding people look at him, is running on the platform of conservative values. Which is utterly uninteresting."

"Really? Attacking people's freedom and rights is uninteresting?"

Crystal's smile looked like it had fed off of this question and knew exactly what the words tasted like. "Darling, men challenging people's rights to breathe, read, vote, and procreate or not is the oldest villain story in history."

Ursula frowned. "Right," she said slowly. "But we still have to do something. Fight it." How could this wise woman across from her be so blase about something so horrific?

Crystal tilted her head, her eyes looking over the younger woman softly. "Of course we fight it," she said, the matter-of-fact words confusing Ursula. But then her smile grew with a gentle sort of knowing that made Ursula want to lean forward and ask all the questions women in their late thirties needed answers to. "Fighting it isn't the question. It's how. Being angry and bothered is only the thing that will motivate us to do something. But fighting it angry and bothered will only drive their convictions deeper." She flitted a thin hand through the air, all of the cares floating there batted away. "We fight with clear heads, our wits, and our ability to do what they are unable to."

What was it? What were they able to do that men like Rob Sandis could not? She needed to know. "Which is?" she prompted.

"Come to the table of discussion with curiosity rather than fear," she said as if it were obvious.

It was not obvious. Fear? These people led charged debates with anything but fear. People like Rob Sandis did not fear people who disagreed with them; they lashed out with pointing fingers and disdain. But before she could respond Crystal's voice lifted and there was a kind of gentle cooing in her tone that drew Ursula's attention to the person she was speaking to.

But when her eyes caught on the one person she could not imagine ever cooing over, she barely held back her own eye roll.

"Ursula honey, have you met our resident bachelor Jenson Lancaster?"

She fought another eye roll but then mumbled, "Unfortunately," she breathed out quietly as she covered it up taking a sip of her coffee.

"What was that?" Crystal asked not hearing her. She leaned over for only Ursula to hear her add, "He's cursed, you know."

She frowned with a tight smile and said in a normal voice, "I have run into him, yes."

He tilted his head, his eyes clashing with hers telling her he had heard her original answer and she swore the tiniest humored twitch of his mouth was fought by his grumpiness, which won unsurprisingly.

He was wearing a long-sleeved navy thermal henley shirt which unfortunately was a great color on him.

"I fixed her porch railing," he said to Crystal.

"Oh, that's right! Me and my old age. Never know what is going to stick around up here," she tapped her temple and winked at Ursula who had a sneaking suspicion she forgot nothing.

Ursula pulled in a deep breath and turned that tight-lipped smile back to the tall man who was looking at her with impressive blankness. She couldn't decipher his look or guess his thoughts with confidence if thousands of dollars were riding on it.

"Would you like to join us?"

Crystal's question pulled an unfiltered groan from Ursula's mouth which she tried to cover with a cough and by taking a sip of her coffee simultaneously as if her mind couldn't decide which costume to put over her reaction. The result was sprayed hot coffee and a coughing fit along with a sweep of embarrassing heat sliding up her skin as she tried to catch her breath.

Crystal reached over to grab abandoned napkins on the table next to them while the asshole himself shocked her by kneeling as his large hand slowly patted her back while she got her coughs under control.

If his hand touching her back wasn't enough, then the hot whisper against her ear did it when she heard, "Looks like you could use a Brawny paper towel." His deep voice and those words made her body give an involuntary shiver.

When she opened her eyes to see his so close to hers, amusement clear in their dark swirling depths, that freckle below his eye so clear, she shrank back from shock at the proximity to the man. And also a smidge of embarrassment. He was warm and smelled good which made something short-circuit in her brain. She did not want his attention on her. It felt out of control.

"I'm fine," she said then cleared her throat and said it more clearly. "I'm fine. I'm good."

The corners of his mouth pulled up slyly at her reaction to him and he raised a mocking brow. "You sure? I can go across the street and grab a roll of the paper towels you like so much." He hitched a thumb over his shoulder to where the grocery store, and slowly dispersing crowd, was.

Her eyes widened a fraction before she narrowed them and straightened her shoulders in a self-collecting gesture. "I'm fine. Your concern is touching, though." She kept his stare with her own icy one unwilling to waver. This man was intense. And he happened to only see her in embarrassing states. Which he was the cause of.

There was something about holding eye contact with another person that was so deeply personal and in this case, unsettling. Not creepy unsettling, but the kind that made little bubbles of hot discomfort fill her, moving from her extremities to her face.

Finally, their stare-off was interrupted by the whine of her large hound who was now leaning against her in what she hoped was comforting solidarity.

His smirk stretched the slightest. "I'm a thoughtful man," he replied as he reached out a hand to run it over Casper's large head.

Casper nudged up trying to get another pet rather than biting him and Ursula cursed the furry traitor.

A snort escaped her at his self-reflecting characterization of himself before she caught it and cleared her throat. "Mhmm. That's the impression I got from you," she said before she smiled and raised her coffee nonchalantly to her lips. She swore his eyes lit at her barb, and something flared in his eyes as he watched her mouth pressed against her coffee, but before he could respond she turned to Crystal, dismissing him. "Crystal, I need to get back. Here's what you asked for and I will talk with you later." She placed the small paper bag of herbs gently on the table and made sure to keep her eyes from wandering to the "thoughtful" man still standing there, his presence and gaze visceral.

As she stood Crystal frowned and reached out a hand to lay it on her wrist. "I will come by later, darling. You're a doll. And you," she leaned over to scratch Casper's head making him lean into her at the attention. "Be good and don't give her any trouble."

"Oh," Ursula remembered the tarot card. "Did you leave one of those cards on one of the graves?"

"No, darling."

"Oh," she said surprised, then shook her head. "It looks like it came from the same deck as the card you gave me."

Crystal sighed with a smile. "Those things have a habit of placing themselves all over this town. Odd little creatures."

She couldn't help but laugh and noticed Jenson smiling fondly at the woman, which made something light inside of her. But when his eyes caught hers his smile melted and in its place was that stoic stare.

Must just be her.

"Come on, boy." Ursula gently tugged on Casper's leash. She could feel Jenson's eyes still on her, burning, and she resisted turning around. She did resist. Until she threw a little peek over her shoulder and then immediately jerked her head back and groaned softly under her breath when she saw his intense face slide into a knowing smirk when she looked back.

He was horrible. He may be a good-looking sonofagun, but if she gave him a rating based on his personality he would score a one out of ten. And that was being generous.

Chapter Ten

WHEN A FAKE HEX IS REAL

Little did these five women know that when they woke up with bubbly stomachs and tender heads, five people would also wake up with their own form of punishment for their drinking in a graveyard under the moonlight.

Jason Harrison spent a good portion of his high school years being a bully and chose, unfortunately, to pick on the two young women in his class with black hair, almond-shaped eyes, and familial ties that were ambiguous to him. They were easy targets to a handsome all-star basketball player who got people to go along with him far too easily and laugh at people far too willingly.

For the last two decades, Jason Harrison swept through life a little less loud in his bullying, as a lot of bullies evolve when they enter the big world that is louder than their misguided rhetoric. He no longer picked on women of Asian background as boldly as he did in his youth. Instead, he got sneakier and smarter. He didn't make fun of their driving or brains, or ask if they were groomed to become a geisha (all things Tilly had to experience from him, including when he posted a photoshopped picture of her as one around the boy's locker room). Instead, he made sure his Asian-American insurance agent worked from home longer than the rest of his team during the pandemic. The other four agents who worked for him came and went as they pleased from the little blue house-turned-business on Apothecary Avenue. Tara Song was graciously offered the opportunity to stay home.

When the team set up a booth at a street fair, which they did every year, to talk about insurance, she was told she didn't need to help out, and that the rest of the team had it covered. She liked working fairs and was confused when she had been the only one given direction to 'take a load off and relax'.

Her glossy and sunny attitude turned overcast when Jason's three-sentence text greeted her the morning of the fair.

Always love your great attitude! I think it's best, though, if you weren't here to remind people about the virus that took so many of their loved ones while trying to sell health insurance. Enjoy a day off! You deserve it!

He married a lovely, if dull, woman named Chloe who spent her days as a former stay-at-home-turned-influencer who documented her lifestyle of living in one of America's most notorious towns.

He got home late most nights and they looked at their phones over dinners she cooked and documented on her page. They had sex two times a month and filled the rest of the time with the needs of their two children.

But this morning, the successful all-star insurance agent woke up as he always did in his navy blue boxers, padded to their en-suite bathroom that looked like it was designed by Homes and Gardens Magazine, and went to do his usual wildly long morning pee when something felt off. Or rather, something felt...furry and ticklish against his leg.

And that was how Jason Harrison looked down to find in absolute horror that he had a lion's tail.

Grady Fletcher had three things in his life that he talked about: his motorcycle, a Ducati DesertX (everyone in town and the three towns surrounding knew because of the 324 posts on his social media page), his motorcycle shop (with 862 posts), and how to make the perfect cup of coffee (Chemex with light roast locally sourced beans).

One thing Grady Fletcher did not talk about was his insecurity when it came to powerful women. At least not with his words.

One way he made it clear that he did not tolerate strong, independent women was by getting Jen kicked off of the town council through a whispered rumor into the slightly large ear of none other than Rob Sandis. While Rob was considered an upstanding citizen, a business owner, and a rising candidate to take over Mayor Cora Acosta's duties, he was also a childhood friend to Grady. They grew up with one blue house between them and many escapades including drunken parties, clingy girlfriends, hobbies, and curating the perfect lives in their beloved northeastern town.

Grady woke up every morning to make his Chemex coffee, then rode his expensive bike into his shop to help other people decide if they should put their lives on the line (obviously, you only live once) to buy a motorcycle or fix theirs up. The name of the shop? Yolo Moto.

When Rob had boasted drunkenly that he would make a better mayor than Cora Acosta, who was one of those women dragging society down into the pits of hell, Grady and their other two drunken friends agreed with the kind of enthusiasm only found at the bottom of too many beers. That and the hubris that comes from being privileged white males.

Now, Jen was kicked off of the town council, creating a domino effect in support of their beloved Mayor who supported the kinds of initiatives that Jen did, like feeding hungry children free lunches in school and diversifying the council so that different ideas and voices could be heard.

Now as it stood, the town council consisted of five men and Cora.

The secret rumor that he whispered into the ear of Rob Sandis that got Jen kicked off of the council? It was rumored that Jen was a bisexual swinger who had ruined more than one marriage.

When her friends asked her with raised eyebrows and caution in their voice if it was true, she gave them neither confirmation nor explanation. And when her true friends, including Cora Acosta and Crystal, simply gave her their time and support, she found peace in letting the town believe whatever they wanted, the truth still a mystery living inside of her head that was held high. This was around the time Crystal folded her into the small group of women that would become her close friends.

And while she no longer had a seat on the town council, her business still thrived and clients sang her praises for helping them find the healthiest version of themselves.

However, that did not stop a seed of resentment from taking hold and growing deep roots inside of her. She swore she could feel the earthy, fibrous roots reach into her ribcage whenever she thought of Grady Fletcher and his conniving ways. He had beef with her from long ago and while she wasn't going to talk about "the incident" that made him want to sabotage her, the threat that she could hovered over him. Bold of him to strike against her and not expect retaliation. So, she retaliated in a moonlit graveyard with tequila in her veins and a strike against something he loved. And there was nothing the man loved more than his motorcycle and coffee.

So, on the same morning that Jen woke up with a tilting world and riotous stomach, Grady woke up to coffee that soured his stomach and made him pass gas so loudly that he could be mistaken for a motorcycle, and an actual motorcycle that would not ride for him. He could turn the powerful bike on, but it wouldn't budge, no matter what he did. He called Devon, his mechanic, to come to his apartment and take a look, and felt relief when Devon was able to get the bike going and take it around the block. But when he tried to get the bike moving, still it sat in its rumbly and stationary way, going nowhere. He would find soon enough out that any motorcycle he sat on wouldn't budge.

Candlelight flickered on the island between the five women, the little licks of light pulsing between them and filling the silence with a quiet intensity.

"Okay, so what do we know?"

"We know that Jason Harrison, who was racist and a complete blow-hard to Tilly, is now part lion." Jen's face was an example of calm feminine rage.

Ursula and Tilly looked at Jen with barely contained exasperation.

Jen threw up one dark hand stirring the air and causing the candles to flicker madly. "What? What about that is wrong?"

"Did any of the other hexes come true?" Kelsea asked looking around the island.

All five women had gathered shortly after Kelsea and Tilly came over. Alcohol was not offered, in a silent agreement that it wouldn't help the situation. So, five mugs of tea were steaming into the air, the various Halloween ceramics merely warm props for fidgety hands as nervous energy was zinging around the dark kitchen.

"I hexed my nephew and his wife," Crystal reminded them. All eyes turned to her.

"Right, they spread rumors about you around town," Tilly said. "And you hexed their farm," she said, her words slowing as they realized what Crystal had said that night.

Crystal's ambitious nephew wanted to cut her out of the family farm business passed down over generations. She had grown up on that farm, tending to chickens, and collecting brown spotted eggs. They owned over one hundred acres with four hundred chickens and the only supplier of organic local eggs for the town. It was a profitable business, to say the least, and her nephew didn't want to share a cut of it, so he and his conniving wife started a rumor around town about his aunt and her mystical ways. The mere suggestion of eccentric Crystal, under-the-moon-dancing Crystal, the one who everyone whispered about and no one knew enough concrete truths about making her a fun character in town that whispers liked to follow, but the exactly wrong character their family wanted connected to their family business. No one knew what happened to her parents, having been raised on the old farm by her great grandparents and grandparents, running around with cousins and second cousins. And she had been dubbed strange since she was five and you were more likely to find her surrounded by chickens than other children. Her grandfather lost his memory shortly after her grandmother passed, and it had been easy enough to write her out of the will.

Easier still, was painting her as some mythical woman, which for a town of superstitious folk might be charming, but for a hard-working, Christian fundamentalist family, which her nephew and his chose to be, just the inkling of someone in their family dabbling in dark arts was enough to ensure she never saw a dime from those chickens.

For her, it wasn't about the money. She didn't care about the profits. She cared about the mornings spent outside with the creatures who gifted them their bounty. She'd grown up walking those fields and wandering over the hills and through the streams, learning what it was to become part of nature. Learning the importance of being quiet so the earth could speak.

When he cut her out and took the farm, they used less organic methods and lifestyles for the chickens, something she pleaded with him and his wife to reconsider. But money was the bottom line for them. The hex for Crystal was more about the cruel treatment of the chickens than anything else.

"So the eggs," Tilly started and trailed off.

Crystal smiled as she lifted her ceramic pumpkin of hot tea to her lips.

"Eggs full of...what was it?" Jen asked looking around at the secret smiles pulling at sneaky mouths.

"Pink exploding glitter," Ursula finished. "Dozens of laid eggs that were empty except for pink glitter."

With wide dark eyes, Jen leaned forward. "Did it come true?"

Crystal smiled. "I cannot admit to sneaking onto the farm to crack one open."

All four women were now leaning so far forward hanging on Crystal's words. Waiting.

"But," she added with a shrug of a delicate shoulder, "I can say he may need to market his eggs for little girls who like Barbies and glitter instead of households making omelets."

Four mouths wide open, four pairs of unblinking and smiling eyes.

"Ohmygod. A farm full of chickens laying Barbie glitter. That is one of the best things I have ever heard," Tilly said.

"What about you, Kelsea?" Ursula asked.

Kelsea's sweet face pulled up in a smirk. "Well, I cursed Chad Weatherby," she reminded them. He was a highly regarded class clown who tripped a girl back when they were in high school named Sarah down the bleachers, filmed it on his phone and laughed with his friends, then posted it on social media. He also got the video cut into the morning video announcements their school did every Monday.

"He lives across town, but I know he works construction and it turns out that he was incredibly clumsy today on the new bookstore's job site. He broke three windows, tripped multiple times, and built a wall frame off by a few feet. They sent him home." She fought a smile as she lifted her mug to her lips. "Not sure that they'll let him back."

"And how did you find this out, sweet Kelsea? Did you happen to sit at The Black..." Jen paused, a look of confusion crossing her face. "The Black," she tried again and shook her head. Everyone watched her with increasing concern as she placed both hands behind her head like ears, as if she were playing a game of charades. "Ohmygosh. I cannot think of the word. You know, the Black..." she groaned. "I can't think of the word. A...house raccoon."

Everyone's confused looks turned deeper.

"The thing that meows. The hissy floof."

"The Black Cat Coffee House?" Tilly guessed.

Jen pointed with excitement and relief. "Yes!"

Realization of what just happened dawned on them. "You can't say the word *cat*!" Kelsea said with a wide smile. The silly hex Jen used as a test on herself had worked.

"Hissy floof!" Crystal barked out laughing. All of the women burst into fits of laughter, including Jen who had her head tipped back and mouth open wide for the raucous sound.

A sobering look came over Jen's features. "I wonder how long this hex will last," she murmured. Crystal patted her arm affectionately.

"So, you were saying," Ursula turned back to Kelsea.

"I may have stopped by and sat at the Black Hissy Floof coffee house," she smiled at Jen who threw a sugar packet at her in response, "across the way while drinking a coffee for two hours and pretending to read," she said. What she didn't say was that she had her reason for hexing the class-clown-turned-construction worker. While he was a popular bully in her class, he also gave her a sexist nickname that followed her for years when she turned down his proposal to prom. He had a habit of responding to rejection with derogatory retaliation so she hexed him for the Sarahs he bullied and the women like her that dared to turn him down and paid a price.

All the women laughed as they turned their attention to Ursula.

"And the last one standing," Jen said. She had a black cat mug with eyes like Sulphur's and Ursula shrugged her shoulders.

"Yeah that guy," Tilly said, pointing at Ursula with a question on her face. "Oh! The one you worked with."

"Felix Smith," Ursula said. "He stole two of my clients after I had finished their coaching work-ups and claimed the work as his. Got a huge commission off of it and my boss couldn't prove that it was my work."

Tilly snapped her fingers. "That's right! Jerk," she muttered. "Okay, so...did he?"

"I'm not sure. I hadn't checked yet," Ursula said. She had been itching to since she clicked on the news story on her porch, but something bubbled inside of her every time her fingers hovered over the keyboard of her computer. If her hex worked, she had effectively changed the course of his life, and while his lack of integrity greatly hurt her, she wasn't sure how she felt about that.

Four pairs of eyes blinked at her in the dark room with candlelight flickering in their depths. "Well, check!" One of them urged.

She pulled out the phone from her back pocket and tapped on the public work media platform that everyone she knew in the working world used. She searched for him, clicked a couple of more times, and then....

"I must confess that I have claimed other's work as my own in the past and profited off of their intellectual data. I have a hard time doing my own work as I am often lazy and not as good as other corporate navigators, so I steal their work to make a name and money for myself."

Ursula looked around the island at the open mouths, held-back laughs, and wide eyes.

"I guess my hex worked too," she said with awe and, to her shock, not an ounce of shame. She felt no shame for this and she wondered if she should. They had worked together for three years. He was the kind of person who made you feel like a friend when you were with him, but when you were out of sight, there was no trusting what he said and did behind your back. A person who was concerned with making everyone happy in their presence often lacked the moral ability to stand up to the eagerness of gossip and in Felix's case, he was happiest adding kindling to that fire. She learned that the hard way.

It was a confusing thing to find someone so damn likable when you're around them, the haze of their friendliness covering up a rather monstrous and selfish personality. It was like being hypnotized in his presence and released the moment you left the room.

"What...what do we do?" Kelsea asked.

"With Ursula's hex graveyard?" Jen asked. She smiled above her mug. "I feel like there's a heck of a lot we could do."

Ursula jolted at the ownership. She supposed, at least for now, it was her graveyard. Odd. A possession she never imagined she would have.

"We cannot just hex whoever we want. This is too much power." Tilly was leaning back in her chair like she was trying to get distance from Jen's words.

"Maybe it doesn't work that way," Ursula said.

"You think that was just a one-off?" Kelsea asked.

"It was a full moon," Crystal offered with a graceful shrug.

Ursula thought of the medicinal plant knowledge she had magically known earlier that day. What kind of powers did this place have? She glanced out the large windows overlooking the back, unable to see the graveyard but still feeling it, like a warm and looming thing. It felt ominous and vast, like a black hole of power they could not understand and it left an unsettled feeling in her fingertips.

"We have to make a pact," Ursula said. Her voice was low, barely cutting through the conversation of the other four women, but the words carried weight. They landed heavily on the old wood slab between them and silence met her as she swung her eyes from the windows to their waiting faces. "We do not hex anyone. Not unless we have a unanimous vote. All five of us have to agree, and only for the most dire circumstances."

Kelsea and Tilly looked to Jen. Jen shifted her eyes toward Crystal who looked at Ursula with shining eyes that took on a sheen of pride.

"I agree," Crystal said, setting down her mug, the thunk of ceramic kissing wood zinging through the air. "We don't understand what happened or if it's even possible to do it again. But we do know something bigger than us is out there and we somehow harnessed it." Her eyes connected with each woman there and her words were met with nods.

"Okay," Jen finally said with a decided nod. She placed her hand on the island, the gold twisting ring on her dark skin shining. "We make a pact. Ursula is right. It's all of us or nothing." She looked up at Ursula who nodded her thanks to the woman across from her. She'd needed Jen's vote for this, she realized in those two minutes. While Crystal was the matriarch here and her wisdom a gentle umbrella over them, Jen was the voice and call to action. So, she gently placed her hand on top of Jen's, followed by Crystal's, Tilly's, and then Kelsea's.

"No hexes, no ambiguous magic unless we all agree," Jen said.

There was a press of warm palms, a whooshing of air and then the door and old windows swung open on a mysterious push of wind that brought in a swathe of twirling leaves making all the women jump or gasp.

When Sulphur jumped up onto the kitchen island, a few screams sounded between the women.

Five women were frozen in various states of fear as moments ticked by with nothing but the gently falling yellow and orange leaves finding their way to the floor, and an unbothered cat licking her paw as if she hadn't just terrified them all. It could have been seconds or minutes but finally, Crystal let out a thick breath with raised eyebrows and an unsteady laugh that caught on cautiously amongst them all.

"Your Prozac dog almost gave five women heart attacks," Jen said.

This time, the laughter was loud and free of fear.

That decided the end of their evening. As Ursula ushered them all out the front door, with Casper at her side, she waved them down the porch steps reluctantly. Crystal was the last to leave, hovering in the doorframe.

"You'll be okay," she said gently. "You're safe here." She must have recognized the fear lingering inside of Ursula at being left alone in a house whose doors magically opened and a graveyard that held the power to hex people.

"How do you know?"

"Because you're you," she said simply. "The house wouldn't have accepted you if your character were in question." She pointed to the steps of the porch. "And you're protected by forces of great magnitude."

When Ursula leaned out the front door to look at where she was pointing, her eyebrows pulled together when she saw six bell jars glowing milky white and silver perched along the wooden steps.

"What are those?"

"Moonlight," she said, in a way that implied the mystery of her words wasn't a mystery at all.

After Crystal left, she gingerly picked one of the jars up, the glass not warm like she imagined, but cool and buzzing as if the swirling, glowing light inside was cool energy.

Crawling into bed Ursula hesitated turning out the bedside lamp. Casper tilted his head and made a soft chuffing noise, the one he made to soothe her, and she smiled gently before cloaking the room in darkness, hoping that Crystal was right.

CHAPTER ELEVEN

THE GRAVEYARD HAS EYES

T he realization that their hexes worked was creating a buzzing text conversation between the women. Updates on a lion's tale being removed, an angry nephew who wasted no time in blaming his aunt's 'mystical oddities', and a motorcycle shop owner leaving town on four wheels were passed around over the next few days. They made plans to get together soon, but in the meantime, Ursula sat on her front porch pouring over the news of Salem reading about their graveyard shenanigans through journalistic ink. She thought of her hex, looking off into nothing while Sulphur licked her black and gold paw on the very top step of the porch. Seeing the black cat next to the bursting mums made her smile and the distraction from this new development was welcome. They would deal with the magical mess that they had created together but for now, she would set it aside.

She suddenly felt excitement for the upcoming Halloween festivities when she realized that she could do something here that she never could before; decorate for the holiday.

Before, any fall decorations stayed in the lane of classical autumn: garlands of leaves, white and yellow mums outside, a few vases of fall-colored flowers sprinkled around the house, and the usual pumpkins. He had never been into the darker decorations.

She pulled out a box that she had put in one of the downstairs bedroom closets and opened the dusty top. Inside were an assortment of collected Halloween decorations she had bought sparingly over the years and hidden away. She wasn't sure why she had done it, other than feeling a zip of rebellion run through her veins whenever she saw something at a store he would hate and make fun of. It was so rudimentary, he had said, to be a woman who celebrated the witchy and dark.

She sighed at the memory, or more at the feelings he had instilled in her through careless remarks that seemed so innocuous at the time but were truly sharpened and well-aimed. It can be easy, too easy, to slip into a world of spoken words and consider them just that: words. The reality was that words spoken by the person closest to you were more potent than weaponry in the hands of someone who didn't know you well enough to aim for your target. And that was dangerous.

They're just words.

Words.

Twenty-six letters rearranged and then strung together by a master at hiding how carefully curated they truly are, feigning insignificance.

But sentences turn into paragraphs. Then paragraphs turn into pages which shift into chapters and bleed into entire books.

And then suddenly, you're in your late thirties and realize that you spent the last decade reading books that had become increasingly darker, filled with hatred on each turning page, inking you into every single one of them.

And they did that to you. And you allowed them.

Ursula sifted through black candles, a gold skull figurine, a soft-feathered raven, a strand of delicate amber beads, and a glass with a fake animal's small skeleton on display. She pulled out a garland of hand-painted pumpkins and another of black leaves thinking about where she would put everything in this house that looked like it had been born for such witchy decor. As she carefully placed black, cream, and burnt orange candles around her house, she allowed her mind to wander to the man she had allowed to burden her with so many chapters about who she should and shouldn't be.

Sometimes, the shame that pressed into her bones at the reminder nearly made her fall to her knees.

Candles sparked to life around her house in every room that she left. When she noticed the flickering wicks that she did not light, she paused as a feeling of something washed over her. It wasn't fear. But it was a presence; similar to how the graveyard had started feeling. Like the souls were coming out of hiding to sit near her more bravely with each visit. But this felt like a kindness; she imagined the offered presence as a balm to her battered heart and smiled at the flickering odes as she passed them.

She wandered to her kitchen which now boasted of black velvet curtains hanging high and dramatic on those large windows looking out to the garden. The need for something warm and seasonal overtook her so she opened the cabinet and frowned when displayed prominently on the shelf was a new mug. A black, matte pumpkin with a curling gold vine as the handle. She pulled it down with a smile, holding the perfectly sized mug in her hand, the weight and shape of it just right. This house and its peculiarities were still jolting.

As she heated cider on the stove with whole cloves, orange peel and cinnamon sticks, and thought of other items she would like to buy and fill the house with, a noise outside pulled her attention from the new black pumpkin mug. She walked over to the windows as the sound came again, a low and gurgling croak.

Casper's head popped up and he slowly got to his feet, stretching and letting out a high-pitched whine as he did so, before he trotted over to where she was pulling the soft black velvet to the side and peering out the window.

The gurgling croak sounded again, a mix between a bird and a toad. She'd never heard anything quite like it. And then something suddenly flew at the window with a loud screech right where her face was nearly pressed to the cool glass causing her to let out a scream and fall back, tripping over Casper's large backend and toppling to the ground.

Casper jumped and barked, his front paws planted high on the windows making him stand over six feet tall. She was scrambling on the floor to get up, her hip smarting with pain, and she called to him.

"What is it, boy? What was that?" She felt for her phone, which was thankfully in her back pocket, and pulled it out ready to call 911, when she saw what had come at the window. A raven sat on the patio next to the floor-to-ceiling windows. He was nearly two feet from tail to head and she stared open-mouthed as she saw him turn his head and in his curved beak, he held a white flower. She peered closer and the moment the pads of her fingers lightly touched the glass, he dropped the large flower to the ground and took off. Her fingers tapped the glass as she waited a moment, then she went outside and tentatively picked up what the bird had left. It was a gardenia. Her mind tingled and she knew she held an August Beauty, not native to this part of the country and the fragrance hit her like she had stepped into a humid garden with these lovely, flowering shrubs. The scent was woodsy mixed with the most spicy sweet smell that put an easy smile on her face. She took it inside and let out a breath.

"Birds are leaving me flowers now," she said to a curious Casper whose nose was pressed into the creamy bloom. Then something shrieked causing her to scream again and drop it to the ground.

The timer on her phone was beeping from the island reminding her to pour the spiced cider, the smell of which had lovingly filled the kitchen with its own spicy warmth.

"I need to work on my reactions, Casper. I am a woman living alone," she said and Casper lifted his head defiantly. "Okay, I am a woman living with a large dog and no one else," she amended, "and I need to get used to this." She put the fragrant flower in a shallow milk-glass bowl of water on the island and stepped back feeling an overwhelm of odd and magical happenings.

The light of the sun had faded until darkness took over the weight of the sky, so the pair from The Lost Souls House made their way along the path they had now trekked dozens of times. Ursula held a jar of moonlight to light their way. The night was getting dark more quickly now. The air was getting cold faster, the apricity of the sun a much more welcome thing when she was out in the garden on blistery days. She was bundled up in a thermal shirt and a puffy vest along with boots and a knit green hat. Casper was too large for any of the dog vests she looked at for him, and wondered if she should pick up knitting, then dismissed the idea when she remembered she once tried to pick up crocheting when she was in college and had mono. The blanket she spent three weeks on unraveled the second time she used it. She took one look at her miniature horse-sized dog and dropped the idea of watching him unravel a lovingly created sweater in minutes.

Once the black headstones were in view, Ursula set the moonlight and herself on the cold ground letting out a long breath. She watched the white puff of breath pushing into the cold night air then tipped her head back to look up at the sky. Tonight was clear, the inkiness dappled with starlight.

"I have been here many times now," she said in a small voice to unseen ghosts, "and I still feel like a stranger walking these grounds. I wish I knew what the others said or did. Did they bring you comfort? Did they talk to you or sing or sit quietly?" She let out another breath and watched Casper sniffing around the grounds slowly, his grey hair looking white in the moonlight.

Ursula held the cool air in her lungs as she debated. She debated sharing pieces of herself she hadn't shared in too long. She imagined having to move around dusty furniture and pull out these pieces that got buried and hidden deep inside the attic of herself.

"Maybe they felt as out of place as I do," she said. And then she hunkered down, pulling her legs up to rest her arms on her knees, words forming shapes inside of her. "I have felt out of place for so long. I don't even think this is what feeling out of place feels like, because before, I lived in a small midwest town with a man who forgot I existed and nothing in that house felt like me. That felt out of place," she said shaking her head. "This, feels..." she looked up at the sky again trying to put into words what was going on inside of her, "this feels like being welcomed somewhere but still feeling cautious because I forgot what it was like to be wanted. Do you know what I mean?" Silence was her answer, but it was the kind of silence that was threaded with life and anticipation. She didn't feel like she was talking to emptiness. She felt like this was a space that suddenly was created for her and her thoughts and it washed over her in a soft blanket of such exquisite comfort that she closed her eyes and rested her cheek on her folded arms.

"I have felt lonely for so long that being around people is like walking out of a dark theater you've been trapped in for two hours and into the sunlight. It's shocking and blinding. Why do we allow that to happen?" she asked softly. And then tentatively she added, "Why did I allow myself to become invisible and then settle in like it's what I deserved?"

A painful memory formed, of throwing those words at her dearest friend who had been asking her to wake up. *"Maybe I don't deserve better. Happily ever after isn't for everyone, El."*

She squeezed her eyes shut tightly at the memory. At the look in her old friend's eyes. For months she would remember that look; disappointment. But she had spent the last few years not remembering and burying it all. She'd been lonely since.

There they were; the words she had kept inside of herself for so long, hidden, even from herself, and now they were out. She watched the white air the words had traveled on dissipate into the world; a sacrifice on the altar of honesty. It scattered quickly leaving behind inky vastness. And suddenly she was exhausted. A large, wiry head nudged her knee and she smiled gently at her companion as he lay beside her. She ran a gloved hand over his head slowly as she felt the weight of those words finally spoken lift from her.

A branch snapped.

Casper jerked upright and she turned toward the direction of the sound, her heart beating harder. The sound of leaves crunching made her heart beat faster and her breath come a little more intensely.

"Hello? Anyone there?"

Casper let out a loud warning bark and ran in the direction of the sound.

"Casper! Come back, boy!" she whisper-yelled. Her eyes were zeroed in on where she had heard the sound and where her hound was staring, his large body hunched and his ears pricked and ready.

Thump thump thump.

She thought about calling out again, but her breath was coming out in shorter puffs, her heartbeat was taking center stage in her ears, and her body was pinned by invisible hands of fear.

And she would swear to anyone who asked that she felt eyes on her. She felt overwhelmed by the feeling of being watched, the pulsing in her veins pressing a staccato of direction telling her to move. Go. Now.

"Let's go, boy," she called out to Casper. "Now!"

Casper looked at her over his sharp grey shoulder blade. He gave one more look to the shadows before he turned his great body and ran over to her where she held out one gloved hand and picked up the moonlight jar with her other. And then they were off, jogging through the dark forest, adrenaline pushing them, thoughts of murder and angry ghosts chasing them lively in her terrified mind.

This was the adult version of running up the stairs in a darkened house when you're a child. Running from the door to your bed because of the monsters under the bed.

Dancing orbs of light bounced above them, guiding and pushing them along.

Nothing sounded behind them and yet she picked up her pace, which Casper matched, and then she saw the break in the forest trail. She ran harder until they were in the back garden and then on the patio. And finally pulling the door open and shoving it closed with the click of the lock.

She let out a breath.

And then another.

She turned around to look out the large windows into the dark garden, but nothing was clear, except for the small round glowing lights dancing off back into the forest leaving behind a night that was too dark making everything look like a hulking shadow of possible danger. She looked at the gold-plated switch next to the door, hesitated, and quickly reached out flicking it up. The backyard was illuminated by the strings of cafe lights and her eyes roved quickly over everything it touched.

Nothing.

But then...

Something dropped to the ground, the dull thud making her jump, her fingers about to make an emergency call. Before she did, she saw what had made the sound as it rolled about half a foot on the ground, tottled back and forth a couple of times, and then settled. It was a Bonnie Brae lemon from her new tree that had grown overnight. A tropical citrus tree that shouldn't survive in the harsh and frigid air of the Northeast.

"What has gotten into me?" she said to no one, her eyes still trained outside and her mind hoping nothing else moved or she feared she would scream and run up the stairs like she was five years old again. But just like when she was five years old, there was nothing to fear.

There was no scary figure standing out there looking in on her. There was no apparition that came from the graveyard.

"I should probably put down the horror novel I'm reading, boy," she said to a dog that had quickly forgotten the last few minutes and was now engaged in a noisy affair of eating his dinner. She made some sleepy vanilla tea, a blend she had curated from her garden, put a splash of bourbon in it for good measure, and then went upstairs. But not before she turned on a couple of lamps around the downstairs that she normally would have kept off before bed. Tonight, however, she was going to double-check that the doors were locked and had a clear, illuminated path through the house, just in case.

She tucked the horror novel she had been enjoying into the bedside table facedown and decided to buy a new genre in town tomorrow.

A trip to the bookshop was exactly what she needed.

And no more horror. Not until she got her newly found fear of   .
living alone in a magical house under control.

She was a grown woman. No one was out there watching them.
She was safe. She was just a little sensitive to this new lifestyle in a new
place.

Still, tonight she invited Casper to sleep in her bed rather than
telling him to stick to his designated dog bed. Just for tonight.

CHAPTER TWELVE

MAGICAL AND POSSIBLY HAUNTED

The next morning came with a brash barging in as her phone rang in a shrill tone that would be dulcet and not unnerving had she gotten a full night of sleep. Instead, she had tossed around, playing a kicking game with her covers and looking toward the door every hour in fear of seeing a looming figure making its way inside. She reached over with a groan grabbing blindly for her phone until it was in her hand and she answered the call.

"Hello?" The word came out reluctantly and her throat was begging for some water.

"Hi, Ursula Cambridge?"

"Yes, this is her," she said, still sounding scratchy and not awake. She cleared her throat and rubbed her eyes.

"Hey, this is Miles."

She frowned, waiting for the name to click. A beat passed and she looked at a snoozing oversized dog lying on his back with his Barbie-long legs in the air and his pink tongue hanging out of the side of his half-opened mouth.

"Miles Greenfield, the art dealer in town," he offered.

She rubbed her forehead. The cute, boyish man who had caught her snooping at his storage art behind the alley.

"Right! Yes. Hey Miles, thanks for calling me back." She sat up, the movement disturbing Casper, who yawned and fell to his side.

"Of course. Can't get on the bad side of the woman at the Lost Souls House," he said with a laughing voice.

She could imagine the puzzled look on her face but laughed with him. "Yeah, don't want me to hex you," she joked. And then she tilted her head with raised eyebrows remembering that she had successfully hexed someone the other night so what she meant as a joke, could be a true warning. Or threat. But Miles didn't need to know that. And thankfully, his laughter let her know he hadn't caught onto the accidental truth.

"So the stained glass piece you wanted to commission, can you let me know what you had in mind if you're still interested?"

She smiled thinking of her burgeoning garden and her newly found green thumb. "Absolutely. Do you have time today to meet for coffee?"

"I'm free after lunch, say about one pm at The Black Cat?"

"Perfect. See you then."

She hung up and looked at the time. She needed to shower fast and get ready for a couple of meetings this morning and she was going to need an extra dose of coffee now to help push her through the day after her sleepless night.

Once she was dressed in a simple black sheath dress with a white collar, black boots, and her hair loosely curled, she called for Casper so she could let him outside while she brewed her coffee. She'd been thinking about what to tell Miles she wanted, dreaming up different pictures in her head, but she was excited. She wanted a greenhouse. Nothing too large; she wanted to start small. But she was imagining a few of the panels as stained glass pieces of art and it got her heart going. She'd always loved the outdoors, something had called to her anytime she went to the mountains, hiked, or found a body of water to enjoy. It was a kind of worship being without man-made material between her boots and the ground. In the last few years, she found fewer reasons to pay homage to something once so alive in her. Maybe it was the wild that kept her indoors; living the life she had and becoming less herself over time had created a box between her and anything that might draw her out, anything that might have beckoned her to wake up again.

She was thinking of that when she walked into her kitchen and stopped. Her body slammed to a complete halt in mid-motion rocking the top of her body forward and requiring her to reach out for an anchor to keep her upright. Just like her body, all thoughts of designing a beautiful greenhouse stopped. Because sitting on her island next to her filled French press was a Bonnie Brae lemon. Next to it lay another dark blue and gold tarot card.

Goosebumps erupted along the skin of her arms making the fabric of her sleeves feel scratchy and tight.

"Hello?" she called out tentatively, hoping no one would answer. Casper let out a low whine next to the back door drawing her attention to the lock. But a few hurried steps later she was perplexed, head tilted and hand on the deadbolt still firmly in place where she had clicked it the night before. After letting Casper out she checked the front door. Locked. Windows, also locked.

She dumped the coffee, which was a shame because as it was swirling down the drain she got a sniff of the robust blend and knew it had been measured and steeped exactly right. The tarot card had a gold woman with feathery wings and two horses. The Chariot. She might be starting a new collection. She bit her lip as she opened her laptop, quickly researching what this card meant before she logged into her meetings for the day.

The Chariot, a major arcana card, represents overcoming obstacles, and not without its own challenges and bumps along the way.

She liked that. Then her eyes narrowed on the description for this card concerning love and relationships.

If you are single, The Chariot is an indication that your past relationships have left you battle- weary. The Chariot signifies that you can overcome the pain of your past and move forward in your love life.

She snorted. She had no illusion or hope of moving anywhere in her love life. No, she was content where she was, thank you very much. She yawned, and thought about the coffee she dumped in the sink.

Then that niggling in her mind happened and she was in the garden cutting off a thick root of ginseng and then steeping it in hot water with the mysterious lemon and mint. The taste was slightly bitter, but with the raw honey that Jen had given her, it was a lovely, warm cup to wake her up. This newfound connection with plants wasn't all bad.

Her meetings were easy and predictable, but she needed to get out. She did need a new book, or an armful.

She got Casper settled in the small office on his plaid oversized dog bed with a new bone before she grabbed her favorite camel-colored wide-brim wool hat with the thin, black leather band. Hanging on the peg next to it was her black leather jacket and then she was off.

The day was the brightest one since she had moved here. Tangerine slices of sun pressed through stark-white clouds that looked like they had been tumble-dried and fluffed. The spice of autumn was peppered on the fresh, though slightly sharp, wind, and Ursula pulled in a deep lungful holding it inside of herself while she walked and tried to let go of the last twelve hours mentally. She could feel the unrest and fear start gathering in-between her fingers and toes leaving behind that prickly sensation that seemed to follow a person wherever they went.

She turned around the events in her mind. The stick snapping and the feeling of another presence in the graveyard. The rush of adrenaline as they ran back to the house and the feeling of something dangerous closing in on them if they didn't get to the other side of her back door quickly enough. Just the feeling of flipping on those carefully strung lights wondering between seconds what she would do if they had illuminated a figure that had been chasing them.

She swore she heard every groan and every creak of the house last night when she was too busy letting that gathered fear take over to sleep.

Was someone in the graveyard? Surely, an animal had stepped on a small, dead branch and that had been the catalyst to her now-groggy morning and the need for double the caffeine.

But the lemon. The same one that had fallen to the ground as she watched with childlike trepidation the still backyard. The oblong fruit was on her island and someone had brewed her coffee. That was not something she had made up. But since she had moved in the house had a habit of making things appear. Was the house magically nurturing her or was there something more sinister at play?

"Ursula!"

Someone calling her name from a distance pulled her from her psychological thriller thoughts, and she looked up to see Kelsea seated at an outdoor table on the patio of The Black Cat Coffee. Tall gas heaters were set up around and between the eight tables on the patio. Kelsea was currently occupying the one in the farthest corner where the railing was lined with boxes bursting with burnt orange and white mums. Ursula motioned to the coffee shop, indicating that she would grab a drink and then join her. Inside the coffee shop, which was packed and loud, she pushed her way gently through a small crowd waiting for their drinks while they stared at phones or chatted with someone beside them.

"What can I get you?" The girl behind the counter had dyed black hair that was in two long braids complete with a thick fringe of bangs and a septum piercing. She was slender, petite and pale. Especially so juxtaposed against her thick eyeliner and black hair that Ursula suspected was naturally dark blonde. Ursula had to bite back a small smile. She reminded her of herself when she was sixteen, working her first job at their town's one Starbucks. While her own hair was naturally black, she too had gone through a piercing and heavy eyeliner stage.

"I will do a large coffee. Largest you can get me."

The girl looked at her computer screen and punched a button. "Late night?" she asked without looking up. Her tone was friendly and calm.

"It was uneventful," Ursula said slowly, "but the sleep would not come."

"Ah," she said nodding her head and looking back at Ursula. "How about we do a dead eye?"

Ursula's eyebrows shot up and she laughed. "If I were ten years younger I would love that, but maybe just a shot in the dark?"

The girl's lips quirked up. "A coffee lover. You speak the language. Nice," she said nodding and Ursula couldn't help the pinprick of pride that this teenage girl had given her a stamp of approval. Teenagers were scarce with their praise of adults so she decided to pocket this one and savor it.

Then the girl tilted her head, her eyes squinting as if she was trying to read something small and far away as she stared at Ursula. "Wait, you're that new woman at the haunted house."

"Well, the Lost Souls House," she corrected. "But yeah, that's me. Ursula. Surprised you could single me out with all of the tourists," she said looking around the packed space.

The other side of her mouth quirked up and she got a full smile now. She was really hitting the jackpot. "Oh, we don't get tourists in here," she said simply. "Cool name. And welcome to our little town of horrors. How are you liking your new haunted digs? See any ghosts yet?"

Thoughts of last night came flooding back.

"Oh, it's not, you know, haunted," she said shaking her head and laughing to hide her thoughts.

The girl shrugged. "Pretty sure it is. But I'll get you that shot in the dark so just hold tight. I'm Bess, by the way."

"Nice to meet you, Bess."

"Oh hey, Uncle Jay. I got your text and your coffee is ready," Bess said to someone behind Ursula as she pivoted around a couple of people to get out of the way and wait for her coffee.

She pulled out her phone to check the time and heard Bess say, "Yeah, that new chick who took over the haunted house is here. Pretty dope."

She smiled and shook her head as the girl pointed to where she was standing, hoping that whomever she was talking to didn't want to talk about her "haunted" house. But when she looked at the customer in question, her smile melted into a thin and hard line. Jenson the Jerk was looking directly at her, his dark eyes an abrupt dash of too much this early in the morning without having had her coffee. She *definitely* did not want to talk about her haunted house with him. Or talk about anything with him.

The chariot card and its meaning flashed in her mind and she quickly shoved that into a dark corner. Never to see the light of day.

She quickly looked back at her phone and pleaded under her breath for Bess to get her that coffee so she could slip outside where it was safe from him.

A ding in her email inbox sounded, a sweet sound like the sprinkling of sugar, and the headline caught her eye.

Salem Having a Hex of a Time

But before she could read the article a deep voice sounded from right behind her, the words pressing against the back of her head stirring her thick hair. She had an annoying inkling that had her hair been pulled up, the words would have touched her skin and made her shiver.

"Don't tell me you're one of those magic chasers," the deep voice said with a note of derision. A few notes.

She sighed and rolled her eyes.

"Fine, I won't," she said without turning around to face the handsome man who made her want to punch his square jaw. But also made her heartbeat pick up against her will.

She could just feel him barely restrain himself from rolling his eyes. "You keep showing up where I am. This is a small town, but not that small."

She did finally turn at that and glared up at him. "You think I *want* to be where you are?" she asked with a tone of disbelief. "I would rather spend time with a telemarketer than with you. I would rather walk back to my house with both socks sliding halfway down my feet inside of my boots than run into you." His dark eyes watched her carefully and his full mouth pressed into a hard line. She pointed a red-painted fingernail into his very hard chest, trying to ignore how sculpted it was. "I would rather hex myself to burn my mouth on every first bite I take of hot food than run into you." That hard look on his face turned...curious, mixed with a flash of something else that made her stop.

Why was he looking at her like that? Why did she feel frozen in its path, their eyes locked and her mind and body unable to move or speak? But then it was gone and he blinked once, his dark eyes leaving her face and moving back to that look of indifference as he looked over her head at nothing.

One of his nearly black eyebrows pulled up, disappearing under the dark wave of his hair falling perfectly over his forehead. "That's a little dramatic," he finally said.

And now she wanted to scream. She had never been an over-emoting kind of person, and she was hardly dramatic, but something about this man made her seethe. But before she could say anything in response Bess was calling her name with her much-needed, even more now than before, coffee. She gave him a punctuated glare before she turned around and gently pushed her way through the small group of people waiting.

Bess held out the cup of coffee with a bored face.

Ursula took it and looked around before she leaned over the counter and said with a lowered voice, "Hey, what did Jenson get?"

Her bored look turned to one of suspicion. "My uncle?"

"Right, yeah. Condolences, by the way," she said. The poor girl was related to that ass? "What did he order?"

"A large black coffee," she said slowly, suspicion lacing each word.

"Listen, I will invite you over to the house and you can look around all you want. I'll even make you coffee or tea or a freaking charcuterie board if you give him decaf coffee for the next month."

The suspicious expression quickly shot into a shocked one. The girl looked at Ursula, then her eyes shifted behind her thinking before she looked back at her and smiled. "Deal," she said with a smile that crossed all languages: it was the conspiratorial smile between two women.

"Really?" Ursula was a little surprised the girl went for it. But then The Lost Soul's house was legendary in this already legendary town.

"Yeah. I love the man, and I don't know what Uncle Jay did to you, but he can be a jerk sometimes and he probably deserves it. And you're cool. Plus," she shrugged a shoulder, "I really want to see that house."

Ursula smiled wide. She gave Bess her phone number to set it up and then took her coffee with her as she left the coffee shop, not letting her eyes find Jenson as maniacal glee filled her.

Once she was outside she found Kelsea deeply concentrated on typing.

"Hey," Ursula said. "What are you working on?"

Kelsea looked up and smiled. "Oh, covering the election."

"It's coming up, right?" She took a sip of her coffee and smiled at how strong it was.

"Yeah. Two candidates at this point. Cora, and Rob Sandis," Kelsea frowned then quickly changed subjects giving Ursula a concerned look. "How's your morning going? You look a little tired, and not in an offensive way."

She laughed shaking her head. "None taken. I didn't get much sleep last night."

"Something wrong?"

Ursula paused trying to think through the last twelve hours. Those images flashed through her mind again.

But something was going on at The Lost Souls House.

"This might sound crazy," she started, her words slow and quiet bringing Kelsea forward as she leaned in to hear her better. "But, I think my house may be haunted? And not in the whimsical way the town whispers about it."

She was nuts. Of course, she was.

"That's not crazy at all," Kelsea said. Her tone was serious and she wasn't making fun of Ursula. "Why do you think it's haunted?"

Ursula walked her through the events with the raven and the flower, the graveyard and once she finished with the mysterious lemon, tarot card, and coffee she wondered if she was still blowing it out of proportion. But the young woman surprised her again.

She nodded, her blonde waves moving the way perfectly healthy and young hair does with a flowing caress across the shoulders of her thick sweater. "I have an idea," she said. They chatted and came up with a plan, spending another forty-five minutes on the patio of the coffee shop. Somewhere in that time, a certain stoic Brawny look-alike exited and their eyes connected. She gave him a fake smile and he raised his cup of coffee, decaf unbeknownst to him, and winked.

Damnit, he looked good winking.

Kelsea watched the interaction with a small smile.

"He's an ass," Ursula's voice took on a defensive note. Why she felt she needed to defend anything was not something she wanted to dissect.

"He's handsome as sin," Kelsea said with a knowing smile.

Ursula rolled her eyes. "That doesn't make up for his appalling personality."

Kelsea didn't comment further, simply laughed which abruptly stopped when her eyes caught on something behind Ursula. The sudden change in her demeanor made Ursula swivel in her seat, finding Rob Sandis talking to a couple of townspeople. He was perfectly put together, but there was something about him that made Ursula want to avoid him.

"Speaking of jerks," Kelsea said under her breath.

Ursula leaned forward. "You worked for him, didn't you?"

"He's just," Kelsea's eyes took on a look of memories, then she shook her head and finished, "he's the epitome of a politician."

"Yeah, I get that sense." They watched him shake someone's hand, his smile wide and like a copy-and-paste Ken doll's mouth.

It was nearing noon and Ursula remembered she was supposed to meet Miles, but with her newly devised plans for the evening, she needed to get some work finished today. She shot him an apology text and asked if they could move their meeting to tomorrow.

As she walked home thinking through plans for later that evening, she smiled hoping that Jenson's body was so reliant on caffeine that his day took a lethargic turn.

CHAPTER THIRTEEN

CHAPTER FOURTEEN

DID YOU NOTICE WE SKIPPED CHAPTER 13

"Where did you find sage candles?" Kelsea asked Crystal.

"The Black Flame Candle shop," Crystal said. "I also brought these," she said pulling out black felt witch hats from a thick, square box she had carried inside.

"I love how into this we are getting," Jen said, rubbing her hands together. She had chosen an all-black outfit, like most of them. A black oversized sweater with black jeans and boots. When she put the witchy hat on her head, her hair in braids falling over her shoulders and nearly to her waist, she looked like a witchy goddess not to mess with.

Tilly, choosing a black skater-style dress with orange tights and black boots, placed the hat on her head and smiled. Her red cat-eye glasses and dimples made her a sweet-looking witch whereas Crystal's long flowing white hair over her flowing black dress made her look like the quintessential mother witch.

Kelsea had on a black maxi dress with gold stars that was very hip. Lastly, Ursula chose a long-sleeved black shirt with see-through sleeves, a high neck, and pants that were black and white vertically striped with her favorite pair of oxford-styled heeled boots.

Kelsea coordinated a group picture before they set up on the back patio. The nights were coming faster now. Stars dotted the clear sky and the moon was near-bursting with her light. Bell jars that borrowed milky moonlight sat around the patio and on the sills of windows. Sage and black candles were placed carefully around the bricks where the women gathered in a circle reincarnating every 90's witch movie where women came together to cast a spell or invite spirits to part the veil between the living and the dead.

Sulphur was batting her paw at one of the marigold flames of a sage candle while Casper lay next to her.

"I've never done a seance," Ursula admitted.

"We had also never hexed anyone before and look how that turned out," Jen replied. She pointed to where Sulphur had knocked over a now rolling green candle. "Your apathetic murder puff almost lit her paw on fire."

"Still can't say *cat*, huh?"

"I'm actually having fun finding new words for the creatures," she replied with a shrug.

Tilly's face took on a slightly scared edge. "Yeah, what if this works?"

"That's kind of the goal," Kelsea joined in. "If Ursula's house or land is haunted, we need to find out."

"Of course it's haunted," Crystal said easily.

"Okay," Jen conceded, "bad haunted," she clarified.

"And then do what? We haven't thought this through," Tilly argued.

Ursula silently agreed with Tilly. What would they do?

"I could make us some margaritas," Crystal offered to which four quick voices replied with a unanimous, "No!"

They looked at each other, the mirth flowing freely. "I'm not sure I've recovered from last time," Jen confessed.

"Yeah, that was a rough morning wake-up," Ursula shook her head remembering the thick pounding and nausea.

"Ok, so what do we do if like a spirit shows up?" Tilly asked, her face smooth and solemn.

"We ask what she wants," Crystal said as if she had talked to many spirits before. And Ursula had the suspicion that she was not the only one there wondering if the woman did speak to spirits. It would not surprise her.

Ten minutes later, the candles were all lit, the women were holding hands, and they were silent except for Crystal who invited the spirits in her sage voice, the lilting sound held a reverence that created an atmosphere of peace. Ursula pictured a glass lake, unbothered and still. She felt it fill her. It was like everything in her life, every problem or inconvenience, fear and insecurity, stopped moving and stilled. There was no white noise of those things filling her head and she felt clear and calm.

Was this true peace?

And how did she find this again?

She was absently aware that Crystal had stopped talking, but that calm had overtaken her in a way that felt like a blanket covering her from the crown of her head to her toes. She feared opening her eyes might break this delicious spell. Moments skated into some amount of time that could have been five minutes or five hours, she was entirely uncertain.

The tickling smell of burning sage touched her nose and that prickling sense inside of her told her that it was white sage that had been used in the candles. The deep, earthy aroma floated around them all and she pictured tendrils of smoke wafting and twirling around the night and brushing against their shoulders, caressing their faces, and then dancing off into the night to join the earth.

Then a picture formed in her mind. The smoke danced and twirled until the tendrils pressed together to create forms, bodies that were dancing under the stars. There were ten figures of smoke dancing with arms sluicing through the night air, hair made of smoke blowing softly. It was entrancing, soft and poetic. The night had its natural music of swaying branches and croaking frogs and crickets. The lilting of laughter, young and free, filled her mind. It felt ancient.

And then just like that, a douse of something darker than the night sky scattered the smoke into nothing.

A flickering of all the candles, not caused by the wind, extinguished the world of peace that had been created. Ursula opened her eyes to find the soft daze of the other women. They looked like they were waking from a deep dream. The air was still, not a stirring, not a single disturbance, and yet the candles all flickered together in tandem like a burning coordinated dance.

"Did you see that?"

"The ten girls dancing?" Jen asked, looking around the circle.

Ursula let out a breath and watched as the other women's faces took on a look of relief and awe that they were not alone in their vision.

"I felt..." Tilly's voice was low and smooth, her words trying to find their way.

"Nothing," Jen said, but with a note of awe, like nothing was *something*.

"Yes, but a gentle nothing," Tilly agreed.

"I felt completely at peace like nothing could bother me," Kelsea added.

"Like the spirits welcomed us instead of the other way around," Crystal's warm voice and words brought about nodding and smiles.

"I think that if this place is haunted, maybe it's a good haunting?" Ursula posed.

"I've never heard of a good haunting but I would bet good money that whatever spirits are here want you to stay," Jen said looking directly at Ursula. "And it's a good thing you came when you did because that was not the feeling these spirits emitted before."

"Before?" Ursula asked.

"This just wasn't the most..." Tilly looked to the other women for help, "welcoming place before."

"What she means is," Jen jumped in, probably sensing Ursula's sudden unease, "this was the house and the woods that kids dared each other to visit. Nothing violent happened," she added quickly. "It just had an overall feeling of restlessness before."

Crystal scoffed, pulling all attention to where she stood, a look of knowing on her face. "Restlessness is a mild way of putting it, Jennifer."

Jen groaned. "You're pulling out my full name," she sighed and looked back at Ursula, a pursed mouth holding in words. "Okay, truthfully it was more than restlessness. There was an overall spookiness about the property."

"Try again," Crystal commanded in a tone Ursula had never heard, but always suspected she had inside of her.

Jen groaned again and then those words that she had been holding back finally pushed through the seam of her lips and burst out into the cold air like hanging white clouds. "Fine! This place felt spine-chilling, hair-raisingly scary. There was an undercurrent of threat anytime someone dropped one toe over the property line."

Ursula's eyebrows shot up so high on her forehead she felt the brim of her witch's hat tucking over them.

"Kids would bet each other that they couldn't run from the road to the graveyard and back. No kids ever made it that far without getting too frightened and running right back to the road where the fear immediately would leave them like claws releasing prey," Tilly added in a voice reserved for telling ghost stories.

"Perhaps we should go inside for this conversation," Kelsea proposed, her face white more from fear than the cool air, looking around them. Then, a sudden whip of wind slashed through the air and all the candles went out.

They stared with wide eyes and unnatural silence.

"I made apple crisp before you came," Ursula said hastily, interrupting whatever had just joined them.

"And I'll put on some tea to calm the nerves," Crystal offered as they made their way inside. Thin china plates each with a heap of apple crisp and a scoop of butter pecan ice cream were in front of each woman along with a Halloween-themed mug of orange and cinnamon tea. The newest mug to magically make its way into Ursula's cupboard was black with red lips and vampire teeth, a couple of drops of blood trailing down the side. Kelsea grabbed that one citing her love of a popular vampire show.

"I need you all to tell me the truth about this house, without holding back." Ursula leaned forward, her forearms holding her weight on the island watching as the women shared secret looks. No one went first. "Look," she said, "I spent too much of my life not asking enough questions. And too much of my life not risking my bland, lifeless life to invest in female friendships. And then I moved to an odd, magical town by means of an odd and magical manner, and then you four came along," she said, her voice softening and her eyes resting on each of them briefly. "In a very short time I have come to value this," she pressed the tip of her index finger into the surface of the island. "Please respect me, and trust me," that hand lifted to her chest pressing against her heart, "enough to tell me the truth."

They took her words and made a silent decision together.

"There are a lot of theories about who is buried here," Jen started, "but based on historical evidence the most likely answer is a group of women who lived here in this house in the early 1700s."

"So, after the Salem witch trials," Ursula said.

Jen nodded her head. No one was wearing the witch hats any longer, as they had taken them off and now the kitchen was dotted with the discarded black, pointy hats. "Women were not allowed to own property back then, and this house had been lived in by a widow and her daughter, both of whom were burned at the stake on the charge of being witches."

"Unsurprisingly," Crystal chimed in, wrapping her thin hands around her pumpkin mug, the steam of tea floating up in a thin wisp, "this property was taken over by a wealthy family, but history shows that they didn't live here long. Things started...happening."

"Things?"

"Noises, moved objects, things appearing inside the house that had been outside of the house. There isn't great detail, but a few cases were recorded of strange illnesses leading to death. They seemed to have lasted less than a year before they abandoned it. And then another family moved in. Same thing. The local pastor condemned it, naming it The House of Abaddon."

"Abaddon," Ursula said the odd name trying to place it. It sounded foreign but familiar.

"Devil," Crystal said, the word thick and punctuated. The air became heavier.

"No one was allowed to live in this house who claimed to be a Christian," Jen said and looked at Crystal.

Crystal shrugged her shoulders and Ursula watched as the woman took a sip of her tea before setting it back down and continuing. "Two women, runaway nuns from Europe, moved into the house a handful of years later, cleaned up the place, and turned it into a home for young women who no longer had a place in the world."

"Like no family?" Ursula asked.

"Mmm...that or escaped one that was abusive, or a marriage that was. Again, there was no great record kept of who lived here, most believe for their security, but they were heavily persecuted by the town. The trials may have been over by then, but they were called witches, or worse, and brandished as tainted. And as they had none of the mysterious and scary happenings, like previous tenants, they were labeled as evil. Clearly, they were in alliance with the devil himself."

Ursula made a face and Kelsea shook her head.

"They lived there for over a decade," Jen said. "They grew their food and probably stayed away from town as much as possible, but again not much was known about them or what they did here. Most records from that time mysteriously," she wiggled her fingers in the air, "vanished. And then," she shook her head, her eyes looking at nothing over Ursula's shoulder, "one day they were gone. Just like that. No bodies were found, but everything was left exactly in its place as if they vanished mid-breath. Animals left behind, knitting that looked like it was dropped with the needles still hoping to finish, a meal half-prepared."

"No one ever found them, not even a trace of them?"

"Nothing," Crystal said. "But, I suspect no one looked very carefully," she added.

"And since then, the only people who could peacefully live in this house had to be invited. And part of the deal for them living here is to keep the lost souls at peace," Jen finished.

Silence resounded loudly.

"And nothing was known about these women, or how many there were? There are ten gravestones."

Jen shrugged. "I would guess that there were ten of them living here and there was some kind of foul play that was kept secret by the town."

"Eight young women and two nuns," Crystal said nodding her head.

"The ten figures of smoke," Tilly said, a spooky feeling filling the space at her words. They looked around at each other at the implication. Had they witnessed an apparition of these lost souls?

"What happened to the last tenant?"

All four of them shared another round of secretive looks. Ursula let out a sigh for all of them to hear. Jen looked to Tilly, passing over the story.

"They were a couple. Husband and wife. The wife became obsessed with the history of this place and trying to figure out who the lost souls are."

"That doesn't sound so bad," Ursula said, thinking of her own desire to find out the same thing. "Wouldn't that put them at rest?"

"Maybe, but the way she was going about it, probably not," Kelsea said. "She got into some really weird stuff, like dark stuff. There were animal bones and blood found after they left." Ursula shivered at that. "She ended up having an affair with someone in town," Kelsea added.

"No she didn't," Jen disagreed.

"Well, then how do you explain the drastic change in her behavior and their constant and very loud fighting that led to the police being called? Twice?" Kelsea countered.

Jen waved a hand through the air like she was swatting away that idea. "That was a rumor. And maybe she had an affair, maybe she didn't. But she was obsessed with someone in town, said she found his name all over some book she discovered in the the house from a previous tenant. She created this whole story in her head about him and it was like she transferred that obsession to him, which her husband didn't take well, and the house didn't seem to take well either. He tried to burn the house down with her in it."

Ursula's mouth hung open. "Tried?"

"This house cannot be destroyed," Crystal said. "Luckily, for his wife," she added.

Ursula shook her head

"And what about the other man? I take it he didn't return the obsession?"

Jen laughed. Crystal smirked. Kelsea and Tilly, both wide-eyed, shook their heads.

"Not at all," Tilly said. "He's the most bachelor a guy can get without sleeping around and acting like a playboy."

Those words created a picture in Ursula's head. A familiar one. A sinking feeling filled her.

"Yeah, a grumpy, hot bachelor who doesn't date," Jen said looking at the others for confirmation.

Ursula frowned as that picture became more familiar and she quickly looked to where Crystal sat, her eyes already on Ursula and that smirk gone with a thin-lipped line in its place. The memory of Crystal whispering that he was cursed surfaced.

"Jenson Lancaster. Salem's hottest, forever bachelor," Jen said.

"Of course," Ursula said with a sigh, this time at having too much information. Jenson Lancaster, the Brawny man, was tied to this house and Ursula couldn't have named a worse person.

The women made their leave once nerves were settled and Crystal placed the last of the hand-washed mugs on the drying rack.

"I will see you later, darling. You know you're not being haunted?"

Ursula answered slowly. "I don't feel like the spirits here are haunting me. I feel calm and honestly welcomed by them. It's just something else. I don't know what it is or how to put my finger on it."

"It will all work out in the end," she said. "The gardenia is lovely. An august beauty, right? Means someone has a secret admirer," she winked as her index finger lightly twirled the white flower in the bowl of water.

"You think a bird has a crush on me?" Ursula's smirk stretched across her face, the feeling welcome after the last couple of days.

"Birds are messengers, darling. I'll see you later!" She wiggled her fingers in the air as she floated down the hallway leaving Ursula looking down at the gardenia as the white petals opened in a floral yawn.

CHAPTER FIFTEEN

THE DEBATE

U rsula pulled out her water bottle to combat her parched throat as she stood next to Tilly, Kelsea, and Crystal in a crowd that was getting thicker by the moment. Today was the first debate between mayoral candidates and Jen had brought them all t-shirts that said, "I think, therefore I'm with Cora".

Though the sun was out and strong today, Ursula was glad for the thick flannel she put on and the puffy navy vest layered on top. Halloween wasn't far away and unlike in the Midwest where Halloween could range from shorts and t-shirt weather to snow gear, here it was crisp and cold.

"So, do you all know Cora very well?" Ursula asked, having to pitch her voice harder in the crowd of people humming with excited chatter.

"Well, she's Jen's best friend. They grew up together, so she comes around now and then. Kickass woman," Kelsea said. Kelsea was sporting the athleisure style and a matching winter hat with a pom-pom.

Jen joined them right as the debate began. This wasn't a typical political debate with the correct time allotments and a mediator asking questions and keeping the candidates on task. Jen pointed out Cora, who wore a brilliant bright blue blazer. Her hair was a perfectly styled puff of coiled curls that bluntly cut off right below her sharp jaw. She was tall, and in heels, she was taller than her opponent, Rob Sandis, who was sporting a nice blazer, button-down, and expensive leather shoes. He looked exactly like a politician would in a movie: handsome, charismatic, with eyes that were keen and calculating.

So far, they had discussed the town's growing problem with the public school system. More kids were being held at home for home-schooling than ever before. Teachers were quitting more frequently than they had in the last ten years combined. Books were a hot topic.

"We have to protect our children and that starts in the schools," Rob said, doing his signature slamming of hands on the podium. It was now the second time Ursula had witnessed the firm gesture. People around them cheered.

Cora tilted her head toward him in response. "If you believed that, then where have you been in meetings about gun violence, Rob?"

Another round of cheers sounded for her quick question.

"I, like most home-rooted Americans, believe in our constitution. If we cannot uphold the constitution and its clearly stated rights fought for by our fathers, then we are no longer the America that fought for its independence!" Cheers, and waving of the star-spangled flag through the crowd was loud and thick.

"Times are changing," Cora started, trying to speak over the crowd. But then a look took over Rob's face, one that reminded Ursula of a bully about to pull something sinister and cruel.

"Is that why you, a strong woman, think you can lead a town in a value-led campaign?"

"Yes," she replied without pause.

"And you think the times have changed *so* much," he emphasized, his eyes looking out over the crowd in a way that said he knew how to work a crowd; it was in his blood, "that a woman that left a marriage in divorce with no children, no family, could lead a town that is looking for a way to raise their family? A woman who had an affair," he said, the sweeping words a death blow over his opponent, a catalyst for sharp intakes of breath throughout the crowd like a breathing wave.

Cora's face blanched visibly from where she stood. Her hand on the podium clenched and she blinked a few times at the unexpected sling from her opponent. Ursula turned her head sharply to where Jen stood, who had a different look in her eyes, the look that overcomes a best friend when her person is being attacked.

"You've got to be kidding me," Kelsea said shaking her head.

Rob continued, talking where Cora couldn't find the words, so thrown was she from the mud he had thrown her way. He talked about raising a family in this town, coming from the oldest bloodline in Salem, a stoic and proud Cherry Sandis standing austerely behind him like a talisman, and wanting to move the town forward in a family-oriented way. He knew how. Because he had a family.

She was a single, childless woman who was divorced and with a skeleton in her closet.

She tried to recover, return his sharp attacks with her own parries, to steer the conversation away from the personal.

But the personal was always so much more interesting when it painted a woman as human. Women were to be infallible. End stop. No room for grace. And Ursula stood there feeling helpless, even though she did not know this woman, she *knew* this woman. To be a woman was nearly impossible. To be a woman in the spotlight was like what she used to believe about magic: not tangible.

Sometime later the rally ended, and people dispersed to various restaurants around the town or went home or to work. A somber group of five women waited for Cora, but Jen got a text from her telling her that she would catch up with her later.

"Need anything?" Tilly asked Jen.

"Actually," Jen said thoughtfully, her eyes narrowed on something in the distance. The women turned to see her glaring at Rob Sandis in the distance. "Impromptu dinner club tonight? I'm going to see if I can convince Cora to come. Let off some steam."

"I'm in," Tilly and Kelsea said easily.

Ursula felt a sweeping warmth then, standing there in the cold, dim outside with these four ladies as they made plans to come to her house and break bread together as a way to heal one of their friends.

"Homemade pizza night? I'll make a homemade sauce from the garden."

"Hell yes. You are a genius," Jen said pointing at Ursula. "Everyone bring your favorite toppings."

"I'll bring the dough," Crystal offered with a childlike smile. "I haven't worked my hands in some good bread making in a while."

"I'll bring a few different cheeses and Tilly, you bring the honey wine, babe. And hopefully, I will have Cora in tow."

They made plans to meet at Ursula's around seven that evening giving her the rest of the day.

She had plans with Miles to talk about commissioning that pane for her greenhouse, so she made her way to The Black Cat Coffee.

Bess saw her step up to the counter and nearly smiled, but mid-mouth movement she stopped the expression before she let on that she was excited to see Ursula. To be a teenager and put all your energy into seeming not to care about things. Those were the days.

"Hey Bess," she greeted her with a smile. She, being in her late thirties, learned only recently to not only give in to what she enjoyed but lean into it. And this young woman with her dyed black hair and air of indifference reminded her of a cat. One that pretended not to need attention, but really, needed it more than most.

"Hey, Ursula. How's the house?" she asked nonchalantly.

"Beautiful and haunted," she replied.

Intrigue lit the girl's dark eyes but she pursed her lips, keeping a reaction from springing out. "Cool. So, what can I get for you? Another shot in the dark?"

"Sounds perfect after this morning."

Bess was writing on a pink to-go cup and trying not to look too interested. "The rally?"

"It was a little upsetting, to be honest."

Bess snorted and set the cup on the counter for the guy who reminded Ursula of Gomez Adams to grab and start making the drink. "Rob Sandis is a douche nozzle and he doesn't actually care about our town. He just feels like he has a right to run it since his blood runs back to basically the Mayflower. He has white knight syndrome in a non-medieval way."

Her words were aimed and ready at this man like an angry teenager, but they were poignant and sharpened to a point with intention. She wore a half-smirk that reminded Ursula a lot of the girl's uncle. She shook that vision out of her head.

"I'm having some women over for pizza tonight. You want to come?" The offer was out of her mouth before she could second-guess it. Maybe inviting a teenager over with a group of adult women who had accidentally, successfully hexed a handful of people while drunk in a graveyard wasn't the best move. But they wouldn't hex anyone tonight and they wouldn't be drinking any of Crystal's lethal margaritas. And hopefully, nothing spooky or too magical that Ursula couldn't explain away would happen.

Bess's eyes widened, an unfiltered response to her invitation and Ursula watched her mouth open then close as she collected her cool self.

"I mean, I don't have anything tonight so, yeah. I can do that."

Ursula's mouth itched to break out into a large grin but she kept it under control as Gomez Adams called her name. "Great, you know where it is. Seven tonight."

Before Bess could respond a voice barged in too close to Ursula.

"Beth," a snap of fingers, and incorrect name, made the teenager glare at the politician they had just been talking about. "Black coffee if you've got it, babe." He turned to where Ursula was looking at him without veiling her disgust and blinded her with his mega-watt smile. "Ursula! I thought I saw you in the crowd," he took in her t-shirt and made a *tsking* noise. "Rooting for the other team, I see. No worries, all friendly fire," he laughed.

Bess didn't move to get his demanded coffee and instead leaned forward with her elbows on the counter and her face the look of a bored teenager.

"Beth? Coffee? I need to get back out there."

"The name is Bess," she said slowly like she was talking to a toddler, "and you need to wait in line." She pointed to the long, spindly line of caffeine addicts.

He made an overly apologetic face and leaned forward. "I know, I am breaking rules, but I could really use your magic coffee to get me through today. I may be running for mayor, but I'm a weak man for strong coffee," he said, his voice dripping with charm.

Bess put on a plastic smile and straightened like she was a robot. Ursula watched with amusement as she said, in a robotic voice, "Absolutely, sir. Your wish is my command," and completed it with a salute.

The sarcasm was either lost on him, or he didn't care as he turned back to Ursula. "I know you're friends with Cora and her gang, but I want you to know you're welcome here and I take great pride in that house and its history."

She nodded her head with a close-lipped smile. Then Bess called out, "Black coffee for Rob Sandis who puts himself literally above others!" The words were shouted as if he were somewhere seated rather than standing right in front of her.

People turned to stare and Rob laughed awkwardly.

"Teens and their humor," he said waving to everyone as he took the coffee and glared at Bess.

"I'll see you around, Ursula. Would love to come by and check out the house. Haven't seen it in years."

"Oh yeah, come on by," she said with a fake smile. He was striding out with his bravado when she added under her breath, "I'll warn the ghosts before you come." Bess smiled at her words and Ursula leaned over the counter whispering, "You gave him decaf, right?"

Bess took on an *of course* look and replied, "Oh yeah. I've never given that dude real caffeine ever."

Ursula laughed and reminded her of the time tonight as she walked away.

"Cool," she said and waved awkwardly.

Ursula looked around trying to find a seat. She was fifteen minutes early for her meeting with Miles and the prospects for seating did not look good outside, or inside. There was a staircase in the back of the shop and when she looked up she saw a balcony with what she hoped were some tables and chairs. The space was cozy and close to the ceiling making this an impossible walking adventure for anyone over six feet tall, but thankfully she was barely pushing five feet and two inches with her olive green duck boots. She sat at one of the two tables and unloaded her bag with the new, not scary, book she was reading.

Looking around she took in this little coffee loft. There was a small, but tidy, station against the back corner for someone to add accoutrements to their coffee. The side wall was made up of beautiful bookshelves that looked handcrafted. They were stained a beautiful walnut color and the spines of the books had been lovingly placed in a whimsical lack of organization. There were two chairs snuggled up on either side of the bookcases, both made of leather a few shades darker than the bookcases complete with a small table between them. A coffee and a book were sitting on that table, indicating someone was there.

She had gone to the bookstore to pick out a book and left with a canvas bag with a few literary quotes printed on it filled with eight. So, she had blindly reached in this morning before leaving and grabbed two so she wouldn't stand in her living room deliberating too long over which one she was in the mood for. One was historical fiction, a genre she hadn't indulged in much but was interested in. It claimed to be an 'epic romance that will have readers gasping for breath' according to the back blurb. She could use a little romance in her life of the fictional variety. Real romance was off the table. Just the thought of meeting someone and giving away pieces of herself again made her squirm in her seat. The second was a thin reprint of Edgar Allan Poe's *The Raven*. She'd never indulged much past the required readings of his, but when she found it at the bookshop, her fingertips grabbing it without pause her heart clenched at the reminder of her friend who had loved his macabre stories. Since she had opened a small door talking about her past in the graveyard, she felt small pieces of herself fitting back into place, memories no longer having the door slam on them in her mind.

She was getting into the backstory of the book when a presence made itself known. Looking up expecting to see Miles, she couldn't help but roll her eyes when instead she was looking up into the dark eyes of a certain broody man.

"I love when a woman's response to seeing me is rolling her eyes."

She looked back down at her book hoping that he would take the hint as she responded, "I'm sure you've gotten used to it by now."

When he didn't respond and he also didn't move she sighed and looked back up at him with an annoyed expression.

"My niece said you invited her over to your house." He said it as a statement, his stoic features unreadable, though based on his overall grumpy demeanor and their short, but brumous history of interactions, she could guess what he was saying.

She placed the free bookmark the bookstore had given her into the book and closed it with a perfunctory clip.

"I just figured, being the niece of a grumpy and terrible conversationalist like you, who probably would have to take a course on smiling if he ever wanted to try, she could use some sunshine and positive discourse in her life." She gave him a taunting smile of her own and she watched, amazingly, as his lips lifted in the slightest of...well, not exactly a smile, but something smile-adjacent. He tilted his head, that same thoughtful look coming over his frustratingly handsome features before he pulled in a deep breath and everything went right back to his usual unamused self.

"She's had a rough life. Just be careful."

Her eyebrows pulled together with a little frown as she considered his words, thinking of a comeback about how he was most likely the source of that rough life when something in his eyes made her stop.

Instead, she nodded and simply said, "Alright. I will." It was a promise stamped between them. The first moment of relational collateral that the two shared, and probably would ever share, but a young woman who had a rough life was not a toy to fight over.

His eyes glanced down at the book in front of her. "I wouldn't have taken you for an Edgar Allan Poe fan," he said.

"But I'm so morose and ill-tempered like you," she shot back.

Another slight smile moved his hard face and she wondered what it would be like to get a full smile from this man. Probably devastating.

Just then, Miles made his entrance walking up into the loft, his open face looking around until he found Ursula, his mouth easily breaking out into a smile.

"Hey! Sorry I'm late. You know artists," he said with a laugh. He looked at Jenson then, who had to stoop just the slightest so that the top of his head didn't brush the wood-paneled ceiling and his smile turned tighter. "Jenson," he said in a way of greeting.

"Miles," Jenson's deep voice reverberated back without inflection. He turned back to Ursula where she sat awkwardly looking up at two men who suddenly felt like they took up a lot of space. "I'll leave you to your date," he said dryly.

And once again, she had the overwhelming urge to roll her eyes at him. This man made her reach back to her teenage years of disgruntled responses making her feel less than grounded as an adult woman.

Jenson's head had just disappeared down the stairs after he grabbed his coffee and book from the little table by the bookshelves when Miles shook his head and said, "Sorry I was late and had to leave you open for that man's sourness. He's touted as our town's anchor, so dependable, but he's just an ass with a pickup truck and the ability to swing a hammer."

She smiled tightly. She despised when someone felt the need to diminish someone's character behind their back in the name of connecting. It was, to her, craven, speaking volumes about their character rather than their subject's. She remembered that though Jenson wasn't pleasant, he had fixed her porch without asking for anything in return, and he was protective of his young niece with a rough past.

"He's fine," she dismissed his unkind words and moved away from the topic of Jenson Lancaster. "So, I have some ideas I printed out for what I am looking for."

He rubbed his hands together, his boyishly handsome face showing excitement. "Great! Let's dive in."

She was a little jolted by the juxtaposing personalities between this artful man in front of her and the brooding one who just left, though there seemed to be more to both men. As he talked about light and colors for stained glass, she absently looked to where he was exiting the coffee shop. When he paused and looked back up at her, her face heated as their eyes connected, his intense and communicating secrets, and she quickly turned back to the conversation at hand.

CHAPTER SIXTEEN

IF WALLS COULD TALK, THEY'D GOSSIP

H oney wine was poured, and seven women were gathered around the island sprinkling and placing their preferred toppings on the oblong shapes of uncooked dough in front of them. When Ursula had told them upon the first sips of honey wine that she invited Bess, a fifteen-year-old barista with a gothic Barbie vibe, they'd surprised her by responding with excitement. Trepidation, confusion and even being protective of their little group, would have made more sense to her.

Instead, Crystal smiled and nodded her head like it was exactly what she had been hoping for.

Kelsea and Tilly said, "Oh good. She's a good young woman,".

Jen and Cora exchanged some kind of knowing look that Ursula could only interpret as happiness at the addition when Jen replied with a raise of her amber goblet, "Thank goodness,".

But she couldn't ask any follow-up questions because the "good young woman" had then rang the doorbell that sounded like starlight.

Bess clearly felt embarrassed that she hadn't brought anything to share, as everyone else had, but Ursula hadn't wanted her to be weighed down yet by social niceties at her age. She wanted her to come and be. And the other women, of course, made that clear as well, bustling her in, pulling her into conversation and jokes, not giving her time to silently watch and wonder if she fit in the room she was currently in. How much time had they all wasted wondering that very thing, standing at a party silently, trying to find the right words or response in conversation, or internally weighing their entire worth against mere snapshots of the glamour the others carefully curated for all to see?

Crystal slid her amber glass of honey wine silently over with her delicate hand to sit in front of a shocked Bess. Ursula quickly reached out as she was passing behind them, scooped up the glass, and looked the beautifully wise woman in the eyes.

"No wine for the minor. Sorry, Bess," she said before handing it back to Crystal with a punctuated look.

Bess looked like she had been caught doing something wrong. Crystal looked like the Cheshire Cat.

"Alright, pizzas are in," Ursula announced. "I got a bonfire going out back with a pile of blankets in the basket out there," she said directing everyone's attention out the Dutch door and large windows. A couple of them wondered out loud if it would be too cold, even with a fire and blankets, to sit outside.

But once they each were settled, soft blankets of various patterns draped and tucked strategically over laps, their faces gentled into looks of warm contentment. The bonfire, perfectly engineered by Ursula and Tilly who had come early, was indeed warm, but each woman sensed without saying it out loud that magic pulled the heat from the flames and stretched it further around and over them. Should they step outside the circle of seven chairs, they knew they would be immediately plunged into a shivering night.

Ursula had been surprised that Cora, the mayor, had come. But after a few minutes of talking with her, it was easy to tell that this strong woman found comfort in the presence of other women, bringing with her a calming touch.

Conversation was slow as the women basked in the stretching warmth of the fire, letting it seep into their skin. Then they were talking about the debate, a topic they had wordlessly agreed to avoid when Jen told them that Cora would be joining them for a much-needed women's night. But after some easy conversation and soft laughter Cora sat forward, her perfectly angled hair gleaming in the flickering light and her presence strong.

"I did have an affair," were her words. And then all eyes, softly-held breaths, and open hearts were present.

Jen, ever the protective friend, placed a hand on Cora's knee and said, "You don't have to talk about it."

"I know," Cora said straightly. "But if my story is going to come out, then I'd like to be the narrator."

Jen nodded and sat back.

"We were different at first. That couple that laughed a lot, acted like best friends, the most important things weren't that important to us if it didn't bring us closer to each other." She was sitting on the edge of her Adirondack chair, her eyes focused on the fire and her words caressing old memories. "And when we, to our own surprise, decided to start having kids, we would talk about how it wouldn't change anything. We wouldn't lose ourselves trying. We wouldn't forget how to be us if we became parents. But then, a few years went by and I never got pregnant. I jokingly said maybe I should see a specialist and he jokingly agreed. And we both knew there was no joke about it." There was a pain, a deep longing lost that crossed over her smooth features, and each woman, regardless of her age or desire to carry a child, understood it. It's something that lines a woman's insides, this fear or knowledge of being unable to bear a child.

Ursula had never wanted children and always thought she was horribly mangled during some impressively formative years for that to come over her. Each woman sat in firelight with their own thoughts.

Tilly still carried a desire inside of herself to bring life into the world, but she didn't speak of it because it felt fragile. Crystal had carried and lost a child once, long ago, but sometimes it was moments ago the way the memory grabbed hold of her in a choking wrapping around her throat. Jen firmly stood in the camp of wanting to adopt one day if she ever found the right partner. Kelsea had an abortion when she was too young to imagine being a mom that would be judged and ostracized from society because of her poor choices, something that she had never shared with anyone for fear of a different kind of judgment. And Bess was young, but she understood that one day she would have to make that decision for herself. Over and over and over, because it's never just once that a woman is faced with this deeply personal thing.

"I can't have children," she said the words forcefully like she needed the reminder. "And one day he joked about how it was just going to be him and me because I was broken." She laughed without mirth. Ursula closed her eyes at the heartbreak. The other women silently responded in their outraged silence. "And then his jokes became more pointed, aimed, and often. And then all of a sudden," she raised the hand not holding her honey wine in the air, palm up like she was holding some imaginary thing; the memory of losing herself there, coiled tightly and dangerously. "I believed I was broken. I believed every joke he never meant as a joke."

She stopped talking and everyone watched as that hand curled into a fist, firm and tight, her eyes piercing the licking flames as the memories painfully pressed out of her from somewhere she had kept deep, deep inside of herself. The silence was so layered with all of the women's thoughts, hopes, hurts, regrets, and anger. That was the beautiful thing about women gathering together; they could gather all of the pieces of grief that they carried inside of themselves, all of the broken shards of who they once were or who they thought that they should be, and they could sew them together to create something beautiful and protective. There was nothing else quite like a group of women allowing each other to heal in their presence by simply being.

"And then he found Kimberlynn," she said. These words came out softer, like they had once started out as sharp glass and then over time they became smoother, weathered down until they weren't dangerous. "And I knew he was cheating, of course I knew. We usually do. And a man who I worked with made me feel not damaged and not broken." She shrugged her shoulders and then let out a long, heavy breath. "We both cheated and I don't excuse myself from the weight of having an affair, regardless of the circumstances," she said. "But I love who I am now. He has three children with her and every few years when he comes back home I will run into him and there's no resentment or hate, but it's like running into someone who no longer knows you. He only knew a version of me and in those moments he looks at me like he can't quite figure out how he knows me, you know?" She sat back now, pulling the blanket up more firmly around her waist.

The crackling fire filled in the spaces as everyone sat there thinking, mourning for a woman most of them knew casually, one of them knew deeply and one of them had never exchanged more than a hello with.

And now they were connected, for however long it lasted, tonight it was a true and devastatingly intimate tie that bound them together.

"Let's kill him," came the startling words that pulled all attention to the teenager with a knit hat over black braids draped over teenage shoulders that carried the weight of learning what it was to be a woman.

Ursula slid a look to Crystal who was biting back a smile. And then Cora broke the seal of laughter which opened the box for all seven voices to ring through the night in a unified circle of relief. And it was a relief, to bear witness to something so heartbreaking and then find themselves inside a world of levity.

"I mean, I know we can't actually kill him," Bess said, a content smile on her face. She looked at Cora with a nearly sheepish air and added softly. "But like, you know he's the worst, right?"

Cora's mouth flashed in a perfect white smile that was warm as she leaned over and squeezed Bess's coat-covered arm affectionately.

"I may lose the election to that mud-slinging man who pretends he is riding on high morals, but if I lose, then that's what Salem wants," Cora said. Just like the kind of political figure people didn't see often enough anymore. The kind of government advocates that we should seek out more because they did it for the people, not for the self.

"Nah, we're not giving up," Jen said.

"Absolutely not, darling," Crystal joined and raised her glass for everyone else to follow. Once all seven glasses of honey wine and one glass of sparkling peach water were raised, Crystal said with her head tilted back and her pearly white hair dancing on the wind, "To good and strong women, may we take over the world and turn it more beautiful."

"Here here!"

"Amen."

Sulphur jumped onto Bess's lap and Jen pointed, "Ah, our Indifferent yarn-chaser has made a new friend."

Bess gave her a quizzical look and Tilly explained, "Jen can't say the words *cat* or *feline.*"

"Ah," Bess said nodding her head, that befuddled look still in place.

Ursula's phone rang with the timer for their pizzas, breaking the moment.

Sips and smiles followed by laughter and more sharing of hearts but on a lighter note filled the evening. They burst into the warm kitchen that carried the smell of their homemade pizzas on the tide of large belly laughs and holding each other up, the way that women do.

It was getting late an hour after pizza was eaten, with discarded crusts, and Ursula noticed Bess looking at her phone every few minutes. Cora and Jen had left a bit ago and the other three were currently bundled up and working their way to the front door while chatting, hands full of leftover pizza and ingredients they had brought.

With the sound of their voices muffled and fading behind the closed door, Ursula walked back to the kitchen where Bess was cleaning up the goblets and small plates.

"Hey, you don't have to do that," she said sidling up next to her at the sink and using the dish towel to dry the amber goblet Bess placed on the drying mat.

"I don't mind," she said with a shrug. "I should probably get going though," she said, her voice reluctant.

An inkling hit her. Jenson's mention of her rough life, checking her phone nervously.

"Will you let me drive you home? I know it's probably not very cool, but I don't want you walking home in the dark," Ursula said, keeping her tone light. She noticed something in this girl she understood too well: the fear of being a burden. She'd learned it well and deeply as a child herself.

"Oh, well, yeah, I guess that would be ok," Bess replied.

"Thank you," she smiled. "Get your coat and there's a skull cookie jar up there," Ursula pointed to the top of a cabinet. "Will you grab us each a cookie for the road? They're maple snickerdoodles."

The corner of Bess's mouth tipped up and she nodded as Ursula put her coat and hat back on.

Once they were in her car, with Casper in the back, Ursula asked for directions and wondered how much she should dig, and how many questions she should ask this young woman who was clearly not excited to go home.

"So, do you have any siblings?"

"Not that I know of," the words came out in a teenage mumble. "But, I mean, my dad ran out so he probably has a few somewhere."

"I'm sorry to hear that."

Another shrug.

"So, just you and your mom?"

"Yeah." And then she added more softly, "Sometimes."

Something pinched inside of Ursula as she drove slowly down a backstreet around downtown. She still wasn't familiar with the town and had never been this way before, but the houses were small one-story boxes, lights on the porches, and lights out inside with only the flickering of televisions. It felt smaller and tighter down these streets like the town had run out of room as they built this neighborhood.

"What does your mom do?"

A sigh escaped Bess and Ursula wondered if she had pushed a button. But before Bess could answer, the red and blue oscillating lights of a police car swirled around the houses of the tight street. The commotion was a block away still, but Ursula stopped driving, trying to peer down the dark street and discern if she could get around them. Casper poked his large head over the console as all three looked on. When she noticed out of the corner of her eye Bess clutching her phone she looked over to see the girl's face washed in panic, a look that took away the edge of age and nonchalance on her teenage face. She looked small and vulnerable.

As Ursula's car came up to the stop sign, now only a couple of houses away from where the two cop cars were parked, they watched as a woman in a leopard-print bathrobe was guided down a couple of concrete steps by a police officer at her back while another police officer was talking to a couple at the house next to it. The lights of the police cars brushed the house number over and over, washing it and highlighting it. It was Bess's house. The woman being taken to the squad car was Bess's mom.

Suddenly Bess's phone started ringing and they looked at it silently and then at each other. Bess answered it, biting her lip, and holding her breath.

"Hey," she said.

Ursula didn't want to intrude, but she had a fifteen-year-old who she barely knew in her car and was watching the girl's only, she assumed, guardian being arrested. Her mind was reeling with what to do because this wasn't a common sense situation.

"I'm with Ursula and we actually just drove down our street," she said sneaking a look at Ursula next to her. She waited for whatever the other person was saying and then said, "Yeah. Ok, I'll tell her. Oh," she said, then turned to Ursula and held out the phone. "Um, My Uncle Jay wants to talk to you," she said.

Ursula looked at the phone Bess placed in her hand and gave Bess a tight smile as she held the phone up to her ear. "Hello?"

"Ursula," the deep voice said. Ursula would not admit that hearing a deep, rumbly voice that sounded like it was made to voice the male main character in a romance novel saying her name would be something she thought about often.

"Jenson," she said back, trying to shake his deeply affective voice.

"I got a call from Tennyson," he said. "Police chief," he clarified.

"Our police chief is named Tennyson? Like Lord Tennyson?"

A sigh resounded across the phone and she could picture his stoic and frustrated face. "Just bring Bess to my house."

Not a 'please' or a nice request; just a command.

"Yes sir," she replied mockingly.

A rumbling growl rolled through the phone and she, again, would not admit that did something to her. But she did smile at annoying him nearly as much as he did her.

"See you in ten," he said then abruptly hung up.

She shook her head and handed the phone back to Bess. "Your uncle sure is a charmer," she said as she put her car back into gear to turn them around. "Will you direct me?"

"Make a left up here, then at the roundabout, you'll take the third exit," she said. She knew the route well, and that simple fact made something inside Ursula pinch again.

"So my uncle is oddly interested in you," Bess said which pulled an unfiltered snort from Ursula.

"If by interested you mean he's a grumpy jerk who for some reason likes to hit a quota of annoying me anytime we're in the same vicinity, then sure." And then the words, which fell out of her mouth without a filter, echoed back to her in the silent car and she quickly slid a look to where Bess was merely a shadow in the passenger seat. "Sorry," she said quietly. "I know he's your uncle."

The silence made her tighten her hold on the steering wheel and internally berate herself for being so callous to this obviously struggling young teen. And the man was willing to step in when Bess needed it, which Ursula could guess was more often than not. Being unkind about that kind of support system for Bess was not the best move she could make here.

But then the sound of Bess laughing softly floated over from the passenger seat and that tight clutching inside of Ursula loosened the slightest.

"No offense taken. He's...difficult," she said thoughtfully. After a pause, she continued. "But for me, he's the one who has always saved me."

Bess's words warmed Ursula. The man wasn't her fan, but he was this girl's hero. "You don't have to talk about it if you don't want to, but I'm here if you need anything. And I'm glad you have your uncle, regardless of my feelings for him," she added.

"Thank you," the very gentle and small reply came. "And he's actually a really great guy. Probably the greatest guy I know. And you definitely get under his skin," her voice held an obvious smile.

"I imagine most people get under his skin."

"Not really. I mean, he's naturally kind of grumpy," she replied. "But I mean, he's cursed and he just keeps to himself when it comes to women usually. But you? He is *particularly* bothered by you," she said, her voice taking on a cajoling tone.

There it was again, the second time she had heard that Jenson Lancaster was cursed. She should ask but truthfully, she didn't have the energy right now.

They didn't speak the rest of the short drive and when Ursula pulled up to a craftsman-style house, a large, wrap-around porch hugging it with lights leading up the walkway, she parked the car and let out a breath.

The front door opened and a large figure, darkened by the light burning behind him, leaned against the doorframe.

"Looks like he's waiting for you."

Bess nodded quietly then turned back to her. "Will you walk me up?"

It seemed like an odd request from a teenager who put on a tough front, but she wasn't going to question it. She was going to jump out of the car as smoothly as possible and prove to her that she was and would remain there for her.

The house was nice. Really nice. It was hard to tell colors in the dark, but there was a well-maintained yard meticulously cut at an angle, wood shingles on the upper level looked like they would be a honey color in the daylight with darker colored siding and white windows and trim.

When they made it up the steps and onto the wide porch she tried to find what words she would say to the grumpy Brawny Man, but Bess ran to him, wrapping her arms around his middle and Ursula watched in awe as he easily pulled her in, his large arms embracing her without hesitation as he rested his chin on the top of her dark head. His eyes opened and landed on Ursula who suddenly felt like an intruder at this tender moment but something in his dark eyes said something else. They were both intense and gentle and it paused the breath in her lungs.

Bess pulled back and smiled widely at Ursula, a look of pure contentment on her face. She was safe. "Ursula is awesome, Uncle Jay. And she let me look around her house. My friends are going to freak."

He smiled down at her and the look was gut-clenching for her to witness. The man was handsome when scowling. But he was world-tilting when he smiled. This girl meant a lot to him. It shouldn't soften her towards the man, but the Lord help her, because it did.

"Well, you're welcome anytime. I should get Casper home," she threw her thumb over her shoulder. They all looked to see the grey hound pressing his face up against the back window like someone arrested in the back of a cop car. That thought sobered the moment as realization over why she was standing on Jenson Lancaster's front porch at night punched her. She waved and turned toward the steps as Jenson told Bess she would come to his house after school but he would be home late after he finished a job at a town she assumed was close to Salem. An idea perked in her mind as her boot hit the first step and she turned around before she thought better of it.

"She could come over to my house. If, well, if you wanted to. I work from home and I was planning on making eggplant parmesan. I could pick her up at school." Bess had a look of excitement and hope on her face while Jenson turned back to his usual scowling. She held up a hand. "I don't want to intrude, just an offer."

Bess looked up at Jenson, her young face hopeful. "Please? Eggplant parmesan is one of my favorites and she's responsible. She didn't even let me drink wine."

His eyes widened at that and he looked at Ursula who held a hand up.

"Which I would never let you do. Until you're twenty-one," she quickly explained.

Slightly appeased, if that was possible, he looked over Bess's face trying to make a responsible decision. "Fine," he said. Ursula wasn't sure if there was a note of reluctance, which was fair since she was still enough of a stranger to them to weigh giving the precious responsibility of his niece to her. He looked at Ursula. "If her mom calls her, I don't want her going home just yet. Not exactly sure what is going to happen, but I'd like to keep Bess out of it for now."

"I'm not a baby," she grumbled. But the conversation seemed like one they had tired out before; the argument like thin, worn linen.

"I know. Get inside. Your room is ready for you," he said.

Her room. She had a room at her uncle's house in case she needed it.

Bess smiled at Ursula and thanked her before she headed inside. Jenson's hands were tucked into the front pockets of his jeans and he had a thoughtful expression on his face.

"Ok, well, I will drop her off tomorrow night. You just text her when you're back."

"I'll come get her from you."

Did he not trust her to drive? "Okay," she said slowly. "Whatever works. See you later," she turned to walk back down to her car and resisted the urge to look over her shoulder because she knew by the feeling on her back that he was still standing there on his porch watching her.

"Ursula," he called. The one-name command made her stop and turn with a question on her face. "Thank you," he said. It wasn't gentle and it wasn't said with a smile, but it was said. And it was earnest. And she would take it.

She nodded her head once and without another word got into her car trying, and losing, not to think of the handsome man who took care of his teenage niece, who people said was cursed and had a particular gruffness with Ursula. Oh, and was the rumored center of an affair with the last tenant of The Lost Souls House before her husband tried to burn her down inside of it.

CHAPTER SEVENTEEN

IN OTHER MAGICAL NEWS

The next morning came with clouds and rain, which Ursula loved in her pluviophile way. She slipped on thick black leggings and warm wool socks along with a worn college shirt and a long black cardigan. Her black hair she let go wavy and a little wild.

On her way through the kitchen to let Casper out she stopped when she saw sitting on the island a plump eggplant, six large tomatoes, and a bunch of fresh basil. She nodded her head silently then said to no one, or whoever was gently haunting them, "This is getting a little creepy now!" She sighed and added, "But thank you!"

After letting Casper out she made herself coffee and carried that into her little office after drying Casper from the rain. She didn't have any meetings today, but she had a lot of administrative work to catch up on so she hunkered in while the rain tiptoed along the roof of the house and down the windows.

Her phone buzzed next to her laptop sometime later and she picked it up, noticing it was a text from an unknown number.

Unknown: I should be by your house around 7 tonight

She frowned trying to think of who it could be.

Ursula: Sorry, I don't have this number saved. Who is this?

Unknown: I didn't give you my number, so that's a relief.

She rolled her eyes and let out a long breath.

Ursula: Ah. I gather from the overwhelming grinch energy that this is Jenson.

Unknown: Thank you for confirming that I'm entrusting my niece to someone who knows how to make an educated guess

"Ohmygosh. I could just..." she made squeezing motions with both hands while letting out a little growl. Casper stirred from his nap and sent her a questioning tilted look. She would be a bigger person.

Ursula: 7 is fine. See you then.

Unknown: Ok

"He is the worst," she said to Casper who made a grunting sound before he flopped over onto his back to catch more sleep. When her phone buzzed again she frowned at it.

Unknown: Are you going to save my name as Brawny Man in your phone?

Ursula: Bold of you to assume I need to save your number at all

A few minutes later he texted back.

Unknown: That's fair.

Unknown: I would, though. Save my number. You can decide between Brawny Man and Asshole

Ursula smiled at the unexpected response.

Ursula: So you know you're an asshole?

She became reabsorbed into the project she had been working on before he had texted her, before he replied.

Unknown: Maybe I'm cursed.

She bit her lip. "Yeah, I'm going to need someone to explain that to me soon," she said to no one.

Unknown: Maybe I'm only an asshole around beautiful, intriguing women

She read the words and then re-read them. She flipped her phone over and sat back in the chair, the springs squeaking underneath the movement. His words frustrated her, not an unusual thing for his words to do, but still. Beautiful? He thought she was beautiful and intriguing. Curses and hexes and magic...none of that was ever a possibility to her until she had opened her mailbox. For him to say he was cursed seemed almost like a slap in the face or a taunt. Either way, she was not going to respond. Either way, she was not going to let her thoughts settle on the way her heart flipped at his words.

Lunch came and went. She ate soup with her romance novel and when the doorbell chimed she opened the door and reared back when she saw Sulphur sitting there with a swishing tail and what looked like a paper mache skull. The cat nuzzled it before using a marbled paw to bat it into the house through the door opening and then sashayed away disappearing through the railing on the side of the porch.

When she closed the door, she looked for the weird skull but found in its place a newspaper and smiled. So, with another cup of coffee and the magical newspaper in hand, she snuggled into the corner of her cognac velvet couch with a blue and green plaid blanket and read.

There was a deal for anyone who presented this phrase to Michelle at his pastry shop : *Trick or Treat, be so sweet, give me something good to eat.*

The deal promised a free pumpkin meringue kiss on Halloween, so she tucked that knowledge away.

There was news about the upcoming Halloween festival and a story dedicated to the magical floating candles that dazzle thousands every year. People have guessed for years how the illusion is done, but it's simply magic.

Then a smaller story still followed a handful of hexes around town. She sat up when her eyes caught on the headline. Jason Harrison's surgery to remove the lion tail he mysteriously woke up with went well and he was recovering.

An article about the pink, sparkly eggs was below that one, dubbing the farm: Barbie Farm. Crystal's nephew was quoted accusing her of meddling, calling her a 'new age witchy sort with a grudge.' Ursula cringed, hoping that nothing happened to Crystal. But what could anyone prove, really?

She wondered how the others were faring from their graveyard margarita hexes. She fished out her phone and looked at the professional networking platform typing in Felix Smith's name. When his profile said he was 'Open to Work' she cringed again.

She hadn't wanted to ruin his life. Had she?

She put the newspaper down, which shriveled up the moment it touched the coffee table, and then puffed into a cloud of sparkles.

"Huh," Ursula responded to the drama. She put out a small piece of salmon for Sulphur on the porch and then looked at the time. She needed to start making the marinara sauce for dinner now if she wanted it to be ready with good, deep flavors. Music played in the kitchen, the marinara sauce was bubbling perfectly, and she had the eggplant slices dredged in egg and a breadcrumb and basil breading ready to pan-fry once she picked up Bess.

The school was a typical three-story, slightly darker-than-beige building with a line of nearly red bricks running horizontally through each story to break up the monotony. It actually looked a lot like the high school she attended back in the Midwest. Bess was talking to two other girls when she spotted Ursula's car. She said goodbye to her friends and then broke from the trio walking to where she was idling. Ursula watched as the two girls stared at her, or her car. She wasn't sure that they could see her sitting inside but it was clear that they were intrigued by something.

"Hey," Bess said, a little breathlessly as she put her backpack on the floor before buckling herself in. "What?" she asked when she saw Ursula squinting out the window.

"Why are your friends staring at us? Don't most teenagers ignore the world and stare at their phones?"

"Usually, but you're more fascinating than their phones."

Ursula turned her attention to Bess. "I am? I am incredibly boring."

Bess held up a finger. "But you live in The Lost Souls House," she said explaining it all away.

"Ah," she said, putting the car into gear. "Still getting used to that."

"So where did you live before here?"

"The Midwest," she said.

"Isn't the Midwest pretty big?"

Ursula thought about it for a second and nodded her head. "Ohio," she answered.

"So what was in Ohio?"

"Nothing," she replied. There was no vehemence in her answer, no mysterious tone, just simple and honest. "There were a lot of 'maybe's' and 'hopefully's' and 'I wishes' that I left there. But truly, nothing real was left behind." She asked Bess about her day. It was easier to think that she'd left nothing behind rather than try and process the truth out loud with a teenager.

An hour later the kitchen swirled with the smells of rich marinara sauce and fresh herbs. She let Bess choose music to play while they cooked, and surprisingly the girl had a thing for "vintage jazz." Also surprisingly that meant that Norah Jones was playing, her smooth and deep dulcet tones weaving around the kitchen and Ursula was a little traumatized that this was considered "vintage." Cooking with Bess was easy, fun. She was rather talented in the kitchen causing her to wonder how many meals she had been in charge of for herself when she shouldn't have been.

Since she came here, she found herself stopping now and then while in a moment with these women she had become friends with. She reveled in the camaraderie, in the brushing of shoulders without apology as they made food side-by-side, in the easy laughter and the eye contact when she told a story. They were all such incredibly simple things and yet they felt anything but. They felt significant.

"This is probably the best eggplant parmesan I have ever had," Bess said around a mouthful. "Even better than Michelangelo's."

"Local Italian place?"

"Mhmm. You should go some time. Though, it's pretty romantic. I went on a date there last year," she said proudly.

"You went on a date to a nice Italian restaurant when you were fourteen?"

She shrugged a shoulder. "Mom didn't really care," she said. "Uncle Jay scared him off, though."

Ursula snorted. "Shocker. Though, if a guy can't handle your uncle's surliness, then he probably isn't the right guy."

"Oh no. Like, Uncle Jay lit into him. Told him never to come around me again or he'd bury him in a foundation of concrete at one of his job sites."

"Holy," Ursula bit her tongue from finishing that and said instead, "your uncle needs to learn how to be civil. He grew up with a pack of wolves, didn't he? You don't have to tell me, just blink twice if he's a werewolf."

Bess shook her head laughing. "To be fair, the guy was nineteen, dropped out of college, and liked hanging around young high school girls."

Something like vitriol filled Ursula immediately, the feeling hard and swift.

"Oh. Then, I would have helped your uncle dump his body and then poured the concrete myself."

Bess laughed again and ate more of her meal. She looked thoughtful as she chewed a bite of the eggplant before swallowing and said, "I guess I just wanted my mom's attention. It was stupid."

Ursula tilted her head as she swallowed the bite of food she had taken and took in the girl across from her. Her black hair was pulled into a half pony and the roots gave away their lighter shade of dark blonde. She wore a cropped green sweater with wide-leg jeans and white tennis shoes. She was sweet and young with an edge of indifference that was covering up something else far more tender.

"You have homework?" she asked because it was the responsible adult thing to do.

"Yeah," she replied. "I have some algebra and English. Can I do it here after I help you clean up?"

"How about I clean up, you do it here, we crank up Norah, which I still cannot believe you called 'vintage,' and then I have some apple pie bars we can eat with tea."

Bess smiled a real smile that made something swoop inside of Ursula. There was a soft harmony that took over the kitchen as Ursula cleaned up and packaged leftovers, while Bess worked on her homework. They were now sitting side-by-side, Ursula going over resume revisions for a new client and Bess reading over an essay assignment.

Bess made a groaning noise as she leaned back and pushed the paper she was reading away from her.

"Dessert?"

Bess nodded her head eagerly. "Please."

The buttery smell of pie crust mingled with the tart apples and a pinch of cinnamon and clove as she set the dessert plates on the island with two steaming cups of sleepytime tea.

"Do you stay with your uncle often?"

"I mean, now and then. He's always been like the only solid adult in my life."

"You don't have to talk about it if you don't want to, but how are things with your mom?" She almost hit herself with the fork in her hand. Things with her mom were not great, since she was taken away in a police car the other night.

"My mom has some issues with alcohol and pills and anger. Ever since my dad left."

Ursula stayed quiet, trying not to interject or spook her.

Bess pushed around a piece of baked apple across the plate with a raven on it. "My uncle tried to get custody of me once," she admitted in a small voice. "He doesn't know that I know, but," she lifted a small shoulder, her mouth screwed up on one side, "kids always know more than you guys think," she finally said.

"Yeah, you do," Ursula agreed softly.

"My mom isn't a bad person. She's just got a problem and sometimes she can't take care of me."

"I'm really sorry," she said hoping that wasn't the wrong thing to say. Apologies in these situations could sometimes be worse than saying nothing. Bess shrugged again but then her sweet face turned thoughtful and more than a little sad.

"Have you ever just, not felt seen? Like, you're somehow a walking ghost in your own life? Like, I have walked around my empty house and thought no one would know if I was there or if I left, if I ate or cleaned up after myself. When she was gone, sometimes for days, I was just there. A ghost," she finished her internal thoughts, the words coming out slow but honest and Ursula pushed against the urge to pull her into the world's warmest hug. Because her words pinched something inside of her, something she understood better than she cared to admit. But maybe it was time to admit some things out loud.

"I left Ohio and everything there because I wasn't a whole person anymore."

Bess looked up at her and Ursula chewed on her bottom lip for a few moments and made a decision. She could talk about this here, with this young woman, if for nothing else than to tell her what it was like to forget to be seen. She turned fully toward Bess, wrapping a hand around her warm mug of tea.

"I loved someone who forgot to see me," she said softly, her eyes on her dessert plate but unfocused. "It can take years, even for an adult, to stop and recognize that they aren't being loved. I think," she paused, "we are told what love is in various ways through examples, songs, books, and movies, but we aren't always ready to recognize what love isn't. And that may be a little half glass empty," she smiled sadly and pushed her fork through a piece of tender apple, "but I think that's okay when we are talking about one of the most important things in the world: being loved and loving well. I became a ghost too, and I forgot the value of being seen."

She pictured herself eating roasted chicken alone at the dining room table, hope turning to shame when he didn't show up most nights. She remembered asking if he wanted to read with her by the fire one night and he said he was tired and would read in bed. A bed that they shared but didn't. A memory came back of her inviting a skeptical Casper onto the beige couch with her, a place he had never been allowed before but she was desperate for connection.

"There is an entry fee no one tells you about," she looked at Bess, a look of understanding and soft sadness on her face.

"Entry fee to what?" Bess asked, engrossed in this moment; a young woman wanting any bits of wisdom to help her better understand this world.

She smiled sadly. "The entry fee for settling. Which I did. I was a ghost for the last few years. I pulled into myself and walked more quietly. I allowed hello's and goodbye's and have a good day's to be enough. I pushed down everything that made me feel alive. Sometimes I would stop and think, wait...*wait, this isn't enough*." She ran her fingertip along the rim of her mug, the steam becoming thin as her tea cooled. Then she looked at Bess. "Your situation is a little more difficult and you're more vulnerable than I was." Bess gave her a look and she held up a hand. "Not because you're a child, but because there is a system of authority in your situation with your mom. And a parent-child relationship, it's the first place that should allow you to be completely human and leave no room for fear of not being loved." She laid a gentle hand on Bess's on the island. The girl stared at their hands and Ursula watched her blink hard, fighting against the vulnerability she wouldn't allow herself to feel. She squeezed lightly, then drew her hand back to give her room. "But, something I wish someone had taught me young was that it is okay to think about yourself and take care of yourself. There is a fine line between selfishness and self-love, and that isn't taught. But no matter what, you shouldn't have to feel like a ghost. It even cost me my most important friendship, a friendship that had been the closest thing to a soulmate for twenty years."

"What happened?"

It was painful, so painful even years later to think about, let alone talk about. She swallowed a lump in her throat and smiled sadly. "I chose a bad, damaging relationship over her, my best friend. Her name was Eloise, and she couldn't watch me disappear anymore." The fight, the tears, the way that Eloise had held up her hand with a look of broken acceptance like she was watching her best friend die. She cleared her throat. "The trick is to find people who demand that you don't allow yourself to become a ghost."

Bess swallowed. She frowned. "But, how do I not?" Her words came out like half-words, formed but diluted by the sadness she was trying to hold back. It was breaking a little piece inside of Ursula.

"Well, I guess that's where your uncle comes in. And your friends. You build your own family, a family and people that see you and invite you into a space where you feel valued and like you have a witness to your life."

"This is a deep conversation for a fifteen-year-old," Bess joked, one tear escaping her violent hold, as she ate her last bite of the apple dessert. Ursula watched that tear, understood it, and promised herself she would try and be here for this girl if she allowed it.

Ursula laughed softly, sitting back in the chair and nodding, hands wrapped around her warm mug. "Yes, it is."

Just then, Sufhur jumped onto the island and made them both gasp, then look at each other and laugh.

"I forgot you had a cat!" Bess said in delight as she ran a hand over the cat's arching back.

"Comes and goes," she replied.

"What did Jen call her again?"

"A house raccoon," Ursula said with a smile.

"Oh an aloof lint-licker," Bess remembered.

"Hello?" A deep baritone jolted them again as Jenson stepped into the kitchen from the hallway. He must have let himself in.

"Hey, Uncle Jay," Bess said with a wide smile.

Ursula gave him a little smile, unsure if they would be enemies tonight or civil. But there was something soft about his face tonight; it wasn't held as tightly or perhaps he wasn't clenching his granite jaw. The look was nice, relaxed.

"Smells good," he said.

"Ohmygod, Ursula made the best eggplant parmesan. We saved you some. And then apple pie bars." Gone was the heartbroken teenager grappling with life in ways someone so young shouldn't have to.

He nodded with a smile. "Want to grab your stuff? I have the truck running so it's warm."

Bess made a teenage face that said she was annoyed. "I guess that's my dismissal so the grownups can talk."

"Bess," Jenson warned.

"Fine," she grumbled and Ursula had to bite her lower lip so that her smile wouldn't worsen the situation. Teenagers were up and down with their moods and she had forgotten that until this moment. Bess had her backpack swung over one shoulder and she gave Ursula a half smile, still battling with the dark mood Jenson brought into the kitchen, which was not surprising about the man.

"Thanks for having me. And dinner," she said.

Ursula smiled and wondered if she should hug her or not; teenagers were kind of like cats, right? Let them come to you. Feed them. Sit back and watch their moods swing until they leave the room.

"You can come here anytime," she said with a gentleness and smile that she felt was a good replacement for a hug.

Bess gave Jenson another glare and then gave Casper a loving head pet and kiss before loudly walking down the long hallway.

Ursula looked at Jenson who was the embodiment of intense. Gone was the relaxed Jenson, with that signature hard mouth, and unforgiving dark eyes. What could he possibly be mad at her for now? She opened her home to his niece. She thoroughly enjoyed having her, picking her up, making dinner together, being near her while she did her homework and their talk was something precious she knew that Bess had gifted her.

She set her tea on the counter and hopped off the barstool as Jenson leaned his weight onto the island, both hands splayed over the top and she couldn't help but admire them, tan and work-worn. They looked strong. She shook those thoughts from her mind and tilted her head, crossing her arms over her chest as she gave him a look, waiting for whatever unwarranted fight he wanted to have. He looked from the island to her and the look he was giving her was wilder than usual.

She opened her mouth to ask him what his problem was when he pushed off the counter and walked toward her. Stalked toward her. The movement of his large body with his wild stare made whatever words had worked their way to her tongue dissolve and before she knew what was happening, he was reaching out with one of those hands, sliding it behind her head, threading his fingers through her thick hair as his other hand landed on her waist and pulled her into him. Fully.

There was nothing hesitant about the way he wanted her against him, her softer body molding to the lines of him.

She opened her mouth again, not sure what would have come out, but it didn't matter because he stopped those words with his mouth. She gasped as he took her mouth in a kiss so crushing and intense that she had no will, only instinct, as she grappled for solid ground, her hands grabbing onto the lapels of his jacket, still cool from the night air clinging there.

His hands tightened on her as she simply stood there, her body pressed to his, his mouth moving over hers demanding her acquiescence, but she was stunned and could only stand there as he took over. She couldn't think. She couldn't process. Jenson's hard, warm, demanding mouth was on hers and he had her body pressed against his tall, muscular length and all of it felt outrageous. All of it felt incredible. His mouth, like him, was imposing. Even his kiss was severe and dark like him.

Until he gentled just the slightest, his mouth pausing, his breath coming out in a caress over her lips, his hand on her waist lightly running over her hip; those simple and soft touches making her melt, her head tipped back and her mouth parted slightly in invitation, which he took without hesitation.

Where the kiss had started as a passionate ambush, now he took her mouth intentionally, with a sweep of his tongue causing her to let out a small moan, which made him pull her into him more fully as he angled her head and took the kiss deeper.

She didn't have time to think, to wonder what was happening, she could only hold on for her life and give in to whatever this was. And whatever this was, was something she hadn't felt in years. Her body hadn't been here in so long it was like something inside of her ignited, a small pilot light that had been just barely there but never stoked. And she was feeling the heat now, a fast catch-fire, and it was like rolling heat down her entire body. She was going to combust.

When his strong grip kneaded her hip, his thumb running under the hem of her shirt and glancing over her bare skin in the most tender touch she shivered and pressed more fully into him. The deep hum she felt reverberate from his chest was its own move he could patent because she found herself wanting to rub herself all over him to hear it again.

He pulled her bottom lip between his teeth lightly nipping and gave her one more, deep kiss before he slowed, pulled back, and rested his forehead against hers, his harsh breath mixing with her own, their lips resting against each other. Time enveloped them in something soft and quiet as they both tried for their own breath, going from sharing it so deeply to separating and untangling.

And then with a squeeze of his hand on her waist he stepped back from her, her hands falling from their white-knuckled grip on his denim jacket, and he brushed a wayward wave of inky strands from her cheek and tucked it tenderly behind her ear as his eyes moved over her face and hair with a look as if he was trying to understand her, like he was in awe.

Her heart was hammering and she was telling her breath to get it under control as she searched for words. But why should she have to be the first one to respond, after the jerk treated her terribly for weeks and then abruptly, without warning, kissed her with more passion than she had ever experienced in her life? There was no guide for this.

But his eyes finally landed on her stunned ones and she held her breath.

"Thank you," he got out, the sound gravelly and rough, making another scattering of goosebumps break out over her arms and neck. She imagined that voice saying other things to her in moments of passion and had to shake her head to stop the thoughts.

Once a dormant body got going, it was hard to stop its trajectory. She would need to remember that.

And then he walked out of the kitchen and down the hallway, following where Bess had disappeared moments before. Had that only been moments? The front door closed.

Ursula touched her swollen lips and frowned. "What the hell was that?"

Casper tilted his head from where he lay next to his empty food dish. She couldn't even begin to untangle what had just happened.

She pulled in the deep breath her lungs needed after...that...and then she let it out slowly.

"Alright, I am going to bury that deeply for now," she said, knowing full well that her mind would be possessed by memories of that abrupt and incredible kiss for the foreseeable future. Probably until she lay inside the cold earth. But for now, she needed to bundle up and visit the souls.

Chapter Eighteen

MAGIC PUMPKINS

The next morning brought no clarity to what happened the night before, even with the bright sunshine and crisp air that Ursula pulled in deeply to try and force peace on her mind. She was sitting on her front porch with a mug of coffee and bundled up under a thick fleece blanket taking in the beautiful start to the day. She'd woken to thoughts of the kiss, as if the memory had perched itself on the ledge between her sleeping and awake minds, waiting to pounce. Because the first thing she saw in her mind's eye as sleep released its hold on her was Jenson, reaching out his large hand and sliding it into the nape of her hair as his eyes swallowed her. His other hand grasped her waist and then she had been pulled into him.

Lips crashing, demanding, pillaging. Softening, asking then plundering when she answered. His thumb touching the bare skin of her waist. Just barely. Like he couldn't help but touch her, but would only allow himself a glance of her skin.

She had rolled to her back and stared up at the still-dark ceiling, the sun sending promises of being on its way, and she groaned.

But then she hopped out of bed, got herself ready for the day, and decided to start it by breathing in the cool autumn morning, watching the sun unfurl its fingers over her little plot of land and not think of him.

The man who could kiss better than the man in her romance novel. And that was saying something because she imagined he knew what he was doing because he was a fictional character written by a woman. Also, the man who was named as the town's bachelor and may or may not have had an affair with the last resident here. Oh and add to that rumors of him being cursed, whatever that entailed. That was a lot to bounce around a woman's head.

She had thought him an arrogant jerk, but an unscrupulous home-wrecker? That was a different shade to paint someone with.

No, she was not thinking about that. Because then she would ask too many questions and go crazy until she got answers. So, she wrapped her hand around a black pumpkin mug, still hot from the coffee, and watched as Sulphur sashayed her way onto the porch with her swishing tail until she found a thick beam of buttery sunlight laid out on the wood where she delicately plopped herself down.

Her phone chirped and when she looked at the message saw that it was from Miles, telling her he had a preliminary sketch of the stained glass if she wanted to come by the store later and see it. A trill of excitement shot over her as she sipped her coffee. The plants in the back were beginning to grow wild. She would need to spend some serious time taking care of overgrown herbs and trailing vines, harvesting some vegetables and either giving them away or canning them, which she had never done in her life.

There was still the matter of building the greenhouse; she had actually played with the idea of building it herself. She could look up some videos and build something that wasn't too fancy.

Another chirp on her phone, this one from Jen asking for help setting up the Halloween festival that was in two days. Halloween was in a week and Salem held a festival that lasted five days, something she had been looking forward to. She and Kelsea were going to be helping with lighting, and she wasn't sure what that entailed, but she was happy to help Jen, which meant helping Cora.

The campaign against Cora was strong with ads about the town needing a family man to lead them. One campaign ad brazenly asked voters not to vote for someone who had lied in their marriage implying she would lie to the people. Each sign, ad, or commercial Ursula saw that smeared Cora's name felt like a point taken away from her and it was disheartening.

After their bonfire where Cora sat and talked with them, sharing pieces of herself that were deeply hers, Ursula couldn't help but feel a kinship with the woman. She was strong and held herself in a way that most women would spend far too much of their peace on envy to replicate. She admired her, even more so with her faults, because you could see that strength was built on life handing her pieces with which she made something to stand on.

She finished her last sip of coffee, stood up, stretched, and walked back through the house to let Casper out. When she opened the back door and stood on the patio she stopped short. It took a moment for her eyes to realize what she was looking at but when she did she laughed, the sound a gentle and clear echo. Plopped along a verdant vine of curling green were squat pumpkins, but not just any pumpkins, these were black. That tickling in her mind and down her neck happened as she walked toward them.

Dark Knight pumpkins. She crouched down and ran a hand over one, the morning dew collected along the top ridges and dark stem. This one was the size of a basketball. She looked and there were a dozen more within sight, some elongated, a few that looked squished and filled out.

Held in the hand of a curling piece of vine sat another tarot card. She leaned down and plucked it out looking over the navy and gold picture. She knew this one. The Lovers.

A flash of the movie refusing to stop in her mind played. His hard, warm lips taking hers. His strong hands bold and not asking, but commanding. She let out a misty breath and tucked the card in her back pocket.

Casper moseyed over to where she was squatting, and when her knees and legs begged her to get up, getting older was wildly inconvenient, she stood and then felt something. She stopped and looked sharply around the bright space; what had been wide and open when she moved here a few months ago was now bursting with plant life along the edges and moving in. She feared she would have a jungle if she didn't start controlling things. But right now something else was niggling her mind, a feeling. Not unlike that feeling she got the other night when she felt like someone had been watching her at the graveyard. She hadn't felt it since then, though she had been on alert for a day or two after. But now, something felt off, like attention was gathered on her and she felt exposed.

And there was something else. The peace she normally felt was disturbed. She thought of the contract and unwelcome guests, a shiver running through her veins.

She didn't want to alert the intruder if there was one, so she stretched her shoulders, raised her face to the sun pretending to drink in the morning, and then with a voice she masked in easy calm, called for Casper to come with her inside.

Once the door was closed and locked she took a deep breath and shook her head. It was probably nothing.

She was glad that she had a lot of work to do today. A few honey-do's from Jen for the festival, and Tilly was stopping by later this afternoon to grab an old journal she had found in the attic the other day for a radio story segment about The Lost Soul's House. She had also found a smaller journal, the size of her palm, that opened after some tugging and cajoling. But only the front cover and back cover would open. It was as if the pages were glued shut, though she could run her fingernail along the edges of the pages and hear that fast flickering the paper of a well-loved book makes.

The thought crossed her mind that it was enchanted and could not be opened. It was a deep forest green, handmade leather, and well-bound. When she flipped open the front cover, she saw thin handwritten words at the top. Cradling it gently, she pulled it close to her face and tipped it toward more light as she made out the words: Fannie McGovern. It didn't ring a bell. She'd put it inside the drawer of her side table for safekeeping until she figured out what to do with it.

She picked up the journal that Tilly was going to borrow and gingerly turned the pages as she sat at her desk. Another mention of the name Fannie McGovern, but this handwriting was different than the smaller journal. She pulled her laptop onto her lap and got lost in searches and history.

There were quite a few records with that name, but only one that matched the timing of this house and this town flitted across the screen and made her pause.

The entry was for a nun who left the church in Western Europe and came over in the late 1600s, but not much else was known about her. Ursula got lost in research of the Catholic church's influence in Colonial America, which wasn't until a few decades later. Fannie was here before her church's time. No other mention of anyone else with her, no mention of this house.

She remembered the rumor about Jenson and the last tenant here and bit her nail as she thought. *Did she want to delve into that?*

She did.

An hour later she'd found out that Jenson came from a long bloodline in Salem. His parents were long ago deceased when he was a teenager and his younger sister, Tori, was only twelve. His sister Tori Russell was married to a man named Ben Russell and together they had a daughter named Bess.

She felt odd, researching him and his family, like she was peeking behind a door in a house she hadn't been invited into. But the curiosity was buzzing and strong.

An article in The Salem Settler from twelve years ago highlighted the devastation of a young woman named Diane Perry, who was engaged to a Jenson Lancaster. Their wedding was planned, then her hopes and dreams were dashed when he called it off. The bachelor disappeared for a few weeks, only to come back and pick back up with his job working in construction as if nothing ever happened. The young woman picked up and left town, never to come back from the shame of her heartbreak.

An article dating five years before that piqued Ursula's attention, as it was about a woman named Cassidy Parker who lived in The Lost Souls House nearly two decades ago. It popped up because there was one mention of a Jenson Lancaster. She read through the article quickly, not gleaning much more than that she inherited the house from a grandmother and moved to town from a few hours away straight out of high school to take care of the property. Jenson was mentioned as a handyman who had helped her with some repairs, which then turned into a summer romance.

Ursula brewed chamomile tea as she thought about the romantic entanglements that Jenson Lancaster was involved in. She ate a light lunch on her porch as she poured over more articles about Cassidy Parker.

There was a mysterious shroud around her in the four short articles she'd found, but what she gathered was that she'd lived in the house for five years, keeping a low profile and prompting articles of suspicion about who she really was and what she did at The Lost Souls House. It seemed she was rather reclusive and it all felt very Emily Dickinson as one article called her *The White Ghost,* who was rarely seen and usually only by curious and brave children who were dared to run up to the property.

An abrupt end to her courtship with Jenson Lancaster was noted in the gossip column followed by her quick departure and the then empty house.

She sighed and shook her head, as she put together the kind of man that Jenson was.

Resident bachelor. Seemed to date and then abandon women. The rumor that he had an affair with the last tenant here only damned him further, making him exactly the kind of man that Ursula did not want to get involved with. No matter how expertly he could kiss her.

Ursula Cambridge had never been one to think much on the fight of good versus evil. Having lived a humdrum Midwestern life over the last couple of decades with little to no swirls of whimsy or darkness, she'd lived somewhere in the middle. Of course there were good and bad happenings, but not like what she read in books. She had an inkling when she answered the magical pumpkin newspaper ad that living in the middle of a humdrum life was going to be a thing of her past, but now she was both feet in to a world where whimsy and darkness were more than stories; they were landmarks here in this new adventure.

The grocery in town was small, mostly filled with local food staples, and had a small deli and baked goods section. She felt a small warmth every time she entered one of Salem's small, local stores, like crossing over a threshold into a room with a welcoming and roaring fire. She'd noticed it at the soup and sandwich place and Michelle's patisserie. Tilly had told her the town lore is that every small and local town shop is enchanted by protection and good fortune. As she moseyed through the small aisles picking out canned chickpeas and a small satchel of curried spices, she smiled at the feeling of protection and peace. Maybe they were enchanted and maybe not, but either way she enjoyed the atmosphere.

"Hi. Ursula, right?"

The thin voice pulled Ursula's attention to that woman she had met at the soup place in her first few days in Salem. What was her name? She smiled as her mind searched through drawers and cabinets.

"Jessica!" she finally pulled out and felt relief wash over her when the woman smiled at being remembered. "Nice to see you. And yes, it's Ursula."

The woman was exactly as she remembered, down to the perfectly styled hair. She even made the long, light blue wool peacoat look like a fashion statement rather than a way to keep herself warm. Diamond earrings sparkled from her earlobes.

She looked into Ursula's basket. "Getting things for dinner?"

"Mhmm. I'm terrible at grocery shopping and planning so I make multiple small trips a week. It's a horrible habit," she laughed at herself.

Jessica's smile was tight, and it may have been because of medical help, because this woman whose age was indeterminate, did not have one line on her face. Or it may have been something else. Ursula remembered feeling like this woman was holding herself tightly, like she was afraid something would release with one false step.

"I'm an over-planner, and it's honestly not a better habit," she smiled a little sadly.

That right there, that's what she remembered about Jessica; she seemed tightly pressed in on herself and sad. Put together perfectly, but maybe that was hiding something on the inside.

Ursula made a snap decision. After moving here and starting over, she found she had capacity and room for people in a way she never had before. Or wasn't allowed to have before.

"Would you like to come over for dinner? I know it's last minute, and I don't even know if you have kids or anything, but..." she pulled her lips up into a lopsided smile, "You're welcome. I'm making a chick-pea curry dish. Nothing special but it's cozy."

Jessica's eyebrows raised as much as her forehead would allow them to, but she genuinely looked shocked. "I," she started and paused, pulled out her phone that was in a sleek pearl case checking something. "Well, we don't have a lot going on this evening. Would seven tonight work?"

Ursula nodded her head. "Yeah, that's perfect."

"I'll bring a side and dessert?"

"I have dessert, but a side would be wonderful."

"Great," Jessica said nodding her head, the look of a woman who had twenty-four mental tabs open on her face. "I look forward to it," she added with a smile.

They waved each other off and then Ursula made her sweep through the produce aisle for anything her backyard wasn't already magically producing for her before checking out. She wondered at the peculiar pull she felt towards Jessica. There was something there that she connected with but she couldn't put her finger on it.

As she was checking out, the woman scanning her items was eyeing her, a look of wariness on her face. Ursula ignored it and gave her a friendly smile, but by the end of scanning her groceries the woman, in her late fifties, leaned back and crossed her thick arms over her chest.

"You're that Lost Souls Witch, aren't ya?"

The question caught Ursula completely off-guard.

"I'm not a witch," she said slowly, never having thought that she'd have to say that. "My name is Ursula and I do live in the Lost Souls House."

The woman, whose name tag read Melissa, nodded her head causing her overly bleached hair that was a short pouf of thin strands to stick up chasing the dry air. "Right. The witch."

She shook her head, frowning as a young man in his teens was bagging her groceries and darting his bespeckled eyes from where he was quickly placing items in brown paper bags to where Melissa was glaring at Ursula.

She cleared her throat. "I'm really not a witch. I just took over the house and-"

"And you're here to stir up what our town is tryin' to forget," the angry woman interrupted, her words spitting and drenched in unfair vexation. "We don't need more of your kind here. We're tryin' to rebuild something wholesome and good in Salem, keep our families grounded in what's virtuous."

Ursula was floored, her heart pounding at the hatred pouring from this stranger who didn't know anything about her. She opened her mouth, about to say something when her eyes caught on the metal button on the woman's red polo shirt. She closed her mouth tightly, paid for her groceries, and told Melissa to have a good day, to which the woman glared in return.

She walked to her car, the interaction playing in her mind. She was so unsettled that when she went to reverse she didn't realize she had put her car in drive instead and when she went to back up, her car went forward instead and bumped against the front bumper of another car. She put her car in park, closed her eyes, and let out a long sigh, then got out to inspect the damage.

There was a small indent the size of a dime on the other SUV and looking around she didn't see anyone, so she left a note with her phone number under the wiper blade.

This day was a mixed bag and she decided she needed to take control.

On a whim she called Tilly.

"Hey, want to meet me at the hardware store and I can give you the journal and you can help me get supplies? I'm building a greenhouse."

She smiled when she hung up the phone, plans made. What was more empowering than taking control and inviting another woman along with you?

But Ursula would soon learn that sometimes you couldn't control the world of good and evil.

CHAPTER NINETEEN

AN UNEXPECTED GUEST

C lear fiberglass panels, sturdy pine two-by-fours, paint, screws, nails, a few necessary tools, and Tom at the hardware store's promise to let Ursula borrow some of his power tools. Over the last two hours she and Tilly had managed to collect all of these things.

"Is there a reason we're rage-buying supplies to build a greenhouse?"

"I wouldn't say it's rage-buying," Ursula defended.

Tilly held up a bucket of nails and a hammer. "I didn't even know what 'galvanized' meant until forty-five minutes ago."

"We're single women who need to know how to do these things, Tilly." She'd decided to keep Jenson's wild kiss to herself for now. And the incident where she had been accused of being a witch at the local grocery store. However, there was an itch, something old and familiar that she hadn't felt in too long when she was with another woman. It was that itch to hunker down and talk about everything in her head, spill it out like a handful of beads, pick them up, and study them with another feminine soul until there was a better understanding and a string of jewelry made from the pieces.

Still. Something held her back.

Tilly nodded with narrowed eyes that made her look like an all-knowing teacher with her cute red cat-eye glasses. "So this is a feminist thing?"

Ursula snorted. "No. I mean, is it feminist to want to know how to build something?"

Tilly considered the question as they walked the supplies out to the car.

"You almost bought one of those power drill things and a power saw thing because Tom said you didn't need to invest in power tools."

"It just seemed a little patronizing," Ursula replied holding up a finger. "Until I saw the price."

Tilly chuckled and stepped back as Ursula closed the tailgate of her car.

"Hey, thanks for letting me borrow the journal. People go nuts for anything new about The Lost Souls House around Halloween."

"Not sure there's anything new in there for you to spin into a good radio segment, but happy to help. Actually," she paused as a thought came to mind, "do you know much about the tenants of the house over the years?"

"Mmm, just a little here and there."

"Did you know a Cassidy Parker?"

She nodded slowly, her face taking on the look of trying to find memories. "Yeah, I was a senior in high school when she moved to town and took over the house. She was pretty private. The town even had a moniker for her, though I don't remember what it was."

"The White Ghost," Ursula supplied.

"Right! Yeah. She was kind of a recluse. I never saw her. Don't even know what she looks like. She didn't live in the house for more than a few years."

Ursula almost didn't ask the next question, not wanting Tilly to become suspicious about Jenson, but her curiosity won out.

"Did Jenson Lancaster date her?"

Tilly's eyes got wide and bright. "Oh yeah. They were hot and heavy for a bit. He was her handyman, that's how he started in construction years ago before he worked his way up to owning his own company. But the rumor was they had an intense falling out." She snapped her fingers as a lightbulb went off in her head. "You know, that's around the time when the town started saying he was cursed."

"Okay, what does that mean? I have heard that a few times about him," Ursula said, trying not to sound overly interested, but when people offhandedly remark on his cursed nature, himself included, and then said man kisses you like the leading man in a romance novel, the curiosity was bound to be extreme.

"I don't know. I just always assumed he was cursed in love," she said shrugging her shoulders, the response a disappointing deflation. "That kind of thing is pretty common here," she added.

She wanted to ask about his involvement with the last tenant at the house, but too many questions about the man and the incident from last night was bound to burst from her.

"Really digging into the history of the house, huh?" Tilly asked with a smile.

"Well, finding the journal in the attic kind of stirred things up."

"If nothing else, we can link pictures of the journal to our social media page for people to check out."

"Thanks for helping with my rage-buying, which it definitely was," Ursula said with a small smile.

"Everything okay?"

Ursula fidgeted with her keychain as she thought about what to share, and what to keep to herself. She didn't want to talk about Jenson and the confusing things going on her her head. And she didn't want to bother Tilly about such a trivial and in Ursula's opinion, juvenile, matter.

"Nah, just working through some things. Nothing I can't handle with more coffee and my new handy hammer," she said with a smile.

But Tilly didn't smile back, instead, she looked at Ursula with an openly worried expression. "You know you can talk to us, right?"

It jolted her, that question. Because of course, she knew she could. But something told her not to. "Yeah," she said easily, waving a hand through the air pushing Tilly's offer aside. "Of course. You are all so wonderful and supportive."

"I mean, you don't tell us much about you," she said gently, testing out the waters slowly. "You don't talk about your life before moving here and you seem like you've always got something going on up there," she said pointing to Ursula's head.

Ursula felt caged, pushed into a corner, and she got the feeling that Tilly had been thinking this for a while. She wondered if the other women thought the same, or worse, had talked about it together. She felt a surge of defensiveness at the picture of them sitting together talking about how Ursula was secretive and didn't share more.

Sure, she didn't talk much about herself, but why was that a bad thing? Wasn't that good? It gave other women more time and space to talk about their stuff. If anything, she was doing them a favor by not talking about her silly issues.

An edged memory of someone she had once shared everything with sliced through her. You can give the most vulnerable pieces of yourself to someone and then they can leave. What happens to those pieces?

She'd wondered that from time to time. Did the person you gave them to still carry them? She imagined an auburn-haired woman scattering what Ursula had given her over years; ashes in the wind, no longer hers to take care of.

"I'm fine, Tilly," she said with a cutting edge to her voice. When Tilly's body physically moved back at the harsh reply Ursula pulled in a breath and put on a smile. "Nothing crazy is going on. I'm just still getting adjusted here in this new life and trying to find new hobbies and ways to spend my time." She hoped that would appease her, though her words were still slightly sharp.

Tilly gave her a half smile. "Sure," she said and Ursula could tell she was choosing her battles. "Alright, well, I'll talk to you later." She started walking toward her car then turned back, "If you need anything let me know. I'm here."

Something pounded in Ursula's heart at the words. She gave Tilly a grateful smile that was over the top but she couldn't seem to stop it and thanked her before jumping into the front seat of her car where that smile dropped and she leaned her head back and let out a deep breath.

What was wrong with her? Tilly, one of the nicest people she had ever met, knew she was lying about something and Ursula had snapped at her. Tilly looked like she had been verbally punched.

But it was her business. She didn't need to air it out and talk about it for hours with other people just to come to zero conclusions. She did not need to be a victim. Her mother had been that, she had watched her push friendships away, ruin work relationships, and put everyone on edge around her with her 'woe is me' mentality.

Ursula had watched that and grown a thick skin. She could handle things on her own and be there for other women. That was good. It made more room for them. And she was more introverted than these other women. That wasn't a bad thing.

She would apologize for snapping at Tilly and thank her for her concern. Tilly was being a good friend, something she wasn't used to; it was something she hadn't had in a long time.

Work was finished and the bright morning that she had welcomed the day with slid into a moody and dark sky with the promise of rain. She started one of her favorite cozy fall meals, sweet corn and cannellini soup with chili flakes and curried chickpeas. Once she had that going, she pulled the bread dough out of the resting bowl, patting it into a round loaf, and used her bread lame to gently slice a design of scrolling flowers along the face. She put it in the oven and stirred the soup, the smells swirling around and creating a warm and comforting atmosphere.

She had about an hour until Jessica came over so she grabbed her book and hunkered into her couch in the living room with the fire crackling and a vanilla candle burning on the coffee table. Casper plopped down onto the rug next to where she sat and she opened her book. A few minutes passed and she realized she was still reading the same paragraph over and over, her mind dropping the words from the page, unread and unwanted.

Her day had been a series of compartmentalized productivity. One of her clients shared a concern over one of the companies she matched him with and she'd been short with him in response. She sent him an email an hour later with an apology saying if he was concerned, she should have listened and set up time for them to talk over his thoughts. And then she kept moving.

She hadn't stopped all day. She'd moved from project to project, keeping herself busy and now she was here, sitting in the most comfortable setting, the sound of the rain and the fire the perfect backdrop for an evening of reading and she couldn't enjoy it.

Jenson Lancaster ruined the quintessential reading night, a lovely pleasure that doesn't always present itself, and she couldn't enjoy the incredible cozy love story trying to unfold.

She slammed her book shut and dropped it on the coffee table, making Casper jolt and look up at her in surprise.

"What kind of man kisses the life out of you and then doesn't so much as send a text?" she asked her grey companion, who let out a huff then put his head back down and closed his eyes. She answered her question in her head: the kind of man who was a serial dater and heart-breaker. She needed to find a way not to let her mind get lost in thinking of him because she couldn't afford to waste any of herself on the kind of man who used women without thought of consequence.

She let out a groan, the kind of sound that had been born and growing for a while inside of a person. The room stilled as she let her anger and frustration press its sound into the corners of the room until it was silent except for the fire and the rain.

She sighed, closing her eyes. She was losing it. Yelling at no one, snapping at someone who she cared about, cutting off a client, and giving him bad advice. What was going on?

Her doorbell rang then and she was the one who jumped. She peeked through the moon-stained glass and saw that Jessica was early.

She opened the door with a perfectly welcoming smile and Jessica gave her a bashful look.

"I'm early, I know. But the kids were in the perfect zone and no one needed me so I just...left." She held up a hand. "And I brought wine."

"Then you have the ticket for early admission," Ursula said, ushering her inside, grateful for the distraction from her self-sabotaging thoughts. The woman looked perfectly poised in an expensive linen suit and low but classy high heels, all of which were the color of Robin's egg blue. She even smelled expensive.

"You look beautiful," Ursula said. She tried not to compare herself to this posh woman, but it was hard when she was wearing dark jeans, a black tank top with a long black cardigan. Her socks were not matching.

"Oh, thank you. I um, I guess I overdressed. I don't know what to wear sometimes."

Ursula laughed, an ease filling her veins at the sound of this woman's insecurity. What a silent and deadly disease, insecurity, that afflicted even the most unsuspecting. She led her down the hallway and into the kitchen which was dancing in the most beautifully warm smells from the simmering soup and the baking bread.

She pulled down two of her amber wine goblets and the wine opener.

"When I don't know what to wear it's always because I am under-dressed. Not dressed to look like a professional, gorgeous model." She watched Jessica's face turn pink and her eyes dart to the left as a sign of being unsure. "Oh, that was a compliment! I am so sorry, I didn't mean to make you feel bad or embarrass you," she rushed to try and fix what her words had done. She was making a mess of every interaction she had today. She slowed down and took a breath. "You look so lovely and I've been bungling my entire day. I'm kind of a disaster today," she admitted.

The relief she felt when Jessica smiled empathetically was swift. It wasn't forced, covering anything up like concealer. She felt this was the first real smile Ursula had seen from her, and it was like a wall had been breached.

"I understand disaster days," she said gently.

"Really?" she asked skeptical. "Because I cannot imagine you as anything but," she gestured up and down Jessica, "well, that. Perfect."

Jessica rolled her eyes and pointed to the velvet high-backed chair. "May I?"

"Of course." Ursula opened the wine and poured each a half glass, then took the seat opposite. "Okay, tell me about one of your disaster days, because I will not believe you until I have details," Ursula urged with a good-natured smile.

"That's very rude, not believing a brand new guest you hardly know," she teased matching Ursula's energy.

Ursula laughed after swallowing a sip of the white wine, which was so crisp and light without that sour hint she usually found disagreeable when drinking white. "Come on," she teased lightly. "Your hair is in a chignon and I am pretty sure you don't have pores."

Jessica shook her head with a soft laugh as she sipped her wine. "These wine glasses are gorgeous. Are they the Mario Novella crystal line from Saks Fifth?"

Ursula held one up and looked at it in horror. "Oh, I hope not. They came with the house," she said, laying it very gently on the island counter, and then added, "Kind of."

"Kind of?"

"Well, I mean, this is a very peculiar house," she said, suddenly unsure what she should or shouldn't divulge. The memory of the cashier calling her a witch with disdain earlier bubbled to the surface of her mind, souring the sip of wine she swallowed.

Jessica, already sitting with excellent posture, straightened and looked around the kitchen, taking in details as she delicately sipped from her glass. "This house is the talk of the town and has been for over two centuries. The history here is deeply embedded in the foundation. And I'm impressed with what you've done with it," she praised. The compliment sounded genuine, with a hint of admiration. "The colors are bold and rich. There's nothing timid about the way you decorated or brought the bones of this place to life," she said.

Ursula looked around at the details and smiled, a flush of pride filling her. "This is the first time I got to make a house mine," she admitted.

Jessica's admiring look turned wistful, a look of dreaming. Ursula knew that look intimately, she could feel the ghost of it on herself when she would see houses full of personality and color, rooms that weren't the simple grey or beige she had been pushed into settling on before. She felt that connection to Jessica again, and the curiosity to understand her better felt like a wave.

"Do you like to decorate? I cannot imagine your house being anything less than impeccable taste."

She laughed, bright white teeth flashing, the look, had it not belonged to this woman with a beautiful face, might have been feral. But then she shook her head and drank more wine. "My house is perfectly decorated. But not by me. We hired someone."

"Oh," Ursula said, a little surprised, but why she was surprised was beyond her. Someone like Jessica with an expensive linen outfit and diamond earrings would have a decorator. "Well, that's pretty neat. You can just pick what you want and they get it done," she said with a snap of her fingers.

"You've never worked with a decorator," she joked. "Color and decor is a deeply personal thing. Decorators take the soul out of it. My husband jokes that it's trifling," her slim fingers painted a pale pink danced in the air with the word. "But I think one day I would like to create my own space."

"What would you do? With a room that is only yours?"

Jessica's face took on that dreamy look and suddenly her posture gave way to relaxation, as if Ursula had pushed a button and released a build-up of pressure. She leaned her forearms on the island top and the apples of her cheeks caught a hue of color. It was comforting to see her folding over with repose.

"I would choose a barely pink color for the walls. Like the pink is just a whispered suggestion, but it's there. Dark cream drapes and the perfect dusty rose bedding with cream sheets and a thick cream knit blanket. Landscape pictures on the walls of rolling green hills and castles."

Ursula listened to her talk, her dulcet voice in that space of dreaming and falling in love with something perhaps that could be. Isn't that one of the most lovely attributes of a woman? A woman knows instinctively how to look forward into a realm of possibility that creates beauty and peace, sometimes even romance.

How many times had she herself sat on her beige couch thinking of what color curtains she would choose with a different color palette and a personality she didn't dull down?

"It's silly though, isn't it? Dreaming of a different life."

The words hit Ursula because she had thought them many times over the years. This posh woman carried the same pain on her shoulders that Ursula understood deeply. They were more alike than their outsides would suggest.

"Well, a different room isn't so different, is it?"

That dreamy smile faltered the slightest. "Yes," she said, but Ursula had the niggling thought that wasn't what she meant. "So," she waggled her blonde eyebrows, "have you learned any of the secrets of the house? Years and years, multiple tenants, and still no one has unearthed the identity of the graves or who lived here and what happened."

"Actually," Ursula's excitement sparked as she leaned forward, "I found a small book in the attic and I'm not sure who the graves are for, but I think the woman that lived here was named Fannie McGovern."

Jessica sat back, no longer that gentle repose in her frame, as she took a sip and nodded telling her to go on.

"I've heard that one or two women took in troubled young women who either ran away from home or were kicked out and that something happened to them. This book I found, I don't know, I can't get it open, but maybe it would tell us who lived here, tell us their stories. Have you ever heard that name?"

"Fannie McGovern?" She pursed her lips shaking her head. "No, it sounds like a perfectly suitable name from the 1700's, though."

"Yeah. I think I'll ask around about her." Ursula remembered the smoke tendrils creating the figures dancing behind her eyelids during their seance, wondering if they would ever know who those eight were.

"Just be careful," Jessica cautioned but when Ursula asked her what she meant the fearful look vanished as she shook her head and smiled, waving it away. "Oh, nothing. I'm just superstitious about these things, especially in a town like Salem."

"I'm beginning to see why. The history here feels deeper, darker, more ancient."

"Yeah," Jessica agreed looking at her finger drawing patterns on the island top. "History has a way of repeating itself."

It felt like she wasn't saying something.

"Have you heard other theories about this house and the graves?"

Jessica laughed gently. "There are so many theories from a house full of witches who would hex people in town until the town got their revenge, to a group of Native Indian women who were eventually run out of town. Up and left everything how it was. The theories are vast and colorful, but I'm afraid they're just that; theories." She looked around thoughtfully. "This place does feel alive, though," she said thoughtfully. "Do you ever feel like it's listening and watching you?"

She thought about how the house had decorated itself for her, harvested food from her garden, and made her feel safe and protected.

"Yeah," she said softly and with a smile.

"Well, I don't know that we will ever know the history of this place, but I'm glad the new tenant is you and that you've made it yours."

Ursula let the theories roll around her mind as she thought about what Crystal had shared. She wasn't sure what Fannie McGovern had to do with the graves, if anything, but she was a part of this house's history. Of that she was certain.

The bread was now rested and the soup was ready to ladle, so she served it for them along with the fall salad Jessica brought as she asked over her shoulder, "So, what does your husband do?"

"Oh," she cleared her throat, "he owns a couple of businesses. Nothing exciting," she replied easily. "He's one of those Salem royalties. His bloodline runs back to the early settling of this town."

"Oh yeah? Maybe I should ask him about this house."

She made a face and shook her head. "He's not a history buff. He just likes the notoriety of that thick, Salem blood."

She wondered if Jessica's husband was one of those Mayflower aristocrats who cared more about their perceived royal blood than the true history of this country. Or the blood it was built on. But saying that to Jessica probably wouldn't be the way to forge their friendship.

When Ursula turned around with a midnight blue bowl of soup and a thick slice of bread Jessica's face lit up. "That looks fantastic. I haven't made bread in years!"

"Oh me either. It's something I decided to start doing when I moved here and it's very relaxing. I get some incredible produce and herbs from my garden so I'm learning new ways to put them to use," she wouldn't tell her that she suddenly had a shocking amount of knowledge about the plants in her garden, or that her backyard was producing food it made no sense to produce. She'd already been called a witch once today. She placed some butter and a tiny white ramekin holding sparkling black sea salt on the table.

"Alright, bon appetit!"

They ate and talked about Jessica's kids. She had three between the ages of thirteen and five years old. She was an art history major, which she never put to use, but one of her favorite things to do was visit art galleries and museums if she found the time.

Ursula got the sense that the woman sitting across from her didn't have many spaces to talk about herself and the tentative way she unfurled, slowly and then with a sweet enthusiasm was like watching one of her delicate moonflowers bloom under the night sky.

"You come from somewhere in the Midwest, Ohio?"

"Word does travel about newcomers," Ursula said still not used to being known before being met.

"Tight-knit community and all that."

"Ohio, yes. Nothing spectacular."

"No one left behind?"

The question was innocent; obvious, even, when getting to know someone, but still it felt intrusive. Ursula took her last sip of wine, which she realized was her second glass, one glass more than she usually partook in. She was feeling the alcohol slide its silky fingers through her system and she pulled in a centering breath and told the thoughts of defensiveness to step back. Why was it so difficult to be known? Did she not want to be known?

"No, no one really. You know, the usual ties from a place you've been for a long time." Jessica opened her mouth, and unsure of what would come next and feeling a slight panic inside of her, Ursula cut her off. "Oh, I have strawberry shortcake. It was my favorite as a kid and I have these gorgeous, plump strawberries growing all over the place that I wanted to use." She got up to gather the sweet biscuits and sliced strawberries she had put in a ceramic bowl with a tablespoon of reduced bourbon and a sprinkle of sugar. A little container of homemade whipped cream was pulled out of the refrigerator and then she served the desserts on her small plates with black ravens.

"Wow, you are impressive," Jessica complimented. "And these dishes are very Edgar Allan Poe," she added.

"I saw a set of dishes years ago with ravens on them and almost got them but held back."

"Why?"

Her brow pulled in and she let a bite of the sweet and buttery biscuit with the bourbon-spiced strawberries take hold of her taste buds. "They fell into my 'pink room' category," she said simply, leaving out that everything about her previous life fell into that same category.

Jessica got a puzzled look on her smooth face. "You said you have strawberries growing? How in the world are strawberries still growing in this weather?"

"Oh! So," so....how did she explain this one? "Greenhouse," she finally landed on. "Heated greenhouse."

"I love greenhouses. Will you show me?"

She mentally cursed.

"Uh, I had to move some things because I am currently in the process of building a larger greenhouse and adding on, so you know, lots of construction. Can't take anyone out there," she said. The lie was not well-constructed, but it was all she could mentally grab at in moments. And she did have all of the wood out there and the tools sitting on the ground in the corner which she pointed toward. She mentally thanked Tom for bringing it all over this afternoon. That man deserved a pie.

"Wow. That's a big project," she replied after looking at the tools. "I am embarrassed to admit I have never hammered anything," she laughed, the sound that had been elegant earlier, grating on Ursula now.

Maybe she needed to recharge away from people and work through some of her emotions before trying with another human for a bit. Her track record today wasn't looking great.

Just then her doorbell rang, surprising both of them.

"I should probably get that. Excuse me for a second," Ursula said, trying to think if there was a way to send out a universal message to all: *Beware of my inability to people right now. I am tripping over relationships like I have two left feet.*

"No problem," Jessica said brightly. "Could you point me to the restroom?" her voice came out high and squeaky. Was she okay or was Ursula in need of a people re-set?

Ursula gave Jessica a half smile and pointed her to the bathroom before she made her way down the hallway. Her eyes trailed along the floral wallpaper and stopped for a moment peering closely. Were the ferns curling up? She stepped toward the wall, her toes touching the baseboard, and delicately, with trepidation, slid the tip of her index finger along one of the fronds. Before, they were unfurled and fanned out over the pattern creating a strong, forest-like background where the flowers and berries were displayed gloriously. But these looked like they were shrinking in, leaving a more open and bare black background.

She was crazy.

A knock sounded on the door and she jumped back, placing a palm to her chest. "You've got this. Just don't snap at anyone or show that you're in an unnaturally annoyed state." She walked towards the door. "And do not give off witch vibes." Her pep talk ended with a fake smile as she opened the old wood door. But the moment she did, her fake smile melted.

Chapter Twenty

A Note

"Bess," what are you doing here?" Ursula peered around the sullen-looking teenager with half a hope and half a fear in her chest. When she didn't see anyone else there, specifically a broody tall man who could kiss like the devil, she looked back at the girl, a thick, light blue quarter zip sweatshirt that had splatters of rain covering it with black jeans and boots, a beanie over her hair braided hair, similar to the first time she had met her behind the coffee counter.

"Mom got home this afternoon," she said. The nearly undetectable lines through her makeup that ran over the apples of her youthful cheeks made sense.

Ursula nodded her head and opened the door wider, stepping back.

"Why don't you get settled on the couch over here? I need to go take care of something," she said. Bess dropped her backpack on the ground next to the couch and sat down on the edge, her posture anything but settled.

She walked back to the kitchen, amazed that the teenager had come to her. When she didn't see Jessica back from the bathroom yet, she went to find her phone but stopped short when she saw movement out her back windows. Her pulse immediately kicked up and she inched closer, reaching out to swipe her phone from the counter as she crept toward the window. Slick little beads trickled down the clear panes, making it hard to see. She saw what looked like a blue arm raise and her brow furrowed as she watched Jessica holding her phone out.

"What the...", she murmured as she opened the door, her pulse no longer beating harshly with fear, but confusion and something that tasted like suspicion. Stepping out onto the patio, she was immediately chilled by icy droplets and a billowy wind whipping her hair.

"What are you doing?"

Jessica dropped her phone as she swung around, her face white and a hand pressed to her chest. Then she let out a laugh of relief. "Ursula! You scared me," her words rolled into an odd-sounding laugh that was more nervous than mirth. This was the first time she had seen this woman less than perfectly put together, a piece of hair darkened by the rain was hanging limp and wet along her cheek, which was pale and there was a thin run of black makeup under her left eye. Her exquisite outfit was collecting dollops of wet spots and she wondered if the material was ruined or if an expensive trip to the dry cleaners was in Jessica's future.

Ursula looked around quickly, not much visible in the dark, especially since she hadn't turned the string of lights on overhead. When she looked back at Jessica, she had her phone in hand and was straightening from where she had bent to grab it.

"Why are you out here in the freezing rain?"

"I am so sorry, I didn't listen to you," her voice was lowered, filled with remorse. "I'm interested in your garden and you said couldn't show me around but I couldn't help myself."

She sounded sorry but it was still odd. And something wasn't sitting right. The air around her felt off like someone had jammed a puzzle piece where it didn't quite fit. The trilling of an eastern screech owl filled the night, its territorial cry like a warning. Even the bell jars of moonlight looked dim and cool. The natural world was telling her something was wrong, and she needed to listen.

"I would be happy to show you around when it's less," she looked up at the sky and felt a pelt of icy water hit her eyelid, "Wuthering Heights outside," she finished looking back at Jessica. She wiped at her face and gestured for an unsure and scared Jessica, to go back inside. Jessica didn't move at first, her eyes flitting to the door and then back to where Ursula stood as if calculating. The dark made it difficult to read the look on her face, but she swore whatever was making her hesitate was a darkness of some kind. Whether she was facing it or it was inside of her, Ursula was unsure, and inviting her back into her home was a gamble. "Come inside. Get out of the cold."

Finally, she moved, putting more distance than necessary between them as she passed through the door. Ursula closed it behind her and looked at Jessica who was straight-backed and tall, though her eyes didn't match her bravery.

"I really am sorry. I should not have disrespected your wishes, especially as you've welcomed me into your home so kindly."

The words struck her as...strange. Not in a spurious fashion, rather like they were old words, ones she had born long ago and dusted off.

"Are you okay? I mean," she looked out the window behind her and then back at Jessica, "yeah, I would rather you have respected what I had said earlier, but it's not a big deal and you can come back anytime to look at the garden."

She blinked in quick succession. Her throat cleared and she nodded her head, a thin layer of ice firmly over her features now. "I understand if you don't want to continue pursuing a friendship with me."

Ursula frowned, completely taken aback by the largeness of her words. How big they felt, like the words had been holstered in a pocket of fear inside of her. Ursula took a step forward. "Jessica, I don't understand what is happening, but this isn't a big deal. And apology accepted. We are good and I would like to be friends," she said, carefully hawk-eyeing Jessica's expression, which was still tight, but her eyes looked hazy, sad, and the slightest shade of hopeful. "Even though you're way out of my friend league," she finished with a quirked mouth, her mind reaching out and trying to connect with Jessica's in lightheartedness.

A breathless laugh pressed through Jessica's mouth and a look of surprise; a tight balloon relieved of the pressure. Her posture relaxed by a few degrees. Then she she blinked and a look like she remembered something took over her demeanor.

"Was someone here?"

"Oh, yeah, I need to go check on her," she replied thinking of the teenage girl sitting in tears on her couch.

Jessica glanced at her phone and frowned then turned it into a bright smile making Ursula shake her head. She was going through so many demeanors and she was barely able to keep up. And still, that vertiginous feeling, tilted and off, was pressing in.

"I actually should get going," her words matched her newly bright attitude. "My husband texted and the kids are having a difficult time going down without me there."

"Okay," Ursula said easily. "I'm really glad you came over. Next time you bring dessert. I bet it's better than mine."

That shiny, bright exterior dropped the slightest, the break in character showing a soft underbelly of hope, and happiness. Then she nodded and smiled a small but true smile. "I, think I'll go out this way so I don't disturb your guest," she walked toward the back door.

"Oh, you don't have to do that," Ursula said, though she moved out of her way letting her take the exit she could feel the woman needed.

That small, but true smile was still there in the corner of her mouth as she held the door handle and looked at Ursula. "This was nice. You're surprising and I like you." And then she was out the door, into the biting autumn rain leaving behind a confused and astonished Ursula.

Who was this woman? Ursula shook her head and laughed as she moved quickly to the living room. When she got there, she smiled when she saw that Bess was curled up into the deep back corner of the couch with a blanket over her lap and Casper's head lolling on top as she pet him gently. The fire flickered over the sweet picture and she waited a few more beats before she broke the magical barrier of peace, which she bet this young girl experienced very little of.

Then she stepped forward slowly, a hand held up and a penitent smile at the young girl whose head had snapped toward her at the movement.

"Hey, honey. Can I sit?"

Bess pulled her knees up tighter against her chest and she nodded. "Are you going to make me go home?"

"I'm going to sit here and listen to you, about what happened and what you're feeling, and then we will go from there," she said.

When Bess burst into tears, pressing her eyes against her arms folded on top of her knees, Ursula immediately scooted until she was there, wrapping an arm around the smaller-than-usual teenager. "Shhh. It's okay, honey. You are safe here. You're okay."

Once her tears were silent and she could talk, Bess said, "She was home when I got home from school, and the first thing she said to me, she," she paused as a new hold of tears came. "She said I'm too much. That I turned her from a woman into a mom and she would pay for it forever."

Damn it. Ursula looked up at the ceiling and shook her head at the foolish, harmful words that this poor girl's mother shot at her like weapons. This would last, reverberate through every momentous part of this girl's life, forcing her to ask this question over and over and over: am I too much? Every relationship she has will be built on the charcoal drawing of that foundation. Every time she feels the sting of rejection she learns a new or firmer way to cope. She will forever wonder if she is worth enough, and sometimes anything at all.

All because a few hungover, shame-filled words that were bred inside of her mother came bursting out of her and forever tainting Bess.

Careless we can be, when we speak words we assume are as fictional to them as they are to us. We know our most shameful thoughts and fears are built on lies. We know because we never fully give up hope that they are. So when we spout our fears so carelessly, we do not realize that they sometimes land on someone else's skin as though they are true.

A roll of thunder, both gentle and strong, sounded around them, cocooning them inside this little, warm world for now. That off-kilter feeling from before was gone, she realized. And Ursula was learning that moments like these, fleeting and never lasting, were worth stopping and protecting.

The fire was getting weaker, Casper was asleep on the floor with his long body pressed against the couch and the rain was steady with random interruptions of the sky rumbling its deep baritone.

"Does anyone know where you are?"

Bess slipped off her hat and wrung it between her pale hands. The hair underneath lay flat and her light roots showed. She wondered what she would look like with her natural hair color.

"I just left the house once she started drinking again," she said softly.

Ursula nodded her head. "Why didn't you go to your uncle's?" Just the mention of him made her insides wobble.

"He's away at a job site. He stays there overnight when they're trying to get through a difficult part of a job. And I just," she swallowed harshly. "I didn't want to be alone."

The words were so big, and said in a small voice, clenching Ursula's heart.

"Okay," she said trying to think.

"And there's something about this house," she continued and Ursula watched her look around the room like she was memorizing something beautiful. "When I was here with you and your friends, it was like, the first time I felt in place. I don't know how to describe it. But it felt like if the house had feelings, then it was glad I was here." She turned to Ursula, a vulnerable shaking look in her eyes. "Is that totally weird?"

She smiled. "Not at all. That's a really good way to put it," she said, taking her turn to look around the room. "I hadn't found a way to put into words how I feel when I'm here, but the house being glad is true."

She looked back at Bess.

She couldn't just keep a teenager here without an adult in her life knowing about it. She barely knew Bess. "I'm going to make some tea for us and then we will figure this out," she said.

Bess's relaxed figure jumped into a position of fear as her eyes got wide. "Are you taking me back to my mom's?"

"Don't worry about that right now. Tea, and then we go from there."

She tucked Bess into the corner urging her to relax again before she put on the kettle and stared at her phone. After a few moments, she sighed and hit 'call'.

She leaned back against the island as the phone rang once, but before she could brace herself a thick, low voice filled her ear.

"Ursula," he said.

Why did his saying her name make her feel like her insides were suddenly getting warmer? His tone was authoritative and unfairly sexy and then she remembered that he kissed her and then hadn't so much as texted her after. That was the reminder that she needed. She pressed her shoulders back.

"Jenson, hi. I have Bess here," she said. Her voice didn't waver and she wasn't hiding behind anything so she was going to give herself a point.

"Bess? Is she okay?"

"Well, her mom got home today and it didn't go well. She ended up on my front porch about half an hour ago."

He cursed and she could hear something rustling around in the background. "I'm forty-five minutes out but I'll come and get her."

"Actually," she said, unsure of how he would take this or even if it was a wise move, "she's cozy on the couch and Casper is keeping her company. I have plenty of guest rooms and if you're okay with it, I'm good with her staying. I can drive her to school tomorrow and pick her up."

The pause on the other end was heavy and she wondered if she had overstepped or thought she was doing this for him.

"This has nothing to do with you or us. Not that there is an us," she closed her eyes and pursed her lips at the words tripping over themselves so clumsily.

"You're not being nice to my niece and giving her a safe place so that I'll kiss you again?" His words sparked embarrassment inside of her.

"No! That's..." Her cheeks heated when she heard his low rumbling laughter that hardly qualified as laughing, more of a sound of seducing a thirty-eight-year-old woman. "Funny. Listen, you can come get her, drive all the way here, and take her to your house which would end up being late, or you can let her crash here and deal with all of this tomorrow." Another beat of silence followed.

"Tell her I'll pick her up from school," he finally said. His words were gentle, curling around his adoration for his niece and it melted some of the frustration she was feeling toward him.

"I will."

"Ursula," he called before she could hang up. She waited, her heart beating hard in the moments between him saying her name and what he said next. Would he bring up the kiss without it being a joke? She wasn't sure if she wanted him to or not. But then his words let her down and she had her answer. "Thank you. She's lucky to have you."

The words were sweet, landing softly along her ribs as she let out a breath. "She's a wonderful young woman. See you, Jenson." Then she hung up and put the phone on the island staring at the background of fall leaves she had as her wallpaper.

With two mugs of chamomile and rose petal tea in her hands and a change of clothes hanging over her forearm, she walked to where she found Bess reading a thick novel on the couch.

"What are you reading?" she asked as she placed the mummy mug on the coffee table near Bess who looked calm, her eyes still a little puffy from earlier, but a veil of peace covering her nonetheless.

"The Scarlet Letter," she said.

"Ah. The curriculum of dead white male writers is still going strong I see."

Bess rolled her eyes and sat up to reach for her tea. "Honestly, who picks what we should read? They suck at their job."

Ursula laughed and settled into the other corner of the couch. She pointed to the fresh, clean clothes. "Those are for you. So listen,

I talked with your uncle," she held up a hand when Bess's mouth opened, "and we decided you are free to stay here tonight and I can take you to school tomorrow. He will pick you up from school."

"Really? Am I putting you out?"

"No. Not even a little," she said honestly. "I might have some extra stuff in the guest bathroom down here, and I will get you a towel. The bed is ready for you and I'll wake you up for breakfast before school."

"We have a late start tomorrow for teacher meetings so I start two hours later."

"Perfect. We can go into town, grab some breakfast. Sound good?"

Bess's face lit up and she nodded her head. She looked so young and pale and Ursula wanted to hug her and tell her everything would be okay.

"Why don't you finish your tea, read some more of that wonderful classic," she said dryly, "and then head to bed?"

She nodded again and let out a sigh. It was the kind of sigh that had been harbored precariously inside of her, waiting with hope and fear and then finally released in relief. Ursula patted her knee affectionately before she got up and rummaged through the guest bathroom.

The bathroom was earthy with cream wainscoting at the bottom and mossy green tiles taking up the rest of the walls. The sink vanity matched the cream wainscoting with golden snail cabinet pulls and a large, gold oval mirror above it in the shape of an owl. The shower looked modern with a black frame and frosted glass. She opened the two drawers in the vanity and was unsurprised when they were empty. She may have to do without a toothbrush tonight. She pulled out a fluffy grey towel from under the sink and when she placed it neatly next to where the dark floral hand towel hung on a gold bar, something tinkled like little bells and she paused.

She opened the drawer to her right again and found an unopened purple toothbrush next to a new travel-size toothpaste. She smiled as she placed them next to the towel and laughed at this magical house.

This house liked to create spaces of beauty and home, take care of others, and invite rest.

She got Bess settled into one of the guest rooms, all of which were decorated in dark, moody themes matching the rest of the house. This one was dark blue, the night sky right before pitch black took over. The hanging chandelier was like a burst of gold and blue stars. Lace curtains with stars and planets hung high and draped to the floor in a delicate sweep. The bed was a sumptuous queen with a fluffy white comforter and a dark blue thick-knit blanket at the foot.

"Wow," Bess said. "If I could have picked out a room for myself this would be it." She sat on the edge of the bed, running a hand over the top of the duvet.

"I'm glad you like it," Ursula said, wondering if the house somehow had known of this particular future guest. "Listen, I need you to promise me that you will talk with your uncle about things at home. He is a jack," she stopped herself before she called him a name and recovered quickly, "of all trades and one of those trades is caring for you." Smooth. She mentally high-fived herself for that improvising gymnastics.

Bess gave her an odd look but nodded her head. "Yeah. I need to talk to him. I just don't want to be a bother. Put him in the middle," she said.

"Hon," Ursula sat next to her. "He may be a grumpy, Brawny man, but he loves you and would want you to be honest with him and put him in the middle." He also might be behind the last tenant leaving The Lost Souls House, a voice whispered in her mind.

"Yeah, I know. What is with you and him, by the way?"

The sudden shift of topic and the suspicious way the girl looked at her made her feel like a microscope was on her. She stood up and smoothed down her shirt.

"Your uncle and me? Nothing. He's just a guy I barely know who is confusing as hell and even grumpier than he is confusing. Why is he so grumpy?" Maybe he was born that way. Are people born grumpy? She saw the corner of Bess's mouth had quirked up and she quickly waved a hand through the air. "Ohmygosh. Don't answer that. Your uncle is, quite frankly, a jerk but you are our common ground and that's enough for me."

"He's cursed."

"What?"

"My uncle. He's grumpy because he's cursed."

Her eyes narrowed. Would she finally get the story? She wanted to know but didn't want to sound too interested.

"He's cursed. By like, a witch?"

Bess shrugged. "No one has ever given me the full story, but all I know is that he avoids women like the plague. Women tend to turn real..." her youthful face scrunched up and her fingers danced in the air, "weird around him. Like crazy."

"Huh. Well, no need to worry about that from me. Alright kiddo, sleep tight. Toothbrush and towels are in the bathroom. Make yourself at home."

"Thanks, Ursula," she said softly then before she could close the door she said, "Oh hey, sorry that I ruined your dinner. She didn't have to leave, you know."

"Oh, no. It's fine. The night was winding down anyway," she said, suddenly remembering the oddity of how the dinner ended. A picture of Jessica in her beautiful outfit standing outside in the freezing rain taking a picture in the dark on her phone flashed through her mind.

"What was Jessica doing here anyway? I kind of had you pegged as a Cora supporter."

"I am," Ursula began, confusion wrapping around her words. "Wait, you know Jessica?"

Bess made a harumphing sound. "Well yeah. Everyone does. I mean, she's nice enough. She's always polite, if a little standoffish when she comes into Black Cat. I just do not know how anyone could be married to that cretin Rob." She made a show of shivering and made an ick face sticking her tongue out.

"Hold up. Jessica is Rob Sandis's wife? She's Jessica Sandis?"

"Yeah. You didn't know?"

She did not. She most certainly did not have that pivotal piece of information.

CHAPTER TWENTY-ONE

THE PULL OF THE MOON

B ess was in her celestial room, fast asleep, Casper curled up in the bed next to her keeping guard. But Ursula felt a restlessness, something warm and buzzing through her.

The jolting news about who Jessica was had been a sledgehammer to the evening, and her thoughts were too tangled and uncertain for her to imagine trying to chase sleep.

So, she did what she found herself doing most nights in The Lost Souls house when she couldn't sleep; she bundled up with a blanket and more hot tea with rose petals and mint, then curled up on the old porch swing.

She loved the sound of the old chains rubbing. The sound was nostalgic, a summer sound like an old screened porch door opening and closing. She closed her eyes and could imagine the sounds of summer crickets and cicadas singing. A soft hope bloomed in her chest where hope had been unwelcome for so long; maybe she could stay. Maybe she could make this her home.

She wasn't sure how long she sat there, the gentle swooping of the swing rocking her, but for unexplainable reasons she wasn't surprised when another presence joined her.

Maybe he couldn't stay away and not check on Bess. Or maybe he too felt the pull of something he couldn't name.

Maybe he was cursed and there was magic on this hallowed ground that called to him too.

The gentle dip of the swing as he sat next to her made her heart beat harder. They sat silently for a spell, nothing but the sounds of nighttime dancing around them. He gently moved them back and forth with his long legs.

"Sometimes I think the moon has magic and that's what poets and writers mean when they talk of her pull."

His words were smooth, low and the perfect harmony to this dark night, lacing beautifully with the creaking of the swing. She turned to watch his profile, the moon he spoke of washing his dark features in gentle light.

"Did you feel pulled here?"

He turned toward her then and his eyes roved over her face, tenderly, like a lover.

"Yes," was his simple reply.

"Bess is okay," she said softly. "She's asleep and I even made her brush her teeth."

One side of his mouth tipped up but he shook his head and reached out a hand, gently sliding a piece of her hair behind her ear. "I know," he replied.

What he didn't say was that wasn't why he was here. He didn't have to.

"Are you cursed?" she asked bravely. She had spent so much of her life forgetting how to speak her mind. "Sorry," she laughed softly when his dark eyebrow lifted at her boldness. She looked back up at the moon. "I had a friend once who was horribly straightforward in the most refreshing way. She had this way about her that was reckless, but she knew exactly when to be reckless, when it would leave the most beautiful impact on someone, like telling them they were beautiful and that someone was magical or that they had hurt her." She felt a rush of love for her lost friend thinking back on her. "She taught me to balance truth with gentleness and that recklessness is sometimes necessary in a world full of bubble-wrapped honesty."

"She sounds like a good friend."

She nodded then looked back at him. "She was."

"Was?"

She shook her head silently and he understood not to press.

"What if I said that I am cursed?" His question was careful, words made of glass.

"Then I would ask how I could help," she replied and his eyes took on a gentleness that was breathtaking.

"Can we sit here for tonight? I think I just need to be here, near you."

She recognized that he wasn't ready to talk about curses or anything else that mattered right now. But he was asking if he could simply be, sit near her, give into the pull of the moon. She could give him that.

She nodded her head in answer and they both looked back up at the moon, her body brighter than before. The swing pushed back and forth in the perfect rhythm and a cool breeze brought the sweet scent of basil, lush strawberries, and thyme. Lemon balm and tantalizing Desdemona roses chased closely after them, brushing against their skin, filling their lungs with growing life.

She pulled in a big breath of her garden air when she felt him lace his strong, warm fingers with hers.

"I think you're beautiful, in the most reckless, honest way a person can be," his words startled her and she looked at him, but he was still looking up at the moon. "And I don't feel cursed around you."

She didn't know what to say but knew he didn't need words. So she curled her hand into his and rested in this nighttime moment with him.

Maybe one day he would explain, give her answers. But for now, he was asking her to sit with him in his darkness for a spell. And she could do that.

She woke up sometime later, in her bed with the covers pulled up to her chin, her clothes on and her boots lovingly placed on the floor next to her nightstand.

She couldn't be absolutely sure that her nighttime swing with Jenson hadn't been a dream, though she felt it hadn't. But what a lovely feeling, to waver between the knowing and the dream world.

CHAPTER TWENTY-TWO

PAINTED SKULLS

U rsula got up earlier than usual, having spent most of the night sliding from one side of the bed to the other as thoughts pounded through her brain. Jessica Sandis. She was Rob's wife. Had she used Ursula, and why? What could she possibly have gained by keeping her identity a secret? She spent hours poring over their conversations and realizing that she had been a master of answering questions just enough to not give away that she was married to the man running for mayor.

She, herself, had barely interacted with Rob. But her friends had deeper roots here. Maybe Rob used the new woman in town to try and get information? She had none. She had met Cora twice and couldn't say that they were friends.

Finally, when the early grey light crept its way into the windows, she got up and took a hot shower, washing off the tiredness the best she could. This was becoming a habit, not sleeping, and it was starting to wear on her. Her bones were feeling heavier. Her steps felt like they required more intention. When she got out of the shower and wrapped a towel around her, she noticed a small notification on her phone. When she saw that it was from Jenson and that it was from last night, she frowned. Opening it up her eyebrows shot up when she read the texts.

Brawny Man: Good Morning

Brawny Man: How is Bess?

Brawny man: And how are you?

She bit her bottom lip, her fingers hovering over her phone trying to fit the grumpy, stoic ass with this guy who was a concerned and loving uncle. Which was dangerous because this guy, sending her a good morning text, checking on his niece, and checking on her? The man who held her hand while they sat on a swing under the autumn moonlight could be the kind of man she would invite into her life. That intentionality and softness did things like make her want to kiss him again. Did she want to kiss him again? The memory alone screamed yes. But her heart was wary and unsure.

She decided not to respond to his text.

After her third cup of coffee, she knocked on the door where Bess was sleeping and told her it was time to get up. She wasn't sure how much time she would need, but based on herself as a teenager, waking in the morning was one of the hardest parts of the day. She went upstairs to change out of her robe and fully get ready. She threw on a black floral dress with small ravens on it. It was short-sleeved and buttoned up the front with a tie around the waist, landing around her mid-calf. She paired it with ankle boots and would put on her black felt hat hanging by the door.

One thing that had changed over the last few months was her wardrobe. The clothes themselves weren't different, but she wore the ones she wouldn't dare put on before. The ones tucked away in the back of her closet that she wished she had places to wear. The truth was, she had been afraid of being looked at. She'd gotten used to not being seen; anything more than a passing glance would feel intrusive.

But now, she pulled those clothes out and put them on with a flourish.

Her long black hair was lightly waved and hung loose and her thick bangs, which were growing out, she decided to wisp to the sides in a curtain today. She enjoyed dressing up and for herself. It did something to her soul, knowing that her frame was dressed in something she loved. Something for her.

When she walked into the kitchen, Bess was drinking freshly pressed coffee from the black cat mug and scrolling through her phone.

"You ready to go?"

Bess looked up from her phone and smiled, her eyebrows raised as she scanned Ursula. "I love your dress. I'm not a dress person, but I like that one," Bess gushed. "Ohmygod, where did you get those boots?"

Ursule kicked one up. "These are one of my favorite pairs. Advice to you from an older woman, invest in good quality shoes and fashion. Fast fashion won't last, is terrible for the environment, and when you put on something of quality, you feel like quality."

Bess hopped off the stool, wearing the same outfit from last night. She threw on a pair of dirty white Converse shoes and washed her mug.

"Ready!"

"Have a place in mind?"

"Yeah, the Lazy Snail. They have coffee-infused french toast that is insane."

Ursula smiled and nodded her head behind her toward the front door.

"Ok, we're going to have to walk because downtown is taped off."

"Oh yeah, don't even try to drive down to the main strip in October. This town becomes a tourist thing that we have to take back once November hits."

"Noted."

She grabbed her black hat, a black wool coat, and her purse. Sulphur was lounging on the outdoor rug batting at a ribbon that was dangling from a package left on the coffee table.

Ursula frowned and picked it up. The rectangle was wrapped in brown paper and had a lacy black ribbon, which she untied and dropped next to Sulphur who attacked it with a targeted pounce.

"What's that?"

"I'm not sure," Ursula uttered. She slid open the carefully taped seam and peeled back the paper revealing a brown, thin book. It was old. What had probably been nice leather was cracked and worn and there was a thin string of leather wrapped around it and tied in the front. She was about to open it but thought better of it. She had better leave this for later in case it was something important. She wanted to enjoy her time with Bess and she already had a lot on her mind, which was all being muddled by lack of sleep.

"I'm going to put this inside and we can be off."

The Lazy Snail was a breakfast spot on the back corner of the main street, not easily visible unless you knew to look for it. In fact, there was no sign, the sidewalk was cracked with weeds growing through, and the windows were boarded up. There was nothing to distinguish this place except for the crooked gold number forty-three.

Ursula looked around perplexed. "Uh..."

Bess smiled and walked up to the black door and threw over her shoulder before heaving it open, "Trust me."

Ursula threw one last look around the already crowding Salem street and then followed her. When she stepped over the rusted threshold, her mouth dropped open. This was like falling into a rabbit hole because the outside with the slightly crooked forty-three was anything but derelict and abandoned. Inside was...adorably magical. There were twinkle lights strung up high along a tunnel of bursting greenery above them. Ferns puffed their way along the top of the rounded tunnel while ivy climbed and wove in between creating a world of lush forest. A few tall trees that looked real pressed up to the high ceilings and looked as though the floor had been built around them. One had a treehouse in it!

"Is that?"

"Oh, that's my favorite spot, but you can only reserve the treehouse table for special occasions," Bess's voice was chipper and excited. The treehouse had a rope ladder that disappeared into the bottom of the structure, which was incredibly detailed. There was a sloping roof and a chimney. A little pile of logs rested against one side of the house and the siding was worn, cozy beachwood. There were two windows that she could see, both large and round and she could barely make out a crystal chandelier inside. A small porch wrapped around the front to one side with small chairs and a railing. It was extraordinary. There were tables made of live wood scattered around the space and servers walking around with black aprons.

Bess picked out a table underneath the treehouse, to Ursula's delight, and she couldn't help but study it as she opened the menu, finding more minute details every time she looked.

"Okay, this place is..."

"Amazing?" Bess smiled widely, the Cheshire cat in teenage form.

"Understatement," Ursula agreed.

"It turns into a nightclub called The Dancing Snail at eight pm."

"You're kidding," she shook her head amazed as she looked around. Crystal chandeliers dotted the fluffy greenery above them, instrumental music played melodically creating a soft and easy atmosphere. "Alright, what is good here?"

"Just about everything. I recommend the French toast. The pancakes actually kind of suck, though."

"Hey now," a voice chimed in drawing Ursula's attention to a tall redhead who looked like she could be a pinup girl. Her red hair was done up in a pinup style and she was wearing a blue and white striped top with a black skirt and tights. She was stunning. "She's not wrong though. The pancakes are weird. Why Joe thought putting cranberries and pistachios in pancakes was a good idea with an unflinching stance on not making plain ones for the normal people, is beyond me."

"Hey Shirley," Bess pointed to Ursula. "This is-"

"Ursula Cambridge," she finished for her. She leaned down and wrapped both arms around Ursula's shoulders, knocking the brim of her hat in a familiar hug that took her by surprise. Shirley pulled back and pulled a pen out of her hair. "You're famous. And you were described as mysteriously beautiful with black hair. You fit the bill perfectly," she winked and Ursula stared wide-eyed at her before she laughed.

"It is a pleasure to meet you," Ursula looked around. "This is quite an experience."

"Yep. Joe, my older brother, owns the place. He wanted to create a space that non-locals wouldn't know about. Only us Salem-dwellers."

"And word has never gotten out?"

"I swear he found a witch and paid her with an organ or something equally macabre to put a secret-keeping spell on this place. Four years and not a single non-local has waltzed in here."

"That's impressive," she agreed.

"You want the French toast?"

"Yes please."

"You need a minute?"

"Actually, I will do the same. With a large coffee. Huge coffee."

Shirley winked and walked away. She had to be over six feet tall. Ursula envied the legs on that woman. She stopped growing in seventh grade, never making it past the five-foot two-inch mark.

"How are you doing this morning?" Ursula kept her tone light and gentle, not wanting to spook the teenager into talking about her feelings too much.

But Bess surprised her when she took on a serious look and replied, "I'm okay. I talked with my two best friends a little last night and we're going to get together before tomorrow's festival."

"That's great." Ursula smiled, remembering how those young, tender friendships could heal just about anything. Bess looked happier and lighter today. She wasn't sure she was that grounded when she was Bess's age. Actually she knew she wasn't. The memory of snapping at Tilly in response to Tilly's kindness sharply pricked her. She wasn't even that grounded right now.

"Yeah, I mean, they're my girls, you know? Like, they're there and they get me and they let me just be when I need it, or to unpack and after I unpack my crap with them I literally feel lighter. Just like you and Jen and Tilly and them. Don't you just feel like you can breathe when you're with them and then breathe easier after you've let them carry some of your emotional baggage?"

Good Lord, this girl was wise beyond her years and her words punctured a balloon of pressured regret and fear inside of her. She leaned forward and lowered her voice to a whisper, "Are you actually forty-five years old in a teenage body?"

"Yes," she whispered back seriously and they shared a laugh.

"Ladies," a familiar voice greeted drawing their attention to a smiling Miles.

"Oh hey, Miles," Ursula smiled.

"You ladies having a girl's morning?"

"Late start school," Bess said, her expression flat but her dark eyes trained on Miles in a hawkish manner.

Ursula studied her new mood with curiosity then looked back at Miles who didn't seem to be affected by a teenage girl's lack of enthusiasm.

"I have a late start day too," he joked.

"Don't all artists have a late start every day?"

Ursula's eyebrows raised as she took in this interesting, and rather sharp, manner that Bess had suddenly donned.

Miles laughed good-naturedly, but a look of annoyance briefly crossed his eyes. He pointed to a chair. "May I? It's pretty slammed today."

He wasn't wrong. Every table was covered by people so she smiled and told him to have a seat. Bess rolled her eyes, which thankfully Miles missed.

He was dressed in a nice light blue quarter zip sweater and his hair was gelled. He looked more like a corporate CFO than an artist.

"You both look nice today. Bess, right?" It was the first time he gave his attention to the annoyed-looking teenager.

Bess nodded her head and started scrolling through her phone. Dismissed. Ursula did not want to be on the receiving end of Bess's icing out.

"Teenagers," he mocked lightly, shaking his head with a smile. His front two teeth were slightly overlapping, giving him an unkempt look. She smiled tightly, recognizing that the nice morning they were having had suddenly shifted.

And then it shifted again.

"Morning," a deep voice resonated deep inside of Ursula, and before she even had to look up to its owner she knew exactly who it was. She thought of the softness and boldness of last night, sitting with him on the old, creaking swing. His eyes held hers long enough for her to know it hadn't been a dream.

But even so, it had been like a time-out, a period where they weren't fully themselves with their animosity. In the light of day, she was left unsure and no longer that bold, reckless woman who sat under the moonlight with him.

"Hey, Uncle Jay!" And just like that, Bess had turned another corner. "I told him we were coming here," she explained to Ursula and she smelled suspicious intent but left it alone.

"Hey, B." He took a seat across from Ursula without asking or being invited. "I didn't realize you had a breakfast date," he drawled.

Ursula looked up from where her eyes had been trained on pressing her cuticles down. The moment her eyes landed on him she felt a thump in her chest to see his dark eyes zoned in on her.

"Not a date. Bess and I came here like I told you," she explained, feeling a defensiveness spring up.

"And then Artsy over here barged in," Bess added spearing Miles with a dead look.

He glared momentarily before he nodded at Jenson. "Jenson."

"Miles," he nodded back, his tone unreadable.

"I saw two beautiful women sitting alone, damsels in distress," he laughed.

Bess and Ursula both frowned at his remix of events.

"And since it's so busy, I thought I could keep them company and talk with Ursula about the art she commissioned me to do for her."

Jenson's gaze swung back to her. "How nice." That tone was readable and she wanted to take her iced water and throw it at him.

"Yeah, thank you so much for saving us from our silly feminine loneliness," Bess's words dripped with so much sarcasm that Ursula gave her a reprimanding look. Jenson smirked.

Miles ignored her and turned his attention to Ursula who was tapping on her knee, hoping that her coffee would be delivered soon.

Jenson wore a denim shirt and his dark hair was in disarray in the most attractive way. The stubble on his jaw made her think of sandpaper. The feel of it against her skin when he had kissed her was suddenly taking over her mind and she felt a blush coming on, so she quickly took a sip of her iced water. Where was that coffee?

"So, I'm working on the drawing of your project and I think you're going to like it." Miles felt closer to her. Had he moved closer?

She cleared her throat and gave him a tense smile, hoping it didn't look tense.

"I can't wait to see it," she said. She turned to Bess wanting to make sure she felt part of the conversation. This had been their morning and she wondered if Bess felt suddenly shoved aside. And for some reason, she felt the need to reiterate that Miles and she were not stealing a romantic moment together. "Miles is designing a few panels of stained glass for me for the greenhouse I'm building," she explained.

"Cool," Bess said without looking up from where her attention was scrolling on her phone again.

"Kids and art. No appreciation yet," Miles said shaking his head as he reached an arm up to signal Shirley. Ursula watched as Shirley clocked him, a moment of steeling herself was not unnoticed before she walked over.

"You're building a greenhouse?" Jenson's question rumbled over the tabletop.

"Mhmm," she acknowledged, her mouth tightly sealed around the straw of her water glass.

"You know, I can help you design it," Miles offered as he put a hand on her forearm. A low sound was emitted from across the table and Ursula didn't dare look in Jenson's direction. Instead, she pulled the arm away from Miles and feigned looking in her purse for something.

"Miles, what can I get for you?"

"Hey, Shirley. I will take an herbal tea and the granola bowl."

"Got it," she said, without her previous sunny disposition. "Hey Jenson," her voice became chipper once again.

"Shirley," he drawled. "Coffee for me and a breakfast sandwich, please."

"Make sure it's not fruity tea," Miles added without looking at her, his attention glued to something on his phone.

This guy was giving Ursula a feeling, and it was not a pleasant one. This entire situation was giving her so many different feelings.

Suddenly Bess leaned forward, a glint in her youthful eyes and a slant to one of her light eyebrows. "So Miles, I heard you were sponsoring Rob Sandis and his run for mayor."

Interesting. "Art and a conservative agenda don't typically mix."

Ursula cautiously watched her. Jenson kept his eyes on Ursula and she could feel it and had no idea what to do with it. Her body was responding to him by heating up, and she was concerned with this prolonged effect, something would go wrong inside of her. This much adrenaline-pushing blood through her body surely was bad for her heart. Or her capillaries. Maybe both. She might die.

She felt something prod her foot under the table and when she looked up Jenson had a concerned look on his face as he watched her. She could read him asking her if she was okay. And there was a moment of connection, of hearing a silent question being asked. She gave him a soft smile and nodded as she came back to the conversation. Miles was talking.

"You heard correctly. He's a good man. I've known him since we were in middle school together."

Jenson leaned back, drawing her attention again, thankful that his heavy eyes were now on Miles. She wondered at their obvious disdain for each other.

"Isn't it true that he is backing the banning of books in our libraries?"

"Well, I wouldn't expect you to understand at your age, but what he is proposing is the appropriate disbursement of reading material for people your age in schools. There is a crisis in our country of young people getting their hands on materials that are too mature, pushing you into a phase of exceeding your understanding and then developing your thoughts and ideas around topics you cannot fully understand until you're older. On a more basic level, his platform is designed to protect you and children younger. There are some incredibly inappropriate materials at the fingertips of our kids in schools."

Bess laughed. "Kids my age and younger are spending their time watching television and on social media. And you think Lord of the Flies is appropriate for us to read and develop our understanding of society?" she asked.

Jenson seemed completely unbothered that his fiery niece was verbally goading Miles. He was leaned back with crossed his arms over his chest in nonchalance. He tilted his head for the show.

"Lord of the Flies is a classic and teaches you,-"

She cut him off. "Lord of the Flies was considered a classic forty years ago and it teaches us the most basic human instincts when stripped down are selfish and about power and survival. From a boy's point of view."

"Which is-

She interrupted him again and Ursula watched with rapt attention, giving Shirley a grateful groan when she set a huge mug of coffee in front of her. She wrapped her hands around the mug and lifted it to her mouth, breathing in the delicious scent with closed eyes before she took a life-supporting sip. Hot, earthy with notes of chocolate coffee slid down her throat and of course, she knew it was too soon to feel the effects, but the serotonin boost was real. When she opened her eyes Jenson's attention was back on her, his eyes watching her drink, that half smirk on his face making him look more good-looking than he had any right to be. She broke their connection and went back to the debate.

"Which is a great study into why men shouldn't rule the world. In fact, William Golding, he's the author in case you didn't know that," her tone was deliciously snarky and she felt Shirley pause to watch the show next to her, "gave us a gift I believe he meant to give us without men recognizing it: men at their most base are carnivorous, power-seeking lone wolves that do not seek harmony or peace in disastrous situations. A man leading a peaceful country is one thing, but a boy trying to keep his power in a time of war is an animal."

"Can we make her queen?" Shirley whispered for only Ursula to hear.

Ursula had to suck in her lips to keep from laughing. Shirley's smile was large and approving. Miles had his eyes narrowed on Bess, his hand on the table tapping to an unheard beat aggressively.

"That is a simplistic and one-toned view of the story. And you're clumping all men together, which is distasteful."

Jenson joined the debate, but his voice was collected. "She's not wrong."

"Oh come on. This feminist 'men are evil and dangerous' vitriol is the reason there is so much division here, and you'd do well to teach her otherwise," Miles threw at Jenson, his voice hardly mimicking Jenson's calm.

Jenson leaned forward. "What I teach Bess is simple: not all men are evil, but most could do better. And I do teach her to be careful around men because I have to; not to would be negligent. And this might hurt your fragile ego, but we could stand to see more women taking the lead in our world. It isn't cruel criticism of men that is the problem, Miles, it's our deaf ears when women are speaking."

Bess looked at her uncle like he was a hero. Ursula couldn't help the admiration in her gaze.

Ursula and Jenson's eyes met, and she felt that zinging connection with him again, so she wrapped her hands around the bowl-like mug and took a generous drink.

"I might be young and not know a lot yet," Bess said. "But I do know that Rob Sandis isn't the picture of morality that he claims he is fighting for which is shown in how he is trying to win this race."

Miles leaned forward, "Rob Sandis has more class than you could ever imagine, especially a sulking teenager like you," his lowered voice was pitched in a threatening tone immediately putting Ursula on the defensive.

"Hey, back off." Everyone's attention whipped to her and she stared at Miles unflinchingly. If Ursula Cambridge had learned anything from deep friendship, it was the unwavering willingness to stand up for your friend. "She just put up an excellent argument, regardless of your beliefs and regardless of your take on the book. You insulted her intelligence based on her age and you didn't like it when she rose to the challenge. Which she did beautifully, and in a pedagogical manner that could rival the college level." She gave Bess a smile, who was staring at her wide-eyed. When she looked back at Miles her smile was replaced by a hard look. "Now, how about you take your tea and your granola bowl to the shop with you today? Shirley, can you make his to-go?"

Bess was beaming and Jenson was looking at her in a way that spread warmth throughout her body. Again.

"Absolutely, sugar. Why don't you go on over to the front and I'll bring it to you, Miles?"

Miles shifted back, recognizing the mess he had made, and nodded his head slowly, pushing his lips out in a look of haughty amusement.

He lifted both hands in false surrender. "Alright alright. I recognize when I've stepped into a den of women and made a mess." He got up and laid a hand on Ursula's shoulder. "I apologize. I hope this doesn't taint our relationship."

She tilted her head and gave him an unblinking look. "I'll talk with you later, Miles." Then she turned back to Bess and winked as she dismissed him. He sighed and walked away, dignity straightening his shoulders as he left.

"His platform also covers the public library. That should be a place where no one is allowed to touch the sanctity of learning and exploring," Bess said.

Jenson laid a large hand on the back of Bess's head in a fatherly gesture. "You did good, kid."

The gentleness this girl brought out in him was something to behold. How much he loved her was lovely and made Ursula think of her dad. He'd been the kind of dad who stepped aside for her to find her own ideas and opinions about the world, challenging them at times when he worried about certain dangers, and championing her regardless.

"Here we go, folks. Two French toasts and one breakfast sandwich. Anything else?"

"We're good, Shirley," Jenson spoke for them all as Bess and Ursula dug in.

The plate had four, thick pieces of french toast, the smells of cinnamon wrapped around roasted coffee beans and swirled around in maple syrup wafted up from her plate. The first bite was like a pleasure bomb and she closed her eyes, a soft moan escaping her.

"Good right?" Bess asked around a huge bite of her food, muffling the words.

Ursula laughed and nodded, as she lifted her thumb to her mouth and licked off a dollop of syrup. As she did, she made the mistake of connecting her eyes with Jenson who was watching her intently over his cup of coffee, his eyes tracking her mouth sucking the maple from her finger. She pulled it out of her mouth and cleared her throat, heat blooming on her cheeks and her neck.

Why was he so intense and good-looking?

He was a jerk.

He was a jerk.

He had been less of a jerk lately.

No.

After she repeated that mantra a few times, she asked Bess about school and she mentioned in teenager-fashion her annoyance over a paper she had to write about civil disobedience. As they were finishing breakfast she noticed she had a new string of texts; one from Miles, an apology, which she ignored for now, and a dozen in her group chat with the dinner club.

She had texted them this morning before they left for breakfast about the slightly concerning turn of events of Jessica Sandis befriending her, without her knowing who she was. Since it had kept her up last night, and her sensibilities were beginning to wear thin, she needed to get more information from people she trusted.

The movement of Jenson leaving the table made her look up.

"Ohmygosh I just got it," Bess's voice held a note of enlightenment.

"Got what?"

"Brawny man. You called Uncle Jay the Brawny Man. He totally looks like him!"

Ursula laughed. "He really does."

"I think you guys should date," Bess declared.

Coffee slid down her throat wrong, like it made a snap decision it didn't want to be swallowed, and now Ursula was coughing.

Bess handed her a napkin over the table, concern mixed with a smile.

"He needs someone like you. And you're cool. And pretty, like Shirley said, you're like this intense, mysterious pretty that is cool."

Ursula's throat felt itchy and she coughed a few more times then cleared her throat. Iced water helped a little. "Um, thank you. I think your uncle and I are better off as frenemies, though."

Bess's smile turned mischievous.

"What?"

But before Bess could answer Jenson was back at the table carrying two to-go cups, one of which he handed to Ursula without any words. It had a black stamp of a snail sleeping on a couch. "Ready to go to school?"

Bess nodded. "Hey, thanks for taking me to breakfast and letting me crash your house." Gone was the robust, mischievous teenager, and in her place was a meek young girl afraid to intrude. She hiked her backpack onto her shoulder, the movement jerky and self-conscious. That age was so incredibly volatile and tender.

"Bess, anytime. You are welcome anytime. Alright, I'll go pay and I'll see you later, okay?"

"I already paid."

"Oh," the awkward word came out. "Thank you. You didn't have to do that."

"It was the least I could do since I crashed your date," his words and eyes speared her, and she had to guess if he meant her breakfast date with Bess or Miles.

She narrowed her eyes and no longer felt flustered by his paying. "Well, you did interrupt my date with Bess. She and I will have to try again." There. She dared him with her steady stare to say anything else.

He merely nodded his head once, as if he received a message, and gently guided Bess toward the front door. As he was passing Ursula he bent down and sent a shiver down her neck and body when his mouth almost touched her ear and whispered, "If I got a chance to hear you moan while eating food again, I'd crash every meal you have."

She stopped breathing. Her head began swimming with the noise of blood rushing at his words. Then his mouth did touch her ear, just the barest brush, but it was enough to make her close her eyes and almost need to grab the nearest object for support as he finished with, "And don't ignore my texts. It's rude." His lips pressed against her now hot ear for a beat, his warm breath doing wild things to her and then it was gone.

She watched him walk out with his hand on Bess's shoulder, listening to her chatter, and throwing her a heated look before they pushed through the door.

She lifted her white cup of hot coffee to her lips, which he got without asking, after paying for their meal. She couldn't deny the attraction to being taken care of that way. And then he says *that*?

She pulled in a big breath of air and held it in her lungs as she counted to five, then released it.

As she walked home, she wondered how she had gone from a life of too much beige and silence to one where she had a lumberjack man tossing her left and right with his attention, a group of incredible women whom she was still learning how to open up to, a new friendship that delivered a betrayal plot twist...whatever reason Jessica had to trick her, and a graveyard filled with unrested souls she kept company and who may have been sweetly haunting her.

The sound of another text hitting her phone pulled her attention to a link sent by Jen. She clicked on it and her eyebrows shot up. The link was to an article in *The Salem Settler*.

Is Our Mayor Dabbling in Dark Magic?

Salem's newest resident of The Lost Souls House brings questions and concern.

Four pictures headlined the article. The first was of the five women in a circle in the graveyard that night they drank the potent margaritas and hexed people. The second was a picture of Cora Acosta sitting with them around a fire in Ursula's backyard. The third was a grainy picture of Ursula alone with Casper in the graveyard, which had to have been that night she felt someone there. And the fourth was a gut punch. It was a poorly taken picture of her bursting garden with a line under it that read: lemons and strawberries in the heart of autumn? What kind of magic is our newest resident, Ursula Cambridge, up to?

Alright, add to all of her newfound life excitements political intrigue, and character-smearing.

"Guess that answers the Jessica piece," she murmured out loud.

Jen sent a follow-up text to the group.

My place tonight to paint the pumpkins and talk?

She sighed and sent a thumbs up, a sagging feeling in her stomach. She had done that. She had aided in creating a headline that could ruin Cora's run for mayor. Her beige life wasn't looking so dull anymore.

Chapter Twenty-Three

When Feelings Turn Into Knives

They were an hour into painting pumpkins at Jen's house, a small white cottage with two bedrooms and decorated exactly how Ursula would have guessed: modern but cozy. They were spread out in the living room with a tarp covering the ground and the couch and loveseat pushed back while they each took on painting their way through the huge pile of various-sized and colored pumpkins that Jen had. Ursula brought five black pumpkins she thought would look haunting with white paint. They would line the mile-long sides of the festival along with the hundreds of pumpkins the elementary and middle school kids carved in their classes filled with flickering candles.

When Ursula arrived a little later than the other women, a knot of anxiety was tight in her stomach. Insecurities were set free from the cage of control she'd had them in before. But the moment she stepped into the warm kitchen, they met her in welcome and empathy. Conversation over breadsticks, salad, honey wine and tea ensued, the way that only women do: abundantly, and with the intention to leave each other better than how they came.

The one person she felt any strain with was Jen; her hug was stiff, she barely made eye contact with her, and she'd immediately busied herself with the task at hand once they started discussing the double agent act Jessica had performed. But, it was probably nothing and Ursula may have been projecting her own fears bubbling inside her onto Jen.

Now that they were painting their pumpkins, and Ursula's worry had been mostly slayed by their support, she asked a question that had been digging into her since she met Jessica.

"Do any of you know Jessica well?"

"Not really," Jen said with a shrug. "Nothing about Rob Sandis interests me." Her tone was flat and the simple remark landed uncomfortably for Ursula. Tilly said she only knew her from a few town events they'd worked on together and one time when she'd accompanied Rob on a radio show that he came in for.

Kelsea just shook her head and concentrated on the detailed Victorian haunted house she was painting.

"She moved here after college, which is where she met Rob," Crystal mused as she leaned back in the armchair and drank a mug of tea. "She was much more amicable back then, more enthusiastic and I remember her inviting me for dessert but we never did get together."

"Why not?"

A thoughtful look crossed Crystal's graceful features. Tonight her silvery hair was down, loose around her shoulders. "She had to cancel and when I tried to reschedule she had just become pregnant with their first and then after that," her shoulders moved up, "I think she poured herself into her children. Wonderful mother."

"Dutiful wife," Jen said in a mocking tone.

It rubbed Ursula the wrong way.

Ursula tried to imagine a younger Jessica, more alive and friendly. Now she seemed careful. Less alive and more surviving.

"Isn't it a little odd, though, that she seems to have kind of disappeared from society?"

The other women looked thoughtful until Jen sighed and put her paintbrush down on the plastic plate, the black paint leaving a stark brush stroke.

"I think it's a little odd that you're so concerned about a woman who lied by omission to get access to your house, which was easy, and now all of a sudden there is a new smear campaign against Cora." The words were harsh, and accusing, and met with silent tension. Kelsea quickly looked away, Tilly looked nervous and Crystal looked concerned.

"I didn't know that would happen," Ursula said, softly.

"Cora is already up against a rich, white guy who is somehow lovable to a certain population and he killed her at the last debate and now this. I'm not saying it's your fault," Jen backpedaled, holding up her hands in a quick gesture, her voice taking on a tone that belied her words, "but, Cora is a good woman, a good leader, and the kind of leader we need for this town. And all of that is being thrown away because of a few headlines, a too-trusting newcomer, and an inexperienced spy who wears diamond earrings."

Ursula nodded, though her mind was running through all the thoughts she carried with her between finding out who Jessica was and coming here tonight.

Ursula recognized something familiar happening, a tightening and a coiling that she hadn't experienced since moving here. The guilt she was trying to tell herself not to feel surged up.

"Cora is a good woman," she said softly. "She doesn't deserve this."

Jen pursed her lips and made a humming sound in agreement. She was clearly placing blame on Ursula, despite what she said.

Her pumpkins were finished and she felt an overwhelming wave of emotion. "Listen, I'm going to go."

A chorus of voices telling her to stay, not to leave, and everything was fine, filled the living room. Jen stayed pointedly silent as she cleaned up her painting area.

She got her coat and smiled tightly, afraid that tears might find their way to the surface if she didn't get out of there soon. "No seriously, I'm exhausted and need to get to the graveyard for my nightly walk and then I need to pass out."

"Just don't let anyone take pictures of you," Jen said from the kitchen. The words struck exactly where she'd aimed and Ursula felt the hit.

"Jennifer," Crystal admonished and Ursula turned away toward the door. She didn't hear Jen respond, but she felt an arm wrap around her gently. Tilly, offering her comfort. Which made it all the worse, as she still owed Tilly an apology. That shame bubbled to the surface and suddenly Ursula was swimming in emotions.

"She's just worried for her friend," Tilly whispered.

She smiled sadly. "I know. And I owe you an apology and a conversation," she added, suddenly wanting so deeply to clear the air that it felt like a living thing inside her. Being at odds with more than one friend was too much.

"Tomorrow before the festival, want to meet?"

"Come over for a pre-festival snack?"

"I'll see you at six." Tilly's smile was divine. It was a small breath in the rocky and vertiginous waves Ursula was currently riding.

"Bye, darling!" Crystal called out.

"Bye, Ursula. See you tomorrow?" Kelsea asked hopefully.

She turned back to give a small wave, a wilted smile. Her eyes connected with Jen's, which held anger before she turned away.

It wasn't late, but she was worn. And after the events of the last couple of days, she felt overtaken. Her emotions felt like they were needles and she was a pincushion; how do you stop the torrent of self-doubt, anger, worry, and shame from swallowing you?

And how did she stop feeling shame when logically, she knew she hadn't done anything wrong? It was still there, lurking inside of her like it had a right to feed off her uncertainty and fears.

She made it home, and as she was locking the front door her eyes caught on the package she'd found waiting on the porch for her that morning. It had completely left her mind until this moment. Casper walked in slowly, stopping to stretch his long front legs giving away that she had woken him from a dog nap.

"Hey buddy, we'll take our walk in a minute."

She picked up the rectangular package and sat on the couch. The thin brown book lay in her hands. Though it was light, there was something about it that felt substantial. She unwrapped the thin, malleable leather string, and opened the front cover. As she did, a puff of sparkly cloud poofed into the air.

"Why does magic have to sneak up on you?" she muttered. Inside the front cover was a thick, small piece of paper with barely legible ink, written by hand. She had to squint and play a slight guessing game at the words but she eventually got it.

Our history cannot be hidden,

no matter the demons, no matter the sins, Amos.

This, too, shall be brought to light.

She frowned and flipped through the book that had no more than fifty pages. They were thick pages, a homemade journal. The writing would take a lot of dissection to be able to read, as the cursive was looping and in places so deeply slanting as if the writer had tilted him or herself. The pen used left ink spots and smears that would make many of the passages difficult to discern.

Every page was filled out with handwritten entries, some of them neat, some of them indecipherable. The last few pages were singed at the bottom right corner and when she turned the book over, she noticed that the leather had been charred leaving behind a rough, partially burned-off cover in parts. A fire had eaten away at this and she wondered when that fire had lived, which led her to wonder when this journal had lived. There were no dates, like a typical journal, so she was left guessing.

She sat there holding this old book in her hands thinking, until her thoughts became tangled and her body reminded her of her exhaustion.

She called for Casper and they made their way to the graveyard, a sleepy hound and a worn-down woman, a jar of moonlight lighting their way through the dark and the sounds of croaking frogs and the ancient language of birds floating along with them.

When she came upon the graveyard her footsteps slowed when she realized there was something on the top of each rounded gravestone. Flowers. She reached out a hand to pick one up, but when the milky moon's glow caught it in its beam she recoiled as the plant's name flitted through her mind with a tingling pinch down her neck and arms.

Oleander.

The pink flowers looked dainty and sweet, a demure mask for something incredibly dark. This plant could kill. Easily, without remorse.

She looked around, holding the jar to each of the stones, finding the same toxic plant gently placed on every one of them.

An ominous, evil feeling overtook the graveyard, something she had never felt here before. She'd been spooked, scared, but never had she felt this crippling fear of darkness, an insidious veil that felt physical. Her jar of moonlight started fading, the glow becoming weaker like it was shrinking back from something.

A small, slinking figure crept in the shadows and she stilled. Another one joined it and when she squinted her eyes made out two black cats licking their paws. She let out a breath and what was left of the beam caught on something written on a headstone. A word.

Burn

She frowned and moved closer, realizing that three of the tombstones had writing on them. She moved closer to inspect them.

Burn

The

Witches

A sound like a gasp filled the air and she realized it came from her.

She looked around, no longer steady, and called for Casper, who had started whining. This place had been disturbed. A dark shadow swooped across her vision and then another, causing her to stumble backward, dropping the jar, the sound of breaking glass shrill. She watched as the moonlight escaped and floated up until it was stretched like a thin, gossamer cloud before it was gone. Sounds, like moaning, eerie and soft, circled the air and she knew she wasn't alone. An un-wanted guest had made their way to this graveyard and disturbed the lost souls.

She frantically called for Casper who raced to her side, pressing his large body against her legs.

"We need to go," she said with a hoarse breath. She gave one last look at the desecration, and then they started running.

Together they raced back to the house, closing behind them she took a deep breath and closed her eyes. The sound of the door locking itself made her open her eyes. The sound of clicking locks, windows and doors shuttered through the house until a feeling of safety cloaked them.

Something was amiss. Something was stirring around them, an unsettled feeling pressing in from all sides, a division of sorts.

Even her temperament and onslaught of fears and anxiety had come in a wave at a coincidental time as had Jessica, the journal, her rift with Jen, and the divide in the town.

What was going on in Salem? Had she brought it here?

She knew, with frustration, that tonight would be another sleepless one. The feeling of helplessness alone was staggering.

Where she had felt like she had a new spark when moving here, now she felt snuffed out and dimmed.

A wet nose and large head pressed into her body between her arm and her side. Casper looked up at her with his big eyes, a soft whine coming from his body as he looked at her in concern. She got on the floor and lay her head against his wiry fur where he stood still as she gathered comfort from another living creature.

She felt alone, yes, but right now she had the reminder that she wasn't alone.

Animals were good at that; letting humans know that they don't have to be alone if they chose not to be.

Sometime later, she was curled up in bed with nighttime tea in a starry mug and Casper curled up on his bed. Peace had settled over her after journaling, the magical ink writing to her that she was safe.

Then she thought of the journal that had been mysteriously placed on her porch. Someone was trying to tell her the truth. Someone was also trying to send a menacing message, but this journal felt more like a helping hand. She flipped through the pages trying to decipher who this person could be.

The name Amos was identifiable twice near the end of the journal entries, so this likely wasn't the journal of Amos. The way that this person wrote read feminine, poetic at times, and often with an air of pleading. They read as letters. It was interesting, what she could make out. And the question remained of who delivered her this journal.

She went to bed that night, hours later than usual, exhausted and yet restless, her mind zigzagging amongst the worries and thoughts that she wished she could turn off like a light. Still, she would just barely wake up remembering a foggy dream of her running, laboriously, almost drunkenly, among bushes and shadows, a mask behind her at every wobbly turn and an eerie whisper calling her a witch.

Chapter Twenty-Four

A Mask Can Hide So Many Things

B lack Cat Coffee House was packed, the hour too late for Bess to be working the early morning rush before school. Bess had texted her that morning, as Ursula staggered out of bed, haggard and sapped. Under-eye concealer was applied in layers. She styled her bangs to pull attention away from her puffy face and knew she would be wearing her black hat today. Bess asked if she could crash at her house after the festival. She decided to run it by Jenson, though the idea of communicating with him in any form still made her insides jittery.

If I got a chance to hear you moan while eating food again, I'd crash every meal you have.

The memory of those words and the heat of his breath touching her skin made her nervously drop her phone into her large brown leather purse after she texted him about Bess staying at her place.

Now, she waited off to the side for her Americano, texting with Tilly about meeting before the festival. A familiar voice made her wince, though she hid it before turning to face him.

"Hey, Ursula. You uh, didn't return my texts, and I get it. I was an ass at breakfast."

Miles stood too close to her and she put her phone back in her purse as she maneuvered her body the only few inches the person next to her would allow. "I was busy," she said, deflecting.

"Will you forgive me?" The words were flirty, a joke, rather than a search for absolution.

She hesitated and then opened her mouth, but before she could respond another familiar face joined them, this one putting her on edge more than Miles could.

"Miss Cambridge, it's nice to see you. I admit I wished I ran into you more often as you're the new celebrity resident in town," Rob Sandis's smile was wide, bright, and false.

"I wouldn't call myself a celebrity," she kept her words and tone simple. His wife conveniently left out who she was married to, befriended her, took pictures of her backyard, and then one of those pictures ended up in a news story trying to paint Cora as a meddler in the dark arts. This man was about as trustworthy as the very lowest stereotypical politician.

"Miles, I hear you're working on a piece for Ursula."

"I am. She's got a creative eye and I am enjoying the challenge. Both of the art and the woman," he winked at her and she cringed. Her mouth pulled up on one side and her eyes held back nothing of what she was thinking. Did Miles think that she wanted more than a working relationship with him? Had she given him that impression?

When she saw the beautiful, and slightly terrifying, face of Cora Acosta walking toward them, with a tight smile, Ursula wanted to scream at the universe. Of course, she would see her fraternizing with these two men, one her polarizing opponent. After compromising and false photos came out.

"Listen," she said pointing a finger at Rob, who immediately stopped smiling and gave her his undivided attention at her fierce tone. She was done and not shading anything in grey. "I am not your friend or your toy to use to win this election. Do not think for a second that I don't know what is going on with your wife and that photoshoot."

"Ursula," he started, a hand to his blazered chest and fake surprise dripping from his mouth but she stepped forward and stopped him. She crossed that invisible line so many women face in their lives; the one that dropped them in a world of sheer ferocity. This was a place where women dropped their placating smiles, and words padded in gentleness that softened blows. This was the place where a woman became a lioness, head down, shoulders sharp, teeth bared.

"No. I am not in the mood for a debate with you and do not insult my intelligence by pretending innocence. You targeted me and you used that to create a false narrative about Cora, and frankly, if that's all you've got then she has nothing to fear. Because if you have to make up stories about her hanging out with witches to win?" She stepped back and gave him a pitying look. "Then you have a hard race ahead of you."

His face, before so wide and carefree, was now a shade of red and a look of danger bled into his features that set off warning bells in Ursula. A mask slipped. Her lioness blood raced. Something primal inside of her wanted to goad him.

Go ahead. Try, the voice wanted to say to him.

"Hello," Cora greeted, her voice smooth and her appearance fierce and impeccable. Today she wore a mustard blazer suit that was gorgeous.

"Cora," Rob nodded his head. "You should probably talk to your friends about how to act diplomatically. Their lack of decorum could hurt you."

"Oh?" she looked at Ursula and Ursula knew from one woman to another what Cora saw: a woman unleashed. Cora's small smile recognized this primal beast and her attention slid back to Rob when she said, "I think diplomacy means something different to you and me because what I heard was my friend standing up to a lying bully. That's diplomacy to me. I heard my friend hold you accountable. That's diplomacy to me. And if you think that branding me, or my friends, as a witch is going to give you this election, you better buckle up, Rob."

"Maybe that won't but you're a childless, philandering woman and those are death sentences for women in politics. And that's not just a theory. This town has worked hard to overcome our history," his eyes ran over Ursula. No longer was there a fake welcoming businessman before her. "A mysterious woman dabbling in magic is rather damning. It's not me," he said pointing to himself. "The town has concerns about your friend that I intend to bring to light if nothing more than to protect our beloved town. I will bring out the truth." It was a threat.

The surrounding area quieted. Ursula looked around as others were now watching them. But then Cora lifted her head with a smile and said, "Do that. Go that route, Rob. I invite you to test that theory at your earliest convenience." She speared him with a look so fiery, Ursula watched in awe. "But remember, Rob, truth is a fickle lover and you've played a philanderer far too much with it."

Then she looped her arm through Ursula's and started to walk away, but Rob threw out another punch like he couldn't contain himself.

"You're getting older with no family prospects in sight. People want a family person with integrity, Cora. You're not that person. Tick tick tick," he said, clicking his finger against the face of his expensive watch.

She paused as his words found their delicate mark. Her body was tight and her face was stone, but then she squared her shoulders and looked back. "I'm sorry, I can't hear my *biological clock* ticking over the sound of my high heels and inner peace. Good day, gentlemen." She nodded once and then walked them out of the coffee shop.

"See? That was diplomatic," Cora said and Ursula laughed, a sudden bubble of anxiety popped and gone.

"I'm so sorry, Cora. I had no idea about his wife."

"Babe, you're fine. I promise. I didn't think for one second that you had anything to do with that. Rob is low and he is dirty. It was just a matter of time before he tried something like this, and honestly? Not impressed. He's desperate."

"Right? Calling you a witch in Salem seems a little too on-brand."

"Too easy."

"Thank you. For not blaming me," she said. The bustling of the thick crowd around them was loud and jostling, but Cora's energy was genuine and there was a softness and peace that calmed.

"You're not conniving. You're good. Anyone who has met you can feel it," she said.

"Well, not anyone," she said, then wished she hadn't. Her chasm with Jen was between Jen and her. "Listen, thank you for taking me out of the wolf den."

"I'll see you later, Ursula. And hey," her voice raised as Ursula was a few yards away, people weaving between them, "Jen will come around. I'm one of her people that she's most protective of. She can act a fool sometimes if I get hurt. I've done the same on her behalf."

Ursula smiled at that. She understood that dynamic well. "She's a good friend," she shouted back.

"See you at the next debate? I plan on crushing Rob."

"Absolutely," she replied with a smile that felt primitive. "Wouldn't miss it."

A strange ray of sunlight pressed its long body through inflated white clouds stark against the sooty sky. It looked like an intruder in a storm-cast sky ready to open up any moment with autumn showers. Sulphur walked alongside her as she made her way home, the pounding in her head from lack of sleep and caffeine getting stronger with each booted step. Her phone rang in her bag and when she fished it out she saw that Tilly was calling her.

"Hey," she answered.

"Hey, are you okay?" Tilly's voice sounded worried and she wondered if she somehow knew about the graveyard incident last night, but she hadn't told anyone.

"Yeah, I'm okay. What's going on?"

"Are you home?"

"No, I left to grab a coffee and get some fresh air. I haven't been sleeping well. What's up?"

"Maybe it happened while you were gone," Tilly said, the words sounding like she was thinking or talking to herself.

"Tilly, what is going on?"

"Did you see your front door?"

"My front door?"

There was a sigh before Tilly answered. "Someone left a message on your front door. The article came out fifteen minutes ago."

She wasn't making sense. "What article?"

"I'll send it to you. Will you call me when you get home or at least let me know you're okay?"

"Of course."

They hung up and there was a link sent to her a few seconds later from Tilly along with a string of texts from their group chat that she ignored as she opened the news article.

Is the Newest Tenant of The Lost Souls House Bringing Back Salem's Dark History?

A picture on the front cover of The Salem Settler with that headline made her stop in her tracks. It was her front porch, or more accurately, her front door which had graffiti in white against the dark wood:

Leave Salem, Witch

"Oh, come on," she said miserably. Sulphur rubbed her body against her legs, and looked up at her with one gold eye and one green. "I'm not a witch," she said to which the cat blinked and rubbed her furry cheek against Ursula's shin before letting out a soft meow and walking on. She sighed and followed the cat home, dreading what she would find. And sure enough, on her front door was the graffiti.

She walked up the steps begrudgingly and ran a finger through one of the letters, which was dry white paint.

The words at the graveyard had been white.

She called the local law enforcement to report the incident, but they seemed unconcerned and unhurried. There was an attack on this house, and she needed to get to the bottom of it if for nothing else than her sanity.

She decided to go to the library to get some work done, get out of the house, and keep herself busy. And maybe she was a little afraid of being here right now with the vandalism.

The library was two stories and looked like it had once been an old bank. The inside was hushed peace, with marble floors and low seating scattered around. Tall shelves spread in rows and the walls were floor-to-ceiling built-ins filled with books. There was an elevator and one spiral staircase that led to a balcony and a second floor of more books. People were milling around and she noticed the far back corner was for children with funky and colorful furniture, a bin of costumes, and a large artificial tree with twinkle lights and cushions underneath where currently a toddler was flipping through a book while chattering to herself.

She set up a workspace and then decided to wander a bit, making her way up the spiraling staircase, the thunking of her boots against the metal steps ringing against the hushed atmosphere.

A small section in a dark corner, through an arched doorway where sunlight couldn't venture was a section of Salem history. It smelled older, ancient here, and when she stepped under the arch she felt a tingling along her arms down to her fingers. It felt as though not a soul had stepped here in ages like the books were on the edge of their shelves at her presence. She ran a fingertip along the spines, gently. These books were old. Too old to be open for touch with anyone and everyone. There were three full shelves, floor to ceiling, ranging from gardening and weather to historical ships coming and going. She pulled out books and gently flipped through them, that perfectly distinct smell of old pages wafting into the air. But then her hand slid over, paused, and slid back to a thin spine with no words.

Something inside of her felt enlightened, a whooshing of warmth as she pulled it from its snuggled position between a book about women's fashion in the 1800s and a horticulture book she decided she would come back to.

The book was a dark red, untitled with no author and nothing to give away what was inside. She looked around and peeked outside of the arched doorway before tucking herself in the corner where she would be hidden out of sight, but the lack of light made it difficult to see anything, much less a handwritten book. She shined her phone flashlight over the pages as she flipped through, trying to decipher what this was. There were dates on the left and then notes on the right.

This was from the early 1700s. Her eyebrows shot up as she read through notes that looked like a town journal with recorded minutes from old town hall meetings. There were names of people she didn't recognize, issues like farming land being taken by a resource-hungry neighbor or a townsperson wanting to open a new storefront. She paused when she heard the ringing of footsteps on the spiral staircase, her heart beating against her ribs. She wasn't sure why she felt as though she was trespassing, but she quickly stuffed her phone in her back pocket and gently put the book in her bag as she left, then she slipped through the arched doorway and wandered lackadaisically down a short hallway between tall rows of bookshelves.

Why did she feel like a spy? This was a public library, for goodness sake. She let out a soft laugh, shaking her head at her silliness as her heart calmed, but when she opened her eyes she swallowed a gasp when she saw someone blocking the exit between shelves. Her eyes widened when she saw who it was as he casually, panther-like walked down the aisle closing the distance between them. This was a dead end, as the wall behind her was made of books.

"What are you doing here?" she asked, cursing herself when her voice came out high and frightened.

Jenson tilted his head as he paused with a mere three feet between them, which might as well be nothing the way she could feel his warmth and overall large presence pressing into her space.

"It's a public library," he replied in his low voice. "I even have a library card and everything." The way he said it was seductive. Or she hadn't been seduced in so long and reading a romantic book was crossing wires inside of her.

But now she had a new weakness: a man who had his own library card. Who knew? But it was deliciously sexy and she had to bite the inside of her cheek to keep from showing that.

"Right," she said. "I need to get one of those."

He smirked and took a step closer as she took a step back making his smirk grow.

"You can borrow mine," he offered as the toes of his boots touched hers. "Are you avoiding me, Ursula?" His eyes were looking down on her as she tilted her head back. She had nowhere to go as her back was now against a wall of books.

"No," she whispered in denial.

The moment he reached both arms out to brace his hands against the shelves, caging her inside of his arms, she told herself to keep her cool, not give in to this dark, sexy man who threw her thoughts and sensibilities into a riot. He might kiss like a fantasy, but there were too many unknowns about him. His dating history and the rumors around him were enough to make a woman like her, who was grappling with what a good man is, run and avoid at all costs.

He raised one dark eyebrow at her refute and she held her breath as he leaned down, closing the distance between them at an achingly slow pace. Her breathing was audible and she was aware of the sound like they were suddenly in an enclosed space. She could smell him, soap and the wood she bought at the hardware store and thought Tom said was cedar, with an underlying scent of warm skin. Looking up into his eyes felt like one of the most intimate things she had done in years. He saw her. This connecting of eyes embodied intentional presence. Something she hadn't felt from a man in too long and now it was like he was touching a raw nerve.

She had to hold herself still, keep her eyes from shutting against this powerful moment. It took courage to stand in a moment like this with a man this intense when her experience with intimacy over the last few years had included no eye contact, engraving the idea she wasn't anything special to look at. And now here she was, held between a man's arms, as he looked down at her like he couldn't get enough. It was a heady thing.

"You're not avoiding me?"

"No," she said again.

She caught her breath when he dipped down brushing her ear with his hot mouth, and whispered darkly, "Liar."

Why was she suddenly so hot? She couldn't breathe normally and her lungs felt sticky, like they couldn't get enough room against her ribs.

"I'm...not," she barely got out.

"Do I make you nervous? Your breathing is off," he whispered in dark amusement as his open lips touched that spot just below her ear making her gasp and then cinch her eyes closed tightly at the embarrassment. "And you're trembling," he added with a nip of her earlobe.

Her breath wooshed out as her hands reached for his chest without her permission, landing there against hard, warm muscle covered in soft flannel as images of what could happen flitted through her mind.

"I can't think."

He ran his lips down the column of her throat slowly as one of his hands gripped her waist, pulling her firmly, slowly against him. The feel of this man alone should be illegal. Her body melted immediately like it was just waiting for his touch and invitation to give up its form and become molten and meld to his whims.

"What's there to think about?" he asked roughly. His mouth was now at her jaw, lightly caressing the skin there and until this moment she had no idea that skin could be so deliciously sensitive. Is that an erogenous zone, because the low pull in her belly was telling her that was an erogenous zone. The tingling in her limbs was muddling her thoughts and all she could picture, all she could stand on the precipice and wait for, was that final descent into madness when his lips took hers.

Did she want that?

Just the memory of how it had felt to be kissed, consumed, by this man had her body screaming for her to lean in, tilt her head perfectly in invitation and give in. Her mind, still, wavered and held up hands of caution.

"You're confusing," she finally got out, but it was barely a whisper as her words were following her body's instructions, and melting.

"Tell me what's confusing, hmm?" his words hummed along her skin and she trembled as she shifted closer to him. "I thought I made myself very clear when I kissed you the other night." And then his lips were at the corner of her mouth, just barely touching; a fraction of a slide would line their lips up perfectly for another kiss, another explosion of sensations she knew would take over her body if she allowed. "I don't know what it is about you," a light touch of the tip of his tongue at the corner of her mouth and her knees gave out which didn't matter as he had her pinned fully between him and the bookshelf. "You make me want to lose control." The rough, low plea poured liquid heat throughout her body and she let out a small whimper. His lips lightly ghosted over hers in a prelude to what would come. But his word, 'control', made her stop, even her logical self that left the moment he stalked toward her heard the word and came to attention.

Control.

She couldn't afford to lose that with him. With anyone. Before his lips could take hers captive again, where she knew she would throw the key away herself and fully give in, she needed to stop this.

"Farrah Rhodes," she blurted. It was what her mind grabbed at as she scrambled for a button, a lever, anything to get herself together.

And he stopped, his mouth hovered, his hands held her still but didn't go further and then he pulled back, looking down at her in a dark question.

"What?"

She let out a breath and licked her lips. "Farrah Rhodes, the last tenant at the Lost Souls House."

"I know who she is," he said slowly.

"You," she didn't want to sound silly or like a gossipmonger, "Did you have an affair with her?"

Everything stopped. The air around them stilled and the passion that had built to a near-wrecking crescendo evaporated as his eyes turned to that stoic, intense look she had become so accustomed to. He dropped his hands from her waist, stepped back a few paces until the distance was just as strong of a feeling as the closeness had been. But this felt cold. The loss of contact was jarring.

She watched his tongue poke out of the side of his mouth as his eyes narrowed on her. Her heart was a riot inside of its cage as she watched, waited, hoped.

"Rumors are fun, aren't they? They could be true or not," his voice was dangerously low and everything around them felt like it was paused. "They could hold a kernel of truth and taint a person just from that small thing."

"You kissed me and then nothing," she said, anger and perhaps a dollop of desperation saturating her words.

The shadow that passed over his face was thick as he tilted his head. "You think I go around kissing women at random?"

"I don't know!" Her whispered words were thrown at him. "I'm sorry," she said quickly, reading that she had just unearthed a darkness in him, but not dangerous. She had found the underbelly of something tender and she felt regret as she read something pained in his harsh eyes. "It's hard not to listen to people when they talk about history. Cassidy Parker and Diane Perry," she added boldly.

And then his face took on a different edge, a smile that looked savage grew on his face. She felt a different kind of heat inside of her at the transformation and sucked in a breath when he took two slow steps toward her, truly a predatory animal now, stalking its prey.

"You have been busy," his voice was rough, taunting. "If you want the truth, the real truth, about my dating history and whether or not I'm a home-wrecker, or a heartbreaker, or a playboy, whatever title you might bestow on me, believe when I say I have heard them all," he drawled. "Do the decent thing and come to the source. I don't have time to waste on trifling gossip or someone who puts value in hollow whispers." He reached out a large hand making her catch her breath, but when he tucked a strand of her hair behind her ear, a gesture she was now going to always attach to him, she opened her eyes wide at the tenderness. "I thought you were different," he said the words like they were tired, weighed down with sadness and disappointment. Then his fingers grasped her chin in a firm hold as his eyes pierced hers, searching, a light of what she could describe as hope flashed for a moment before it went away and all that was left was his dark stare. "See you around, Ursula."

And then he was walking back the way he had come, though this time something inside her told her to call out to him and not hide. To tell him to wait and come back, but another part of her told her to hold her tongue and let him go. Which part was wise and which part of her was scared?

He had a patchy and less-than-golden history with women, and he hadn't come out and answered her question about Farrah. But something told her that he would have, had she asked him without the accusation of assumption that had been the foundation of her question. She'd done the right thing, stopping whatever was happening between them. She wasn't a toy he could play with like a cat with a ribbon. She was a person. A whole woman who just left a relationship that tried to tell her she was worth nothing. She couldn't do that again.

And yet, as she left the library, after getting a temporary card and barely making small talk with the librarian as her thoughts were muddled and rioting, something deep inside her told her she'd just made a mistake. Maybe she had judged and assumed before going before a jury. And maybe the part of her that told her to hold her tongue and let him go was the haunted part of her that needed healing.

CHAPTER TWENTY-FIVE

GOLD MASKS AND HONEST TALK

A delicate gold mask was pulled with a flourish out of Tilly's large tote bag.

"What's this for?"

"The festival is a masquerade and I made a guess that you had not bought one, or have one on hand."

Ursula held the light mask, admiring the intricate gold lace, the smile stretching her face felt like stretching after a long ride in the car. "I do not have a masquerade mask on hand, you guessed correctly."

"Well, there you go. It will go perfectly with your dark hair and green eyes."

"What's your mask?"

"Red jeweled and over the top," she said waggling her eyebrows.

"Perfect," she beamed, but the excitement for tonight dimmed with something more pressing. "Tilly, I am so sorry for the other day."

She nodded, seriousness taking over her features. "Can we talk about it? You don't have to give me details if you don't want, but I would love to walk through your reaction so I can better meet you where you're at."

They were sitting at the island, each with an antique crystal tumbler of bourbon.

"I um," she swirled her drink around twice, "I haven't talked much about the life I left behind. And I didn't think I needed to because I figured, new place new life, starting over, no need to look backward, you know?"

Tilly nodded encouragingly.

"But, turns out that my last relationship might have rewired how I relate to people. And there's no running from that." Thoughts of Jenson's disappointment in her, his whispered hope that she had been different than others weighed like stones in her pockets. She hadn't been able to shake it all afternoon, the movie of that scene on replay. She didn't know his story. She didn't understand what people said when they called him cursed and she didn't have the details, but more importantly, she hadn't heard any of those things from him. He had been right.

"I get that," Tilly empathized. "You don't have to tell me about that relationship."

"No, I want to. I want to start, at least." If she was going to have any kind of relationship, romantic or otherwise, she needed to face the one that grew shame and shadows inside of her first, or she feared she would have many more moments of disappointing people including herself.

She took a small drink of her bourbon, the burn trailing down her throat. "I was in a relationship after college for about a decade, and he was the kind of man who didn't want me to take up too much space.

Had I been able to name that in such a stark way, I don't think I would have spent so many years making myself smaller. It was tricky because he wasn't abusive, he didn't hit me or demean me, though he had his moments of making me feel silly or stupid." She sipped the bourbon, the sweetness bright and fiery. "Even trickier, he was romantic at first and doting. It was like he put on a mask in the beginning but once he had me," she shrugged, "he let the mask slip and he didn't feel the need to try anymore. He was distant, uninterested. I remember him saying once that romance was a lie that women needed to stop believing and I thought," she shook her head, a sad smile on her face, "I thought how sad that was, but maybe he was right. And maybe I was silly for wanting romance and to be wooed. Isn't that sad?" she mused with a little smile."He made me believe I was silly for wanting to be in love."

Tilly dipped her head, a soft look of understanding on her sweet face. "Some people like to tell people to lower their expectations so that they don't have to rise to them."

"Yeah, that was him. I realized in the last few months that I felt more and more like less. I pulled pieces of myself out and got rid of them for him because it seemed easier than not. And I beat myself up over that. I do."

"You shouldn't," she consoled.

"I know. I know that I shouldn't but I do. Because I spent most of my life, not just with him, trying to be strong and I never had enough energy left over to learn how to be happy. Or just to...be," she let out a breath thinking back to her childhood of walking on eggshells around her mother's emotions, growing a thick skin, and learning to be strong and resilient. "I built walls to keep out storms but didn't realize it also kept people out." She lost her best friend because she had let him chip away so much of her there wasn't a lot left to recognize. "And so when you pushed a little the other day, as friends do and should," she pointedly looked at Tilly who smiled at her, "it freaked me out. I had walls for so long, you know?"

"And you weren't seen for a long time, it sounds like. Suddenly being dropped in a small town, in a notorious house, being surrounded by four boisterous women probably felt a little shocking."

Ursula laughed, leaning back against the soft cushion. "You are not wrong. But it's been lovely. To be here, in this house, and be seen by you, and to get to know this boisterous group of women. You all believe in each other and I forgot how much I needed to be believed in."

"I will toast to that," Tilly raised her glass and in an uncharacteristic bravado, she added, "and might I also say about your past man, fuck him. Asshole."

That made Ursula laugh as they clinked glasses and downed their bourbon.

She looked at Tilly, this woman who created a space for her to be without apology and she made a decision.

"Can I tell you something else I'm struggling with?"

"God, yes. Please," she responded. "I've had an uneventful personal life myself lately so bring it on." Her enthusiasm made Ursula smile.

"Jenson Lancaster kissed me and I don't know what to do with it, but his past kind of freaks me out, especially since I haven't been seen by a man in years or made to feel...well, anything in years, and he's like this broody, mysterious, enigma. And I haven't had sex in over a year, maybe longer? Honestly, the sex was never very good so I may have blocked some of it out," her words tumbled out like little gymnasts. But she was on a roll and couldn't stop. "Do you remember the last time you had an orgasm with someone? I could not remember the last time someone gave me one, which is *really* depressing and makes me feel like half of a woman." She shook her head. "But Jenson. I mean, have you seen him? And my body does something feral whenever I'm around him. And he looks like the Brawny Man on the paper towels. He's just so..." she squeezed both hands and made a sound in the back of her throat unable to find words.

Tilly's mouth was wide open.

Ursula pulled her lips in trying not to smile, feeling like fifteen pounds just left her body.

"Jenson kissed you? Jenson Lancaster?"

"Mhmm," she said, nodding her head.

Her mouth slid into a slow, cat-like smile. "Well, I'll be damned. You go girl." She clinked her glass against Ursula's.

She bit her lip. "But I kind of pushed him away too."

"Do you want to push him away?" She held up a hand. "Wait, first, is he a good kisser?"

She let out a groan and dramatically laid down on the island top. "Imagine the best kiss you've ever read in a book or seen on TV. Double it."

"Damn," she said sitting back. "Okay, back to the first question: do you want to push him away?"

"I...don't want to get hurt. And there's so much unknown about him. Also, he was a complete ass to me until the moment he grabbed me and kissed me."

Tilly leaned forward. "There was grabbing?"

"Oh yeah."

"God, I could use some grabbing," she said wistfully then shook her head and sighed. "And in answer to your really out-of-left-pocket question, the last orgasm a man gave me was three years and two months ago."

Ursula nodded, impressed with the math.

"Listen, you don't know if you're going to get hurt or not. And I've known Jenson a long time. He's a good man. I know his past, and the snippets you've heard of it would lean him towards the morally questionable, but if you want a new start you should give him the benefit of the doubt and get more than the snippets."

She thought about asking Tilly to fill in details about Jenson, but his words were still ringing loudly. She should ask the source. Him.

"Thanks," she said softly.

Tilly squeezed her hand and winked. "He is very..." Tilly's words trailed off as she pictured the man.

"Yeah. He is," was all Ursula could say back.

"And you're totally right he looks like the guy on the Brawny paper towels. For what it's worth?" her head tilted as she smiled at Ursula. "I haven't seen the man date or anything flirting-adjacent in a long time."

She pulled in a slow, deep breath trying to let that settle in her bones.

"What if I messed it all up?

She shrugged. "Then he doesn't deserve you. People mess up, and we tend to feel out new relationships with the hands that were burned by the last one."

"You're pretty wise," she remarked.

"I am," Tilly winked. "But honestly, you have us. We're your people. Let us be."

The realization that she had people was a sweetness she hadn't prepared for, but then she thought of her rift with Jen, the sweetness souring a smidgen. She wouldn't bring that up here, with someone else. Regardless of what happened with Jenson, he was right about something: she needed to go to the source.

"Ready for a masquerade festival?"

"I am."

They got their things and were walking down the front steps when she looked back at the words on her door. The police had yet to come and take her report so she would have to keep them there for now.

"Should I be concerned that people in town think I'm a witch?"

Tilly shook her head, flipped her hand through the air. "Naw, last time that happened most people lived."

"Oh, you mean other than the fifteen people that were hanged?"

"It was actually nineteen and out of the hundreds accused, that's a fairly low percentage."

"Excellent," she remarked and pushed her shoulder against Tilly's playfully.

Masks in place, they made their way to the sounds and smells of a Halloween festival in full swing. She checked her phone before the night got swallowed and found a text notification waiting for her. Her heart leaped when she saw it was from Jenson, but when she opened it, she saw that it was a simple text in response to her earlier text about Bess staying with her after the festival.

I'm fine with her staying with you.

She sighed and wondered how, or if, she could repair that. After opening up with Tilly she knew she wanted to, and that scared her.

"Crystal!" Tilly's voice tried to fight the volume of the crowd and music that belonged on the set of Phantom of the Opera. The crowd was heavy, the whole of Salem had to feel more weight tonight than it had in the last three months combined. Everywhere you looked there was something to hold your attention. Fire-eaters, food trucks with food that was more art than food, games with macabre twists like bobbing for apples but bobbing for rubber body parts or throwing ping pong balls into small fish bowls but instead of goldfish there were piranha.

Witches were everywhere, barely a head without a witch hat could be found.

They made their way over to where Crystal was in her own booth, handing out ominous fortunes from her crystal ball or from the cards. She was wearing a diaphanous black robe over a thin gold dress with her glowing hair falling in waves around her shoulders. She looked every bit the mysterious woman with the answers.

"Darlings! Look at you, so renaissance mystique," Crystal cooed.

"How's the night going? Tell anyone their imminent death is coming yet?"

"That happened once, and it was purely coincidental," she remarked with a knowing arch of her brow.

Tilly explained at Ursula's curious expression. "Two years ago, Crystal told Kalia Smith that she was going to die unexpectedly but that her husband and children would prosper. Two weeks later, she died in an accident while riding her bike."

"That's awful," Ursula said.

Crystal gave her a look and added, "After she died, her husband found out that she was having two affairs. One with her married dentist and another with a bartender a town over."

"Oh wow. That sounds, exhausting," Ursula said with a laugh.

"When are you finished tonight?" Tilly asked Crystal.

"I'm afraid I'm here until breakdown. But I saw Jen with Cora over by the caramel apples and Kelsea slipped in a little bit ago, but when I called her name she didn't hear me. She seemed a little frazzled."

"Kelsea? Do you know why?"

"No, but I have a bad feeling. Check on her?" Crystal asked.

"Of course," Tilly agreed. She looked worried, her usual bright eyes crossed with concern. "We'll head to the maze and if we find her, I'll text you," Ursula said.

"Oh, Ursula. This is for you," Crystal said handing her a black velvet pouch. "I think you'll find it helpful though I have no idea what's inside."

The bag was light, the size of her palm. She slid it into her bag and told Crystal they would see her later.

The night was a lucky indigo sky with a white moon near-to-bursting with her light and a hazy covering of see-through clouds coming and going. The smells of bonfire and festival food mixed with the sounds of the haunting music. The push of bodies was overwhelming and the hats and masks made everything feel not quite real.

She looked overhead at the lights masterfully strung, a delicate canopy of a spiderweb with dew drops. Little baubles of lights moved in a slow dance inside the web making the sky above them look like fireflies had gathered and were serenading them all. As she took it in, admiring the beauty of it, she was jostled forward, pitching her body almost causing her to fall. Catching herself, and with Tilly's help, she righted herself. But she felt dizzy, her vision blurring, and it took a moment to fully come back into focus.

"You okay?"

She shook her head. "Fine. I just," she swallowed and took a breath. She was fine. This was just the lack of sleep. "Actually, could we find some water?"

They didn't find water after walking down the booths, but she settled for pumpkin beer. They were standing in line when Miles walked up to them, a smile on his maskless face. She had the thought that he smiled too much.

"Ursula," he greeted them. "How are you liking the festival?"

"It's nice," she replied, trying to make her tone kind but not overly inviting. Why did she keep bumping into this man?

"I could tell it was you because of your hair. You have pretty identifiable hair," he laughed and looked at Tilly like he was looking for
support.

"Well, we're just getting a drink and then meeting some people,"
Ursula said. Tilly glanced at her but said nothing, thankfully. It wasn't
exactly a lie.

"I'll get it for you," he offered. He looked hopeful, overly eager and
something in Ursula twisted.

"Please," he added, "I still feel awful about that confrontation the
other morning. It was not my best look."

She looked at Tilly who tilted her head but continued to stay silent
then she sighed and looked at him. "Fine. But you don't owe me an
apology. You owe Bess one."

"Not that I need an apology from her, but she kind of wiped the
floor with me in that debate," he said with a crooked grin.

"She did, and I gave her a high five for that."

He chuckled. "Well, next time I'm at the coffee shop I will be sure
to apologize to her."

"Good."

"Let me get you ladies those drinks?"

She thought it over for a few seconds and then conceded. "We'll be
over at the benches," she pointed to where she spotted a few.

"Miles isn't the worst," Tilly said as they found two small empty
seats. They were nearly sitting on top of each other.

Ursula gave her a pointed look, as pointed as one could get behind
a gold mask. "Not the worst is one of the worst reviews for a man."

Tilly laughed. She smiled and reveled in this moment. She was sitting at a festival with a friend, having gotten through a fight, laughing
about guys. It was like she had jumped back a couple of decades and
she felt more full than she had in years.

Miles came over carrying two beers, but shortly after they had both taken a few sips he got a call and stepped away from the crowd to take it.

"So, Miles?"

"Is designing stained glass panels for my greenhouse. That's it."

"He's cute in that football jock way," Tilly observed. "Though, his chosen friend group could use some trimming," she murmured.

Ursula nodded. He wasn't the man who encroached on her thoughts unexpectedly. And there was something about him that didn't settle well.

"He reminds me of those guys who get stuck in their high school glory days with the same guys they hung out with, still wearing the gold class ring with their jersey number on the side." She leaned her shoulder against Tilly's. "I bet you a thousand dollars if we took a peek in his closet we would find his letter jacket and it wouldn't be dusty."

"Think he wears it around his house?" Tilly joked.

"I absolutely think he wears it around his house while streaming the top hits during his senior year," she replied with a wide smile.

"Ladies, I apologize. There is some trouble at the art studio and I need to go check it out."

"Hope everything is okay," Tilly said.

"Yeah, I'm sure everything will be fine," he said. "Can I come by this week to talk about the panels?"

She hadn't been sure if she was going to continue working with him but joking aside, he was trying and being nice. "Yeah, that sounds good." She lifted her beer. "Thanks for these."

He winked but it came off as overdone rather than charming.

"Okay, pumpkin beer is weird," Ursula finally said looking at the liquid that had a slightly bitter aftertaste.

"Have you noticed Kelsea being odd lately?" Tilly asked after they swallowed their sips of beer each making faces.

"I don't think I'm the one to ask," she replied honestly. "From meeting her to now, though, I would say she's less..." she weighed her words, trying to find the right way to describe what she knew about Kelsea. "I guess, shiny. She seems like she's pulled back, but again, I've only been here for a minute so I would ask Jen or Crystal."

Tilly looked thoughtful and then lifted her cup to Ursula's. "To terrible fall beer and good friends." They clinked plastic cups, took one more sip and then threw them away. When they turned around, Ursula paused as Cora and Jen walked toward them. Cora, with a wide smile, and Jen, with a closed-off look only a woman who was angry could pull off.

"Hey," Cora greeted. She looked like a goddess with her coiled hair slicked through with gold that matched her gold mask hanging around her neck. Jen had a black lace mask around her wrist with her braids hanging down to just below her shoulders, the ends of her braids a vibrant red.

"Hey guys," Tilly said, everyone passing around hugs. Jen and Ursula hesitated, but when Ursula was about to step forward in a peace offering, Jen turned toward Tilly cutting off the action. It cut Ursula but she held it quietly inside.

"Hey, I heard about your door. Everything okay?" Cora's concern was soft.

"Yeah, though the police don't seem that concerned," she replied with a shrug.

"Oh, they probably think it's kids. Trick or treat season," Cora offered lightly and Ursula hoped she was right, but knew deep down it was more sinister than teenagers playing with spray paint and dares.

"Did you see Kelsea? She was acting strange when we ran into her a bit ago."

"No, but Crystal said the same thing."

"Anyone call or text her?" Ursula suggested

Jen held up her phone with raised eyebrows. "That's obviously the first thing I did."

Her snide reply was felt among the four women, strings of tension running between them. Ursula felt a pitch of anger toward Jen's unjust treatment. Being hurt and accepting that quietly until the right time was one thing; but outwardly being contemptuous was another.

"Okay, well, I say we split up and look for her," Tilly said, trying to cut that tension.

"Fine with me," Jen said, her shoulders set back and chin tilted up. It was grating on Ursula but she was choosing the peaceful route. When Jen wanted to talk, she would be more than willing to do that. Clearly, she needed to feel her feelings. Plus, her head was starting to ache.

"I'll head to the end of the street vendors. Jen, you take the east street. Tilly, you take the west street vendors, and Ursula, why don't you ask around the corn maze."

Ursula nodded, looking toward where she had seen the corn arch earlier.

"Everyone keep in contact with each other through text and call one of us if you find her," Cora instructed.

"Don't get lost in the maze," Jen said, a slight taunting to her tone with a glint in her eyes. Ursula pulled in a breath and counted before she smiled brightly in response. Because frankly, she wished she were holding that pumpkin beer right now. The thought of Jen's reaction if she threw it at her was incredibly cathartic. She was regressing to her teenage years if she was allowing her emotions to take her hostage.

"Jen, knock it off," Cora said sharply.

Tilly shifted uncomfortably and Jen looked admonished, though she pursed her lips and turned her head. The gesture only highlighted Jen's phenomenal bone structure. Ursula wanted to roll her eyes because yes, Jen was being unfair, but also, the woman had better bone structure than Johnny Depp and that was frustrating.

"Alright, convene back here no later than forty-five minutes. Deal?"

All heads nodded and Ursula made her way to the corn maze. The large arch made up of corn stalks, lights, and a sign that welcomed you to "Get Lost", was a few yards ahead but as she made her way, her steps faltered. She paused to pull in a deep breath and close her eyes. Not sleeping was truly getting to her. She would help find Kelsea and then she would call it an early night, head home, take an over-the-counter sleep aid, and crash. Now that she had a plan in place, she nodded to herself and headed for the arch.

"Hey, witch," someone said under their breath as they passed Ursula. She looked sharply at them, unable to recognize who they were with their mask and quickly retreating steps.

She was feeling more unsteady and she paused to grab a lungful of cool air to center herself. When she saw the arch a little ways off, she gave herself a pep talk. But as she started that way, she caught sight of the side of Kelsea's face, her dark mask pushed onto the top of her head talking with someone obscured by a lamppost and high-piled bales of hay.

She was about to text the group that she had found her when she paused because Kelsea held up a slim hand and her body was in a stance that said she was angry as she talked quickly. She couldn't tell what she was saying from this distance so she started closing it and then stopped abruptly when she saw the person she was talking to. She recognized the blue wool coat. Jessica Sandis.

Before she made it to them, her voice wouldn't have carried had she yelled, Kelsea shook her head vehemently and then ran off. Ursula watched her run into the corn maze, disappearing under the arch, and then was swallowed by the darkness.

She groaned as she texted the group.

Found her going into the maze. Looked like she was arguing with Jessica Sandis. Will find her.

She slipped her phone into her bag and went off to find her friend. She thought about going after Jessica and asking, demanding, to know what they were talking about. For all she knew, Jessica had a hand in the words on the graveyard or her door. But time wasn't on her side, and her head was feeling more and more discombobulated. So, off into the maze she would go.

CHAPTER TWENTY-SIX

HOW TO SEE COLORS

U rsula was a few turns into the maze, the sounds of children screeching jolting her every so often, but what was most disconcerting was her lack of sense of direction. She stopped once she turned a corner to the right and looked around.

She thought back in her mind to the last few turns she had taken and could guess which direction she was headed, but with the only insight into cardinal direction being the sky above them, she wasn't confident of her guess. The sky above was nearly pitch black, the slightest blue tinge had been at the bottom edges, but she couldn't see that now. Now it was ink. Now the moon was hiding and the stars were only a suggestion behind the covering clouds.

And her head was starting to pound and was the ground tilting? She reached out a hand to brace herself on the unsound tower of hay bales that were sprinkled throughout the maze with trash cans and signs pointing in unknown directions.

As her head began to feel fuzzy, she was beginning to regret the few sips of that beer she'd had.

Did someone call her name? She turned her head and then cursed as her vision barely followed her body's movement. It felt like she was drunk, which wasn't right. She needed to get out of here and sit down.

Someone in a completely white mask that covered their entire face caught her off guard and she gasped. It was eerie as they looked at her steadily and silently but maybe they knew which way she needed to go.

"Do you know the way out?"

The person in the mask, a little over average height, nodded and tilted their head to the side. There was a narrow walkway that spilled into a long, clear row. She thanked the person as they doubled back the way they had come and she realized the person worked there. The narrow space he had led her down must have been one of the quick exits that the workers knew about.

She continued down a long hallway made of towering stalks of corn, but as she walked, she swore that the end pushed further and further out. She could make it. There was no one in front of or behind her and the sounds of people talking and laughing seemed distant. Very distant. She looked up, barely making out a star in the vast and hazy sky, and then she felt her stomach pitch as she doubled over down to her hands and knees. Everything that had been in her stomach in the last couple of hours made its way onto the slightly wet and muddy ground. She was aware of the wet mud digging into her knees and hands but didn't care as the coolness of it felt grounding.

She sat back on her haunches and wiped her mouth with the back of her sleeve, taking off her mask at the same time and letting it hang limp and loose on her arm.

Breathe in.

Breathe out.

Breathe in.

She was going to be sick again. She was shaking and every muscle in her body felt constricted.

Then she heard something up ahead and lifted her head. The man with the full white mask was standing at the end of the row. Hands clasped so casually in front of him. He was wearing all black and she had to squint through the tears in her eyes but she was sure he was the one who led her here. And where was here?

There were no other people around. She hadn't been wrong that they sounded distant and far away.

The sounds of creaking stalks made her turn, slowly so she wouldn't heave again, and when she looked behind her she let out a weak scream, barely a scratchy sound coming out of her dry throat when she saw that there was another man, wearing all black and an all-white mask.

She watched with a pounding head, a turning stomach, and rising fear as he lifted one finger to his mouth in a shushing gesture. The eeriness of it made her insides clench. Then the sound of slow, but sure, footsteps reached her ears and she didn't know which way to look. She needed to get out of here. She needed to run.

Danger was lifting every hair on her body, her brain was screaming for her to get up, push herself out of this place pinned between two men in white masks who she now believed did not work the corn maze.

They were closing in.

She didn't dare move her head to look behind her but she knew he was closing in, she could feel the energy of him getting closer and closer.

"What do we have here? A witch?" Though muffled by the mask the words were clear.

A deeper voice from the man behind her answered, "Witches in this town don't have a good history."

Laughter behind her and in front of her.

The man in front of her still didn't move. He tilted his head slowly. Then he bent down to his haunches and said, "I wouldn't put your witchy nose in town business if I were you." The words were said flatly, no inflection and it sent a river of chills throughout her body. "This town has a way of getting rid of infections." He tilted his head again, assessing and calculating.

And she wasn't going to find out what.

Suddenly, with everything inside of her, she jumped up and pushed through the wall of corn, pressing her body against the thin, but sturdy, stalks until they gave way to her exploding energy. She gritted her teeth against the roiling in her stomach, the beads of sweat pouring over her temples like gentle strokes of cool fingers along her face.

She needed out.

Everything was closing in. The sounds of the world around her were stretching like they were morphing her vision. She was seeing sound, the waves of conversation low and like loose strings, the sound of laughter up high and static like jolts of a mountain top. Why was she seeing sound? The smell of popcorn was bright yellow with a golden hazy glow and she almost smiled at the happiness of it. It was so beautiful!

She pressed through another line of skinny stalks of corn then stumbled into an open row where people jumped back in shock. She looked around at the open mouths and the wide eyes behind masks. Some of the people had wings. That would be so nice if you were in a corn maze, just fly your way up, up, up over it all and look down on everyone stuck in their own back and forth. Like life. So many people just stuck. Stuck.

Everything was so loud. She stumbled through the thin crowd of people and covered her ears. She was overheating and felt like sweat was running down her body in a shower. After shrugging off her jacket and handing it to a confused bystander, she continued wonkily until she was free.

Oh thank God she was out in the wild open and she lifted her arms up slowly and high into the sky, grabbing fresh air and space and smiling at the now shining moon. It was shining for her.

"Ursula?"

She wanted to taste the moon. She knew that it would taste like sweet, condensed milk and she smiled and laughed.

"Ursula."

Someone was saying her name. She didn't care. She was underneath the moon goddess and taking in the bright gold popcorn smell, the creamy sweetness of the moon a perfect cap and that gentle wave of cool air against her skin was soothing her pounding head and stomach. Was she still laughing? Something bright popped and flashed and she covered her face with an arm.

Then a voice, dark, dipped in honey so golden and smooth she wanted to drown in it brushed against her ear. And a warmth so encapsulating wrapped around her body as words were pouring into her ears. She imagined someone laying her on the ground, holding her head gently as they dropped words into her ear until her brain filled up with them. What an astonishing way to collect words.

And then she was weightless. Maybe she had wings like those other lucky people in the maze! Perhaps she could fly? She tilted her head and looked into two dark, beguiling eyes, so deep and mesmerizing that she wanted to ask what religion they were so that she could kneel at the altar. She reached out a shaky hand and ran her buzzing fingertips along a rough jaw.

But then she started drooping, her limbs felt like stones. Had someone opened up a hole inside of her and poured in molten lead? Who would do that? She could barely hold up her head and the solid warmth holding her had a cozy place for her. It brushed against her cheek and cradled what she could no longer hold up. The smell was clean and sultry and she sucked it into her lungs that felt like they too were filling up with something more than air.

"I can't move," she said. Did she say it out loud? She didn't feel like laughing anymore. Where was the moon and her glowing body? She couldn't move her head to look for her comfort.

"Shh. I've got you. Close your eyes, Ursula."

She wasn't sure if they were open or closed but she burrowed into the soft and strong pillow. "The white masks. Did they find me? They were looking for a witch," she slurred.

"Shh. I'm taking you home. Go to sleep."

And there was something in that voice, a picture of a shiny butterscotch button candy, the taste of it revived from her deepest girlhood memories. It calmed her and she let out a breath as she let her leaden body relax in the cocoon of safety.

Her body was shaking. Shivers and wracks of cold, strong icy fingers dragging their claws down her back. She opened her eyes, just a crack, and then moaned, slamming them shut when the air touching her eyeballs burned.

"You're okay. You're safe," a deep voice said. "You're freezing and damp. I need to get you out of these clothes and into a hot shower."

It was that smooth butterscotch voice that she had fallen asleep to earlier. A resounding thump in her head kept time with a ticking clock somewhere and she wanted it to be silenced. She could barely get words out but tried opening her eyes again, this time slowly.

When she did, she saw that she was lying in her room, on her bed. The bed, she knew, was soft but it felt rock hard and agitating against her skin. She was simultaneously hot and freezing and whoever had spoken was right, she was shivering uncontrollably.

Her surroundings came into focus, though she let it happen gradually so she didn't strain her already bleating head.

"Water," she got out. Did she? She heard it reverberate in her head, but did the butterscotch voice also hear it?

She got her answer when she was slowly lifted up and forward, pulling a little groan from her as the pain shot through her body. But that pain was forgotten the moment cool glass touched her dry lips. She opened immediately and took a sip, too fast, trying to draw too much into her mouth and down her sandpaper throat. She choked and coughed.

"Easy, easy. Just a small sip at a time, sweetheart."

She got her bearings and then tried again, taking the smallest sip of the perfect, most delicious water. It nearly tasted sweet, like a drop of honey was mixed in with it as her body soaked it up and demanded more. She drank a few sips over the next few minutes until she felt partially sated and then let her head roll back, the effort of keeping it up finally giving way. She was gently laid down and the sound of someone moving around was on the periphery of her awareness.

A distant sound of spraying water touched her ears. She may have drifted for a few moments, her body trying to find some comfort but everything felt so cold and so hot and she was itchy why couldn't she stop shivering?

"I need to get you cleaned up and get you warm. You may wake up and hate me for this." She was aware, and grateful, that she no longer felt nauseous or like a live animal was trying to claw its way out of her stomach. She must have thrown up a lot in that cornfield.

The cornfield. The men in white masks. She opened her eyes in a jolt at the memory but then every thought came to a halt as she was doused with what felt like the heaviest water in history. Can water have different weights? She didn't think so. Why did this pelting of rain feel so dense?

"Ahhh," she mumbled pathetically. She was sitting on the floor of her shower, her body barely able to hold itself up and the water was trying to pin her down.

She heard the voice curse and then the door was opened and closed, a flash of cool air hit her making her gasp, and then a large body slid behind her. A thick arm banded firmly, though gently, around her middle as two long legs encased her on either side. She looked at the legs and should have been concerned that they most definitely belonged to a man, but at this exact moment, she felt safe and protected. The water that was burdensome before became a light, warm summer rain. The heat at her back made her feel like when she was a child and would lay on the hot blacktop of her driveway in the middle of a summer storm. The memory of that smell permeated her senses and she felt sheltered and secure.

"I'm going to wash your hair," the deep voice said, his words caressing her neck and making her shiver for a completely different reason now.

A pop sounded in the enclosed glass and strong hands gently massaged her hair, the smell of eucalyptus and vanilla bursting into the small space. It was heaven and she leaned back into the motion.

Something was said about needing her to keep her eyes closed as he grasped her chin lightly between his fingers and tipped her head back, the warm spray of the water sinking and sliding deliciously over her scalp and through her mass of hair, rinsing away the soap and the night.

The pain and the wracking shivers had subsided.

"You're going to be okay," he crooned, his mouth pressed against her ear, another shiver overtaking her body. She hoped that he credited the shiver to whatever was going on with her because the embarrassment right now wasn't something she could work through mentally. But his rough cheek against her wet smooth one, his firm body holding hers protectively as the water baptised her brought a myriad of sensations she wasn't sure how to describe. She felt guarded and alive and like she wanted more but didn't know what that meant or how to ask.

Before she could think further on that, he picked her up slowly, seemingly effortlessly, turned off the water, and then wrapped her in a towel. It was then that she realized she was wearing only a bra and underwear. She couldn't picture which bra or underwear she had put on before the festival but she was praying that they weren't the ratty ones she found so comfortable even though they were worn and passed their retirement date.

"Can you take those off by yourself? I'm going to get you some dry clothes."

She nodded her head slowly and he left. She wouldn't torture herself by looking in the mirror. So, she dropped the towel and somehow got the wet bra and underwear off without toppling over, though she did have to lean on the linen closet for support. She couldn't reach the towel on the ground without falling.

"Are you ready?"

"Yes," she called, her voice still weak.

The door opened again and then his butterscotch voice cursed low. He wrapped the towel around her and then placed clean clothes on the countertop. "I'll be right outside if you need me. Just call out."

She reached for the neat pile of clothes, surprised to find them warm, but after she got them on, with some difficulty, she sighed in delight at the warmth they brought. She padded to the door, opened it slowly, and peeked her head out. There, sitting on the edge of her large bed was Jenson Lancaster, his wrists dangling between his knees and his dark head down. She knew on some level that it was Jenson taking care of her, but seeing him in her room, on her bed no less, made something inside her squirm. Seeing him with a flannel shirt unbuttoned and hanging open, with jeans and bare feet made her feel a lot of things. It felt familiar in the way a soft, worn-in relationship could.

"Um, I'm finished," she said, her voice sounding small. She felt whittled down to the smallest version of herself, vulnerable and naked.

But when his head lifted at her voice, his dark chocolate eyes hit hers with that intensity that, right now, grounded her. He looked at her like he'd had his head bowed in prayer for her. His eyes never left hers as he stood up from her bed and walked toward her, his gait strong and steady. When he reached out and lifted her chin, turning her head from one side slowly to the other, his eyes assessing her, she held her breath.

Then, to her absolute surprise, he wrapped both of his arms around her, encapsulating her body with his. It was the kind of hug that said he would protect her. It was the embodiment of him communicating that she was treasured, important, and safe. She held on because she needed to. No confusing emotions muddled this moment because right now he was a human telling her that she could relax, that she was out of danger. She held on because she needed everything else to fade away; she needed to be pressed together by someone else.

She almost cried when he pulled back, but then she almost cried out of relief and a sweeping sense of sweetness when his large hands framed her face and he leaned down to kiss her forehead, his lips warm and promising against her skin. Her eyes closed at that contact, at the unexpected touch of her soul.

She thought briefly, that if men only knew what an unexpected forehead kiss could do to a woman, they would have unspeakable power at their fingertips.

"Come on. You need to get to bed."

He scooped her up making her gasp and wrap her arms around his neck, but too soon he was laying her down on her turned-down bed then tucking her fluffy comforter around her. It reminded her of the night she woke up after their quiet moonlit swing, the comforter pulled up to her chin like she'd been tucked in like a child.

He looked at her like he wanted to say something like he wanted to say everything, but was holding back.

"What.." she couldn't form words. She wanted to ask what was wrong with her, why she could barely move or talk. She was about to try again but her eyelids closed as a heaviness she wasn't sure she'd ever experienced before took over her body and her mind. She felt like a warm weight was pressing her down against the bed.

He shook his head and brushed her hair out of her face. "We'll talk later. Bess is coming over in a little while, but I'm going to stay downstairs until she gets here. You need to sleep, but your phone is next to you on the nightstand," he pointed to where he must have placed her phone. "Call me if you need me. Don't get up on your own," his deep command wasn't gentle, but it was kind.

She nodded her head, she hoped she nodded her head. He was being so...gentle. This soft side of him was a drug. Or more potent than a drug, it felt like home. She tried to pick at that string in the mess of the tapestry of her thoughts, but she couldn't quite grab ahold of it.

A thumb stroked over her cheekbone, leaving behind a small lick of flame, and then he was walking to the door. She didn't want to let go of this gentleness.

"Wait," she called, praying her voice moved past her mind. He paused and turned around.

She wasn't sure if he said anything but she could feel, even behind her closed eyelids that he was still there. "Jenson?"

"Sleep," he ordered with a sigh.

"I don't want to," she got out, the fear of being alone, of seeing white masks and hearing whispers of being a witch winning out over her pride.

She wasn't sure what his face was saying, couldn't imagine what he was thinking. But when he stretched out his long body next to hers, on top of the bedding, she felt immediate relief.

"Butterscotch," she whispered. "You remind me of butterscotch and I think you're all darkness but in the lightest way." She wasn't sure if her words were coming out, but her mind was pulling that string out of the mess, trying to create a picture to understand him. "I think you make me feel things I'm scared to feel." She sighed, hoping her words made sense. Or hoping they weren't making it to his ears at all. But she couldn't stop her thoughts from coming whether they stayed silently inside of her or not. "I think you're right, that the moon has magic and I think she pulled me to you." She wanted to be back on that swing with him. His silence felt like a blessing, like its own love poem. "I'm sorry you found my clumsy heart," she said, feeling a sadness well there like a lagoon. "I don't know if I remember how to be seen."

And then she pictured the graveyard, ten girls dancing and laughing, raising their arms up to the moon, the look of hope on their faces as they learned the lesson of what it is to be a woman in this world: that it wishes to tame the wildness until they feel shame for wanting to dance and be seen. She let sleep wrap his arms around her gently then, a smile on her face as she hoped that they all would find their own path to that brave wild.

Dreams cascaded like dropping velvet curtains. Taunting voices over the background of the slow strum of dramatic music, laughing and pointing.

A voice from tonight, which felt like so long ago, tormented her.

Witches in this town don't have a good history.

And what she now knew was a warning:

I wouldn't put your witchy nose in town business if I were you.

Chapter Twenty-Seven

ARE YOU TRACKING?

U rsula had slept through the night and until the next morning at nine a.m. She was usually an early riser, never able to sleep past the seven a.m. mark, but when she finally opened her eyes, blinking against the soft light of the lamp in her room she groaned and sat up trying to orient herself.

"Hi," a voice called from the corner making her shriek and jump. Bess was curled up on her cream velvet chaise, Casper somehow squished his large body onto the chair with her and the sight was sweet.

Everything from the night before surfaced. Her head didn't hurt anymore, her stomach didn't feel wobbly, and when she pulled off the comforter and sheets, found the floor with her bare feet, and stood, she nearly sank in relief when she felt steady.

"How are you feeling?" Bess asked as she awkwardly tried to maneuver her way off of the chaise and out from under Casper's long grey legs.

"Honestly, good. I need water and food, but I feel pretty good. You didn't sleep here all night did you?"

"No, I slept in the guest room, but I came in here around six this morning to check on you when Uncle Jay came down."

The mention of Jenson made heat bloom in her cheeks and her stomach. She thought of him putting her in the shower, and then getting into the shower with her in only his boxer-briefs. Or boxers. She had no idea what kind of underwear he wore but the fact that she was thinking about it now with a low pitch in her stomach meant that she was definitely doing better and definitely needed coffee and to *not* think about that.

Oh god, he'd seen her naked.

She closed her eyes against the mortification.

"School," she blurted. "You have school, don't you?"

She smiled. "Uncle Jay called the school and told them that I would be late."

"I'm going to get dressed and then want some coffee?"

Bess perked up with a smile. "I'll go make it while you get dressed."

"You're a dream," Ursula said with a soft smile then walked into the bathroom where she found her partially damp hair frizzy and wavy in parts, straight and curled at the ends in other parts like she had been tumbling through dreams and nightmares. She brushed it out, then dried it. Fifteen minutes later, with wavy hair, a cream sweater, and jeans and wool socks, she padded downstairs and could hear Jenson talking in low tones to someone in the living room.

"Hey," she called, slight trepidation in her voice. But when her feet hit the landing her eyebrows rose at what she saw. Her friends were all sitting around the room in equal states of disarray. Tilly and Kelsea were on the couch, both wearing pajamas and messy hair. Tilly didn't have her red eyeglasses on and she looked so young and innocent as she looked at Ursula with wide, concerned eyes. Crystal was in a cream robe and wide cream lounge pants with her hair in a braid trailing her shoulder. She looked like the kind of woman who woke up easily with a smile, requiring very little to make her presentable to the world.

On the coffee table was a crystal vase of red tulips. Kelsea, no doubt, had brought chocolate brownies dusted with powdered sugar, and a tin of something Ursula suspected was tea sat next to the plate.

Her friends had come here and stayed the night in her home. They'd come, quite literally, around her in her time of tumultuous need.

"You guys," she shook her head, a smile she couldn't hold back, a smile against all odds of the last twenty-four hours breaking over her face. Then her eyes found Jen as she stood from where Ursula hadn't seen her perched in the cognac-colored armchair.

The fierce look on her face stopped Ursula's smile from moving on her face. Everyone paused, looks of elation and happiness frozen in place as Jen pushed her way through the living room, even lightly bumping Jenson out of the way as she made her way to Ursula. Her fierce brown eyes took her in before she crushed her in a hug so powerful that Ursula could imagine her little broken pieces being pushed back together. She smelled like sugar and cloves and Ursula felt as she dragged in a breath of her that she was healing.

"I was a bitch," Jen said, uncaring if anyone and everyone could hear her. "Don't even try to say that I wasn't or that it's okay because I was and it wasn't okay." She pulled back to look at Ursula. She had on a red silk pajama set that made her look beautifully royal. "I am a black woman who feels her feelings in a lot of big ways but sometimes I feel them too big and this time got the better of me. I am so sorry. You are not and never were, to blame for Rob Sandis's idiotic antics. That man is a fool and was one long before you were a name we even knew to love." She placed her hand on Ursula's cheek, the gesture loving, another wave of healing. "Can you forgive me?"

Ursula smiled and felt the warmth of tears in her eyes bloom. "Of course." And then she laughed. "You are *really* good at apologies."

"Baby, I am also really good at fucking up," she said with attitude and her perfectly arched eyebrows raised.

"Aren't we all?" Tilly said behind them and everything felt pieced together as they talked, words indecipherable as Ursula's eyes sought out Jenson's.

When her mouth hitched up in a small, tenuous smile, he nodded his head and winked at her.

And that was enough. Ursula's dad used to say that a good relationship, no matter the kind, understood that fighting was about finding common ground through something difficult. Not winning, not making someone else lose. And if you did it right, you would find yourselves with a deeper foundation than before.

She'd never felt that with anyone, not really. Until now, here in Salem. She realized as they bustled into the kitchen with Bess pouring coffee, chatter tripping over chatter, laughter and gasps, that she was learning how to make space for rich relationship, which meant some pain and mistakes. But also this. Community.

About halfway through her cup of coffee, she set her ghost mug down when she realized that Jenson was nowhere to be seen. She excused herself as they continued talking, the happy sound behind her as she walked down the hallway. She found him sitting on the couch, his own mug of coffee in his strong hand as he was looking at something on his phone. A small smile touched her lips when she noticed this was a new addition to her mysterious mug collection; a simple dark brown mug that looked like it was made from tree bark with a thick, twig handle. It was a grey, rainy day, and the man looked completely at peace sitting easily and unbothered.

"Hey," she said.

He looked up and something in his eyes made her want to run to him, made her want to ask if he would keep her safe. And that terrified her because she hadn't wanted or needed that in so long. Also, she felt vertiginous, and there were probably things that needed to be said still, stories that needed to be told. She had a gossamer memory of asking him to sleep next to her. Of his large body folding over the other side of the bed and possibly whispered words that wouldn't form in the light of day. She hoped she hadn't embarrassed herself. She hoped she hadn't pushed him further away.

He stood up slowly, unfurling his long body. His flannel was buttoned today, to her disappointment, but he looked roguish and so handsome, with his dark hair falling in disarray. He stopped a few short feet from her so she had to look up to meet his eyes. And his were running over her face like he was making sure she was all there.

"How are you feeling?"

She took in a deep breath and nodded her head. "I feel like... I'm angry and like there is a target on my back for some reason and I don't know why. And I don't feel fully safe. But I also feel happy and full, because when I needed it, my friends showed up. You," she added gently, "showed up." She felt sheepish. She wanted to mend what she had done to...well, to whatever their relationship was, as confusing as it may be. "You stayed."

His simple nod gave away nothing of what he was thinking or feeling and she wasn't sure if it was a punishment or if he was simply being there, not rocking the boat.

"I'm sorry," she said softly. And she hoped he knew she was apologizing for something more important than the shallow burden of asking him to sleep next to her. She hoped he heard in her words that she was sorry she had made assumptions about him and pressed fear and insecurity from her fingertips to his skin when all he had done was offer her something honest.

"I have to go to a site today to finish up a project, tie up loose ends. But I'll be back tomorrow. Can Bess stay with you again tonight? Her mom disappeared a few days ago and I filed for custody."

The sudden change in subject felt like whiplash. She couldn't stop the pang of hurt that he wouldn't respond to her apology. Maybe she'd ruined what he saw in her. She couldn't shake the way he'd looked at her in the library, the disappointment.

She shook that aside and gave him a brave smile.

"That's amazing, Jenson. And yes, of course she can stay."

He nodded his head, opened his mouth as if to say something then thought better of it and closed it. He tucked a piece of her black hair behind her ear, the way she was getting used to, and then walked out of her house, closing the door behind him.

She let out a big push of breath and shook her head. She would need a study guide on Jenson Lancaster.

"Hey, Ursula? You better come in here," Jen called.

The oddness of her voice pushed all thoughts of Jenson out of her mind and she immediately went to the kitchen to find the pajama-party women all hunched over the counter looking at something. She pushed her way in and gasped when she saw a video of her running around from last night. She looked crazed. Her hair was a frazzled mess like she hadn't brushed it in years, her clothes were rumpled and her eyes looked wide and wild.

"Ohmygosh," she exclaimed.

"They're calling you the Wicked Witch of The Lost Soul's House," Tilly said, a note of fear in her voice, her eyes deeply concerned behind her red glasses.

"What the hell?"

"It gets worse," Jen said.

"How?! I look like the bird lady who talks to ravens and only speaks in Edgar Allan Poe quotes."

"That," Kelsea interjected pointing at Ursula, "would be both really cool and really annoying."

"Rob is using this and connecting the other articles about us dabbling in witchcraft to say that Cora is into drugs and witchcraft, which is not a good family platform," Jen said, though this time there was no anger directed at Ursula.

Ursula groaned and laid her head on the island.

"We will figure this out," Crystal said, rubbing her hand over Ursula's back. "The truth will come out."

"Someone drugged me," Ursula suddenly said looking up as something clicked. "I knew it wasn't just exhaustion." Everyone was watching her and she shook her head adding, "I haven't been sleeping for a couple of weeks, this stupid perimenopause and everything going on, and it was starting to mess with me. But last night I was on something. Like, I could see colors and smell sounds."

"Sounds like LSD," Crystal said nodding her head. "What?" she asked shrugging her shoulders at curious stares. "I lived through the seventies."

They laughed, all except for Ursula who turned to Jen. "But Cora, her campaign."

"We will figure it out. But there's something else," she added slowly.

A stone sank in her belly. "Oh come on, what?"

They looked at each other and then slowly parted. She frowned and then her eyes widened when she saw, written on her large windows, the velvet drapes now slid to the side, in dark red:

History always repeats itself.

"Jenson kept us updated last night when he brought you home."

"We immediately came over then," Tilly said, reaching over and squeezing Ursula's hand.

Jen continued, "And then he let Crystal know when he found that on your window. He took pictures of it, sent it to Taylor White."

"Who?"

"Local officer. Very handsome," Tilly said with a smirk.

"I thought you didn't like men in uniform," Jen said, crossing her arms over her chest.

"I don't," she replied with a shrug. "Doesn't mean I can't think one is handsome. He has one of those deep dimples when he smiles," she pressed her pointer finger into the side of her cheek.

"Anyways," Crystal brought the subject back to the emergency on hand, "Taylor will be by later to take your statement and you may want to tell him that you think you were drugged."

"What if he doesn't believe me?"

The women looked at each other and then Kelsea's sweet voice piped in. "There's no possibility of him believing you if you don't at least tell him."

"Taylor is pretty cool," Bess added. She was in an olive green crop top and matching sweatpants, her dark hair in a high messy ponytail. She shrugged as the women gave her varying looks of question. "Druggie mom who likes to sing to the neighborhood and yell a lot, remember?"

Ursula wrapped an arm around her shoulders at her glib words. Glib to protect her young heart. Bess laid her head on Ursula's shoulder, the act soft and causing her heart to squeeze a few tears into her eyes.

And then she remembered why they had split up in the first place last night. "Kelsea," she suddenly said, worry dripping from her. "Are you okay? We were worried about you."

She smiled sheepishly and shook her head. "I'm fine. I just had a bad day. We can talk about it later, but honestly," she looked around at each of them, "thank you."

"We're not used to seeing you anxious, pumpkin," Crystal said in her nurturing way, her arm wrapped around Kelsea pulling her into her side. Kelsea's anxiety melted away, her body relaxing and her face smiling softly. Ursula watched her, feeling like there was still something there, something the young woman was hiding. And she was sure she had seen her talking with Jessica Sandis, but she had made it clear she wasn't ready to talk about it.

"Okay, so this officer is coming here to talk to me, take my statement, and then what? Someone is after me, and trying to ruin Cora's career. The two seem very integrated."

"We don't think that they are separate," Jen said. "Someone posted on my business website that I'm a witch and to not trust anything I say or offer as a nutritionist."

Ursula's mouth opened and her eyes widened in shock.

"I was asked to step out of the journalism limelight until things calm down," Kelsea said. Her face looked defeated and Ursula wondered if that had been part of her bad day.

Tilly raised her hand. "We've had multiple callers at the radio station on live air talking about our coven and telling people not to support Cora."

"You're kidding. This," Ursula shook her head in disbelief, "this is insane."

"This," Crystal said, deadpan and with the air of undoubted wisdom, "is a witch hunt."

Silence covered the room, a sacred kind of dark thing hovering like this place knew what they were embarking on.

"Now," Crystal said raising a hand as her cream sleeve fluttered, "who is up for apple brandy french toast?"

And the women continued playing high-school-girl-sleep-over-dress-up filling the kitchen with more laughter and shared tasks to bring a meal together. That ominous feeling was swept away by the smell of cinnamon apples and maple sugar and the magic that happens when women find community.

CHAPTER TWENTY-EIGHT

THE LANGUAGE OF FLOWERS

Taylor White, the handsome detective with the deep dimple when he smiles, from the Salem Police Department, came to take her statement an hour after the women had left her with hugs and promises that they would get through this.

Never would Ursula have guessed months ago that she would be at the center of a real witch hunt, repeating history. She sat at her island, a vanilla tobacco candle burning next to her and another cup of coffee as she stared at the red writing stating just that. The journal someone mysteriously left on her porch lay open next to the ledger she got from the library. There were so many pieces and she felt the more she gathered, the closer she came to putting them together, the more attacks came.

Luckily, Detective White had been kind and did his job well and thoroughly. Something he asked her was twirling around her mind as she sat thinking.

"Why would anyone target you? Wouldn't it be easier to target Cora if this were about the election?"

And that was it. He was right because this couldn't simply be about the election. Something else, bigger, possibly more sinister, was at work.

Rob Sandis was at the center of all of this, she was sure, though there wasn't any evidence linking him, even if they found drugs in her system after taking her blood, it would be hard to pin the mayoral candidate of any wrongdoing.

So, as she stared at the words, she wondered if they were a threat or a mere warning. She tapped her pen on the open journal lying in front of her. She thought about the questions he'd asked her, running them and her answers through the hamster wheel of her mind.

Had anyone had access to drug her?

Yes, Miles had when he got her and Tilly pumpkin beers.

Why would he drug her?

To make her look crazy, like those videos (there were multiple popping up from people taking videos with their phones), and further prove Rob's stance that she was involved in dark happenings. It was brilliant, she would give him that, because even if for some the idea that she was practicing witchcraft was too outlandish, her doing drugs was not. If enough people believed she was bad news for their town, targeting her as a pariah and running her out of town wouldn't be too lofty a goal.

The detective hadn't been sold on Miles drugging her without evidence, but he promised to look into it. She wasn't even sure she was sold on it.

She pulled her journal forward and wrote all of it down.

Goal: Get her out of town, and also by extension take the election from Cora.

Why?: "I wouldn't put your witchy nose in town business if I were you."

"This town has a way of getting rid of infections." The words from the man in the white mask had been on replay in her mind.

Ten graves.

Ten smoke figures dancing.

Oleander Flowers.

Amos.

Amos...she frowned as the name triggered something in her mind. She grabbed the ledger she'd checked out from the library and flipped through the brittle pages carefully. There...Amos.

Reverend Amos Beckwith brings to the town council the removal of The Devil House from their town's limits.

Ursula hunched over the counter, running her finger gently over the page reading over the meeting notes.

Claims Fannie McGovern has come to Salem on the heels of leaving her homeland of England and her church to foster unseemly and unfaithful women in the house that the town has cast as evil. He has a suspicion that Fannie McGovern is seducing these young girls, even from their homes in Salem, to live in the house and commit indecorous acts. Accounts of three young pregnant women seen coming and going from the whorehouse.

A vote will be taken by the council to ban anyone from said house from entering their town and any Salem folk from doing business or trade with them.

Vote: 9 Yea 0 Nay

Ursula sat back as she picked up her tea. Did the town think this was a whorehouse? Regardless, they voted to ostracize the women from their town. Her pen tapped on her journal as she thought, then moved easily, the script flowing with the words and fears in her mind as the dark purple ink found its ground. It was revitalizing to empty her mind where these words felt like a pacing animal in the cage of her silence. It was interesting how the written word could be so freeing and cathartic.

She was at the bottom of the page so she flipped it and stopped. Her breath caught when she saw the different script appear on the blank page. An answer to one of her questions in the middle of her thought-dump. Who was Fannie McGovern? Who were the girls that lived here?

Speak her name in the graveyard when the moon is high.

"Fannie McGovern," she said to an empty kitchen. Her candle flame flickered and blew out causing chills to traipse down her shoulders and over her arms. She groaned and laid her head on the wood counter. Between the mystery of this house, the accusations against her, and the mess that was between her and Jenson, she was afraid any moment she would unravel. "I'm not sure my last boring decade of life prepared me for this."

A cool, wet nose pressed into her neck making her laugh and wrap her arms around Casper. She pulled back and looked into his big eyes. "We're going to go to the graveyard tonight to possibly find answers." She tilted her head. "And also possibly summon a ghost with magic-laced words. Who really knows at this point? You in?"

As always, her loyal hound nudged closer, a promise to stay by her side.

When her doorbell rang as she lost herself in a work project, she looked at a growling Casper with a scrunched brow. He never growled. The gentle giant would welcome a burglar into the house if they offered him a body scratch.

She got up from her desk, peeked out of the stained glass moon and stepped back sharply as her mind raced.

What was he doing here? Should she call for someone? She looked around then pulled her phone out, texting the group what was going on asking them to call her should she not update them within fifteen minutes. She could ignore him, but truly, her curiosity was overwhelming. She had the thought last second to push record and slid it into her back pocket carefully so that the speaker wasn't muffled by her jeans. She let out a breath, braced herself, and opened the door to a dutifully concerned-looking Rob Sandis.

She didn't bother with a smile.

He did. Wide and beguiling. He was holding a pot of red begonias and their meaning was not lost on her.

"Ursula. I heard about your mishap last night at the festival."

"Before or after it happened?" she asked with a saccharine smile.

His smile twitched, but his eyes hardened. "You're funny," he said with a lilting laugh.

"I have my moments. What do you want, Rob?"

He held up a hand. "Hey now, I just came to check on you."

"As you can see, I'm alive and no longer drugged against my will."

He feigned a look of concern. The man had always made her feel uneasy, but now it was like watching an actor over-act. How did anyone fall for this man's antics?

"It's absolutely appalling that someone might consider drugging you. I cannot imagine anyone in this town doing that."

"Maybe you should work on your imagination, then."

"Ah, at least your wit is still with you."

"Well, I have some damage control to do with my reputation, and wit is such a crowd pleaser," she answered drily.

His smile widened. "I just think, you know, we've had tenants come and go from here and the ones that seem to last the longest don't meddle."

She made a humming sound and nodded her head.

"I would hate for you to get chased out of town like the last couple because they just had to know about the lost souls here. The lost souls are more of a," he swirled a tanned hand through the air with a flourish, reminding her of a circus ringmaster, "town legend. Old folklore, if you will."

"Mhmm," she said nodding her head again.

"It's nothing but myth and fable, you see. A waste of time."

She pulled in a breath and then tilted her head, her eyes pinned to his. "If it's all so trifling, then why would anyone chase them out of town?" She stepped forward, feeling a rage well inside of her. She knew this feeling, being told that she was silly, little, not even worth the importance of being seen. "If the lost souls and this house are nothing but myth and fable, a waste of time, then why are you here with a pot of ill-meaning flowers and a warning behind your poorly veiled concern, Rob?"

The fakeness cracked. A hammer hitting glass. And the smile was gone. Now the only expression on his face was annoyance with an edge of anger. The air felt dangerous. And somehow she could feel that the house was at attention. She was thankful for the recording on her phone but knew that if that anger took over, it wouldn't protect her in the moment.

He lowered his voice, his eyes narrowing. "Just take this as a gentle warning."

His use of 'gentle' made her scoff and he stepped forward until there was a mere two feet between them.

"There's nothing 'gentle' about being drugged. I know Miles is behind it. We have proof and Detective White has it now," she said, pushing her theory.

His eyes narrowed. "You can't tie the tracker to him. Or to me, for that matter." He smiled wickedly, but his statement had triggered a thought for Ursula. "This town does not take kindly to intruders who don't belong here trying to stir up old things that do more harm than good."

A rumble of thunder sounded, the vibrating roll of it pressing up from the porch throwing him off balance the slightest. His hand caught the table holding a fluffy fern to steady himself.

She smiled slowly and then stepped back so that the door's threshold was firmly between them. A line and a fortress.

"I have an inkling that old things would do certain people more harm and others some good. So nice of you to check in on me, Rob." She was about to shut the door then added, "And say hello to Jessica for me."

Then something happened. Another rumble rolled and shook the porch, and Ursula watched in awe as the porch's floorboards groaned and moved, as if a large animal were running underneath the house. Rob yelled when the ground beneath his feet lifted up, throwing him to the side, then a plank of wood directly between his loafers shot up and hit him squarely in the crotch. The house shimmied, shoved, and then rolled him off of the porch and down the steps until he was laying on the ground. Her mouth was open and eyes wide as the man who had been spitting threats at her moments ago was cradling his crown jewels and curled up, his handsome face pinched and red like a baby about to cry.

"Huh," she said as she closed the door. "I guess Rob was an unwanted visitor." She locked it and smiled.

She fished her phone out of her back pocket, pushed stop on the recording, and then called Tilly to let her know she was okay.

"He's definitely behind this. Rob Sandis does not want the history of this house to come out."

"He has to know the history, then."

An idea struck her. "Can you bring the book I found in the attic by later?"

"Of course. I have a late segment tonight, so I'll drop it by around dinnertime."

"Thanks, Tilly."

She walked into her kitchen, a renewed spring in her step and a token Rob hadn't known he'd given her in her possession. She pulled her leather tote from the chair in the kitchen and dumped its contents on the island, the sound of everything falling and landing a loud clash that matched the noise in her head. Her hands pushed the items around until she found it. She grabbed it and held it up; a small, square tracker.

She shook her head thinking about how often she had 'run into' Miles over the last couple of weeks. Coincidence and a small town disguising hidden evil intent. She removed the small battery finding the barely visible numbers, typed them out in a text, and sent that along with a picture to the group text.

A text came in from Jenson and her heart lifted.

Brawny Man: Did Taylor come take your statement?

Ursula: Yeah, he did.

Brawny Man: Good. Have any insights?

Ursula: No

She then thought of Bess coming over, to the house that was vandalized and visited with a smiling threat from Rob.

Ursula: But maybe my house isn't the safest place for Bess until things are sorted. Between the vandalism and Rob's visit, I don't want her in danger.

Though frankly, Rob probably had more to fear than anyone if he stepped foot on this property again. She saw that he read it and waited but he didn't respond. She slowly sipped her tea as her thoughts swirled, and when he finally did reply her heart sank at his flat words.

Brawny Man: I'll be home early, so Bess can stay with me.

Alright. So, she had ruined whatever didn't even start between them. Her red fingernail ran along the rim of her mug as tea billowed into the air while she let the disappointment sit. And then the disappointment turned to something else. Sure, she'd made some assumptions, but she'd done so in a bid to protect herself and she hardly knew Jenson. He had been an ass from the moment he literally ran into her, and then had confused her at every turn, but her lack of trust was what pushed him over the edge?

She grabbed her phone before she allowed her anger to cool and sent him a reply.

Ursula: Ok.

Ursula: And by the way, I was cautious with you because I have some baggage. Also, you're confusing. And you're kind of an ass. I am sorry for listening to rumors but you didn't even give me the grace to fumble. So I'm done—no more back and forth. I don't want to play anymore.

She set her phone down, staring wide-eyed at the vehement text sent without one filter, and bit her lip. She let out a groan and picked it up, quickly typing an assuage for her outburst.

Ursula: I'm sorry. Ignore that. I appreciate you making sure I was safe last night and taking care of me. Will you let Bess know I'll have her over when all of this blows over?

She felt better, though a little silly, for her up-and-down show of emotions. She prided herself on keeping herself cool, even in tumultuous times, but Jenson Lancaster brought out a less-than-sure-footed side of her that she wasn't sure she understood or liked. He didn't respond, and that was just as well. She needed to push him out of her mind and the less confusing communication from him the better. She needed to move, get out of this space, and keep her mind busy, so she called Jen and asked if she could come over with pie while she got through neglected work. Her gratefulness for friends who could heal with their mere presence was overflowing.

Ursula was stirring the pot on the stove with cannellini beans, sweet potato, and caramelized onions as she sprinkled in spices and fresh herbs from her garden with music sliding around the fragrant kitchen. She raised the glass of white wine to her lips and danced to the upbeat notes of music, singing along and letting the stress of the last twenty-four hours melt away.

She could be thinking about Rob and what he knew about the history of this house that he was so hellbent on keeping a secret that he was willing to send in his wife as a spy, track, and drug her, and then threaten her with begonias. She could be thinking about how delicately Jenson had taken care of her last night, the memory of his lips on her forehead, the juxtaposing way he had a habit of tucking an errant piece of hair behind her ear that clashed with his intense and sometimes harsh personality. Or the way his kiss had awoken something in her that she had forgotten lived deep and low. And the overwhelming realization she would never feel that kind of kiss from him again.

She could admit that after last night, she had allowed a well of hope to open inside of her that she'd kept closed and empty for years. But after he left and their brief text conversation, which he hadn't responded to, that well of hope now felt like an open wound. And she had enough pride not to reach over the chasm that was Jenson Lancaster's personality and ask for attention.

She had spent too much of her life waiting for attention.

Instead of allowing any of those thoughts to consume her, she made one of her favorite fall soups, another loaf of artisan bread, and swayed to music with a glass of wine. She cut a piece of the local white cheddar she'd bought earlier, popping it into her mouth and letting the sharp taste take over her taste buds. Wine and cheese were a magical pairing.

But, as a woman's mind has the uncanny ability to often do, instead of the peace she was seeking her mind flipped back to pictures of Jenson kissing her. That damn intense stare. The aching gentleness of his actions and then his stark silence.

She set down her phone and groaned as she finished the last gulp of her wine, deliberating if she should take on another glass. She didn't normally drink more than one, and she didn't feel tipsy, just a little warm and loose. *Let it go, Ursula*, was the mantra in her head as she turned up the music and finished cooking her dinner.

She was pouring her sautéed mixture into a blender when a loud knock sounded on her back door making her whip around. A dark figure filled out the top of the dutch door window and she reached for her phone when it pushed open, a gush of cold wind and the sound of whipping rain drowned out her harsh beating heart.

In stepped a wet and angry-looking Jenson, his denim jacket a shade darker in most spots from the cold, autumn northeastern weather.

He shut the door behind him and she let out a heavy breath as she pressed a hand to her heart.

"What is the matter with you?" she accused.

"Why didn't you tell me Rob came here?" His voice was deadly soft and she shifted uneasily.

"Why are you angry?"

"Because the man responsible for scaring you," he closed his eyes as though the next words physically hurt him, "for hurting you," his eyes opened and she could feel the dark depths of them. "Was here. On your property where you're alone."

She shifted again, unsure why that affected him so deeply. "I know. I was here. And to be fair, the house literally kicked him out, so I'm not exactly alone."

His eyes flashed. "Don't."

His command was strong and did something to her. She lifted her head. "Don't what?"

"Don't play with your safety and don't be glib with me now."

She let out a humorless laugh. "I don't know how to be with you," she admitted. "Why are you angry? You still didn't answer my first question: why are you here?"

He took a step toward her and it felt like its own statement. "Because you said you don't know how to be seen anymore."

Confusion crossed her face. "What?"

Another step. "You apologized for your clumsy heart."

The memory of those vulnerable words made her clench her jaw.

"The night I kissed you? I heard you talking with Bess about being a ghost. And I know what that's like. And I have my own apologies to make to you, but right now I need you to understand one thing."

Her heart was now pounding. She wasn't sure if it was fear, or that feeling of being dangled over the ledge of something knowing that the next move was big, important.

"What?" she asked, barely getting the word out.

He was closer. Close. Her body was reacting as a warmth started buzzing under her skin.

"I see you. I have seen you. You're all I've seen since you ran into me."

"You ran into me," she countered.

He let out a deep sound that vibrated low, a warning.

"You don't want to play anymore?" He repeated her unfiltered words. His voice was heated, his eyes even more so.

She frowned and shook her head.

"I came to check on you but now I have something else in mind," he said, his words and slow prowl toward her ratcheting up her heartbeat again.

She took two instinctual steps backward until she was pressed against the kitchen island as he advanced, the distance between them becoming smaller and smaller.

"I've been confusing and unclear, Ursula." Another step. "Mostly because I have a lot of insane baggage and it's clear you do too," she frowned, about to respond when he finally closed the distance and she had to tip her head back to look up at him towering over her, his dark hair nearly black like hers from being wet and his eyes molten. "But I'm done playing too, honey. And now I'm going to make it really fucking clear, got me?"

She couldn't get a word out of her mouth because she was stunned, her mind trying to figure out what was going on and her body was trembling. Jenson was here in her kitchen, his large body trapping hers against the counter.

He tipped her chin up. "Answer me, Ursula."

The way he said her name was unfair.

"I, what?" was all she could think to say.

His mouth hitched up slightly on one side at her inability to talk. "No words? That's fine with me." And then his mouth was on hers. It was harsh, demanding, hot. She opened without needing much coaxing because admit it or not, she had been craving this since he kissed her that night weeks ago.

The way he kissed, the way he took over, was something she didn't know could live outside of a steamy romance novel. Her body responded like a sigh of relief, a releasing of something pent up for too long that could now roam free.

When he swept his tongue inside of her mouth he groaned, the sound reverberating through her. She could taste it, the sound of his absolute satisfaction. One of his hands tangled in her hair, pulling out the pin holding it up, the sound of it dropping to the ground a mere plink in the onslaught of all of her roaring blood and emotions.

His other hand was on her waist, his grip firm. There was nothing tentative about him and she would admit that was what she needed when it came to passion.

No questions, no guessing. Taking, giving, unapologetic touch and need. This was what intimacy should be: unfettered. Being able to feel something click exactly into place with someone and know that you can let go with absolute abandon. There was a weightlessness to releasing and giving in that alone could be its own high.

Suddenly his hands were under her arms as she was lifted from the ground and her butt landed on the countertop. She looked up at him dazed, her mouth open and her swollen lips wanting his demanding ones back, as he used a hand to spread her legs and then fit himself between them as his other hand grabbed her ass to drag her against him, leaving no question about what he wanted.

His eyes caught hers for the briefest of moments, a heavy pause that felt like everything. He communicated in one second, one heated, the-moment-before-combustion-second, that he saw her. And God help her because it was like experiencing being worshipped.

And then his lips were on hers again, but now her body was wrapped around his in a tilting up and down, the friction drawing out a moan from her throat that he answered with his own groan as his hips pressed harder into her.

Neither of them could have kept time as they burned and moved against each other. The autumn storm was their background noise as a curse was broken in The Lost Souls kitchen that night.

Jenson Lancaster, from the moment that he ran into Ursula Cambridge, had felt for the first time in too long a connection to someone without the strange undercurrent of the curse. It was always there, buzzing a reminder that he couldn't love and couldn't be loved in return. But the moment her green eyes looked into his, something was different. And he hadn't figured it out. It was agitating in its peacefulness, as sometimes peace can be for someone so used to war.

He fought it, fought her, but it had become undeniable. Ursula was the person the curse could not touch.

The couple, spent and lying in each other's arms on the copper rug of the kitchen, looked up at the ceiling, her fingers wrapped in his as the storm continued its serenade. He turned to his side, propping his head on his hand and looked down at her.

"When I ran into you, that first day, everything stopped for me," his voice rumbled like it was trying to smooth itself out. She watched his face as he held her, his eyes roving over her features like they were art. "I never was allowed the luxury of this," his fingertips lightly brushed over her collarbones, "of holding someone I wanted."

She frowned at his words and wondered if they were about his curse.

He shook his head, a look of disbelief in his eyes. "I made peace, violent peace, with knowing I would be alone. And then you came here. The moment I found you," he paused, a war waging, words trying to make sense, "I had no idea what peace was. And it scared the hell out of me. What I want is this," his thumb brushed over her kiss-swollen lips. "You. This peace, this outrageous miracle."

Her heart, it was swelling. It was filling the cavity of her ribs too quickly and she was so scared that it would pop with the next shoe. He wanted her. She wasn't sure if she could trust this. "We fight like crazy."

He smiled. God, that devastating smile that made him look like a God, lighting up the room and warming her. It was unfair how just this could trip up her heart and make her nestle into him. "Yeah, baby. But that's because I was an asshole who didn't know what the hell to do with a beautiful gift like you. Now I do."

Her eyes widened. She was on the precipice of something big and vast. "What's that?"

That smile turned into a smirk, a shadow of something seductive and honest covered his eyes. "Keep you. And earn the right to keep doing this." He leaned down and captured her mouth in the kind of kiss they had never had before. Before it had been passion, lust, storms, and chills. This was worship, him building a shelter in reverence and telling her soul she could simply be. It felt like they were creating the catalyst for something that could outlast time.

When he pulled back, she pulled in a vanilla lemon breath and held it deep inside of her lungs as she kept her eyes closed relishing in this absolution. Magic.

When she opened her eyes he was watching her with patience and a calm resolution that let her know he was safe. She smiled and cupped his face, feeling the beginning of his thick scruff after a long day. When he closed his eyes and leaned into her touch, a large, powerful creature seeking out softness, the simple intimacy of the moment rushed over her.

"Okay, I need more," he said, but before she could ask what he meant he got up and reached down to pick her up and slung her over his shoulder making her gasp.

"Jenson!" she shrieked and kicked at the sudden movement.

"Bedroom, baby."

"You can put me down," she said with a laugh.

"No," he answered as he strode out of the kitchen and down the hallway. "Not letting you go for a while."

And she smiled because she liked that. Having someone not wanting to let you go? That had to be a love language on its own because it filled her near-to-bursting.

"Okay, up the stairs and first room on the left," she said.

"I know," he said as he squeezed her bare ass, making another rush of desire flood her. "going to do round two properly in your bed, then we'll shower."

"Oh yeah? What if I had plans?" she asked as she bounced on his shoulder up the stairs.

"Cancel them."

"That's a little demanding."

He spanked her right cheek and she gasped. "I've lost too much time."

And that, she could understand. Years with the wrong person can take something so deep from a person. But time with the right one? There wouldn't be enough time.

CHAPTER TWENTY-NINE

LIGHT IN THE GRAVEYARD

Two jars of moonlight, an Irish Wolfhound, and a journal visited the graveyard that night after the storm had cleared and the two new lovers untangled themselves. An hour ago Ursula had been in Jenson's arms, running her fingertips over his chest as she asked him to tell her about his curse. She wasn't sure what she expected from him. That was the beauty of getting to know someone; every reaction they had was a surprise.

He told her in a calm voice a story of nearly falling in love with a witch in Salem, twenty years ago. But when that "nearly" never turned to blossoming love, and he broke off the relationship, the young woman who had an audience with magic came to this very graveyard and cursed him. Her name was Cassidy Parker and she lived in The Lost Souls House almost two decades ago, losing herself in the mystery and magic rooted here. When the man she fell in love with didn't return her passion, she dug up the magic from the dirt and hexed him with the two things that lay on either side of love: loneliness or obsession. It was a dark magic, the kind of magic that is twisted from the natural world by the desires of someone wielding it with malicious intent.

He would turn the heads of women, and the only thing they would fall into with him was obsession; the dark, dramatic, and shadowed step-sibling to love.

He told her stories of his past and how the curse came to grab hold of him until he no longer looked for love or even hoped for it.

One of his girlfriends, whom he had dated for a short month, moved into his house without asking. He came home from his first job in construction, to a one-bedroom apartment in a historic Salem house, to find her boxes and things neatly stacked in his tiny living room. When he told her they weren't ready for that, bewildered she would do such a thing, she screamed and tied herself to his bed.

He shook it off as a fluke.

But then the next woman he dated invited him to her place on their fifth date, and unbeknownst to him, he walked in to find her parents were there with champagne and a deposit had been put down for their wedding venue. Every year the curse seemed to get stronger. A woman's obsession could spark from a one-night stand, sometimes a mere flirtation.

And the previous tenant? Farah and Brody Rhodes. She came into town to scope out the Lost Soul's House, wandering into a town fundraiser square dance, where she got swept away with the town's charm and swept under the curse of Jenson Lancaster.

"Is there any rhyme or reason to someone falling prey to the curse?"

"Some people are just more prone to being persuaded by that kind of magic," he answered.

"Why aren't you worried that I will be?"

He smirked as he wrapped her thick, black hair around his fist and pulled her into him for a kiss under the moonlight streaming in from her gothic windows. When he looked down at her, his eyes those intense dark pools, he replied, "I learned to feel for the curse catching hold of someone. It would feel like static." At the questioning look he released his hold on her hair and wrapped his hand around the side of her neck, his warm palm holding her pulse. "You know when your mind feels like it has too many tabs open and it becomes overwhelming, all of this information trying to talk over each other so that nothing is clear or makes sense, so the best thing would be to just close them all?"

"I'm a woman. We rarely close all the tabs. We're more likely to open another one researching how to better organize all of the tabs."

He gave her neck a squeeze and a gentle smile. "The curse feels like that."

"And I don't feel like that?"

He looked up over her shoulder as he searched for words, his thumb running a pattern over the skin of her neck causing shivers to run down her body. He looked back at her and said, "You're like silence. Even that first day when you ran into me."

"You ran into me," she corrected and he hushed her. She smiled.

"Even that first day, it was like suddenly the background noise went away. A complete wash of comfort. Like I could unfurl, relax, not hold myself together so tightly."

She had to suck in a breath at his words because she had felt that exact thing in his arms. She could just be.

They showered, and took their time as new lovers do, mapping out each other's bodies with curious hands and awe-filled smiles. And then they bundled up, grabbed two moonlight lanterns, the journal, and Casper and now found themselves in the company of ten black graves.

"Now, what are we supposed to do with these lost souls?"

She smiled and turned to where the graves sat on the cold, wet ground. "We talk to them. Keep them company. For a while, I was reading them Mary Oliver."

"The poet?"

"You know Mary Oliver?"

He shrugged a large shoulder. "There is a lot we don't know about each other," was his simple reply. And it was a promise.

"Well, tonight I brought this journal that mysteriously ended up in my care and will sometimes leave me notes."

"Intriguing."

It had been clear: ask the lost souls about Fannie McGovern.

She set her jar on a headstone, the glowing light showing off the slowly swirling fog. With the journal open in her hands she asked, "Who was Fannie McGovern? Was she the lady of The Lost Souls House?"

Fog began to swirl harder until it billowed out in a flourish that revealed the ground giving way to bushes with light pink flowers. They watched, her heart thundering and her mind racing as the same poisonous flowers sprouted at each of the graves.

"Is that?"

"Oleander," she finished. "I saw it here before and in my kitchen. I thought it had been a warning but now," she shook her head trying to think.

Jenson's fingers brushed the journal she was holding. "Look," he said.

She looked down and her eyes widened as tight, black script scrolled across the page.

History has a way of repeating itself. When the sons do not care to learn, they set in motion the flipping back of pages in time, to repeat the sins of the father.

"What is it?" he asked when he saw the look on her face. She felt an odd prickle on the back of her neck, something whispering in her mind to focus, connect everything.

She shook her head. "I feel like this is a key. I've heard this now a few times, about history."

Casper barked drawing their attention to where the flowers suddenly burst into flames. Jenson's arm pushed her behind him. She tucked the front of her body into Jenson's back as she peered around him at the eerie sight. Every grave had a burning bush, a crackling bouquet of poison.

"We need to leave. We can't breathe that in," he said, his hand wrapping around her smaller one. "Let's go, Casper!" he called out to the hound who immediately obeyed his deep command and they didn't waste any time running out of the clearing and into the woods to her house. The image of the black skeletal remains of the flowers burned into her mind.

Once they were in her kitchen, she pulled off her knit hat and coat, placing it on the back of the chair and a memory hit her.

Jessica sitting in this chair. Them talking about the history of the house and something she said with a distinctly thoughtful look in her eyes.

"History has a way of repeating itself."

"Oh my god," she said softly, her mind raking over that evening, her odd behavior, the betrayal, and yet something about her still calling to the empathetic side of Ursula. "I think I know who left that journal on my porch. It was Jessica."

Jenson crossed his arms over his chest and leaned back against the fridge. The one where he had her body pressed against while he was deep inside of her hours ago. She could not think of that right now. She mentally berated herself even as a flush of heat wove through her.

"Jessica Sandis who lied to you?"

"There's something about her, a woundedness. And the way she left that night, it was like she felt remorse, hated what she had done, or was about to do."

"Okay, so she felt guilt," he shrugged. "Most people do."

She was still piecing it together. "I'm not sure," she admitted finally. She wasn't ready to paint the woman as a villain.

When the doorbell chimed, Casper went loping to the front in excitement leading the way for her and Jenson. Peeking through the glass she frowned when she saw Kelsea and Tilly standing on the porch.

"Hey," she said pulling the door open. "What's going on?"

Kelsea had her head down and Tilly had a grave look on her face. "Can we come in? I think we have a way to take Rob Sandis down."

CHAPTER THIRTY

HISTORY HAS A WAY OF REPEATING ITSELF

"Hey Jenson," Tilly said with a suspicious tone in her voice, her eyes bouncing between him and Ursula.

She didn't know what to say. She didn't know what they were doing, but he was a pretty private man with that grumpy air about him that said he didn't want other people in his business.

"Tilly," he responded with a nod of his head and nodded to Kelsea who smiled tightly at him. "I'll leave you ladies to talk. I need to go check on Bess." And then he shocked three women, when he wrapped a large hand around the side of her neck, and the other at her waist pulling her into him and tipping her chin up with his thumb before taking her mouth in a very heated kiss. Her body molded to his and her mouth answered his demand without question. Heat engulfed her body hoping for the promise his kiss was making. When he pulled back she looked up at him dazed. So much for not telling anyone his business. "I'll check on you later. Do not go back out to the graveyard tonight. And do not do anything stupid."

She rolled her eyes at his demand. "You can't just start telling me what to do."

"I'm not. I'm telling you what not to do." He kissed her lips hard one more time then left behind three bewildered women.

Finally, once the door was closed behind him, Kelsea was smiling and Tilly looked at her with raised eyebrows behind her red glasses. "We will talk about *that* later." She nodded her head at Kelsea motioning for her to follow her into the kitchen.

"Is this a tea or bourbon conversation?" Ursula asked following them.

"Bourbon. Definitely bourbon," Tilly replied.

An hour later the three women were sitting quietly around the island after Kelsea shared her story.

"This needs to come out," Tilly urged.

Ursula watched Kelsea's face fill with dread and panic. "You know why I can't say anything," she said, an urgency in her voice.

"Hey, shh. It's okay. We'll figure it out," Ursula promised. Still, as Kelsea had talked with them, Ursula had listened as her mind whirled, her anger simmered, her thoughts trying to piece together as she swirled the amber bourbon in her glass.

"How?" Kelsea asked. Kelsea usually looked like a twenty-something who knew how to make looking fashionable easy. Tonight, her blonde hair was twisted into a messy bun, falling out in places. The bags under her eyes were deep-set giving away that she hadn't been sleeping well.

This young woman shared her broken story with them, only after finding herself in a hopeless position. Rage ran through Ursula in rivers and Tilly was right: they needed to do something. But to protect Kelsea they would need to do this covertly.

"I have an idea but it's a little crazy and you're going to have to trust me," she said, her eyes connecting with both Kelsea's and then Tilly's. "I think we need to invite Jessica over."

Kelsea's eyes bugged out, their light blue color with the bruised skin underneath them making her look a little wild and harried.

"Jessica Sandis?"

"Ursula," Tilly said, a dark warning in her voice.

"I think she's the one who gave me Fannie McGovern's journal," she said. "It doesn't make sense. I've been thinking about it for awhile and going over the evening she came over. When I found out who she was, something she said jumped out at me. She said, 'history has a way of repeating itself,' which keeps popping up. She seemed despondent, scared of her life, like she's stuck in it," she explained, her eyes watching the bourbon in her glass as she worked through the puzzle pieces. She remembered the way Jessica had left that night, what she had said to Ursula as though she wished Ursula had been different, harder to like. "What if she knows exactly what Kelsea is going through?" She looked up at them and they were staring at her, Tilly with a look of concentration and Kelsea with a look of trepidation.

"That's a big risk," Tilly said.

She wasn't wrong. It was a huge risk. She nodded her head slowly, took the last sip of her bourbon and set the glass down. "Let's call the girls."

One text and one hour later it had been decided amongst the group of women what they would do. An hour after that? The doorbell rang, its delightful ring juxtaposed the dark and tenuous atmosphere.

Ursula looked around at the four women. Jen gave her a nod and then she walked down the hallway and opened the door to their invited guest.

"Thank you for coming," she said gently to the woman who wasn't wearing a chic, color-coordinated outfit tonight. Tonight she was in leggings and a long wool jacket, her hair pulled up into a frazzled ponytail.

"I almost didn't," she admitted.

Ursula nodded her head and led her into the kitchen where her four friends sat, with open expressions on their faces, and an air of invitation. Jessica walked in like a baby lamb coming upon adult lions. Ursula paused and hoped this would go better than anticipated and then Jen stood up, and walked around the island, the sound of her steps loud in the quiet and tense kitchen. She stopped in front of Jessica, the wife of the man who was sabotaging her best friend, and wrapped her arms around her and whispered something in her ear. They couldn't hear what it was, but instantly Jessica's shoulders relaxed and the air pulsed with a feeling of that magical peace.

"Ready?" Jen asked everyone to which they all nodded. Though the fear and tenuous feeling had left the air, what remained was something stronger: resilience and the rage of women who were done with the battles waged against them, and ready to wage war to finish it.

CHAPTER THIRTY-ONE

THIS IS WHERE KARMA SMILES

"I don't think I was drunk enough," Tilly whispered to Jen who rubbed at her bloodshot eyes.

"Are you serious? I'm so hungover I think I might still be drunk." Jen leaned back and eyed Ursula who looked pretty good for having stood in a graveyard at midnight with Crystal's deadly margaritas running loose between the six women.

Ursula passed Jen the thermos. When she gave her a questioning look she said, "Trust me. Gave some to Tilly before we walked over."

Jen opened the lid and peered inside, made a face then drank. She looked like she was going to throw up after half of it was gone. Ursula looked at Kelsea who wore anxiety like a sweater.

"What if it didn't work?" she asked, her eyes scanning the crowd, the signs for Rob loud and many of them starkly against Cora. A few of the signs were bold enough to call her a witch.

"I don't know. If not, then we'll figure something out," Jen said adamantly.

"I can't," Kelsea started, her voice breaking and Ursula put an arm around the young woman's waist.

"We know," she soothed.

Then the volume of the crowd took on a new level as the two candidates made their way up the wooden stage. Cora was regal in a horizon blue suit, lips red like blood and her eyes sharp.

Rob smiled to the crowd cheering for him, his teeth too white, his smile too bold.

A woman with a white swirl of thick hair on top of her head like a vanilla soft serve ice cream cone stood at the front of the stage and raised one hand into the air as she spoke into the microphone. Rob's mom.

"Beautiful day for our final debate before we vote in the new mayor of Salem!"

Ursula's eyes went to the side of the stage and down the stairs where she found Jessica and her three children standing nobly. She looked glorious, the perfect politician's wife. Ursula smiled remembering the woman knocking back her second margarita and losing a sharpness to her, laughing without apology. It had been a side of her that Ursula understood: released and free. Letting go of the pain she had collected against her ribs because a man made her believe it was her job to.

The truth of Rob Sandis came out last night, between sips of tequila, and dancing with souls who knew Jessica's pain.

But now, she was the picture of a dutiful wife, hiding the lies of their life behind perfectly tailored clothes and children who looked like they knew the consequences of acting like children.

"How do you think she's doing?" Tilly whispered, her own cat-eyes on Jessica.

"That woman is one hell of a surprise and she will get through this," Jen announced. Jen was the kind of woman who made you believe in yourself because anything else wasn't an option.

"Do you think she hates me?" Kelsea asked, and not for the first time.

"No," all three of them announced. It was an easy answer.

"I'd hate me," she mumbled.

Ursula squeezed her closer and replied, "No you wouldn't. Because this is not about you, or her. This is about him."

"We will get started if both candidates will step forward," Mrs. Salem royalty announced as Cora and Rob took their places behind their respective lecterns.

The four women were pressed close together all holding hope in their fingertips.

They started debating about the town budget, talking about where they would spend the money and what programs they would focus on.

They touched on crime rates and tourism. It felt like hours and also only minutes. Every word he said, was somehow barbed and landed against Cora's skin inflicting and branding her. He found ways to draw out the fact that she was a divorced single woman with no children in just about every topic.

A few people in the crowd yelled out, "Witch!" here and there. The name Tituba was yelled and Ursula wrapped her hand around Jen's tense fist, linking their fingers together.

"Let's talk about family," Rob said, a keen look in his eyes.

"Okay, let's," Cora agreed amicably. She was holding strong even through the hits she had taken over the last hour. If this was a battle, Rob was winning. Her armor was battered and his was shining.

"You said you would spend money on a family planning center," he said. She nodded her head, her eyes saying she was ready. Ursula could see the nearly imperceptible movements of a woman mentally putting on more armor; shoulders moving back and down a fraction, chin tipped up, eyes hard. "You have to admit, all these young girls and even young women not ready to be mothers, getting themselves pregnant," he paused looking out over the crowd, "it's reckless and shameful. Building and investing in a center that would give them an out would only enforce their reckless behavior as something that can simply be," he waved his hand in the air with a flourish, "taken care of."

Cora looked at Rob. "I thought you were Christian, Rob," she said.

He smiled. "I am. You know I am."

"Then how can you believe all these young, reckless women are having immaculate conceptions?"

The crowd went silent.

His smile tightened the slightest. "You know what I mean."

"No, I do not. Please explain," she said simply, easily.

"This isn't about feminism," he said, his hands grabbing the sides of the podium. "Actually, let's talk about that, because my opponent seems to be running on a toxic feminist platform. This is about protecting the foundation of our country: good, healthy families and their values."

Cheers went up all around them.

"Let's talk about that," she said, leaning into the small microphone waiting for the cheers to die down. "I'm a toxic feminist because I bring up and focus on equality and how far our society, including Salem, still needs to go? Female firefighters are paid eighty cents to the dollar of their male colleagues."

"Hold on now, I am all for equality. That's the American dream. It's feminism I have a problem with."

"That's like saying you're for H2O but not water."

Laughter rumbled through the crowd and Rob's smile faltered. A point to his opponent was unacceptable, even if he was clearly wiping the floor with her.

"What you believe is not a representation of what everyone in Salem believes, Rob. To create a system and a town that caters to only a fraction of ideals and religion is not democratic."

"Oh, you wouldn't know democracy if you took a class on it," he retorted, his voice taking on a new edge, like he was starting to slip.

"I'm glad you brought that up because I did take a class on it. I have my masters in political analysis and strategy. Or did you spend all of your research dollars and time on who I hang out with rather than what my degree and qualifications are?"

Another wave of laughter at his expense. Ursula looked at Jessica who was watching the debate tightly. She wondered what was going on inside of her head.

"She needs to ask him," Tilly mumbled.

Jen cut her a look. "She will."

"She has to say her name," Ursula said, a tightness in her chest.

Again, Jen said, "She will."

"Who a person spends their time with, the life that they build and the people in that life are a direct reflection of a person's character," Rob said, lifting his head. A gleam entered his eyes and Ursula felt like a caged animal was inside of her. "And you've chosen an outsider with a questionable lifestyle. Drugs, witchcraft, spending time in a graveyard. That house is an abomination to our town! It's a reminder of this town's dark history, holding an evil inside of its bounds that needs to be brought down and demolished. Once. And. For. All."

He punctuated the words with his fist on the podium. People agreed with hands in the air, wildly waving signs. More names and slurs flung anonymously through the crowd landed on Cora who kept her head high.

"We need to get rid of the Lost Soul's House and give this town a fresh start, a family-first, moralistic rebrand!" Soft Serve was smiling triumphantly, an air of superiority highlighting her sharp cheekbones as she silently supported her blood.

Cora looked out over the crowd of people, the air wild and frantic. The women crowded closer together, feeling the animosity. Could he win this? What if he took power? Ursula thought of the Lost Soul's House, of what she now knew about who the gravestones were marking, what was done to them.

"Let's talk about the Lost Souls, Rob," Cora said calmly. It was hard to hear over the crowd. She waited then continued. "The history of those young women, cast out of society and shamed, taken in by Fannie McGovern."

At the name leaving Cora's red lips Rob's entire body stopped, like someone pointed a remote at him and paused him on screen while everything else around him moved. A shade of color left his skin. Ursula bit her lip. Jen's hand squeezed around hers. Kelsea's entire body was strung like a bow's string.

"You know that name, don't you Rob? Fannie McGovern, the woman who took in young women who were pregnant and abused, kicked out of their homes, shamed and called the worst of names in a society that blasphemed them and glossed over the men who had a hand in getting them there. Like Amos Beckwith. Your own blood, the very blood that you tout as the royalty which runs through your veins. The very respectable and honorable Reverend."

"Stop," Rob barely got through his tight lips.

"He was so respectable that he got a thirteen year old girl pregnant, didn't he?"

The crowd was silent, so hooked on her words and on the sight of Rob losing all pretense of political control. His mother's face no longer held pride, but a shade of worry.

"Thirteen years old, she was cast out from her family home, ran to the only place she knew: the Lost Soul's House, rumored to be a last hope that took in girls just like her. Protected girls like her. From men like Amos Beckwith, the God-fearing and religious man holding up family values."

"Stop talking. This isn't," he faltered, his mouth opening and nothing coming out. They watched with bated breath as he was silenced from speaking lies. "It's...that..." he mouthed air, like a fish caught out of water.

"He ordered men in town to sneak into that house, poison all of the women with oleander and then buried their bodies in the middle of the night. Children. One baby. Three pregnant women. Fannie McGovern. The girl your blood raped and got pregnant. All to keep his secret and uphold those very pure family and religious values."

Rob's mother's face was red as she started up the stairs, a desperation in her movements but three men stepped from the shadows of the stage and blocked her. No one was paying attention to her fraught energy.

Rob still couldn't talk. He took a shaky drink of the water on his podium, a desperate hand clawing at his throat.

"She's going to say it," Jen said, her eyes bright and shining, breath held tightly in her chest.

Ursula heard Kelsea praying next to her.

Cora tilted her head watching Rob as he choked on his lies, a look of a woman about to deal a death blow. "And history has a way of repeating itself, doesn't it, Rob?"

A tinkling of bells sounded so gently no one in the crowd would have discerned them. A new feeling came over the entire crowd, it was the feeling of a precipice. Something was about to tilt everything over an edge no one saw coming.

Suddenly, as if he was attached to strings like a puppet, Rob straightened and his face looked out over the crowd and he cleared his throat. "I have an admission to make," his words came out direct. Ursula's heart pounded. "Years ago I had an affair. I speak of standing on a platform of family values and demonize pro choice, but when I was working on my first campaign, I had an affair with a young woman who was eighteen years old. She was caught in a snare I had set, my being older and knowing what I was doing, her innocent and unable to name the imbalance of power. She got pregnant with my child and I paid in secret to get her an abortion. Then I threatened her mother's business, which I invested heavily in as a way to control this information not getting out. This isn't the only affair I've had and I have brought shame on my wife and children. On my parents."

All four women looked at Jessica who had her arms around her children, a lioness protecting her cubs, her head up high, the sun shining on her blank face.

Nervous, excited faces looked to where his mother, no longer trying to get on the stage was standing with her mouth open in shock. Ursula watched her eyes cut to her daughter-in-law, a look of pain taking over the shock. This wasn't the look of a woman ready to protect her son.

"Holy shit, it's working," Jen whispered.

Tilly laughed excitedly and Kelsea had a bewildered look on her face.

"I've had five total affairs," he continued, like he was reading from the honest script that was written for him under moonlight with lost souls breathing magic into it. "I have not acted as the man I put before you, a man of honor. I have led a shameful life in the shadows and cursed myself and my family. My wife has stood by my side, not out of duty, but because I held her with threats. I have ensured that she can never take my children from me and behind closed doors I have kept her in fear under my control."

Murmuring tinkled through the crowd, words of disbelief, anger, confusion. Jessica gave her husband one more look before she turned and ushered her children out of the crowd, which parted for her as she walked away from him with her head held high. Her eyes connected with Ursula's, a sheen of clear happiness and relief ringing there, gratefulness and freedom. Ursula nodded once with a smile and then Jessica was gone.

Rob's mother was nowhere to be seen.

And then as if a cloud dissipated over Rob, he shook his head and blinked his eyes rapidly. He looked shocked, then terrified. He looked out at the crowd who was watching him with various looks of disgust and mortification. He leaned forward, his words throwing themselves into the microphone too loudly, too desperately.

"Wait, that was," he tried to get words out but they wouldn't come. And the six women who stood in the graveyard last night knew that lies would form from his soul but wouldn't be able to leave the cage of his bones. "It's all, it's...it's.." he stuttered then blurted, "true! It's all true." He shook his head in frustration and grasped the podium. "We can still make this town great together! I still believe everything I have said!"

But he had lost them. They were shaking their heads and Cora was watching him unravel. Then she took back control, the way she knew how, with honesty and hope.

"Let me be clear," she said looking out over the crowd. "I shame no religion, I shame no belief system. I believe in bringing our differences, ideals and beliefs, backgrounds and cultures, together. Pro choice, pro life, choose your lane and stand by your beliefs and I ask everyone to respect that. Rob," she said pointing a manicured finger at the man who no longer looked regal, no longer had anything holding his head up other than spitting anger, "says that he is building his platform on family values, but let's call it what it really is. He has built his platform on shame. Shaming anyone who doesn't share his own beliefs and then living in hypocrisy at its finest."

She shook her head sadly, giving him one last look then dismissing him.

"I have built my platform the same as before, hopefully with lessons learned and a stronger charge forward towards one goal: an invitation to grow together as a community. I do not have all of the answers, and I will make some mistakes. I will ruffle some feathers. But I will also stand on a platform of honesty and respect. Let's cultivate the garden of Salem. Let's grow something beautiful together."

There was no hesitation in the cheers, the hands raised, the hope shining out. The signs that had been raised and shaking earlier were gone, lowered by the sinking admission of who they thought they were following. Not everyone would change their loyalty, but the women stood there in the crowd knowing that enough would.

Sometime in the middle of Cora's final speech, Rob had been escorted off of the platform like the disgraced man he was, head held up only by hubris.

"I can't believe it worked," Kelsea breathed out, looking at them with awe.

Tilly wrapped her in her arms.

"How are you?" Ursula asked, still concerned. Her name hadn't come out, but it still could and probably would.

"Fucking elated," Kelsea said, surprising them and making Jen laugh loudly, head thrown back, throat bobbing with the force of her happiness. They gathered together and then Crystal joined them from where she had been silently standing guard near Jessica.

"Back to no more hexing?" Tilly asked.

"Until another moraless person decides to come along."

"There are plenty of those," Crystal said sagely.

"Okay, but if we ever decide as a coven to try another hex for dire circumstances, can we try without Crystal's deadly tequila?" Jen asked, still looking puny and pained.

"What if it's the combo that makes the hexes work?" Kelsea asked.

"Maybe hexes go well with tequila," Ursula said with a smile.

CHAPTER THIRTY-TWO

A WORD LIKE "US"

U rsula walked away from the loosening crowd, the air different than when she had walked in. Hope and victory sang sweetly, like verbena and peach blossoms. A red pickup truck was parked on a side street that would lead her home and a man leaned against the bed with arms crossed over his flanneled chest.

She walked up to him feeling a heat creep slowly inside of her as his dark eyes swept over her in a clear look of desire. Jenson Lancaster was a conundrum, but one that she looked forward to getting to know.

"I hear there was a shocking upset at the debate," his deep voice said.

"It was positively scandalous," she replied stopping in front of him.

His hands found her waist like they were made to fit there. "Sounds like it."

She was looking up at him, feeling everything she forgot to feel for years.

"Were you waiting for me?"

"I knew you'd be walking this way soon."

"Creeper. Always ending up where I am," she said with a cheeky smile.

His hands tightened on her waist and pulled her flush against him, pulling out a small gasp. His hard body was making her softer one flush. "Call it what you want, but I know what I want so you'll be seeing a lot of me."

She smiled up at him, biting her bottom lip as his words washed over her. Feeling wanted was a heady thing. That was a form of magic she could get used to.

"Come home with me," he said, sliding a hand into her loose hair. "I'll make dinner for us and Bess and then we can watch a movie."

"How's she doing? Still staying with you?"

He nodded. "Judge ordered she could stay with me until she rules whether I can have custody."

She smiled. "Alright. I need to go let Casper out and then I can come over."

"I went and grabbed him," he said nodding his head back and she leaned over to see that her hound was in the cab of the truck his face pressed against the back window.

She looked back at Jenson with raised eyebrow. "You broke into my house and stole my dog?"

He shrugged. "Report me."

"You are frustrating," she said with an eye roll.

He answered by fisting her hair and pulling her up into him as his mouth took hers in a kiss that went straight through her entire body to her core. She grabbed onto his chest as she kissed him back, their mouths moving together like they knew exactly what to do. Like they had been made to dance together.

When he finally pulled back, he ran a thumb over her lip. "Come home with me. Stay the night at my place tonight and then we'll go from there."

He helped her up into the cab as she scooched in next to a happy Casper.

"You're very demanding, Brawny Man."

He speared her with his eyes. "A cursed man who finds a woman who can break that curse is going to fight for that woman. Get used to it." And then he closed the door.

She smiled, still feeling his kiss on her swollen lips. Imagine that. Being fought for by a man who wants her was not exclusive to characters in books.

"Ready?"

She smiled. "Yeah. I am."

He drove slowly through the edge of town as the sun set behind them, the fingers of autumn orange and gold leaving behind a new glow over a town turning the page to write a future that learned from its history.

"Hey," she said, a thought flitting into her mind, "what do you think will happen with the souls now that the truth is out?"

Jenson looked over at her, the concern on her face making him reach out a large hand and squeeze her leg. "Maybe they're at peace now."

She made a humming sound, hoping he was right. And hoping it wouldn't change much about the house. "I think I'll miss them," she said wistfully.

"Well, if someone misses them then they're not lost anymore. They have a witness now to who they were."

She smiled, something warm blooming inside of her. Like her, they were nameless ghosts, wandering around a graveyard at night hoping to be seen, known, recognized. She had finally found her peace here, with friends who she could drink deadly margaritas with, tell her secrets to, be seen and loved at the end of the day. She looked over at Jenson, his strong profile backlit by the orange glow of the setting sun. She smiled as peace washed over her with a tinkling of bells and a warmth that settled in deep.

Chapter Thirty-Three

An Unexpected Visit

W eeks went by, the election was won by Cora Acosta and she settled into her second term as Mayor of Salem.

No evidence could support Rob or Miles's hand in drugging Ursula or the vandalism, but she felt he got his due.

After his timely and shocking confession, footage of the debate made national news.

While Jenson hadn't had an affair with Farrah Rhodes, her obsession with him was sated by an affair with Rob, who tried to control her curiosity and the dark secrets of the lost souls. A rumor whispered around town that Rob had been the one to start the fire at The Lost Souls house, though the truth of that might never come to light.

To everyone's shock, Rob's mother disowned him and gave Jessica all of the support she needed in leaving him with their three children. It turned out that royal blood did not make Rob infallible to his own mother, who found his indiscretions distasteful. More than that, the truth of how he treated his wife and children came out, solidifying her arm around Jessica in support. Rob left town. No one knows where he went. Three weeks after he was reported driving out of Salem, Miles Greenfield closed up shop and quietly left to an unknown destination.

As for Ursula Cambridge, she started cutting back on her hours for work and dove head-first into what started out as a magical hobby and was now a slowly growing business. She drew up plans to have not one, but three greenhouses, built around the property, each of them bursting with life and color.

The morning she finished the final revision of her blueprint (she was self-taught in the art of construction blueprint and it wasn't half bad), her pencil lifted and she was looking down at her design with elation when Sulphur dropped a thick cream envelope next to her before sashaying away.

She opened it and pulled out a thick monogrammed card. Inside there was a message- one that lifted something that had been heavy inside her.

Ursula-

I hope this ivory double-embossed note finds you well. I am afraid that I owe you a sincere apology. I have been doing quite a lot of self-reflection lately and I have come to realize that while I hurt a lot of people with my selfishness and lies, some of them deserved it. Remember Kevin Banks? I don't care how rich you are; you cannot use "summer" as a verb and then snidely remind everyone how poor they are because they didn't marry into old money.

But you, Ursula, you didn't deserve what I did to you. Taking your hard work as my own, I must say that is my most villainous moment. You are under no obligation to forgive me, and you should not unless it will benefit you and make your skin glow. (I will also send along a pumpkin facemask I recently discovered. Girl. Life changing.) But I want you to know how deeply sorry I am.

I think you are the only person I authentically like. Have the time of your life, you witchy little minx.

Best and worst-

Felix

She smiled. It stretched across her face as she made coffee and thought of her old work friend. She'd considered him a foe after what he had done, but now...well, perhaps even good people have, as he said, villainous moments. She hoped he sent the mask. She hoped he found peace.

She'd walked out of her kitchen with a steaming mug of coffee, a thin layer of snow dusting the ground and found Jenson and three of his men putting up glass panes.

"What are you doing?" she called out to him. "I have a plan and I was going to do this," her voice was miffed, though she wouldn't admit that her plans had not looked this good in her mind.

"You were doing it wrong," he said, and she rolled her eyes.

"You're such a bossy ass," she said making his three workers grin and Jenson's dangerous smile flash.

He stopped what he was doing, walked up to where she stood wearing a blanket like a shawl, and pulled her in with a gloved hand for a hard kiss. The man didn't touch her without passion. And she wouldn't have it any other way.

"I got you something," he said then pulled out a huge, thin box that had been leaning against the side of her house. After carefully opening it, he slowly pulled out a large pane of stained glass. It was hard to depict what it was at first, but then she smiled at the gorgeous trees and the black house that looked just like The Lost Souls House. She paused as something else became obvious. She looked up at him to find him staring at her.

"Is that...?"

He ran his gloved hand gently over the woman with long, black hair in a floral dress. "I had them put you and Casper in it." He looked back at her. "Now, for however long this greenhouse lasts, you will never not be seen."

She stepped forward in awe, running a cold, red-tipped finger reverently over the cool glass, following the expertly crafted stained glass figure of herself and the large, majestic Irish wolfhound standing next to her. "When did you..." she shook her head, trying to find words as emotion overwhelmed her.

"After the first night I kissed you," he replied.

She got up on her tiptoes and kissed him, saying with her mouth what her words wouldn't be able to convey. He saw her. And he wanted her to be seen. That was a kind of love she hadn't even known to hope for.

"Get back inside, babe. We should have this together in the next couple of hours."

She was thankful for the unnatural warmth that seemed to be encapsulated on her property like a snow globe. It wasn't warm exactly, but the temperature wouldn't make it impossible for the men to work or her magical plants to grow.

"The girls are all coming over for dinner club and I'll let them know four burly men will be joining us," she said smiling up at him.

"Sounds good. I'm staying the night," he said as he gently put the pane back in the box where it would be safe.

"Do you not know how to ask?"

He tucked a piece of her hair behind her ear and smiled down at her in that wicked way that made her toes curl. "I could, but then you won't roll your eyes at me and get all persnickety, which is a sexy look on you."

She stared flatly at him and he kissed her forehead. "Get inside, honey," he said for the second time, and this time she listened. She paused, then turned to the side as she saw something reaching into her peripheral vision. She frowned when she saw a completely mature peach tree. "Huh," she said to herself. Even for her magic garden, a mature peach tree weeks away from handing her lush peaches was peculiar.

Thoughts of browned butter peaches and cream swirled in her mind and she shook the thoughts as she went in.

A black velvet pouch sitting on the island caught her eye. When she picked it up she realized it was the pouch Crystal had given her the night of the festival. She'd forgotten about it. When she opened it, she pulled out a card and a small piece of paper.

The tarot card was the Eight of Cups sitting between her fingers upright. She'd been studying how to use and interpret tarot cards. The Eight of Cups was about walking away, letting go, searching for truth. Turn it upside down and it represented stagnation and accepting less. The saying that had stuck with her when studying this particular card caught her in the ribs: *You are coming to the realization that you must step away from what is familiar.* Her mouth curved into a soft smile then froze when she saw the other piece of paper that had been tucked into the velvet pouch.

It was a note. A note she knew well, from her life before.

"I love you always and forever. Maybe one day we can start over."
-E

Her heart pounded. How...where had this come from? As her thoughts were racing her doorbell twinkled. She frowned and looked at the time. It was a couple of hours before the girls were supposed to be here. She made her way to the front door, looking out of the moon-phase stained glass seeing a stranger's profile. She opened the door with that hesitant smile everyone puts on when they're faced with an unexpected visitor on their doorstep, but as this stranger turned her head, her red-brown hair falling in familiar waves over her shoulders and her amber glass eyes connecting with Ursula's, her smile froze and her mind went deathly quiet.

"Hey, Pretty Sea Witch," a voice she heard in distant memories said with the nickname she hadn't heard in years. A voice she would know in a pitch-black room. Ursula watched in wonder as the friend she'd lost years ago shrugged her shoulders. "I heard you were starting over and I thought I could join the adventure."

"Eloise," she said on a rush of breath.

Milton Keynes UK
Ingram Content Group UK Ltd.
UKHW030151051224
452010UK00010B/537

9 798990 893917